I0562492

Vampire's Queens

by

Evelyn Silver

The Bloodline Chronicles

Vampire's Queens

Cover Art by *Lisa Dawn MacDonald*

The Wild Rose Press, Inc.
PO Box 708
Adams Basin, NY 14410-0708
Visit us at www.thewildrosepress.com

Publishing History
First Edition, 2025
Trade Paperback Print ISBN 978-1-5092-6351-6
Digital ISBN 978-1-5092-6352-3

The Bloodline Chronicles
Published in the United States of America

Dedication

For Evan, Ashley, and Rachel
Special thanks to Kerry, Kelsey, Ana, and Heather

Author's Note

Vampire's Queens is intended for adult audiences due to subject matter including explicit sexual content, violence, death, suicide, mention of abuse, discussion of sexual assault, general adulty topics, and LOTS of very delicious blood. Reader discretion is advised.

Chapter One

Therapy

Queen Consort Sarai Meir of the secret vampire kingdom of New Ulster pushed open the throne room doors and let them swing shut behind her. The chandeliers above were dark with unlit candles, and the only light in the room came from lines of red sunset under the thick curtains adorning tall windows.

She stepped as quietly as she could across the marble floor. The room felt haunted despite the absence of ghosts. It was meant to be such a busy room. Was she permitted inside when it was so empty? Still, she was a queen, and it was her palace. She was permitted wherever she liked.

That said, the throne wasn't hers, not exactly. It was a marble throne carved with Celtic knotwork designs and decorated with gold paint, with an animal skin laid over it—a throne for her Iron Age warlord of a vampire-king husband, Setanta. He was the regent, not her. Still. No one else was there. And the throne would one day belong to the baby in her belly.

She climbed the dais and ran her fingers over the chair, then sat. It was comfortable, if a bit large. Sitting helped relieve some of the pressure on her lower back.

"Everything the light touches is your kingdom," she joked, patting her abdomen. "Or maybe everything the shadows touch. You are a vampire."

Having the room to herself was nice. She'd just come from therapy, of all things, and her mind was swimming. Luckily, the psychologist she frequented was a human who'd once worked donating blood as a source for vampires, so she knew about the world Sarai was a part of, but Sarai's issues were still so much to work through that she worried the poor doctor was out of her depth. How could a mere doctor understand the horror of being nearly possessed by a demonic, extra-planar monster that shattered her mind and required memory-removal magic to be managed? She could barely remember her own wedding to Setanta, like it had happened in a fog. But her latest therapy session had revealed something very important to her.

Sarai was frustrated. Horny. And she needed her lovers, both Setanta and her co-queen the vampire Marcelle, to stop treating her like glass just because she was pregnant. And sure, the pregnancy felt awful, and perhaps kinky, vampire sex wasn't good for the baby…but Sarai needed it desperately.

The door to the throne room opened a crack at the far end, and a pale head with a long, messy braid peeked inside. Red lips smiled, and Marcelle de Sauveterre came striding down the hall as the door swung shut behind her.

"Hey," Sarai said, smiling at her lover. As Marcelle got closer, she noticed the vampire's signature red lipstick was smudged and her hair was messy as if she'd just rolled out of her bed. Or someone's bed. A slight scent of smoke distinct to a pyromancer witch and the only mortal counted among the knights of New Ulster gave away whose bed. "Coming back from Lochlan's?"

Marcelle grinned. "Couldn't help myself."

"How are things with him?"

"Good. He left me peckish, though. He wasn't in the mood for bites."

"Don't tease me like that." Sarai sighed. "If he doesn't want it, you know I do."

"A few more months, my love, and I'll bite you anytime you'd like." Marcelle climbed the dais and leaned in to whisper, "Anywhere and everywhere you'd like."

Sarai whimpered as Marcelle planted a slow, sensual kiss on her lips, then pulled back a little.

"I wanted to talk to you about that," Sarai managed to say, only for Marcelle to kiss her again and steal her air.

"Yes?" Another kiss from Marcelle and a gasp for air from Sarai.

"See, I was talking to Dr. Chandler—" Kiss. Gasp. "—and she said—" A flick of Marcelle's tongue, and Sarai inhaled the scent of smoldering smoke from Lochlan's pyromancy and rosewater from Marcelle's perfume and makeup. And the savory scent of orgasms and sex. Pregnancy hormones had turned Sarai into a sex-obsessed bloodhound. She lost her train of thought.

"What did she say, my love?" Marcelle asked.

"You're making it very hard to focus," Sarai accused, giving a playful shove.

Marcelle grinned. "Well, I'm listening, my little witch. Tell me all about what the venerable Dr. Chandler said."

"A few things. She…made me wonder what we are to each other."

"Hm?"

"Am I your girlfriend? I realized we married

Setanta. Not each other. So what are we? Officially?"

"What would you like us to be?" Marcelle sat on the armrest of the throne, caressing her finger down Sarai's cheek.

"I don't know if I've figured that out yet, but I'm working on it."

"If you want something, tell me and you'll have it."

That felt good to hear. "Okay. Yeah. I'll think about what I want. Also, I…I'm horny, Marcelle. All the time. And you and Setanta, you're too nice to me. That first night we were together was so intense, and then I got pregnant, and you're treating me like I can't do anything."

"We're not pulling out the whips or ripping into the veins of a pregnant lady."

"No, I know. That's not what I want. It is, but I understand. I want that itch scratched, you know? Dr. Chandler suggested I talk to you and Setanta about trying some safe kink. It can't all be dangerous to the baby."

Marcelle let out a long sigh. "I suppose. It's new territory for me, if I'm being honest. And last time Setanta had a pregnant wife, I don't think the term 'kink' had been invented yet. I'll do some thinking on the subject. We'll scratch that itch for you." She leaned down and gave Sarai yet another long, lingering, and needful kiss. "Are you feeling unsatisfied right now?"

Sarai let out a slow breath to steady herself. "I could use a little more satisfaction."

Marcelle slid down to kneel on the floor in front of the throne and snapped open the button at the top of Sarai's pants.

"Will Setanta mind us using his throne like this?" Sarai wondered as the vampire pulled down clothes so that her bare bottom rested against the fur-covered throne.

"He'll just be jealous he wasn't invited. Now, don't worry your pretty head about what he might think. You focus on me. On my voice. My touch. Nothing else exists but us. Nothing exists but me."

It was a perfect moment, and Sarai quivered with anticipation, feeling Marcelle's light, cool breath so close to her skin. She knew it was purposeful since Marcelle didn't need to breathe. That light fluttering was part of the vampire's practiced teasing technique to make Sarai crave her.

Fingers slid against her sex without penetrating her, taunting her. "You're wet, *ma petite sorcière*," Marcelle whispered. "Is that for me?"

"Please. You know I need you. I need more."

And so Marcelle gave her more.

Chapter Two

New Blood

Sarai was satisfied. Being served by Marcelle while sitting on their husband's throne was so exquisite that the multiple climaxes she reached left her content, for the moment. Her wild hormones would demand more soon enough, but being satisfied was a wonderful feeling.

Marcelle curled up against her on the throne, the two of them entwined happily, basking in the moment, in what the French vampire liked to call "the little death" after pleasure.

"What are your plans tonight?" Sarai nuzzled her lover. "People will be waking up soon."

"They will, yes. Much the pity. But I do have some rather important plans. Final tryouts for Angela's replacement are today."

Sarai's heart stung at those words. She hadn't been very close to Angela but knew her enough that her death at the hands of the late Reinhart coven stung with a mix of loss and survivor's guilt. "It took a long time for you to replace her," she remarked.

"It's an important role, being a knight of the realm. I put Bear in charge since Angela was his fighting partner, but he couldn't find anyone he liked. I narrowed it down to three to present today." Marcelle paused for a moment before she added, "You know, knights of the realm serve the monarchy. Specialty missions, bodyguards. Personal protection. This one will be joining Bear as your personal bodyguard. Would you like to be there for the trials? They should see who they're protecting. You could knight the victor."

Sarai hadn't considered that. "I can? Am I allowed to do that? I thought I was just a queen consort. I don't have any real power, right?"

"In general, yes, Setanta is the one with ruling power. One of the exceptions to that is in appointing your own protector. You can knight someone in his name to keep you and our child safe." Marcelle gave her a smile and slid down Sarai's body to place a loving kiss on Sarai's belly. "Would you like that?"

"I do have tutoring tonight…but yes. I'd much rather do this."

Her first exertion of any royal authority. It was exciting.

After Marcelle cleaned herself up so she didn't smell too much like sex, both women changed clothes. Sarai into a long-sleeved, turtleneck dress the vampire chose for her that felt a little stiff but kept out enough of the cold, and Marcelle into tight clothes that would allow for the most movement.

Marcelle also made a point of wearing the official dagger with a wolf-head symbol at her waist, with symbols that indicated her rank. She also carried a second similar dagger, one befitting a knight, to be given to the winner of the new position.

"You're missing one small thing." Marcelle picked up two thin, ornate, gold, nearly matching circlets. One had a star ruby in the center, the other a star sapphire. She put the one with a ruby on her own head, then placed the other nestled atop Sarai's wild gold-brown curls. "There. My queen, officially." Her voice held a reverence of respect.

They made their way to a large basement, a level above the dungeon, where the knights and other vampires would train and spar with each other. The knights awaited their arrival. Sarai recognized a few. Bear, of course. He was an incredibly tall and muscular Mi'kmaq Native American vampire with a thousand years of experience, long black hair, geometric tattoos, and the personality of a teddy bear. Crispin was an English vampire with a prosthetic leg and an eye patch, whom she suspected had once been a pirate. She knew several others by face and a few by name. Oddly, though, Lochlan appeared to be missing. He was the only mortal to ever be given a knighthood in the vampire kingdom, so she had expected to see him.

Among the knights were three new faces she'd never seen before. They were different from the rest in that they did not have any symbols of rank and wore plain, black, sleeveless uniforms.

Crispin at the front door offered to announce the queens, but Marcelle waved him off.

"At attention!" she shouted, her piercing, high-pitched voice vibrating strength throughout the room.

Everyone formed lines as chattering stilled. The three candidates stood with feet shoulder-width apart and arms clasped behind them, eyes downcast. They knelt in unison with practiced precision.

All the formality and the people bowing made Sarai uncomfortable. But Marcelle's ease at taking control was hot. She liked that very much, and it helped her to keep her own head high. They were queens. These were their people. She had to behave as if she were worthy of their respect. The more she acted, the more she began to believe it as well.

"Behold your queens," Marcelle said. "Tonight, we will decide which of you deserves to shed their blood for us. Who deserves to serve us and our heir. The two who fail will be allowed to try for positions serving our dukes or duchesses or return to your current posts. Stand."

Sarai eyed the vampires as they stood. One woman had brown hair cut into a bob fashionable perhaps in the 1920s. One was an Asian man with a sharp, powerful, square jawline, facial hair in the style of a mustache and small goatee, and unusual long hair styled into two braided loops falling out from under a knitted ski cap. The last was a sick-looking pale man with no hair at all, a gaunt face worthy of a corpse, and limbs that were too long for his body. Sarai wondered at their ages. The pale man, she couldn't tell, but the other two had distinctive hairstyles that could have only come from certain time periods. Hair was almost always the easiest way to determine a vampire's age since they could never cut or grow it after being turned without the hair returning to its original length.

Marcelle called forth the first two to introduce themselves. The flapper, Janet, boasted about her hand-to-hand combat skills. The pale man, Gedeon, had specialization in language, stealth, and explosives, who had pivoted from service to their spymaster, Lilly, in the interest of something new.

Then there was Temuulen Borjigin.

"Borjigin Temuulen," the Asian vampire corrected as he stepped forward. "Clan before personal name."

Sarai looked him up and down. He wasn't tall, no

more than five foot six, but that wasn't a problem for her. She was four foot eleven. She found the prospect of not needing to stand on tiptoe to kiss someone his height quite nice, then she felt her face flush with intense heat as she blushed at the thought and pushed it from her mind.

"Apol… Wait." Marcelle paused. "Duke Borjigin?"

Sarai blinked. A duke? That meant he had authority already. Why would he want a downgrade to simple knighthood?

He grinned. "There's too much paperwork involved in running Delaware. So here I am, a sixth-generation vampire. I can shoot a man through the eye from horseback at a thousand paces with a bow or a gun. I can also ride and snipe from a motorbike if the horse is impractical. I speak seven languages. Oh, and Chinggis Khan, or as you know him Genghis Khan, was my father."

Sarai widened her eyes. That was a historical name she knew, and it did impress her.

Marcelle appeared less impressed as she raised an eyebrow. "I'm sure you are. And I'm an illegitimate daughter of King Charlemagne. Weren't you claiming to be the *grandson* of Genghis Khan just last decade?"

"You caught me." He gave the queens a wide, mischievous grin that made Sarai's cheeks flush with heat as she blushed again. "He's *my* grandson."

Sarai rolled her eyes. Something told her that he and Bear, the other notorious joker, would be good friends. She made a mental note not to believe anything he said without an outside confirmation.

"All right, meet and greet is over. Janet Grimes, Gedeon Katz, Borjigin Temuulen," Marcelle barked.

"You are presented today with the great honor of fighting for the right to serve your kingdom as a knight of the realm. I will draw lots, and each of you will face off against your opponent in the order I call you. I already know how you fight fellow vampires, so that is not the test. You'll be fighting a witch."

The three glanced around in what Sarai assumed was confusion. Sarai noticed their gazes lingered on her form and wondered if any of them would actually fight her if she had stepped up, or if their morals and submission to vampire hierarchy would prevent them from fighting a pregnant queen. Sarai smiled at their reactions. She knew where this was going.

Lochlan stepped out from the shadows, a bow and a quiver of arrows on his back, an hourglass talisman hooked to his belt that Sarai could see surged with magic power, and a hound-headed dagger in his hand. He had shoulder-length purple hair, scruff on his chin, eyes dyed by a potion to match his hair, purple fingernails, and round glasses. He gave a grin and sheathed the weapon, drawing the incredulous reactions of all four vampires. In Sarai's interactions with vampires since Lochlan's knighthood ceremony, she'd discovered that the fact that a witch worked alongside the knights of the realm as one of them had spread as a rumor most vampires didn't believe until they saw him in person.

"Sup, leeches," he said to the vampires. "I'm your taskmaster today, and yes, I outrank all three of you. 'Cept maybe his dukeness." He tapped the dagger at his belt that only a knight of the realm was permitted to carry.

"Actually, you do outrank the Duke of Delaware in matters of New Ulster security," Marcelle said.

"Well now, fancy that," mused the duke.

Lochlan was good. He'd been training with Marcelle and learning new magic to keep up with his vampire coworkers. But Sarai wasn't sure he could take on three vampires in a row, especially not ones he was antagonizing with insults. The new vampires appeared to agree with that sentiment, as they looked a little more confident, even smirking.

"Now, I don't want you to worry too much," Lochlan said. "You don't have to beat me. You just need to show us what you've got."

"And if I do beat you? What will be left for those who come after me?" Janet with the bob cut asked.

Lochlan smirked. "Don't worry, sweetheart. There's plenty of me to fuck up every single one of you."

"Rules," Marcelle said. "No lethal strikes from any opponent. You three, no biting. If you bite him, you're disqualified. This is a fight until one side yields, so first blood drawn doesn't matter. No fighting outside the ring. Understood?"

"Yes, Queen," the three said in unison.

Marcelle drew a lot to determine the first fighter. "All right. Janet Grimes. Prove yourself."

The rest backed off and gave Lochlan and Janet space in a roped-off ring while Janet picked out a spear for her fight and Lochlan flipped the hourglass on his belt.

"Are you sure that's safe?" Sarai murmured to Marcelle. "I mean, I know he's powerful, and you guys have sent him on a few big missions, but how strong are these vampires? Facing all of them one after the other is a lot."

"Trust me. We've been tutoring him." Pride flashed

in her eyes. "He's developed some interesting anti-vampire techniques. I know you heard about his mission in Maine, and now you'll get to see for yourself."

Bear rang a bell, but the fight didn't start. Janet was eyeing Lochlan, as if trying to figure out what his gimmick might be. Then she launched forward. She was fast, almost as fast as Marcelle. But Lochlan sidestepped before Janet had moved, and she landed face first on the floor. Lochlan had an arrow notched and aimed at her but fired to the side of her head. It was a shot he easily could have made, but he was making it clear he was toying with her. She spun around, and her spear caught the bow to fling it from his hands, which he allowed her to do. Sarai found it obvious why—the bow was a distraction. He focused, and the metal of the spear became red with heat. She yelped, dropping it, then glared at him and continued her battle.

After being deflected again and again, Janet visibly dropped her decorum; her fangs emerged, and her eyes turned red. She rushed forward with her mouth open, and Marcelle intervened, grabbing her by the throat and throwing her to the ground.

"You're done," Marcelle snapped. "Get out."

"I had her," Lochlan muttered as Janet brushed herself off, glaring at Lochlan.

"I know you did, but I'm kicking her out for lack of control." Marcelle drew a lot with Gedeon's name, holding it up to reveal it to the gathering. "*Next!*"

Sarai eyed Gedeon as he stepped up to the ring and suppressed a gasp. He had a small tattoo on his inner arm of a string of numbers, the kind worn by Holocaust survivors. Though, given that he was a vampire, she wasn't sure she would call him a survivor. No wonder he looked so skeletal. This had to be the Jewish vampire Setanta had once mentioned to her. He could had been persecuted for being Romani, disabled, gay, or a political prisoner rather than Jewish, but the probable conclusion was that he was Jewish. After all, his last name was Katz.

Even if he didn't win the position, Sarai wanted to talk to him. He had to have an interesting story, and she was curious how he balanced kosher rules with the dietary demands of being a vampire.

Gedeon did better than Janet had. His movements were like some sort of cryptid, and he relied on his agility and throwing stars as weapons. Lochlan raised heat in pockets in the air to melt them in a feat Sarai wasn't sure many pyromancers would be capable of, and the molten remains hissed in puddles on the floor.

Ultimately, Gedeon ended the fight lashed down under ropes of fire, sighing at the moment of his defeat before giving a simple statement of, "I yield."

The last one up was Temuulen, who had been silent as he watched Lochlan's fiery victories.

"Wanna pick a weapon?" Lochlan asked.

"I am a weapon," Temuulen replied with a wide smile. "But I know I'm no match for your flames as they are. So perhaps we make this interesting. This isn't about whether I can destroy you or not. Whether I can draw your blood. This is about proving my skills and my determination. This isn't a combat test." He looked around and turned to address Marcelle.

"Isn't it?" she said, a coy tone in her voice.

He scoffed. "Everyone here is more than worthy and capable of fighting for the royal family, or we wouldn't have made it this far. This is a personality test to prove our tenacity." He unsnapped a button around the cuff of a fingerless leather glove, and a shining silver chain dropped from a hidden compartment, charring his flesh with a sizzle when it touched his skin. "So let me prove my mettle."

"Are you trying to trick me into wearing silver to keep me from being able to use my magic?" Lochlan asked. "It's not gonna work. I'll take every advantage I've got, and you should too."

"Not at all."

Lochlan shrugged. "Suit yourself, man."

Temuulen charged like a bull the moment the bell rang, right through a wall of fire from Lochlan, and wrapped his arms around the witch's waist before wrestling him down to the ground, grappling him with powerful legs and arms. Lochlan had a smaller build not quite suited for wrestling someone like Temuulen, but with the silver on the vampire's wrist, he had a shot.

Sarai was no combat expert but felt that Lochlan gave it a good try. He shot out flames constantly, trying to use them to push his opponent back. Each time, new severe burns erupted across the vampire's skin that did not heal due to the contact with silver, but he remained undeterred. They shouted and grunted and pummeled each other with fists until Lochlan managed to gasp, "I yield."

Temuulen, looking like he'd lost a fight with a barbecue, stumbled as pulled himself to his feet and put the silver away in his glove's hidden pocket so that his disfiguring burns began to heal. Lochlan did not have any such healing abilities, so Sarai rushed forward and used one of her two magical gifts, her ability to heal, to fix his split lip, broken ribs, and several beginning-stage bruises. He gave her an appreciative pat on the shoulder.

She took the moment of being closer to the pair to get a good look at Temuulen. As the skin on his arms healed, the definition of his arm muscles was stunning. No doubt he could hold her down with ease. Without the fire involved, the wrestling had looked almost fun. He could pin anyone he wanted to the floor, thrust between her legs, and spread them with his powerful thighs, hold her down by her wrists with those strong arms, make her ache for him. She had never kissed a man with facial hair. What would it feel like? She wanted to taste his lips. To bite down on them, hard. To devour him.

Sarai gave her head a little shake. She had just gotten her satisfaction from Marcelle, and yet her hormones were rearing up again as if she were some sort of irresponsible teenager. She needed to get a grip.

Lochlan offered a hand to Temuulen, and the pair shook.

"That was cool," Lochlan admitted.

"Hot, more like it." Temuulen laughed. "That was without competition one of the most intense fights of my existence. Thank you for that."

"Your thoughts?" Marcelle asked Sarai.

As much as Sarai had been rooting for Gedeon as a fellow Jew she wanted to talk to, she had to admit that Temuulen had performed the best. She hoped that it wasn't just her hormones talking. "Is it really a question?" she mused.

Marcelle nodded in agreement, then offered Sarai a sword from the assorted weapons available. "Do you remember the oath?"

Sarai had a vague memory of her own oath at her coronation. Her memories of Setanta's coronation and Lochlan's knighting were stronger. Luckily, she had been made to memorize the oath as part of her studies. "I think so."

"Shield, sword, and hearth. In King Setanta's name," Marcelle instructed.

Sarai nodded. This was it, her power to express as queen. "Borjigin Temuulen, please kneel."

Temuulen adjusted what was left of his charred ski cap and obeyed, getting down on one knee in front of her as her heart raced. Something about the way he looked up at her as he knelt, his clothes smoldering with smoke rising around him, made her lose her voice for a moment as she opened her mouth to speak, then closed her mouth. He was…literally smoking hot. She rehearsed the lines a few times in her head while everyone stared. Let them stare and wait. She was queen. A queen lost in the thrill of having an attractive man on his knees about to pledge his life in service to her.

"In the name of our regent, King Setanta, I ask. Do you swear to be my shield to the innocent, my sword to our enemies, and my hearth to our allies and for those who need your protection?"

"As shield, sword, and hearth, I do swear."

His eyes locked on hers. As she stared into those deep brown eyes, she forgot what came next.

Marcelle came to the rescue. "Arise, Sir Borjigin Temuulen, knight of New Ulster." She offered a sheathed dagger to him.

He bowed as he accepted it, and all the vampires—and Lochlan—cheered for him.

"Your first assignment is simple," Marcelle told him. "Sarai and our unborn child are your top priorities. You'll join Bear in ensuring their protection."

"It is my honor." And he bowed deeply to Sarai as befitted a knight to his queen.

Chapter Three

Jackie

Once she could, Sarai excused herself and ran off to take a cold shower, then find her human friend Rosaline and get some food. She found it nice to hang out with Rosaline in the human quarter. One of the guys would cook for Sarai whenever she had a craving, and the rest were happy to treat her like one of them. She could feel almost normal.

"A new, hot bodyguard?" Rosaline asked.

"Yeah, you ever hear of him? He's giving up being the Duke of Delaware so he can come do this," Sarai said, her voice muffled as she shoveled pancakes into her mouth.

"Duke of Delaware? I think I have heard of him. He's Genghis Khan's brother, right?"

"He said son. Then grandson. Then grandfather. So you know, take it with a grain of salt."

"Gotcha. One of those vampires with a sense of humor and a mysterious backstory no one can discredit or verify."

"I wonder if they're related. I mean, it's not impossible," Sarai said.

"Who knows. But you said he's cute?"

"Yeah, he wrestled Lochlan. It was…" She'd liked watching it way more than she wanted to admit with a bunch of humans around. "Well, he was very good at wrestling. But I've gotta be going crazy. It's these pregnancy hormones. I'm—" She glanced around and lowered her voice so as to not be heard while one of the source boys named Will made more pancakes. "—horny all the time. Marcelle and Setanta are trying to keep up with me, but I'm going crazy."

As Sarai looked up, she caught sight of someone she didn't recognize standing in the doorway to the dormitories. She was a short woman with a soft, round, brown face framed by a black-haired pixie cut and even bangs. Something about her slight lips and the elegant neck that was too long for her short body was stunning. Like a precious flower with soft petals that needed to be protected and that Sarai wanted to hug and hug and hug to be as close as possible to her. Sarai's cheeks flushed with heat.

Not again. First Temuulen, now her. In fact, something about them was similar. But she wasn't sure what, since they visually had nothing in common.

Rosaline looked up to acknowledge the girl standing there. "Oh! You haven't met the new girl, just transferred from upstate New York. This is Jacqueline. We're calling her Jackie. Come on in, don't stand in the doorway like a gargoyle."

"Sorry," Jackie murmured in a soft tone and crept out like a mouse from the shadows. She sat down at the very edge of one of the empty chairs around the table, fiddling with a charm bracelet that clinked on her wrist under white, lacy, long sleeves.

Sarai had the passing thought that Jacqueline was perhaps an unusual name for someone who looked South Asian, but made no remark since any number of circumstances could have led to such an outcome.

"I didn't think they let pregnant humans be sources." Jackie's gaze flickered down as she spoke to look at Sarai's bump.

"Oh, I'm not a source," Sarai said.

"This is Sarai. She's the vampire queen."

Jackie's expression, which had been cautious and shy, turned to stone. Then confusion. "You don't have red eyes?"

"Nope. Not a vampire. Just married to one. And together with another one." Sarai felt her face burn with heat. "It's, well, vampires do things differently, so we have an open kind of arrangement." She felt very strongly that Jackie needed to be fully aware that Sarai wasn't locked down just because she was married and pregnant.

"That's…" Jackie hesitated, then said, "Unique."

"It's not that weird with vampires, girl. You'll get used to it," Rosaline said. "You don't gotta get involved with any, but you'll at least be hearing about all their sexy shenanigans. It is the best gossip ever."

"But you're mortal?" Jackie asked. "Isn't that dangerous, to be with vampires?"

"Probably, but everyone here has good control," Sarai assured her. "I mean, you know that, right?"

Jackie's eyes widened. "I-I don't…haven't had those kinds of relations."

"Oh! No, I meant because you're a source," Sarai said. "Obviously sex is a little more intense than a bite, but there's some comparison. Do you have anyone regular yet?"

"Regular?"

"You know, a vampire you have regular

appointments with." Rosaline rolled her eyes. "You aren't new to this, are you? A blood virgin? You don't get to be a palace source without a recommendation from one of the dukedoms."

"You mean, one of the states?" Jackie said. "Oh, yeah. Um. I was pretty new in New York. Artemisia wanted me here."

Everyone stopped and stared.

"Artemisia?" Sarai asked. "Princess Artemisia, the pureblood? Who doesn't need human blood because she's a pureblood and they need vampire blood instead?"

"I didn't see any teeth on you, Jackie," Rosaline joked and poked at the woman's arm. "And you feel as warm-blooded as any other human."

Jackie shrugged. "She likes my blood. She asked me to be here for her."

Rosaline made a face. "You're sure it's not a sex thing, right? I know she's thirty or something, but their brains don't age until they choose to let their bodies age, you know. She's still a kid. You're the grown-up here."

"No, no, no, nothing like that," Jackie blurted. "Just blood. I know she's a kid."

"Setanta drinks my blood, you know," Sarai said. "He did when I wasn't pregnant, anyway. Purebloods like our warmth. We're like candy or something to them."

"You're okay with being candy to the vampire king?" Jackie said.

"I mean, aren't you okay with being candy to the vampire princess?"

Jackie laughed a little. "Fair point. It just sounds terrifying. I've heard about him and seen him from a distance. Artemisia is strange in her own way, of course, but all the other purebloods I've heard of sound scarier."

"Well, Sarai's got her witchy-ness," Rosaline said. "So she's not scared of anyone."

"A…witch." Jackie's face was unreadable, but her stare lasted a few moments longer than Sarai was comfortable with. "Sorry, I don't mean to be rude. I've never met a witch who hung around vampires before. You have a gift, then, right?"

"Yeah. Two, actually. I'm one of those weird fluke witches, so I can heal and I'm a necromancer," Sarai explained. "But you know, it's nice to forget about all that and hang out here. Do you, um, do you have any plans? We could all do something. Maybe play cards. Or eat more pancakes?"

"Next batch coming in hot," called Will as he plopped a fresh stack of pancakes in the middle of the table. "Chocolate-chip pancakes."

"Fuck yeah," Sarai said.

"I guess I haven't had dinner yet. Or is it breakfast?" Jackie asked. "If it's dinner, my favorite is chicken alfredo."

"Who knows," Rosaline said. "I think it's late enough to qualify as a midnight lunch."

Sarai reached for a pancake and bumped hands with Jackie, who pulled her hand back, biting her lip.

"Sorry," they both said at the same time.

Rosaline cleared her throat and looked between the two. "Have you had a tour yet?" she asked the new girl.

"No, not yet," Jackie said.

"*Sarai* could give you a tour. It's her palace, so she would give the best tour. You two could go together."

Sarai didn't know what to say. She didn't mind the idea of being alone with Jackie, but something about

Jackie being a human made her nervous. She could imagine flirting with a vampire easily. Most of them were promiscuous and could read body language like a newspaper, so there was no hiding a crush. But a mortal, a regular human woman, was so much more intimidating. Her lips looked so soft, so warm. And the skin of her neck so smooth. Sarai could almost feel the pitter-patter beating in Jackie's veins just from looking at her from a distance.

"That sounds nice," Jackie said. "I think I'd like that."

"You would?" Sarai asked. "I would too. I mean, it would be nice. I'd be happy to show you around."

Someone knocked on the door, and Will opened it to reveal a vampire man with a pageboy haircut. Sarai groaned and hung her head in her hands. It was her tutor.

"Excuse me, is Queen Sarai here?"

"I don't wanna learn," Sarai muttered.

"Learn?" Jackie asked. "What are you learning?"

"How to be a good vampire queen," Sarai said. "Art, history, politics, law, etiquette. Being a vampire queen sounds interesting, but all the preparation and studying can be a lot. It would be interesting if it wasn't so boring to listen to."

"Maybe...I could come with you for your lesson, and you could show me around after?"

That perked her up. A lesson with a cute second student in the class sounded much better than listening to a lecture, and Jackie did seem to want to spend time together.

"All right. Yeah, come learn boring vampire law books with me. It's a date," Sarai joked before she could stop the words. She froze. "Not a *date* date. Just, you know."

Jackie smiled. "That's cute. Let's go to school, queenie."

Sarai's tutoring session went well. At least, she assumed it went well. She was very distracted by Jackie's proximity, the brightness in her eyes as she listened to the tutor. Watching her thirst for knowledge was beautiful. The way she leaned forward, twirled her index finger against the short strands of her black hair, and smiled. She had very straight teeth. They were almost as perfect as veneers. Perhaps she'd had braces at some point, which did surprise Sarai a little. Most humans who worked as sources had some tragic story of difficulty that didn't include family willing to pay for something as expensive as braces. Many were former foster kids who had run away from abusive homes, many were former addicts, and almost all had been unhoused people at the lowest point in their lives when recruited by vampires to donate blood. What was Jackie's story, and how she had ended up serving Artemisia exclusively?

"Damn," Jackie said once the tutoring session wrapped up, the tutor left, and she looked at the clock on the wall. "I do want that tour, but I have to go. I'm supposed to meet the princess in fifteen minutes."

"Oh." She'd been looking forward to being alone with Jackie. "That's okay, no worries. Whenever you're free, I guess?"

"Yeah." Jackie paused, then leaned in for a hug.

The hug lasted longer than a friendly hug would, and Sarai felt dizzy as she basked in her scent. It was some sort of coconut and floral shampoo or conditioner. Her neck was so close, her skin so warm. Sarai wondered what it would be like to be a vampire and sink her teeth into that gorgeous, long neck. To drown in her taste, every drop of her hot blood flooding down Sarai's throat…

As soon as the thought entered her mind, she pulled back, trying to breathe. It was different from the general horniness she'd been obsessive over due to her hormones. It was a violent desire. Yet she didn't want to be violent to this beautiful woman. She wanted to be sensual.

Right?

"Thanks for coming here." Sarai smiled to try to hide her thoughts. "I'll see you around?"

"For sure. See you around, Sarai." Jackie squeezed Sarai's hand, then left to attend her meeting with the princess.

Sarai sank back into her chair, a hand over her pregnant bump. Too much studying, she decided. Learning about vampires was getting to her head. She was starting to think like one.

She didn't want blood. She didn't.

Really, she didn't.

And maybe if she told herself that enough times, she could believe it.

She pushed the thoughts down as deep as she could and took off her crown to stare into the shimmer of the star sapphire. She had more queenly things to focus on than tutoring. Perhaps the trial of those who wronged her would be a good thing. It would help her focus on something, anything, other than lust for sex and, perhaps, for blood.

Chapter Four

A Princess of Rome

With the trial of the former queen looming on the horizon, Marcelle could only distract herself by throwing her mind into her work as the Knight Commander of the Realm by raiding a rural warehouse several states away in the dead of night.

She loved her work. Loved the plotting, the violence, and the thrill of taking down those who would kill her—the Vasi. They were hunters who loathed anything occult, a secret society of humans who for centuries had worked to end the existence of anything they perceived as a threat to humanity and in particular, vampires and witches. Marcelle loved hunting the hunters. And as of late, she loved working with her new witch allies to rescue enslaved witches from their grasp. She found her work much more fulfilling when rescuing live witches from a horrible fate than stomping a Vasi human's head into a bloody puddle, though both had merit.

She especially liked working with Lochlan at her side, and the pair had become quite accomplished. The Ellis Coven witches all knew about Marcelle and Lochlan, how they led teams to do what no others had done in rescuing people. Lochlan's fire had been honed from an out-of-control raging inferno to a precision instrument of war, and Marcelle couldn't have been prouder of her lover.

Yet at one of their more recent attempts to raid a Vasi warehouse, things hadn't gone as planned. The building they found in Ohio had been abandoned with no trace of life at all. The second raid a week later in Maryland had been the same. Nothing. Two was a coincidence.

Three was a pattern.

The third raid more carefully plotted over three more weeks targeted a series of warehouses known to belong to the Vasi. Yet again, when Marcelle and her team broke into the building in Tennessee, they were met with only silence.

The vampires and Lochlan moved with care, along with a small group of witches from the Ellis Coven who joined the mission, using gestures to indicate movements as well as the vampires communicating in tones too low for humans to hear. Yet despite all their care, they found nothing. No Vasi humans, no lights on, not even a scrap of paperwork.

She couldn't think of a different conclusion. The Vasi had been tipped off.

Marcelle cursed and kicked a metal desk, crumpling the side. "They knew," she snapped, looking back at Bear, Crispin, and Lochlan who were close to her. "What other explanation is there? They're watching us somehow."

"Maybe they captured a seer?" Lochlan suggested.

"Unlikely. Between Setanta's protective enchantments on us and the ones you've bolstered, a seer shouldn't be able to see us coming." Marcelle looked at Bear. "Theories?"

"None yet." He paused as he took several moments to analyze the room around them with narrow eyes. "We need to look around more. The air was still when we came in. I didn't see any fresh tire marks outside. They left before yesterday, judging from the rain last night. That would have washed away any tracks. They might just be getting smart, keeping on the move to avoid us, and we've had bad luck to hit their abandoned sites."

"I don't believe in luck, good or bad," Marcelle retorted and ripped open a file cabinet. Empty, once more. "Not even fucking notes. We always find some scrap of something if they leave in a rush, their little recordings of vivisections on witches and vampires. Experimenting with vampire dust and what have you."

"What's a vivisection?" Lochlan asked.

"You don't want to know," Crispin murmured.

"It's a dissection performed on a living subject," she snapped, too irritated to sugarcoat anything. "Yet another reason in a long list of reasons why Vasi are scum."

"Yeah." Lochlan looked sick. "Damn, I didn't know they did that."

"It's a more recent phenomenon. Exploring the science of magic," Marcelle said. "We've been seeing it for a few years now, and they've escalated. Did none of you find anything of interest here?"

"Actually, I wanted to show you one of the cells." Crispin led the group to the basement where they came across rows of open, empty cells. He pointed to the one in the center. "There."

Marcelle stepped in, trying to make sense of what she saw. The floor was covered in something white. "Are those...flower petals?"

No, not flower petals. As she picked one of the white things up, she could see they were hard. Almost like…

"Scales, I think," Crispin said. "Lochlan, you're our resident witch. It's gotta be from one of the Vasi slave witches. Ever see anything like that?"

"Scales?" Lochlan scoffed. "No. We're witches, not lizard people. We don't shed."

"Is there any power you can think of that it might be related to?" Crispin asked.

"Nah. I mean, I guess maybe a shapeshifter who wanted to be like…an albino dinosaur? But shapeshifters have been extinct since before the Middle Ages."

"A little after the Middle Ages," Marcelle said. "There was a werewolf problem in Paris in the fourteen hundreds. But yes, I highly doubt a scaley shapeshifting witch was shedding in here. Perhaps it's the remnants of some new object or weapon they intend to use against us? Whatever it is, we need more information. We need *prisoners*. I want Vasi prisoners in my dungeon so we can find out what they're up to."

"Yes, Your Highness," Bear said.

Lochlan put a hand on her shoulder.

She tensed, then a low warmth grew from his touch, enveloping her like an embrace.

"Let us handle this," he said. "You're stressing yourself out trying to carry it all when you've got people here who can help."

"Of course I'm stressing myself out." She sighed. "I'm the queen now. It was already my responsibility to keep the realm safe before my coronation, but now? If they're planning something and I don't catch it, who knows how many vampires could be hurt. And witches too, for that matter. We should all be stressing out."

"We'll figure it out," Bear said. "But this is the third base we've hit that they've abandoned. We need to go back and revise our strategy before we try again. We keep doing the same thing, and we'll just get more of the same results."

Marcelle nodded. "Yeah, you're right."

"You guys are planning a trip to New York soon, aren't you?" Crispin asked.

"Yes," she said. "To visit Sarai's family. Not until well after the trial, of course."

"Then you've got plenty going on beyond this," he said. "I'll coordinate with Spymaster Lilly, and we'll come up with new plans for you to review and approve when you get back."

She opened her mouth to protest that she should be doing that work, then closed it. She didn't need to micromanage these people. She could trust them. Bear and Crispin were experts of their craft with hundreds of years of experience under their belts, just like her. Lilly was a brilliant spymaster. Lochlan was new to their world but a fast learner and as dedicated to his work as any vampire. She even trusted the Ellis Coven witches to manage without her. She could delegate to all of them. That was what monarchs did. She was no longer just the Knight Commander; she was the queen. Setanta delegated work to her all the time, after all, and these were her subordinates as well as her friends. She had to trust them.

"That sounds like a plan," she said. "Yes. Crispin, after the trial is over and when I come back from New York, we'll work on a new plan of attack. We'll get these bastards."

"Yes, my queen."

31

****

The trial, though stressful, was an exciting prospect to Marcelle.

As it began, she sat on one of three thrones on the dais of the throne room, alongside her husband and Sarai. Normally, court was held without the attendance of the queens, who held social positions rather than a regent's power. But finally, after months of agonizing political back and forth between Setanta and the vampiric Roman Empire, the trial for Setanta's stepmother, the former queen Giovanna, and her brother, Valens, was set. The pair had conspired in a plot that led to the death of one of the knights who served the kingdom, and by proxy kidnapping of Sarai and Marcelle by a coven run by Sarai's now deceased father. Their crimes amounted to treason.

Putting the former queen and a foreign prince on trial was a spectacle unlike any the vampire royal court had seen in a long time. Marcelle didn't feel nervous about the full crowd. She felt vindicated that the woman who had so venomously once threatened Sarai's life and worked to have them both abducted would see justice. After all, Setanta had always been one to champion justice, even if it was a more brutal form of it than modern mortal societies of the twentieth century were used to. Marcelle wasn't sure what Giovanna's sentence would be, but she knew the woman was guilty. She did wonder how the trial would proceed. She'd seen one other vampire trial before at Setanta's court, to judge the guilt of murderous vampires who'd once targeted Lochlan when he was a child. Since those vampires had been undead and of Setanta's bloodline, he had the ability as a pureblood vampire to compel them to speak the truth whether they wanted to or not. Giovanna and Valens were a different issue; they were purebloods themselves and under no obligation to tell the truth. That and, unlike the case of the previous trial, they had a representative on their behalf, their father, who had flown in from Europe to attend the trial.

Giovanna and Valens looked impeccable as they were led in by guards. Given their social standing, they had been afforded some luxuries during their imprisonment. Their clothing was clean, and every hair was in place. Giovanna even wore some of her usual gold jewelry on her ears and around her neck. The only indication that they weren't there of their own free will were the silver cuffs burning black charred marks into their wrists to suppress their magical abilities and vampiric prowess.

As the pair stood tall and proud before the dais, their father, a dark-haired and statuesque prince of Rome with a very straight nose and muscular physique, stepped forward to join them, his arms crossed and an unreadable expression on his face.

Setanta looked down at them coolly, as regal as ever. His red hair was tied back in a ponytail by his usual black ribbon, and the iron circlet marking his status as regent rested on his head. Under his black button-down shirt, a golden torc with hound heads as decoration was visible, as were the start of a network of blue Celtic knotwork tattoos on his pale skin.

"Queen Stepmother Giovanna Aïdōneús of New Ulster and Prince Valens Aïdōneús of Rome," Setanta said in a clear, loud voice. "You stand before the king of New Ulster charged with conspiracy against the throne in a plot to have both of my queens abducted from the palace. This plot led to the unlawful grounding of Queen Marcelle and assault of Queen Sarai through a vile ritual by witches. The charge against—"

"Before we proceed further," interjected the pair's father, "I would like to object to the charge of treason."

Of course he did, Marcelle thought and resisted the urge to roll her eyes.

Setanta frowned. "Prince Marcus, I find it clear as starlight that plotting against the throne held by one's regent is worthy of being called treason."

"It would be," Marcus said, "were my Giovanna still a citizen of New Ulster at the time of the alleged plot. When she became queen, she pledged herself to your father and New Ulster as the queen consort of the king regent. Once she was no longer the queen consort of the king regent, that pledge concluded. Therefore, her more important title is not Queen Mother or Stepmother as you say. She is no longer a subject of New Ulster. She is of Rome. And I have a writ from my grandfather, the emperor of the Roman Empire, claiming her at this time as a recognized Princess of Rome only. So any alleged actions against the throne of New Ulster would not be under the umbrella of treason, but rather under the same classifications as those levied against Prince Valens. A foreign actor, with the protections of a foreign land."

Marcelle scowled. If Rome claimed her, the politics were too delicate for Setanta to refuse. She hadn't expected Giovanna to ever go along with a plan to reduce her title, even if it did lead to some leniency in sentencing.

Marcus handed a scroll of parchment to one of the guards, who brought it up to the dais for Setanta to inspect. The king unrolled it, read the Latin, and nodded.

As Marcelle knew, he couldn't object without an escalation of the international affair into dangerous territory.

"Agreed," he said. "Giovanna Aïdōneús will no longer be referred to as the former queen, having relinquished the responsibilities and rights associated with the position, and will be treated as a Princess of Rome."

And that meant whatever punishment could befall her would be much less severe. Marcelle had hoped to see the former queen grounded, and hoped it was still an option.

"*Princess* Giovanna, you met with and conspired with an enemy witch by the name of Alma Reinhart to have Queen Sarai abducted. You wrote a letter to lure her from the protection of our barrier to enable this. A scheme by Prince Valens sent Marcelle after her, into the arms of the enemy. The enemy witches additionally killed one of my knights, Dame Angela Lupu. What have you to say on the matter?" Setanta asked.

"I reunited a witch with her own family," Giovanna said. "Alma is Sarai's half sister, is she not? The Reinharts are where she belongs."

"That's not your decision to make," Setanta said.

"A mortal witch has no place on the throne, nor does an undead vampire," Giovanna hissed with the venom of a snake. "If anyone should be on trial, it should be you for permitting such a disgrace to vampire traditions. All I admit to is facilitating a family reunion. How that reunion went, well, those are crimes committed outside of my control." She smiled, returning to a calmer and more collected demeanor. "I cannot be punished for the actions of another. The internal bickering of a witch coven should be no business of a royal vampire such as myself, or such as you."

"You maintain your innocence, then?"

"I do. And I demand my rights as royalty."

Marcelle leaned forward in her chair. Whatever plan Giovanna had to walk free had to fail. She needed it to fail.

"What rights do you demand?"

"Trial by combat," she said. "My brother and I demand trial by combat."

Marcelle stood. She could manage that. It was an archaic rule but one Giovanna was entitled to. It had happened twice before in the history of New Ulster, and both times Marcelle had been the champion on behalf of the kingdom, as suited her role as Knight Commander. Of course, Giovanna wouldn't fight for herself. The woman wasn't as well trained in combat as others would be.

"I see," Setanta said, his expression unreadable. "And do you have a champion?"

"I do." She stepped back, and Valens stepped forward with a smile. "My brother is more than capable of defeating your knight commander. He is my champion, as well as his own."

Valens eyed Marcelle, smirking as if he had won already. Marcelle felt her fangs in her mouth and knew her eyes must have turned red as anger trembled in her closed fists.

"I'm more than happy to fight the trial," Valens said with glee. "I look forward to seeing your skills, Marcelle. And to defeating you."

The thought of having the opportunity to fight him gave Marcelle a fantastic rush. She wanted nothing more than to destroy him and pound his smug face into viscera. The problem was he was a pureblood. In almost every instance, a pureblood vampire would win a fight against an undead vampire. They were faster, stronger, and each bloodline had a unique magical gift much like a witch's gift. Setanta's bloodline of born vampires could grow wings, while the Romans were notorious for an intoxicating touch that turned anyone they wished into worshipers. All Valens would have to do was touch Marcelle's bare skin, and the battle would be over. Still, she couldn't back down. She stepped up and opened her mouth to speak, to accept the fight, but Setanta spoke up first.

"My queen, please sit," he said with an eerie calm. "You are a victim of this case, so it would not be suitable for you to fight. Especially against the accused."

Marcelle looked at him, confused. "Sire, it's my duty. Whatever else, I am still your knight commander."

Setanta shook his head. "No. You will not fight." He stood and walked up to Valens, his every footstep echoing against the marble floors until the men were face-to-face, Setanta looking down at the prince. "I will be your opponent."

The smirk melted off Valens's face. Marcelle had to utilize every ounce of careful control she had honed over the centuries not to burst into laughter.

Valens was *fucked*. And she reveled in his terror.

"I have to object," Marcus said, stepping forward. "To all of this. Trial by combat is their right, but no one of royal blood should fight. Choose undead champions as is tradition and let the matter be decided."

"My dear Prince Marcus, is Rome so weak?" Setanta asked.

The foreign vampire blinked twice, then narrowed his eyes. "I beg your pardon?"

"Pardon granted."

"That is not… Rome is not weak," Marcus snarled. "Our empire is the backbone of Europe. The jewel of the Mediterranean. For you from your land of potatoes and bog shit to insult us—"

"It is you who insults yourself," Setanta interrupted, "by implying we royals are so weak as to not be able to fight our own battles. I learned to always fight my own battles, even if I do hail from bog shit. My people respect me for my strength, for my willingness to risk my own body on enemy spears. Or in this case, not to force someone else to fight on my behalf. Your son seems to believe he has that strength. Would you neuter him in front of the world by denying him the fight he has requested?"

Marcus's nostrils flared. When he spoke, a glimpse of fangs was a visible sign of his anger. "To first blood, not to the death." He glanced at the two queens. "It would be regrettable if Valens were to leave your wives as new widows when they have a child on the way."

Marcelle laughed. Coward. Valens had some potential to score the first blood, but to kill Setanta? Not a chance. Still, she knew Setanta's fighting style. He didn't care much to avoid nonlethal or nondisabling attacks, instead relishing in the adrenaline rush and using that fuel to power the rest of a fight. In truth, while powerful and dangerous, Setanta was sloppy. But he didn't seem deterred.

"Tomorrow evening, after sunset," Setanta decreed. "You may choose the weapon. May the best vampire win."

As court ended, Marcelle looked at Sarai and had to stop herself from lurching forward in alarm. The witch's grip on her throne was white-knuckled. She looked ill. Marcelle took her hand and helped her up. That iron grip was stronger than she thought Sarai was capable of as a mortal, yet she could feel something was off. Either the stress of the trial had been too much, or something was wrong with Sarai's health.

"Stay with me," Marcelle said. "Hold my hand. Let's get you upstairs."

Chapter Five

Sweet Caramel and Tinnscra

The walk up to the royal chambers was horrible. Sarai kept her chin up until they were beyond the sight of any citizens. Once it was just Marcelle and Setanta, she let the pretense go.

"I don't feel good," she muttered as her stomach flipped and her knees cracked and crunched in pain with each stair. Yet she couldn't get herself to stop. If she stopped, she wasn't going to keep going.

"Sarai, take a deep breath. We've got you." Marcelle held her close, forcing her to stop. "We're here."

"I..." Sarai wasn't sure if she was going to throw up or if she was starving or if she hurt or if she needed to lie down. She felt horrible and wanted to step out of her body for a minute to take a break from feeling.

"Easy does it," Setanta said.

Marcelle scooped up Sarai in her arms, and Sarai leaned against her soft, pale chest. Her cold skin felt so soothing.

"I've got you."

"Don't go fast," Sarai begged. "I might throw up if you go fast."

"We'll go slow," Marcelle promised. "Rest."

Sarai closed her eyes and curled up like a fetus, focusing on her breathing and the gentle swaying motion of being carried. She felt safe. When the motion stopped, Marcelle laid her down on Setanta's bed, and Setanta presented her with a glass of water. She sat up with help from a pillow Marcelle fluffed behind her and accepted the glass, taking a few slow sips.

"Sorry," she said. "I don't know why it hit me so hard."

"How are you feeling now?" Setanta asked.

"Not good." The water didn't settle her as much as she'd hoped it would. Her throat ached with such a terrible thirst, yet it was as if she'd swallowed sand. She tried to gulp down more but coughed, spitting it up. "I'm so thirsty, but I feel like I'd throw it up."

Setanta and Marcelle exchanged knowing glances. Marcelle hesitated, then bit her own wrist and held it out.

Sarai opened her mouth to protest, to remind Marcelle that she kept kosher, that she wouldn't drink blood, then the scent hit her like a wall of bricks. *Sweetness*. It was the sort of scent one might encounter wafting along a breeze from a bakery mixed with warm caramel, like the most delicious treat in the world. She imagined that sticky, hot caramel drizzling over flaky pastry. Thick. Seductive. Dripping…like blood.

The fetus in her belly fluttered.

"I don't drink blood," Sarai whispered. "It's not kosher."

"You may need to," Setanta said. "What do you smell?"

"Caramel," she answered without hesitation.

He smiled a little. "I know it well. That thirst you're feeling, I've felt it. It's the thirst of a pureblood vampire, the one you're growing in your womb. And that scent of caramel, it isn't the way a mortal would smell blood. It would smell like copper to anyone but a vampire. That's Marcelle's scent as I experience it."

"I didn't consider I'd get cravings like this," Sarai said. "I guess that makes sense. Vampire baby, vampire cravings."

"It may not be just a craving, Sarai," Setanta said gently. "It may be a need. You're a strong witch, and that's why you've lasted this long, but the child is draining more from you than you can stand if you're having these cravings. You need to replenish."

She paused, and a numb fear washed over her. Vampire blood, especially the blood of a pureblood vampire, turned mortals into the undead. She was connected to the vampire inside her via a shared circulatory system. "If my sense of smell is like a vampire's, is this going to turn me? I never agreed to being turned for this. I…" Her vision spotted with white dots, and she couldn't breathe until Marcelle held her hands and snapped her back to reality.

"Easy does it. Take a deep breath," Marcelle reassured her. "You aren't going to turn. Not from this. My understanding is—and correct me if I'm wrong, Setanta—that you're immune to being turned at the moment."

"She's right," Setanta said. "Under normal circumstances, a drop or two of my blood or a drop from any pureblood would be enough to change a mortal into an immortal. But these aren't normal circumstances. I can't imagine a worse hell than being trapped in a body that couldn't undergo physical change while being pregnant, not to mention it would kill the child. So the child protects you."

Sarai took several deep breaths. It might have helped

if it didn't force her to inhale that sweet caramel calling to her and clouding her mind. "That makes sense. So I get, what, a vampire nose out of this?"

"Scent, perhaps some other senses. There's a blend of mortal and living vampire magical blood in your veins. You sit at a most unique intersection, with a blend of magic flowing through you that straddles worlds. Mine and yours," Setanta said.

"Sarai, I can see you salivating," Marcelle said. "It's all right. Really. I do this for Setanta all the time. I'm happy to do this for you. For our child." The wound at her wrist closed, but the blood that had spilled still teased Sarai like fruit ripe on a vine.

She leaned forward, but trembling overtook her. It was too forbidden. Too taboo. "I...can't."

Marcelle sighed. "You had that Jewish fast day back in September you told me about, right? Yom Kippur? But you said the rule was pregnant women are supposed to eat to stay healthy, so you didn't fast. That you don't need to follow rules in conflict with your health. It seems to me that maybe your dietary laws aren't as strict as you're forcing them to be. You need to do what's best for your health, Sarai. Yours and our baby's."

Sarai didn't reply. There was logic in that train of thought. Perhaps Marcelle had a point.

"Setanta, back me up on this," Marcelle said. "You can't let her hurt herself."

Setanta shook his head. "It's your choice to make, Sarai. I understand the gravity of making a pact with a higher power or clinging to traditions to honor your heritage and keep something ancient alive."

"It's not that I don't," Marcelle interjected. "But you have to do what's best for you. Yes, sure, tradition is important. I suppose. But I also know what thirst is like. True thirst. If you're channeling our child's vampirism, it won't get better."

Sarai looked down at her belly. Marcelle was right. "It feels wrong," she said after a pause.

The vampire woman sighed. "You never seem very religious except for this one kosher rule. You still have your candles for Friday nights. You can't let the kosher stuff go?"

"It's not about religion," Sarai insisted. "It's this one piece of heritage that I feel right with. It's a culture I don't have to be ashamed of. My dad's side has all this horror as my inheritance, and then my mom's side feels beautiful. I want that. I need to stay connected to that. I need her with me."

"We can try something else," Setanta suggested.

"What?"

"An IV perhaps. Judaism has no prohibition against donated blood as far as I'm aware. Marcelle, would you be willing to draw blood for us to give to her through a line?"

"I could try to do that, yes," Marcelle said. "But that'll take a little while for me to get enough out since I don't have a pulse. What do we do in the meantime? Leave her here?"

"I can help." As he spoke, Setanta took Sarai's hand and stretched out her arm, running along her veins with a gentle touch. "Will you let me pierce your skin? For a moment, to draw blood."

"What for?" Sarai asked.

"It will help, I promise. I've done it before. But it's not something we should do often, just to play it safe."

"I trust you." Sarai steeled herself for whatever pain

might be waiting for her at Setanta's hands. Somehow, even through the bloodlust, the prospect of making herself vulnerable to her vampire lovers still excited her.

Setanta's fangs extended. He lifted her wrist up to his mouth and bit. The pain pierced her for a moment, then his saliva soothed the harshness with a light numbing tingle.

She stared, transfixed, and wanted to beg for another bite. For Marcelle to bite. For everyone to bite her and have sex with her until she was screaming again and again. Before she could make her request, Setanta did something unexpected. He released her wrist and scratched open the tips of two of his own fingers.

The scent hit her hard and awoke primal, painful cravings in her soul. It didn't smell like food the way Marcelle's blood did. The only way she could think to describe the scent of Setanta's blood was pure power. His blood smelled like air before a lightning strike, and even a few drops drowned away the caramel from before.

Setanta pressed the bleeding wounds together as if injecting her with his blood, and the effect was immediate. Sarai's entire body seized under attack from the sensation. The lightning had struck, and his blood was electricity scorching through her veins. Yet it felt as if the stream of his raw power wasn't able to consume her. Instead, it joined power already inside her. The connection was more intimate in that moment than any sex or blood sharing she'd ever experienced with him before, as if they were one person for that single, intense second. Her blood was his blood, his blood was her blood, and the baby's blood united them both in perfection. Sarai felt her heartbeat slow, matching the pace of Setanta's slow heart, pumping together in harmony.

Then he pulled away, the wounds healing for them both. Sarai lay limp on the bed in complete shock, and Marcelle rushed to cradle her.

"What the hell, Setanta, you could have hurt her," Marcelle snapped. "Giving her *your* blood? You might as well give her an opium pipe while you're at it. Are you all right, Sarai?"

Sarai blinked and gave a slow, lopsided smile. All right? She felt amazing. She could feel those few drops flowing throughout her body, satisfying every craving. The power it gave her was beyond good.

"Trust me," Setanta reassured Marcelle. "I have done this before, though it has been a long time. She's craving magic in blood, and there's none around more powerful than mine. She'll be fine. Isn't that right, Sarai?"

"Oh yeah. I…" She tried to find the words to explain the experience to Marcelle. "I feel like I got hit by lightning but in a good way. Is that what it feels like to turn?"

"Not quite. Turning is like being hit by lightning in a bad way," Marcelle said. "Though if you're lucky like I was, you're dead when it happens. Setanta broke my neck before the worst of the pain could hit me, and I woke up a vampire."

Setanta leaned forward in the bed, holding Sarai's hand. "Would you like to find out one day? What it is to turn?"

Her heart picked up its pace once more, back to a normal human's heartbeat and then quicker from the adrenaline of the question. "I can't say I've thought about it." Sarai paused as she tried to take a moment to think about it. "Is that an offer?"

"It could be," Setanta said. "When we're through having children. Though it's possible you might have some magical longevity of your own without resorting to vampirism, given your healing abilities. We can discuss it some other time or even years from now. Whenever you're ready. But I wouldn't be against gifting you my blood should you ever ask for it."

Sarai nodded. It was a heavy subject, and she wasn't sure how she felt about it.

"On a different note, I'm glad to have you both here. I have something for you. If you'll excuse me a moment." Setanta disappeared too quickly for Sarai to see where he'd went.

Sarai exchanged glances with Marcelle. "Any idea what he's got?"

"I haven't the faintest idea."

He returned with two envelopes, which he handed to each of the women.

"What's this?" Sarai asked.

"*Tinnscra*," he replied.

"*Gesundheit?*" Sarai said, but the scowl on Marcelle's face said she knew what the word meant.

"That's not necessary." Marcelle pushed the envelope back into his hand as she spoke.

"In English, please?" Sarai asked. "What's *tinnscra* mean?"

"It's an old Irish term. A bride price," Marcelle explained. "It's something men would pay the families of their brides. You don't need to buy us, Setanta. This is insulting. You never paid for me like this even when I was for sale, and I don't intend for you to start now."

"It's not an insult. It's practical," he insisted. "If

something were to go wrong, you have something of value of your own so your life can be comfortable without depending on me. I thought you would appreciate this more modern version instead of a herd of cattle to your name."

"A bride price?" Sarai frowned and opened the envelope to reveal two checks for more money than she'd ever seen in her life. They both had far too many zeros. The first was shocking, but the second was obscene. "I thought you told me you don't pay for sex."

Setanta gave an exasperated look. "I'm not paying for you. For either of you. But you are my wives now. Call me old-fashioned, but I see your circumstances, Sarai. You have no job, no land or property to your name, no personal funds, no family to return to. You own nothing. If for whatever reason you decided you didn't wish to be married to me, you might force yourself to endure a situation you don't want for financial security. Especially since there's no court on earth you could summon me before to grant you alimony. That's the purpose of a bride price and behind traditions of giving jewelry to a bride. Should things go poorly or should I die, you have security."

Well, when he put it that way, it made sense. Perhaps the idea of a bride price wasn't as bad as Marcelle made it out to be.

Marcelle glared at him, snatched back the envelope, and flipped it open to look at the contents inside. "Setanta..." She sighed.

"It would make me feel better and reassure me that you're both here with me because you want to be, not because you need to be," he said.

"As if I haven't proven that I'll be by your side until

the end of the world." Marcelle punched his arm. "Why are there two checks?"

"The larger is the bride price." He grimaced and rubbed the spot she hit. "The other is a queen's allowance."

Sarai raised an eyebrow. "I get an allowance?"

"Do we have to call it an allowance?" Marcelle asked. "We're not children."

"We can call it a salary, if you prefer."

"Yeah, that sounds better," Sarai agreed. "I get paid for being your queen?"

"Of course. *Tinnscra* is for security, and this allowance, sorry, this salary is for living. Use it for clothing, restaurants, travel, or fund whatever it is you find yourself in need or want of," he said. "In fact, since one way or another Giovanna will no longer be our problem, now might be a good time to gut her quarters and refurbish them to your liking as befits a queen consort. Use the salary money to that end."

That was something that excited Sarai. She'd known the queen's quarters would be hers but had been sleeping in Marcelle's room for most nights. She had a sketchbook with ideas cut from magazines and doodles that she couldn't wait to share with whoever she was meant to give it to in order to bring it to life.

"Is this replacing my current salary?" Marcelle asked. "I don't need more than I already get. Is this coming from the kingdom's funds?"

"It's from my personal accounts, not the kingdom," he said. "I would feel better if you kept it for yourself. I'd like to be a responsible husband."

Marcelle made a noise somewhere between exasperation and disgust. "I'm not sure how I feel about being all respectable. I don't need respectability, and I never have. You're doing this for you, not me. I'm a whore. A mistress. I'm not upset to be one; I own it."

"When have I ever called you a whore, Marcelle? Not once," he said. "You are now what you've always been in my heart, *mo anam cara*. My queen."

"He's right. You're a wife and soon-to-be mother," Sarai murmured. "Come on, don't make me feel greedy being the only one taking it. Let's be respectable together."

Marcelle sighed. "If you both insist. But I do this under duress. Though I suppose it is nice to have the trappings of respectability. Having a real wedding was wonderful."

Sarai looked away, wishing she could remember what Marcelle had looked like on that day. No doubt she had been a beautiful vampire bride.

"What's wrong?" Marcelle asked.

Sarai looked up to meet her concerned gaze. "Oh, nothing. Just, well, that whole thing with the Myrk. And then when you fixed my memory with that spell, Setanta? It's like everything in that time happened in a movie or to someone else. I don't remember it well."

"You don't remember our wedding?" Marcelle frowned. "That won't do at all."

Sarai shrugged. "It's a one-time thing, right? Not like I get a repeat."

"You could, though," Setanta said. "We could hold another ceremony, something private."

That did sound nice. "Then I would like to do a Jewish ceremony, if you would be okay with it? I'm not sure how that would work or who would be willing to perform it. I could ask my aunts."

Setanta's lips drew taut with what appeared to be displeasure. "I appreciate your heritage, but I'm not one to participate in a religious ceremony calling on a deity I haven't met. I need to participate in a dialogue with them before honoring them directly."

"Oh." Sarai's heart sank like lead in her chest.

"I'll do it," Marcelle said. "It can't be all that different from a Catholic ceremony in essence. And it would make me your wife."

Sarai broke into a grin. "You want to marry me?"

"You're already carrying my child in your womb. It's only decent for me to make a respectable woman out of you," Marcelle teased and got down on one knee in front of Sarai. "Sarai, will you marry me?"

"Yes. Yes, I'll marry you, Marcelle," Sarai said without hesitation.

Marcelle planted the sweetest, most loving kiss on her lips.

Chapter Six

The Firstborn

After a day curled up in her lovers' arms and a second dose of blood from Setanta's fingertips, Sarai felt strong enough to watch the trial by combat. She felt certain of Setanta's victory until she saw the tense look on Marcelle's face. "Why are you looking at him like that?" she asked.

"Because he better not lose," Marcelle replied.

Setanta straightened his shirt. "I don't lose."

"It's to first blood, not to the death. You and I both know your fighting style. You're careless. Reckless. Prone to anger. Not to mention I have no doubt Valens will take a kill shot given the opportunity while you'll be trying not to kill him. Then they could try to put Artemisia on the throne as their puppet, since Lugh has no interest in ruling anymore. You lose, and we lose a lot more than just you."

He stepped close and took her hands. "I appreciate your concern, Marcelle, but you're inventing scenarios that will not come to pass."

"My job is to predict movements of enemies to defend the kingdom," she retorted. "I know there's a chance you'll lose."

"I won't lose. And I won't be killed by an arrogant little Roman shit like Valens. To be frank, I'm insulted that you would even think I could be."

Marcelle raised her hands as if in surrender. "All right, maybe he can't kill you. But he might draw first blood. And then what? You would be required to set him and Giovanna free. Not to do so would cause an even worse international incident. They might not have pulled the trigger themselves, but Angela is dead because of them. Sarai encountered the Myrk because of them. I was buried in a graveyard because of them. I don't want them freed."

"All those who are directly responsible for those actions are dead, except Alma who is atoning."

Atoning, that was a word for it. Sarai did feel a little sympathy for her half sister being turned into a vampire, then compelled by magical command to remain trapped on the destroyed property of their old coven for the next fifty years. Setanta certainly had a draconian sense of justice.

"What happens if Valens does draw first blood?" Sarai asked. "Giovanna scares me. There's no way she wouldn't come after me for revenge."

"I swear to you that regardless of the outcome of the trial, I will not allow her to remain somewhere she can hurt you," Setanta said.

Sarai nodded. That was reassuring. If nothing else, Setanta was a man of his word. While his word was sometimes a monkey paw to people like Alma, she trusted him to have her best interest at heart.

Once dressed and wearing regal circlets befitting their stations, the trio descended through the palace to the outdoors where a space had been made for combat. Everyone was there. The knights, court advisors, the royal family, and the three Roman purebloods. A druid,

Muach, was there to stand as judge for the fight, as they were duty bound to be objective.

Bear released Valens from his chains and offered him a clear bag of blood, which he drained as his wrists healed from the silver. Marcus offered his son a sword, and they stood wordlessly on the other side of the combat field.

Sarai tried to look tough, to not let the glares from Giovanna and her family get to her, but she was nervous. What Marcelle had said about Setanta held some truth. The man was a reckless fighter; she'd seen it on two occasions how he rushed into battle headfirst. No one could kill him, but drawing a bit of blood? That was possible. They might lose.

Setanta was given a sword that matched Valens's and twirled it in one hand.

Valens stepped forward, both hands on his sword's hilt. "No animal wings?" he called across the field. "I was hoping to see the famed CuChulainn's battle form."

"You haven't earned it, boy," Setanta said. "Nor am I foolish enough to give you a larger target. But when I ground you after your loss, I'll have someone carve my battle image into your coffin lid for you to look at for the next century."

Valens looked rattled but appeared able to maintain his focus. "You plan to ground us? Is that the worst you can do? In Rome, we've always been so much more creative in how we deal with prisoners. Did you have a chance to ask your daughter Boudicca what we did to her and her girls before she died?"

Sarai's breath caught in her throat. Boudicca was one of Setanta's many dead children, killed by Romans, and her daughters—Setanta's granddaughters—had been violated at their army's hands. Sarai had seen in his memories due to a spell mishap and felt his anguish as if it were her own. If she could come up with one sure way to provoke Setanta's fury, that was it. His lip twitched.

"You know, I think I remember my great-great-grandfather telling stories of how eager they were," Valens continued. "How soft. How they spread their legs for a legion of Roman soldiers again and again. Your offspring make excellent whores... I hope to meet the next one in Rome someday. Do you think they'll spread their legs for us too? Just like Boudicca and her daughters."

Sarai felt sick and held her belly. *It was just banter*, she told herself. *Nonsense.*

"Setanta, focus," Marcelle warned, but it was too late. The Celtic king rushed forward with a roar, fangs extended, and swords clashed. Sarai couldn't see what was happening; the speed of each strike and parry was too fast to follow. She held on to Marcelle's hand as tightly as she could, her heart racing.

Then Valens was pinned to the ground, sword useless in his broken wrist and Setanta's teeth in his throat. Blood soaked the earth under them as Setanta ripped his fangs free to the sound of gurgling from the prince.

Setanta spat down at Valens as he tried to hold his throat closed with his right hand so it could heal. "If I hear my daughter's name from your tongue again, I will remove it," he growled.

Sarai looked up at Giovanna and Marcus, expecting them to be horrified. Yet they were both smiling.

Valens held up his shaking left hand, his fingertips covered in blood. "Doesn't matter." He gasped. "I won."

Setanta froze and looked down at himself, for the first time appearing to become aware of scratch marks on his side, bleeding through his shirt as they healed.

"Fuck," Marcelle whispered.

"Prince Valens of Rome is the victor of this trial by combat," Muach announced.

Setanta's eyes flashed in anger, and he looked ready to attack the druid but instead threw his sword into the dirt. "Free them," he snapped.

Giovanna was released from her silver chains as Marcus helped his son up from the ground.

"Leave my kingdom now with your lives and consider yourselves fortunate. Never allow your shadows to darken my shores again," Setanta said. "Giovanna, your marriage to my father is dissolved. You will leave unharmed with all you brought with you as you first came. A princess of Rome and nothing more."

Giovanna looked around the crowd until her gaze landed on her daughter, Princess Artemisia, standing next to Setanta's father. "Artemisia, pack your things. We're going to a better home."

Setanta stepped between the former queen and her daughter. "She stays."

Giovanna blinked. "What?"

"Princess Artemisia ni Lugh stays in New Ulster. You did not come here with her; you will not leave here with her. She is first in line for the throne until my child is born and bears the gifts and control of an Ulster pureblood, not a Roman one. She is not yours to keep."

"You beast," Giovanna whispered. "How dare you? The trial is concluded. You have no right to punish me by taking my daughter!"

"Your daughter is a coddled thirty-year-old child

because you raised her poorly, leading to her not aging as she should. Not to mention that on your watch, she was kidnapped and needed to be rescued from Vasi. She is immature and needs to learn what it means to be of Ulster instead of being fed poison from a Roman tit. No, Giovanna, you will leave your life in Ulster behind. Including Artemisia."

"You dog-fucking, potato-shitting, soulless barbarian son of—"

She was stopped by her father putting a hand on her shoulder and yanking her back.

"I apologize for my daughter's words. We accept the not guilty verdict for both my children and will be glad to leave your kingdom." He turned to Giovanna and shouted something in Latin that caused tears to stream down her face.

"I curse you!" She shouted after Setanta as Marcus pulled her away. "I curse you to see every child you ever have die!"

Setanta's eyes narrowed. "Watch your words, woman. I have protective charms embedded in my skin to ward off dark magic and deflect it to the caster."

"I don't need to cast a curse myself," she snapped. "You already carry that curse. You brought it on your own head for killing your own child."

Fury rose in Sarai's throat, and she couldn't help but jump to her husband's defense. "He didn't kill Boudicca. I saw it with magic," she snapped. "You Romans did. And did so much worse. Don't you dare put that at his feet."

Giovanna laughed. "Oh, sweet naive and ignorant girl. Not Boudicca. Connla. Your dear husband killed his firstborn son—"

"That's enough," Setanta said quietly.

"—after he raped the boy's mother."

"*Enough.*"

The grove was silent, and Sarai felt cold. That couldn't be true. It couldn't. Setanta had a dark and violent side, she knew that, but he wasn't that. He couldn't have committed *that* crime, could he? But in the silence, no one denied it.

"You didn't, though," Sarai said, breaking the stillness.

He didn't reply.

Why didn't he reply?

"Sarai, we should leave," Marcelle said, but Sarai stepped around her to confront the vampire king.

"Setanta?" Sarai asked.

"Marcelle, take her inside," he said without looking at her.

"You can't send me to my room like a child. I'm your wife. You need to talk to me about this. *I* need to talk to you about this."

"Do not confuse me for a man who loves you, Sarai," he snarled, blood dripping down his front. "Go. Now."

She felt as if she had jumped headfirst into a frozen river and impaled herself on broken ice. She knew he didn't love her. He'd made it clear before they married and never pretended to her otherwise. But the way he said it, and after what Giovanna revealed without him denying it…

Sarai spun on her heel and fled back into the palace as fast as her pregnant body would allow her.

This was a mistake. This was all a mistake. Vampires, their world, it was too much for her. She couldn't have been thinking clearly when she agreed to any of it, dazzled by pretty dresses and comfort and Marcelle's love. She had the *tinnscra* money. She could go live in the Ellis Coven and be comfortable. But what about the baby, an accused rapist's baby? King Setanta would never let her keep the baby from him.

A hand touched her shoulder, and she jumped a foot into the air before she realized it was Marcelle. "Did you know?" Sarai asked before Marcelle had a chance to speak.

Marcelle didn't say anything for a while, then nodded.

"Is it true? He raped a woman and killed their son?"

"Sarai, what you need to understand is that period of his life was different from—"

"And you're defending it! I can't believe you. With your history, you should be the first to say it's wrong. All this time I spent worrying about my father, and I never noticed Setanta was just a more suave version of him. I'm a naive fool."

"Sarai, listen to me. When he's ready, he'll discuss it with you. It's not my story to tell you. But I want you to ask yourself if I would stay with him if what you heard from Giovanna was the full story."

"There's no justification if it's even a little true," Sarai snapped. "I'm going to find Rosaline. Don't follow me."

Thankfully, Marcelle listened. But unfortunately for Sarai, Rosaline was out doing her work as a maid.

The only one in was Jackie, who smiled when she saw Sarai. "Hey, are you here to give me that tour?" Her cheerful expression turned to one of concern. "Is something wrong?"

"Wrong? Yeah, you could say that," she muttered. "Is Rosaline around? I need my friend."

"She'll be out for a bit, I think. I can be your friend if you want. Tell me what happened?"

"I might be married to a rapist who killed his firstborn child, and no one is denying it," Sarai blurted out. "Setanta didn't deny it, Marcelle didn't deny it, and…you don't look surprised."

"You didn't know?"

Sarai stared at her in cold horror. What was that supposed to mean?

Jackie quickly continued. "I assumed you knew. It's easy enough to research his mythology in a public library. I read everything I could about CuChulainn in the Ulster Cycle and *The Tain* before I transferred here. He seems like the kind of guy to avoid. A 'take what he wants' sort."

Sarai blinked. Everyone knew. It had to be true, then. How had she read books and studied and somehow missed such an important piece of information? "Uh, okay, theoretically, if I was stupid and didn't read up on the easily available information about my husband before agreeing to an arranged marriage with him, what can you tell me? Like, bullet points, the worst red flags."

"Oof. Okay. Bullet points. He's like Irish mythology's version of Hercules. Not the cartoon version, the hardcore bloody version. Has a violent temper. Cheated on his first wife Emer a lot, but she was chill with it except one time. He killed Emer's father for trying to forbid them from marrying after going on a quest to prove himself worthy of her."

"Well, I guess we have that in common."

Jackie raised an eyebrow of concern.

"He did help kill my dad, but trust me it was justified," Sarai explained. "The cheating thing might just be nonmonogamous relationships. I think. That's what we have. There's no cheating because we all are okay with things."

"I'll take your word for that."

"What else? What about his kid?"

"Right. Uh, on that quest he went on, he trained with some battle witch and defeated her sister or her daughter. I can't remember which. Raped the sister or daughter after she failed to knock him out with a potion, and forced her to have his son as some kind of sick punishment."

Sarai blinked a few times and sat down on the couch while she absorbed the information. "Well. That's horrible."

"Yeah. Then when the son grew up and came looking for him as an adult but didn't announce his name or something like that? Anyway, he refused to identify himself, and Setanta killed him, thinking he was a rival."

"It was a mistake?"

"Yeah, but he still killed his son. Who was conceived through rape. Seriously, you didn't know any of this? That's why I was so weirded out when you said he was your husband. It's hard to imagine anyone marrying that guy, knowing all of that."

Sarai shook her head. "My history lessons are more about other countries and which monarch ruled at one time rather than his personal history. I don't know what to do. I'm carrying his child. He's always protected me and been good to me. He made me feel safe. Do I…leave?"

Jackie pursed her lips. "Is he, well, a safe person to

confront? I dunno that I would risk talking to him and asking his side, if you think he might hurt you. The man's a vampire, he could hurt any of us easily, and no one here could stop him. And he's a smart guy. He could manipulate you and lie to your face. We need to sneak you out."

Sarai would have once said Setanta would never hurt her. She felt she knew him. But now she wasn't sure.

Her head was spinning, and she sat down. This was all too much, and she felt as if she were spiraling. Her mind had her flashing back to when she had escaped from her father's clan, getting help from her half sister, Alma. But that had been different. That moment of fleeing had been in response to years of abuse and an active threat to her well-being. That was when she was physically able to be sneaky. Trying to sneak out while heavily pregnant and body creaking with effort would be very difficult, especially since she didn't think she would be allowed to simply leave with no plan.

Was Setanta really similar to her father? No, she'd never been able to sit down and talk to her father about anything. Setanta sat and talked to her all the time. She didn't think he had ever lied to her, though certainly he was the sort who would lie by omission. He had given her money specifically in the case that she might decide to leave him one day. If she wanted to leave him, he had indicated that he would let her.

What would her therapist say?

"I don't think he'd directly lie to me. And I don't think he'd hurt me," Sarai said. "My therapist would tell me to talk to him before doing anything."

"You have a therapist?" Jackie asked with a look of surprise.

"Yeah."

"Well, any therapist worth anything would tell you not to put yourself in danger."

Before Sarai had the chance to reply, someone knocked on the door and Temuulen, her new bodyguard, opened it.

"My queen," he said with a respectful nod of his head. "The king requested your presence and sent me to escort you."

Jackie gripped Sarai's hand from behind. "You can tell the king to shove—"

"It's okay," Sarai said. "Thank you, Jackie. But I'll go. I don't think he would hurt me. If he wanted to hurt me, I think he already would have. But I'm going to get something from my stuff in Marcelle's room first. I won't let him lie to me."

"As you wish, my queen."

Chapter Seven

Lovely Lies

They stopped by Marcelle's room as Sarai instructed, then proceeded to Setanta's study.

"Thank you, Temuulen, that will be all," Setanta said. The new guard left and closed the door behind him.

It was just the two of them. Sarai and CuChulainn, the possible rapist.

"Sarai, I want to apologize—"

"Ah, ah." She held up a small button, the type one would find on a dress shirt, so that Setanta could see it. It was an enchanted gift from Danior, a witch with a gift for discerning truth from lies, and she knew he knew what it was. "Now you can speak."

He looked impressed. "I wanted to apologize for the way I spoke to you after the combat trial. It was wrong of me to be so harsh, and I hope you can forgive me."

"That depends."

He sighed. "You want to know about Connla and...Aife."

"I got a crash course just now. Everyone seems to know but me. It is true, isn't it?"

"Ask me what you want to know, Sarai. You'll learn the truth."

"Did you rape Aife?"

"No."

She looked at the button in her hand. It stayed cool. If he had lied, it would have warmed. She exhaled the longest breath she had ever held and sat down in a chair, hard. "And that's a 'for sure you didn't' and not a 'different time periods didn't count it as rape' no, right?" she pressed to make sure he wasn't using some sort of truth-spell-resistant semantic loophole.

"By no definition did I rape Aife. I never raped her or any other person. I am guilty of many horrors, but I have never raped anyone. I would never inflict that hell on any person."

Sarai breathed a deep sigh of relief and sank into her chair. "I'm sorry. I thought the way everyone reacted meant it was true. Why didn't you deny it?"

He looked away. "Because that is the story I wish people to believe. It is a lie I went along with and spread many centuries ago to hide a truth I felt was more shameful."

"I'm having a hard time imagining a truth that's more shameful than having your name recorded forever in history as a rapist."

"It was a different time. I defeated her in a fight, and it wasn't considered dishonorable at the time for me to claim her as my prize in bed. But that's a story I told once she bore our child and I couldn't ignore what happened."

"Then tell me the truth. What happened?"

He looked as if he had been told to eat a lemon. "I suppose this was inevitable," he murmured.

"I mean, yeah. I'm your wife now, so I need to know that my husband is a good person after having a vindictive Roman bitch shouting at me that I married a child-murdering rapist. I need to know if you're the good man I thought you were, or if I'm going to need that *tinnscra* cash you gave me."

"I don't believe I am a good man," he retorted, then sighed. "Though I can say I don't consider myself an evil one. If you decide I am not to your standards, I will not stop you from leaving me."

She found it to be concerning that the button did not detect a lie in his statement that he wasn't good, but she chalked it up to a matter of it being his opinion. "Get to it. I need to know the truth."

He nodded. "I was on a quest in the Isle of Skye to study under a battle witch named Scathach in order to earn the right to marry a remarkable woman named Emer. Scathach's sister, Aife, took a liking to me after we sparred and I defeated her. Her magical gift was strength not dissimilar to my own, so it intrigued her to meet someone capable of besting her. I turned her down because I was focused on courting Emer. And also, I had my relationships with my friends Ferdiad and Laeg who were rather more than friends." His eyes flickered with what Sarai could only interpret as affection for the men long gone. "Suffice to say my plate was full. Aife wasn't pleased with that. She wanted us to have a child, to combine our strength. And so she slipped a potion into my drink."

"That's what I was just told. It didn't work, so you punished her."

"That is where the lie begins. The potion worked very well and rendered me unconscious. When I woke..." His voice trailed off, and he clenched his jaw for a moment before continuing with the truth. "I woke in silver shackles in a hut somewhere I did not recognize. She kept me chained to a bed for two months. The first night I nearly freed myself and tried to strangle her with my chains, but she slipped a dagger between my ribs. Once she stitched that closed, she force-fed me enchanted poison to keep me weak. To this day if I catch the scent or sight of belladonna, I imagine myself back in that hut whether I want it or not. Sometimes I swear I can still taste those sickly sweet berries on my tongue."

Setanta paused, and his expression went blank, a complete contrast to the disgust that had been in his voice. It was the only hint of the discomfort bottled up and buried inside him. Sarai wanted to jump up and hug him, to tell him he was safe now and she was sorry for forcing him to relive the memories again. But he continued.

"Aife *used* me every night until she got what she wanted. You might think she couldn't if I wasn't inclined, but she had her ways. My desires had nothing to do with what happened. She conceived a child and gave me one last potion. When I woke, I was free and she was gone."

She wasn't sure what to say. He looked so calm, but the story he'd told was so horrific. Her eyes swelled with tears.

As if he realized she wouldn't speak, he said, "You understand why I would be, ah, shall we say, hesitant to tell the real story. To admit to something like that, to admit that she succeeded as the aggressor, was more shameful. *Is* more shameful."

"She raped *you*," she whispered. Guilt washed over her. She'd accused him of the very crime he had been a victim of. He had endured months of torture and violation, only for the world to see him as the cruel one. "There's no shame in that. Not for you. How old were you?"

"Seventeen."

"Fucking *hell*, Setanta. Seventeen?"

He shrugged. "From my people's perspective, I was a man."

"You were a teenager. A boy. How old was she?"

"In her thirties, I believe. I couldn't say for sure; it's been a long time."

"Thirty and you were a kid. Even if she hadn't magically roofied you and you'd gone along with it on your own, that would be statutory nowadays." She shook her head. "You could correct the stories people believe, you know."

"To what end? People would assume the correction was a lie to fit the times and make me palatable to modern folk. And if it was taken to be the truth, I would be seen as weak by my peers in other vampire nations. Even in modern times, it's not accepted that men can be victims, especially of a woman. Emer, Laeg, and Ferdiad knew the truth. Believed the truth. And Marcelle, of course. A rare handful of other lovers over the ages. Aside from them, I have an image to maintain. Maybe one day the truth will come out to the public, but today is not that day."

Politics were terrible.

"What happened to your child? If you don't mind me asking."

"Connla. He was my firstborn child, through Aife."

"Jackie, she's a new source I'm friends with. I was talking to her, and she's read about your history. She said you killed him because you didn't know who he was. That it was an accident."

"That is also a lie," he said.

"You didn't kill him, then?" That was a relief. The

idea of having a child with someone who had killed their own firstborn wasn't one she was comfortable with.

"No. I did kill him. The lie is that I didn't know who he was. I knew who he was, and I meant to kill him. Again, the shameful lie is a disguise for a more shameful truth."

She looked down at the button in her hand and back to him. He had told her the truth, and this time she didn't like it. "Why would you do something like that?"

"Aife, as you can imagine, was not the best mother. She raised him to be entitled due to his superior powers. Which didn't end up working well for her, as he killed her. You know, of course, how purebloods like myself do require blood? Vampire blood of those we create is preferable because the magic is stronger, so we need less. If we take from humans, they do not often survive, with an exception for rare witches. Connla preferred the warmth of mortal blood and did not care whether or not his victims survived or were willing. Humans were cattle to him and nothing more. When he sought me out, he was under the impression I would be like him, drinking my fill because I could regardless of the consequences to those around me. He wanted to rule humans as their tyrant, to have them all as his subjects and sacrifice them to his bloodlust at every whim. He wanted me to join him in becoming a conqueror. He was the worst a vampire can become when left unchecked. When he found me living among humans, found me in love with my human wife Emer and our lover Laeg, he attempted to kill them both to free me of what he called mortal shackles. I tried to reason with him, but in the end, it was a battle to the death, and I killed my son with the very spear I still carry to protect my lovers and my tribe. He did not deserve to live, so I took the mantle of responsibility and rid the world of him."

Sarai didn't know what to say to any of that. She rested her hand over her belly, horrified at the thought of any parent feeling forced to kill their child to save others. She didn't think she could do such a thing. The baby wasn't even born, but she felt such a strong protective bond to it. "I don't think I'd have it in me to do what you did," she murmured.

"It's a moment that still haunts me. I used to be plagued by doubts, and I wondered if he was truly beyond redemption. Perhaps I should have hunted down Aife when he was a child and taken him to raise him with knowledge of how to manage our bloodlust in more civil ways. But what is done is done."

"Are you...still capable of that?"

"I do not know," he admitted. "In all likelihood, yes. But you shouldn't need to worry. The chances of our child growing up to be an irredeemable mass-murdering monster are slim considering we don't intend to raise them to think all human blood is their birthright."

"Yeah, I guess there's that at least. I remember when I was still connected to the Myrk." She glanced at him nervously. "It let me see that part of you. I could sense the darkness, the bloodlust, that something inhuman in you."

"My nature is not a pretty one," he admitted. "Yes, there is something in me, something in all purebloods, that is monstrous. I'm sure that's not the only time you've noticed."

"When I've seen you kill. At the Reinhart coven, you had fun ripping off heads. The way you turned my sister and were planning on letting her feel all the pain, that was terrifying. And sometimes in bed, when you beat Marcelle, bite us, or choke me...you enjoy it. You want to hurt people."

"Have I ever pushed you too far? Have I ever done anything that you did not enjoy or even ask for specifically?"

"No. I do get a thrill from it. Hell, I was complaining to my psychologist the other day that you aren't rough enough with me now that I'm pregnant. But you're a real sadist in every way. Not just in bed."

"Have you ever known me to kill someone who did not earn it or who wasn't an enemy combatant?"

Again, the answer was no.

"I live a brutal life, and I enjoy battle and sadism," Setanta said. "That is my nature. But I am not a mindless slave to my baser instincts. I live by a code, and I love as deeply as I crave the violence. I'm capable of more than death. I know how to channel my desires in appropriate ways. So yes, I am a monster. But I am a monster with self-control and the ability to reason." He reached out and held her hand. "I hope you know; I will never hurt you more than you are willing and able to accept."

She looked at his hand on hers. It was tender, and she believed him. He'd never shown her otherwise or in any way tried to force her to endure something she didn't ask for, such as his fangs. "Do you think...our kids will be like that?" she asked quietly. It had never occurred to her before how much her baby would take after the father. "Have that darkness?"

"Everyone has darkness in them," he stated with a hint of sadness tinging his voice. "Mine is a little more pronounced. I've never known a pureblood who didn't have that side. It can express itself in different ways, so there's no guarantee that a child of mine will crave battle. If it is of any comfort, I can confirm that none of my children that I've had a hand in raising turned out like Connla. Bloodlust is our nature, but how we're nurtured makes a significant difference."

She nodded. "Does Marcelle know about all of this? About Connla? About purebloods?"

"She knows about Connla. And she has been told about purebloods and the creatures that helped create us, but I don't think she can understand the way you can, since she's never encountered one of those creatures. Undead vampires have some small fraction of that bloodlust, but it's a simple thirst, from my understanding. A physical hunger. Not a, well, for lack of a better description, an irrepressible and monstrous sadism. So Marcelle knows, but not truly. Her comprehension is a human one."

Sarai nodded in acknowledgment. Of all the things to share with her husband, it had to be an understanding of why he was a monster. She felt a little guilty with how quickly she had believed Giovanna's lies and how quickly she had leapt to letting Jackie convince her she might not be safe. Certainly, she was an impulsive woman, but it felt worse than usual. She should have understood Setanta. "Are you upset I doubted you?"

"No. It's reasonable for you to believe a lie I myself spread. And forgive me for being a tad sexist, but I haven't known any pregnant women who weren't, shall we say…" He paused a moment in an apparent search for the right word. "Intense and easily riled."

She laughed at that. "Don't go blaming all my shit on hormones. It's still like ninety percent me." She looked down at her pregnant belly. "I guess we'll have to see what happens with the kid. I'm pretty committed to it now, so it is what it is. I didn't think this through, did I?"

"Perhaps I should have explained all that I am more thoroughly before you agreed."

"Yeah. Though, without meeting the Myrk, I don't think I could comprehend more than I already did. Like you said about Marcelle, on a human level. It's not on you. I don't regret it." She had one more issue on her mind, though, before she could feel at ease with all she'd heard. One thing he said, one last thing, she needed to mention. "You said you love just as deeply as you crave violence. I've only seen you crave violence. And what you said out there. That hurt."

"I apologize for hurting you. I could make excuses, but it was wrong, and I won't pretend otherwise to you." He held her hand a little tighter and brought it to his lips to give a gentle kiss. "Please know, I'm not incapable of love. But I am slow to love. I've lost a lot of people. If I loved as easily as a mortal, it would destroy me. But I like you very much, Sarai. I have since the moment you walked barefoot and bloody and stinking of onions into my home."

She laughed. Not the best impression she had ever made. "Is that why you didn't kiss me back that first time we kissed? You didn't want to feel anything? That first time, when we were dancing in Marcelle's room and I kissed you. If you always liked me, then why did you mess with me like that? You were flirting with me. I know I didn't mix up those messages. And I know you and Marcelle can tell when someone has a crush on you."

He chuckled. "To be honest, you surprised me. It's been a long time since someone else made a first move on me."

"But you were flirting with me," she accused.

"Of course. I've been flirting with you since our second meeting, out on the terrace."

Her cheeks burned. "Asshole."

He laughed. "Perhaps. I needed your trust, your cooperation. What better way to get something you want than to make someone want to please you? But it was more a game of manipulation, not something I expected to bear fruit. It did cross my mind that perhaps Marcelle might suggest I make a guest appearance in your bed, after you and she began your trysts. That's standard for her, and I would have enjoyed the dalliance. But I didn't expect the kiss from you. Or for it to lead to all of this."

"I love her, you know." Sarai sighed. "She said she loves me."

"She does. Quite desperately too. You're very important to us."

"Do you think one day you could love me?" She regretted the question the moment it left her lips and hated the ugly silence that followed her words.

"Sarai…"

"Sorry," she murmured. "I didn't mean to spoil the mood."

"Would you like to hear a lie or the truth? I can tell you a lovely lie if you wish to hear it from my lips. But it would be a lie and nothing more."

"Tell me a lovely lie. But make me believe it. I know you know how."

Setanta tilted her chin up with a finger so that her eyes were locked on his intense, red gaze. "Sarai," he murmured her name like a prayer in a way that made her heart catch in her throat. "You are more precious to me than you could ever imagine. You enchant me. Every moment I spend in your presence, I am in awe of you. Of your strength, your valor, your passion. I crave your touch and the feel of your breath against my skin. When I'm not with you, I think of when I'll feel your warm, soft body again. I love you, Sarai."

The words melted her soul and felt like warm molasses, sweet and comforting. But she knew it was a lie. At least, the truth-telling button she held warmed the moment he tried to say he loved her. "This would work better without Danior's button." She felt heat rise to her cheeks. "Though it only warmed at the end. I almost believed you."

He smiled. "The best lies are mostly true."

"Well, thank you. It's a very lovely lie. And you should tell it to me more often."

"Oh?"

"Because if it becomes the truth one day, I'll know. Maybe even before you do."

He nodded. "Fair enough. I love you, Sarai."

And her button warmed.

Chapter Eight

Airplane

After the stress of the trial, Sarai spent as much time with Jackie and the other humans as possible, reassuring them that they had no reason to fear Setanta. The humans had instituted a game night on Mondays, and Sarai looked forward to those hours with Jackie joining them, playing board games and card games together in a group. Yet she didn't know how to bring up anything other than playing games in a group with Jackie. It was too intimidating because she had no way of knowing where she stood or how to proceed with a human.

The focus that preoccupied Sarai was the design of her new rooms. Giovanna's rooms were an overt Roman design that she was more than happy to instruct to be gutted. She asked for a small kitchen area to be added so that she could perhaps learn to cook a little herself instead of needing to go down to the kitchens or the human quarters. Other than focusing on a design honoring her Middle Eastern heritage, she had one other requirement for the vampire interior designer, Lydia.

"A cradle? In your rooms?" she asked. "My queen, should that not be in a separate nursery? We have Artemisia's old nursery that was going to be refurbished."

"That's way too far away for me to hear a baby

crying, though," Sarai said. "How would I know when they need me?"

"You could have a nurse caring for the child."

"No, I'm caring for my own child. The baby goes in my room, next to my bed. Not off in a room by themselves, that's just cruel. In fact, make sure there's nothing breakable at toddler level in my room. I want it baby proof and safe."

"As you wish, my queen."

As her rooms were renovated, Sarai received an invitation. She was invited to dinner.

Not a sexy dinner or a dinner with humans offering blood in ballgowns, just a normal Shabbat dinner with family. Her family—specifically, her lesbian aunts on her mother's side who lived in New York City in an apartment with their daughter. Her aunt Mazal, who was also a healing witch, had been making a few trips to the palace to check on Sarai's pregnancy to ensure all was well, and at her last appointment, she'd insisted that before the baby came, Sarai should visit their New York City apartment while she could still safely travel for dinner with her family, as some of the family who usually were not in town were in town.

Going to New York meant a private plane ride. The movement of the aircraft mixed with the pregnancy made Sarai extra nauseous. Once they were up in the air, she lay across several seats with her head in Setanta's lap while he ran his fingers through her hair, massaging her scalp. Marcelle stood in the aisle, trying to comb her floor-length raven hair to look put together for dinner. The rest of her was impeccable, of course, but her hair had chosen to be difficult.

They had some knights with them as well, playing

cards together at the table at the back of the plane: Bear in a T-shirt featuring a cartoon cat hating Mondays, Temuulen in a leather motorcycle jacket and black ski cap, and Lochlan bundled up for the cold winter weather much the same as Sarai was in several layers of sweaters.

"How can a pyromancer get cold?" Bear wondered.

"I'm not on fire all the time, you know. I'm still just a dude. Go fish."

Sarai closed her eyes. *Fish.* The thought of fish and their pungent odor made bile rise in her throat. "I need someone to keep my mind off wanting to puke and how horrible being pregnant is." She looked up at Marcelle. "Tell me something I don't know about you. I want to know something new about you that most people don't know."

"About me? Or him?" Marcelle asked. "You already know more about both of us than a lot of vampires do."

"Both of you. Not like trauma secrets, fun secrets. Stuff you don't care if the rest of the knights know about. You guys have five hundred years of being a couple. I want in on some stuff. I feel like I only just got a taste of it, and I need to get to know your secrets better if I ever want something resembling equal footing in this relationship."

"Five hundred and seventy, exactly, but who's counting?" Setanta mused.

"You, apparently," Marcelle teased, then got aggravated with her hair and pulled the dagger from her belt.

"If you cut it, you're cleaning the dust." Setanta sighed. "I'd rather not be stuck in a metal tube smelling vampire dust until we land."

Marcelle rolled her eyes and sliced her hair to her

shoulders. The cut hair turned to dust around her feet, and the length regrew from her head, sans tangles. She got a hand vacuum from the back of the plane and cleaned her mess before starting a braid. "A juicy secret about me," she mused. "I can't think of any juicy secret you don't already know. Oh, I once had sex with a vicomte and his mistress in the fountains at Versailles."

"That was hardly a secret." Setanta laughed.

"Well, it was meant to be." Marcelle stuck her tongue out at him. "Weren't you doing the wife?"

"I was. But so was half the court. Including you, if I remember correctly."

Marcelle grinned. "True, I was. They never found out about each other—that was the amusing part of it all. Your turn. A secret she doesn't know."

He paused as he tapped his chin in an exaggerated display of thinking, then chuckled. "All right. Would you like to know my weakness?"

"You have a weakness?" Sarai said. "I assume you don't mean silver."

"No, I don't."

In the back of the plane, the three knighted men were looking up with interest and Bear with a knowing smirk.

Setanta then popped his right eye out of its socket and into his hand.

Sarai shouted in alarm and jumped up as he laughed.

"It's glass," he said with clear amusement. "I lost the real one in a battle ages ago. I was able to find a witch who crafted me this one in exchange for some gold. It doesn't see very well, though, so half my vision is as dull as a human's." He popped the eye back into its socket and blinked as it rolled in the socket before settling, readjusted as if nothing had happened.

"Can you see with it when it's out the way I can move my prosthetic hand when it's not attached?" Sarai leaned forward and analyzed the eye. The enchantment and craftsmanship that had gone into it were superb. She couldn't tell at all the difference between the glass eye and the real eye.

"No, thankfully. That would be rather disorientating, I imagine, as useful as it could be. It does do this trick, though." He tapped his temple four times next to his prosthetic eye, and to Sarai's surprise, the iris turned green, and the color spread across to his real one so that a pair of emerald eyes stared back at her.

"That's a good look on you." As she spoke, she was absolutely certain she was blushing.

He stooped his neck low and kissed her sweetly. "Thank you. I don't care for it because along with the color, my vision changes to human vision, and I'm certain the witch who crafted this was far-sighted. But it has been useful whenever I needed to be more subtle."

"No one suspects a man walking with a cane like a blind man of being a vampire," Marcelle said.

"Like there's anything subtle about you," Sarai scoffed.

He laughed again as he tapped his temple to return his eyes to their natural red coloration.

"Walking with a cane?"

"The witch was very, very far-sighted. By vampire standards, I might as well be half blind. Perhaps even some human standards."

Near the end of the plane ride, Setanta dozed off and Marcelle and Sarai joined their guards to teach Sarai poker using plane napkins and straws instead of tokens to place bets.

"We could make this interesting and play strip poker," Marcelle said, her eyes on Lochlan, though Sarai did notice a flicker of a glance in Temuulen's direction and the way his eyes met hers.

"Not even the possibility of seeing your pretty tits could convince me to take off this sweatshirt at these temperatures," Lochlan retorted. "I hate the cold."

"Mm, I could order you to." The vampire woman had a mischievous twinkle in her eyes.

"Marcelle, I am shocked. Shocked, I tell you. To abuse your power as queen to make your guard get naked." Bear made a disapproving tsk, tsk noise with his tongue.

"I'm down." Temuulen smirked, giving both queens a look of interest that made heat rise in Sarai's cheeks and Marcelle grin.

His bold gaze reminded her of Marcelle and Setanta before they'd started their threefold relationship. The way they could read her body language and knew how to play it to their advantages. They could all sense attraction in mortal bodies, and Sarai never for a moment questioned whether they knew how she felt or not. Temuulen had to know she found him attractive. The flirting, the looks. Sarai recognized it now as a vampire's invitation. All she needed to do was return the invitation and invite him in.

"But how will you get to the apartment without your clothes when I win?" Temuulen asked.

"Bold of you to assume you'd win," Sarai said. "It'll be difficult for you when *I* win and *you're* naked in New York. I'm your queen, so I should get to win if I want, right?"

He winked at her. "Sweetheart, if I have something

you want, all you need to do is ask." And there it was. As blatant an invitation as there ever was.

Bear rolled his eyes. "I will politely decline your debauchery. Hannah wouldn't care for it," he said, referring to the elderly Lakota witch from the Ellis Coven Sarai had once caught him making out with.

"You're no fun when you have a relationship." Marcelle gave a facetious exaggerated pout. "You're going to see her while we're in New York?"

"I am." His tone and demeanor visibly brightened. "There's something special about her. I can feel it."

"Is Hannah your lady love?" Temuulen asked.

"Hannah is my lady love," Bear confirmed.

"What about you, Temuulen? Got a lovely *mademoiselle* or *monsieur* back in Delaware mourning the loss of your dukedom?" Marcelle asked.

"Nah, nothing serious. A bit of fun on the side now and then, but I never clicked with a relationship here in America. I had ten wives back in Mongolia, you know."

Lochlan raised an eyebrow. "And I thought these three were crazy."

"You're a liar, Temuulen." Sarai held up her focus, a magical item unique to all witches that was used to cast spells. Hers was a fingerless leather glove, currently blue. And she had sewn the truth-sensing button into the cuff. It grew warm to the touch to alert her. "It tells me when someone lies." She smirked as his face fell before he broke into laughter.

"Oh, that's cheating for poker."

"Maybe. I think it evens the playing field when you're all highly trained vampire knights who can spot a millisecond expression from a mile away. So spill. How many wives did you actually have?"

Temuulen narrowed his eyes as he stroked his goatee, very clearly inspecting Sarai's face as his gaze swept over her expression. "I'm going to learn all your tells, my queen. Every little millisecond flicker of emotion. I will read you like a book. And truth spell or not, I will be the unknowable mysterious man who knows all about you."

"Cool shtick. Still avoiding the question."

"He didn't have any wives." Setanta came up from behind them and took a chair as he wiped sleep from his eyes, then leaned forward to drape an arm around Marcelle. "He likes men."

Sarai widened her eyes. "No. Come on, he's been flirting with me this whole time. Seriously?"

Temuulen leaned back, a hint of a grin tugging at his lips. There was something open and welcoming about the way he sat back in his chair, a vampire's invitation once more. It was not unlike the flirting he had performed for her. She glanced at Setanta; his eyes were fixated on Temuulen's, his red gaze analytical, yet intrigued.

"Now how would you know that, my liege?" the Mongolian vampire asked.

"Because I can sense that you were turned by my ex, Robert," Setanta replied. "He was with me before I turned Marcelle, and then he ran off with a stable boy to explore Asia while I stayed in Europe. If I know Robert, and I do know Robert intimately well, then you two fucked like wild beasts. He liked some women but preferred men. And the men he preferred generally did not like women. So you prefer men."

"If Robert turned you, that makes you a second-generation vampire, like Bear," Marcelle murmured.

"You lied."

Temuulen sighed in surrender. "You found me out. Yes, Robert turned me. Yes, I lied about what generation I am. I find it best to obscure how strong I am so others underestimate me."

"I don't appreciate being lied to," Marcelle warned, but her expression was amused rather than upset. "But I can appreciate the wisdom in your logic. And how well you managed to hide the truth from me. Don't lie to me again."

"As you command." He bowed his head. "Since I'm being truthful, allow me to make an amendment to his majesty's claim. I lean toward men, true, but I do appreciate a beautiful woman. And there are two very beautiful women here."

"You might want to watch yourself. Those are my queens you're talking about," Setanta warned with a smirk as he got up and walked in front of Temuulen, towering over him.

Marcelle snorted back a laugh. He had a different sort of energy in his stance, but Sarai recognized it even when it wasn't directed at her. It was dominant. But it was also intimate and a challenge. She recognized it as a challenge she met and gave in return an attitude in bed. She held her breath to see how Temuulen would meet the challenge.

"Oh, are they yours?" Temuulen asked. "I was so smitten with the pretty little one, and the dark-haired one knows how to wield authority in the best way. I am curious how they taste. Would you share that knowledge with me, my king?"

"I suppose I am a generous king. They taste very good. In fact, I sampled Marcelle before we got on the plane." Setanta gripped Temuulen by the neck and pulled him up to his feet. "Tell me, does the flavor linger?"

Sarai stared in absolute shock as Setanta planted a forceful kiss on Temuulen's lips.

Temuulen seemed a little surprised but relented in seconds. Lips parted, tongues moved, and Sarai's heart pounded like it would leap out of her chest. She ached between her legs, her need making her body hot. She wanted them. Both of them.

Setanta pulled back. "Well?"

"I can see why Robert was always talking about you," Temuulen murmured, his fangs extended in arousal and his dark eyes now bright red.

"Remember to breathe, Sarai," Setanta said without looking back at her.

"I'm breathing. Mostly fine," she retorted.

Marcelle laughed and leaned over to kiss her. "You are a darling, my little witch."

"You are all vile degenerates." Bear sighed. "Do you mind waiting until I'm off away from you with Hannah to start the orgy?"

"I make no promises," Temuulen said. "No fangs for me, Your Highness?"

Setanta flashed his teeth to reveal he had indeed extended his fangs, then he retracted them as Temuulen looked on with a disappointed expression. "Some other time, perhaps. I might need a source come dawn, and Robert always had good taste. I'm sure your blood would do nicely."

Bear gave a loud, exasperated sigh that made the rest of the group chuckle.

Soon after, they landed and it was time to part ways with the guards, since Sarai was more than safe in the company of her vampire lovers.

Sarai found herself glad for the opportunity to take a trip back to New York City again with Marcelle and Setanta. While their first trip had been less than perfect, Sarai felt at ease without the threat of the Reinhart coven looming over her. Or at least, mostly at ease.

Despite knowing she was welcome, she felt anxious to visit family. She'd had very limited interactions with her aunts and had never met their daughter. An invitation to dinner at their home was nerve wracking. Not in the least because Setanta and Marcelle had also been invited but even more so because her aunt by marriage's older brother, his family, and their parents had also been invited, as well an uncle by blood and his family whom Sarai had never met. She wished she could have had a small, intimate dinner to get to know her aunts better, but her aunts had insisted she needed to be introduced to the family. The whole family.

Since it was a dinner, Sarai's nerves insisted before they went that she needed to bring some sort of food to contribute. But she didn't know if her aunts followed kosher or halal rules in the house, or a combination of both, or if they had no dietary rules at all. It was all a jumble of fear of doing the wrong thing in her head. Bringing food brought the risk that it would be thrown out. And if they were having any sort of meat dish, then she had to make sure what she brought had no dairy, in case of kosher rules. But then she had no idea what halal rules required, other than that also forbade certain foods like pork. She wished she'd thought to ask Mazal about the particulars during one of her checkups at the palace. She decided to stick with the kosher rules since it was what she knew and hoped it would be sufficient for both her aunts. So before leaving for the aunts' apartment, the trio stopped at a kosher market to pick up a nondairy cake.

"You know, I don't believe I've ever been inside a kosher market before," Setanta mused to Marcelle as they followed Sarai around. "Deli yes, market no. The scents are intriguing."

Marcelle shrugged. "It smells fine, I suppose." Of course, food wouldn't smell appetizing to an undead vampire such as Marcelle. Only to a living one, like Setanta.

They walked past the spice aisle, and Marcelle paused. "Saffron, Setanta. Look at all this. Turkish saffron." She picked up a packet of dried, red, flower stigmas to wave at him, then put it back and picked up a jar. "Cardamom pods. All these herbs." She shook her head. "Can you believe how easy this is? Saffron for peasantry. Look, I can just buy nutmeg or vanilla extract or fennel. Chili powder—I don't even know what that's supposed to taste like. All in one place. There's more flavor here than fat King Louis ever tasted in his entire life. And for pocket change."

"Progress is something fantastic to behold," Setanta agreed.

Marcelle popped open the top of the container of chili powder and frowned at the seal but inhaled anyway to try and catch the scent. Her eyes widened. "It's like Lochlan in a bottle. Oh, I would have loved this."

An orthodox Ashkenazi woman wearing a bad wig to cover her hair and modest clothes gave Setanta a disapproving glare and ushered children away from the trio, whispering to them in Hebrew to hurry up. Sarai felt her face flush, feeling almost ashamed of her association

Evelyn Silver

with Setanta in a Jewish environment, as if she'd done something improper by allowing him into the space.

"Is something wrong?" he asked, noting the woman's reaction.

"Your tattoos," she said, trying to put on a joking face as she poked at the blue by his wrist. "Everyone knows you're a goy boy."

"Ah. Yes, that makes sense. Perhaps I should wait for you outside?"

She shook her head. "It's fine." She didn't want him to feel bad on her account. Besides, they weren't getting any more negative attention than passive-aggressive cold shoulders.

She picked out a nondairy cake, a chocolate one that looked like it had tasty frosting, and brought it to the front where Marcelle paid for it. Sarai was relieved to leave the shop. After that orthodox woman's glare and the looks she got from others in the store, she wasn't sure it was someplace she felt she belonged. But they were off to someplace that had people who welcomed her. To her family.

Chapter Nine

The Whole Family

The Ali-Meir household was a nice apartment in the city, well above the busy streets up on the twelfth floor. She was glad that the elevator worked, since there was no chance she would have been able to climb all those stairs with her pregnancy-inflicted back pain and the constant yet annoying pain in her knees.

The moment Sarai knocked on the door, the excited running of fast, small feet trampled through the apartment on the other side accompanied by the happy shouting of, "Mom, Mom, Mom, someone's here!" in a high-pitched child's voice.

The door opened to reveal a little girl, no more than six or seven, grinning from ear to ear, her hands fidgeting with a knee-length pink dress that looked much more appropriate for a formal party than a small dinner gathering. She also wore a tiara with plastic rhinestones in her curly black hair. Her face was a mirror image of Sarai's aunt and her mother and perhaps even herself. They had the same cheekbones, the same nose, the same chin, even the same eye shape, but young. And so much happier than Sarai had ever been at that age.

"Hi, I'm Yaffa, your cousin!" She grabbed Sarai's hand and pulled her inside the house. "My mom's in the kitchen."

Setanta stepped into the home after Sarai, but Marcelle hesitated at the doorway. "It seems they've left a few wards against undead up," she said, glancing at the *mezuzah* in the doorway. "Could I get an invitation, please?"

Sarai's aunt, Mazal, hurried out of the kitchen, looking frazzled as she wiped her hands clean on an apron as she looked at the group. "Oh, you're early." She glanced at a clock on the wall. "No, you're on time. I'm sorry. I lost track of time. You're the first ones, though."

"You're fine. Don't worry," Marcelle said. "If you don't mind?"

"Of course, yes, please, come in," Mazal said. "I'm sorry dinner isn't quite ready yet, and Zeinab is running late, but she'll be here soon."

Now officially invited, the vampire stepped through the protective barrier spell.

"Do you need help with anything?" Setanta offered.

Mazal looked at him with an uncertain expression, as if she wasn't sure whether or not it was a courtesy or a genuine offer.

"You can help me." Yaffa grabbed his hand with her free one, not letting go of Sarai. "I can't reach the plates. I want to set the table."

"I'd be happy to help," he told her, a slight smile on his face as the little girl led them into the kitchen, Marcelle close behind them.

As they walked, Sarai looked around the house. It was cramped compared to what she'd gotten used to at the vampire palace, but full of personality. Display shelves showed Jewish items such as candlesticks, a hanukkiah, and a variety of trinkets that looked Middle Eastern, like a filigree-covered teapot and cups set. The walls had stunning artwork in frames, including Arabic script and an elaborate *ketubah* marriage contract in Hebrew, and a small corner of the room was blocked off with a folding divider, behind which was a short bookshelf with Muslim prayer books and a basket with prayer rugs. The home was a perfect blend of Jewish and Muslim items, and that made it beautiful.

In the kitchen, Sarai was overwhelmed by an amazing smell. She identified at least cumin, ginger, garlic, paprika, lemon, coriander, and who could know how many other scents, and the kitchen was full of food.

"I hope you'll be all right," Mazal said to Marcelle. "I can't offer you anything more than company. You can't eat at all?"

"Not a bite, I'm afraid. Don't worry, I'm not thirsty," Marcelle reassured her. "I wouldn't expect anything from you. Why don't you let us help?"

"This one, not that one," Yaffa instructed Setanta as she pointed up at a cabinet with a sticker labeled *Meat* on it, next to another labeled *Dairy*. "We need..." She counted on her fingers as she muttered to herself. "Nineteen plates. We have nine and ten people today. That's nine and seven more people than we usually have."

Sarai gulped. Nineteen people at dinner. So many new family members, some of whom she had never met. It was terrifying.

"I think eighteen will be enough," Marcelle said. "I won't be eating."

Yaffa's eyebrows furrowed with deep concern. "You don't want dinner?"

"I'm on a special diet," she explained. "You know how your family has special rules about food? I have those too, but a different set of rules, so I have to eat at my home."

Yaffa nodded, and Sarai was impressed with the simplistic explanation that avoided mention of blood. Setanta got the plates down from the shelves, and the girl snatched them from his hands eagerly, struggling to hold the weight of them all.

"Come on, I'll show you where the nice tablecloth and the napkins are and how to set the table. My mom taught me how to set the table so I know how to do it right."

Setanta looked delighted to be ordered around by the child who had no fear of him or concept of his position in their society, and followed along dutifully to the other room with her as if he were her servant.

"The food smells amazing, *Doda*." Sarai looked around at the kitchen and the avalanche of food spread out across every surface area. No wonder it smelled so good.

"I had to go all out, give you a proper Meir meal," Mazal said with a smile. "I have fresh challah bread to celebrate Shabbat, then for the meal we have dolma, Israeli couscous, zaalouk, lentil soup, falafel, hummus with pita, shakshuka, joojeh kabab, and Moroccan lamb shank tajine... Oh, I forgot the salad." She sighed and went to the refrigerator where she got out several tomatoes, cucumbers, parsley, and lemons.

Sarai was daunted by the list of foods she didn't recognize but felt she should. "Wow, that sounds like a lot of food. We brought a chocolate cake. Don't worry; it's nondairy. From a kosher market."

"That's so kind of you, thank you." Mazal smiled as she washed the tomatoes and cucumbers in the sink.

"You can put that anywhere there's room."

Sarai managed to find space on the countertop in between a sack of onions and a jug of olive oil. The oven beeped.

"*Aiyaiyai.*" Mazal rushed to the oven to turn off the timer.

"We can help, if you'd like," Marcelle said. "We can manage the salad; just tell us what to do."

On the list of things Sarai had never thought she'd see was Marcelle preparing a salad.

"I need those diced. That would be wonderful," her aunt said as she pulled on mitts and opened the oven to usher out the most amazing smell of lamb Sarai had ever experienced.

"Sure thing." She got a cutting board and knife and split the work with Marcelle, dicing up the food as instructed while Mazal handled the lamb shank. "You know, I was kinda expecting, like, kugel, gefilte fish, and matza ball soup. That's what I had this one time I went to a Chabad meal for the holidays."

Mazal laughed. "Oh, *motek*, sweetness, no. That's Ashkenazi food. I suppose the authentic stuff with chicken fat and everything pickled has some good, strong flavor. And kugel is good. And matza ball soup too. But this is Sephardic and Mizrahi food, our family's food from Morocco and Iraq, perfected in the Negev Coven. And also some Persian food my mother-in-law taught me to cook. She's been shockingly accepting of us compared to my own mother kicking me out, and we bonded over cooking. You'll love her." She looked up sympathetically as she put down the lamb shanks. "You've never had food from your own culture, have you?"

Sarai felt her face flush with a slight heat as an undeserved sense of shame crept over her. "To be honest, I don't even know what half of what you said you made means. Though the smell reminds me a little of this Indian restaurant I worked at for a bit. I liked the food there a lot."

Mazal nodded and gave her a tour around the kitchen, telling her what each dish was and the origins of the meal. Dolma was stuffed grape leaves with rice, diced vegetables, and ground lamb, a recipe from their Iraqi side that Mazal had learned from Sarai's great-grandmother as a little girl. Israeli couscous was a pearl-sized grain dish. Zaalouk was a Moroccan dish of eggplant-tomato spread, which was served next to a homemade hummus spread and warm pita bread. Falafel Sarai was familiar with, a cross-cultural Mediterranean and Middle Eastern favorite made of fried chickpea balls full of spices. Some of those spices and more, namely cumin, paprika, chili, and cayenne, crossed to the shakshuka, poached eggs in simmering tomato, onions, and garlic. Joojeh kabab was the Persian food Zeinab's Iranian family had introduced, a dish of marinated, grilled chicken on skewers. And of course, the lamb shank was the star of the show, a Moroccan recipe slow cooked to perfection so that it was falling off the bone.

Once Marcelle had finished dicing the tomatoes and cucumbers, Mazal had the pair bring out the platters and bowls of food to the table Setanta and Yaffa had set, while she prepared the salad with lemon juice, olive oil, vinegar, and parsley.

"Oh, ah, I haven't told my in-laws that vampires exist," Mazal said with an awkward laugh as she came out to put the salad on the table, glancing up at Setanta where he sat on the couch with Yaffa, being shown several dolls and their dresses.

Sarai stared in alarm. "What are we telling them exactly? His eyes are a bit of a giveaway that he's not human."

"I can make them green," Setanta said.

"Yeah, but that makes you practically blind," Sarai pointed out.

He shrugged.

"It…should be fine," Mazal said. "They do know about *kesemi* witches. You know, Jewish witches like us. I mentioned that you and your company here would be a little unusual and that you're from the magic communities. So they do know that much and didn't ask any other questions."

"Did you at least tell them that we're not in a regular two-person relationship?" Sarai fought down panic at the thought of having to out herself to people she'd never met who might judge her for it.

"Yes, I mentioned that and the baby. It'll be fine." Mazal dismissed with a wave of her hand. "I just never brought up that vampires exist before and didn't know how to—"

Someone knocked on the door.

"I got it, I got it, I got it!" shouted Yaffa. She ran to the door and flung it open to beam up at the new visitors.

In the doorway was a middle-aged man and his wife, their twin sons who looked a little older than Yaffa, and an older couple who had to be Zeinab's grandparents. Sarai was surprised to note that neither of the women wore hijabs or any form of head covering the way Zeinab did. Mazal greeted them in Arabic as Setanta, Marcelle, and Sarai stood to the side, waiting.

"Please, please, I'm rude. Please, come meet more family! These are my mother and father-in-law, Laila and Samir. Then this is my brother-in-law, Omar; his wife, Katie; and their boys Yusef and Ibrahim. Everyone, this is my long-lost niece, Sarai."

"Welcome to the family." Katie, a tall black woman with short hair, gave Sarai a hug. "Wow, you look so much like Mazal and Yaffa."

"I know, genetics. Crazy right?" Sarai laughed.

"Where is Zeinab?" the mother-in-law, Laila, asked, in an Arabic accent. "I need to talk to her about my computer. We bought a printer, and I don't know how to make it work."

"She should be here soon. She's running a little late from work," Mazal said. "As soon as she and my brother's family get here, we can all sit down and eat."

"Ah, I see you made my dish," Laila said with a smile. "So good, such a good daughter-in-law. Here, we brought a little dessert. I made baghlava." She held up a large tray covered in plastic wrap that presented a flaky honey and pistachio pastry cut into enough large squares to feed an army. It looked so much better than the now sad-looking kosher chocolate cake Sarai had insisted on getting.

Further pleasantries were exchanged, which somehow Sarai felt less comfortable with compared to socializing at the vampire court. Setanta surprised her by speaking to the elderly couple in semi-broken and accented Arabic, which had them fawning over him and applauding his attempts with delight.

"Do you speak any? Arabic, I mean," Sarai asked Marcelle, who shook her head.

"He traveled a lot before we met; that's how he

picked up so many languages. Though I don't think that's Arabic. I'm not an expert, but I'd guess Farsi. Or an older Persian variant. I imagine his dialect is archaic compared to theirs," she replied.

Zeinab finally arrived with circles under her eyes and a look of exhaustion on her face framed by a beautiful green hijab, but she brightened up when she saw the gathered family and the food. Yaffa ran to her for a hug, and Zeinab swung her around before planting her on her feet and setting down her purse and house keys. "I'm so sorry I'm late, everyone." She smiled. "Sarai, it's so good to see you again. How are you?"

"I'm good." Not just good. In fact, Sarai felt great. She was surrounded by so many people, by her cousin and aunt, by Mazal's in-laws, and she was struck for the first time by the realization that she was truly with her family.

"You're here!" Mazal took off her apron and came over to give her wife a peck on the cheek. She didn't have long to stay with Zeinab, though, as the last guests arrived.

The final group was Sarai's uncle, Ezra, along with his wife, Tzipora, and their staggering army of five rambunctious children whose names Sarai could not keep track of if her life had depended on it. The children said polite hellos, then went to play with their cousins and ignore the adults.

These Meirs, like Zeinab's family, seemed more relaxed about modesty, as Tzipora didn't wear a head covering the way Mazal did and wore dress pants instead of an ankle-length skirt. Erza, Sarai's uncle, wore an almost casual polo shirt and cargo shorts, with a kippah decorated to look like a baseball over a bald spot on his head.

"It's amazing to meet you," Ezra gushed in the same Hebrew accent as his sister. "Absolutely amazing, you look so much like your mother. I had pictures of her from growing up in the Negev I meant to bring you, but we were in such a rush getting the kids out the door I left them on the table. I'll bring them for you next time, yes?"

"That would be wonderful." Sarai had no pictures of her mother, so such a treasure had value beyond measure.

"Now we can eat! Come, sit, sit, everyone. Before the food is cold," Mazal insisted.

Chapter Ten

The Healer's Problem

Everyone sat down and quieted. About to ask what
the wait was, Sarai had her question answered when
Zeinab and her family took a moment to quietly pray to
themselves over the food with murmurs of, "*Bismillah*,"
and a longer version Sarai couldn't quite catch from
Zeinab that ended with the word, "*Bismillah*." This was
followed by Mazal lighting Shabbat candles and saying
the Hebrew prayers for the holiday, then Ezra said a
prayer over a cup of wine and another over braided
challah bread.

Sarai was a little surprised to see the wine. When it
was their turn to sip from the glasses in front of them,
she was more surprised to see Zeinab and her family all
drinking from theirs. She took a sip and realized why it
was acceptable. The drink wasn't wine, only grape juice.

Once the prayers were done, it was time to dig in.
Loud chatter erupted at the table as dishes were passed
around for all to take their portions.

"Why don't you eat? Are you unwell?" Laila asked
Marcelle. "Please try some of the lamb. You should have
a lamb. Do you not have a plate?"

"I have a lot of medical needs and allergies, so my
food is difficult to manage," Marcelle lied.

Well, it was sort of a lie, Sarai thought. She wasn't

sure what would happen if Marcelle ate real food, but doubted it would be good. "I ate before coming, don't worry about me."

Laila pursed her lips and looked very disapproving. "No wonder you're so thin, you look sick. You need to eat more food."

"She did eat at home," Sarai vouched. "She's just got a very restrictive diet."

Laila wasn't impressed.

"I would love some of the lamb if you could pass it to me?" Setanta said in a clear attempt to cut the tension.

The old woman gave a broad smile with adorably crooked teeth and heaped a helping of lamb shank onto his plate, saying something in Farsi that made him laugh.

Sarai found it incredibly funny that he charmed the family with such ease. Despite a few uneasy glances at the tattoos at the edge of his wrists and neck, he had been embraced by all. *He so easily fits the role of whatever social situation he finds himself in*, Sarai thought. He was humble but firm when engaging in diplomacy with witches, dominant and commanding at the vampire court, flirtatious and charming when he saw a person he desired, and now he fit the part of the perfect son- or brother-in-law guest. He reflected his surroundings, mirroring the mannerisms of those around him to put them at ease. What was he like when the masks were all removed? Perhaps the truest expression of his inner self was when they lay all together, when he could take his pleasures how he desired them. Or perhaps it was when he was in the throes of a battle, soaked in blood.

Sarai glanced at Marcelle and gave her hand a squeeze. The vampire woman was not so easily immersed in the new culture. She could weave herself through vampire politics and battles with ease, but a dinner had her on her head. She stood out like a very pale sore thumb with her plate-less, empty table setting, unable to participate in their hosts' hospitality.

Sarai needed a way to show them that her wife, her love, was a part of them. A part of the family. "*Doda* Mazal, Marcelle and I were talking," she said. "We wanted to do something special, for us. She wants to do a Jewish wedding ceremony with me."

Mazal clapped her hands over her mouth. "Yes! That would be beautiful. Oh, we have to throw a party. We'll get that Reform Ashkenazi lady rabbi who did ours. She'll be okay with two women. And the party, there's so much to plan."

"You have to let us cook for the party," Laila insisted, excitement in her voice. "Mazal, you'll help me?"

"Oh, I'd love to," Sarai's aunt replied. "We'll have a henna ceremony, a beautiful *ketubah*, lots and lots of food and dancing. Sarai, Marcelle, you must let us plan this all for you."

"I've no objections." Marcelle put her hand over her heart as she agreed to the plans. "It would be the honor of my life." And like that, the energy of the room shifted, finally welcoming Marcelle.

"But I don't think I know anyone willing to do a wedding for three people," Mazal said, glancing at Setanta.

"Don't worry, this is just for the ladies to enjoy. I'll be a spectator. And if you're doing the food, I'll be more than content. You're an excellent cook." He raised his glass as if in toast toward Mazal.

"Oh, it's nothing." Her voice was dismissive, yet her

expression was that of a woman beaming with pride. "Though I suppose it's better than haggis and boiled potatoes?"

He laughed. "You're thinking of the Scots. But yes, it's a touch more flavorful than most Irish cooking."

"Only most?" Zeinab asked.

"You'll never hear me say a word against a good Irish game stew," he said.

"Did you try the kabab yet?" Laila said. "It's my recipe, and Mazal did good. Please, try, try. And take some dolma—it has lamb. You need meat for all those big muscles, young man."

Sarai almost snorted into her hummus.

"If it's not what you're used to while living here in America, would you like to put some ketchup on it?" Mazal teased, and the entire table burst into laughter.

"I would never disgrace your cooking in such a way," he promised.

"And you, Sarai, you need to eat more too," the woman insisted, putting lamb onto her plate, then adding two falafel balls and some more hummus before she could object.

Sarai was convinced she would end up rolling out of the apartment at the rate she was being fed. But it would be rude not to have a bite, and she hadn't tried the falafel yet. She picked up her fork and knife and began to cut into it.

Tzipora laughed, and everyone loudly joined her in the joke Sarai didn't get.

"Oh, no, sweetie, put down the knife. Like this." She picked one of them up, dipped it into her hummus, and ate with her hands.

Sarai felt her face blush as heat flooded her cheeks.

"Oh, right."

"Do you want more? You should have more," Laila insisted. "You're eating for two, and you're too skinny. You need more food for the baby. Are you gaining enough weight? How much do you weigh?"

"Uh…" Sarai felt very self-conscious about discussing her weight at a table full of relative strangers, even if they were family.

"When I was pregnant with Yehuda, I swear overnight I gained fifty pounds," Tzipora said. "I could not stop eating cheese all the time. Then with the breastfeeding, zip! It all melted off. Then the same thing with Aviv and Shir, but with Uri and Rivka it wasn't so easy. I thought I was going to be a hippopotamus forever!"

"Yusef was such an easy pregnancy," Katie said. "It was such a relief, honestly, eating whatever I felt like whenever I wanted and having this one"—she nudged her husband's arm—"running out to get me food. Tomatoes and olives, that's what it was for me. What about you, Sarai? How are your cravings?"

Well, she was craving blood and getting small infusions from Marcelle to manage it. A glance at Mazal's non-magical in-laws reminded her that not everyone present knew vampires existed, so she decided she shouldn't mention it. "Well, now I'm going to be craving all this food," she deflected with a smile.

"I am going to give you my recipes," Laila said very seriously. "And Mazal, Zeinab, you need to send her home with as much as she can carry."

By the end of the meal, Sarai had never felt more stuffed with delicious food and more welcomed in her life. The conversation around them was so loud compared to what Sarai was used to with vampires. That made sense of course, considering vampires tended to be a touch quieter with their sensitive hearing, but the family was louder than even mortal witches at the Ellis Coven. Everyone talked over each other, made loud sounds and exclamations, and interjected points into each other's conversations in a manner that might have been considered rude to others but was organic and commonplace to them. Setanta seemed to keep up the best compared to Marcelle, and Sarai fell into the ebb and flow of conversation easier as the night progressed.

Omar and his wife helped pack away the leftovers, and Mazal busied herself making a large pot of tea to bring to the table to be served with the baghlava and chocolate cake. Sarai offered to help despite objections that she needed to relax as a pregnant guest, in part because the familiar ache in her knees had returned, and she wanted to catch Mazal alone for a moment in the kitchen to talk to her about it, healing witch to healing witch.

"Hey, *Doda*? Could I ask you something?" Sarai said.

"Mm, of course, what is it?" Mazal closed the refrigerator on the leftovers as she continued to speak. "About the wedding, about the food?"

"About magic. I think something's wrong with my healing gift. Since you're a healer too, I thought maybe you could help."

"Something wrong with your gift?" Mazal frowned as she looked up and turned off the water. "What do you mean?"

"I've had this pain in my knees a lot lately. I don't know if that's a pregnancy thing or what, but I'm not a fan. And my gift usually fixes anything that's wrong with me. So I was wondering maybe you could help me out a little since you've got medical knowledge."

"Your knees, you say." Her eyes filled with sympathy as she nodded. "Sit, sit, let's take a look."

Sarai sat down on a chair at the small kitchen table, and Mazal pulled one up across from her, where she proceeded to pick up Sarai's leg in her lap and run her hands over her niece's left knee.

"Hm. When did this start?"

"It's been... I'm not sure. It comes and it goes? A bit for the past few weeks. It's not terrible. It's mostly annoying. There was one night where I had trouble with stairs, though. Like, I needed to hold the railing."

A warm glow of healing magic emanated from Mazal's hand, and to Sarai's surprise, the ache felt worse.

"That didn't help, did it?"

"No." Sarai made a face. "That hurt more."

Mazal nodded, then sighed. "It's a common ailment among healing witches. We can't get sick or hurt but..." She patted Sarai's knee. "What sort of medical knowledge do you have? Any studies? Have you learned about autoimmune disorders?"

"No." And the thought that maybe she should have been studying medicine made her feel inadequate. "I just work off instinct."

"I'll explain basics for you, then. Your healing is too good, too strong. And because it's too good, your gift thinks it needs to work harder than it does, needs to fight more than it should. You understand?"

"Wouldn't that be a good thing? If I've got a super immune system, that means I'm super protected, right?"

Mazal shook her head. "Not in this case. Your immune system has decided to attack your own tissue. Your joints. That's why your knees hurt, why more healing magic hurts, because your body is fighting itself. You have healer's arthritis, Sarai."

Arthritis? She almost laughed. That was an old person's disease as far as she knew. And not something that should affect a witch. It had to be a joke. Except the expression on Mazal's face was serious as it could be.

"I have arthritis," Sarai repeated. "That's got to be a mistake. I'm not even thirty yet—I can't have arthritis."

"Young people can have arthritis too. The elderly are more prone to it, but it can happen. Healers like us are prone to it. Your *safta*, your grandma? She couldn't walk some days. Her joints were so painful. I have it as well."

A coldness tingled in Sarai's fingers and toes. "But...we're magic. There's a cure, right?"

The silence from Mazal as she shook her head made the cold dread spread through her whole body.

"It can be managed, though," Mazal said. "I've developed a magically amplified turmeric, black pepper, ginger, and cinnamon tea I drink myself. It reduces inflammation and pain, slows the progression."

"Slows. Doesn't stop, slows." Sarai sat for a moment as she absorbed the meaning of what she'd been told. "I want to stop it. I don't want to have arthritis."

"No one does, Sarai." Mazal reached out to hold her hand. "Magic is wonderful, but it can't solve all problems. Bodies are tricky things, and magic gifts are tricky things. But don't worry, it's not all that bad."

Sarai slumped back into her chair, staring at the wood grain of the kitchen cabinets, at the little stickers on them that said either *meat* or *dairy* in red or blue. Everything felt like it was swimming. No cure, progression… She had arthritis, and it was going to get worse. She'd been handed a sentence of chronic pain for the rest of her life. She was a witch. She was supposed to be immune to this sort of mundane concern. This was all wrong.

And what would her spouses think? Vampires with no flaws, no physical defects. Would Marcelle still love her if she couldn't keep up with them? Would Setanta, who she knew didn't love her, replace her the moment he had the chance? She thought of hiding it from them, but that was foolish. With their hearing, they'd already heard the entire conversation from the other room.

Sarai put her leg down and rubbed her knees. It was cruel. How dare her body betray her in such a way? A sob gripped her chest, and she wasn't sure if she was more angry or sad.

Mazal fetched a glass of water and held it out. "Here, here. You'll be okay, Sarai. You have people who care for you, *ken*? You have your vampires, you have me, and you have your family here. It isn't fun, no, but it's not the end of the world."

Sarai took a shuddering sip of the water. The cool liquid running down her throat helped steady and relax her, if only a little. "You said there's a tea?"

"Of course, yes, my tea. You can take it home with you; I have plenty. I'll get you a jar, okay? It's one spoon of the mix seeped for seven minutes in hot water, one cup a day." Mazal got up again to go through her cupboard and pull out a large mason jar full of the tea. "This jar will fill back up when you empty it, so you'll always have your tea. No charge for *mishpacha*, for family."

Sarai unscrewed the lid and took a sniff. It smelled very nice, the fragrance of the spices like a melody. "One spoon, seven minutes, one cup a day."

"And no pain." Mazal gave her niece a contagious smile.

"And no pain," Sarai agreed, closing the lid. "It's okay to drink with the pregnancy, right?"

"Yes, I promise," her aunt assured her. "I did when I had Yaffa. It's good for you, really, because you don't want your body overreacting more and attacking the fetus. Healer's arthritis can be milder or more aggressive than mundane human arthritis, so it's best to stay on top of things so the autoimmune reaction doesn't spread beyond your joints."

Sarai hadn't even thought of that as a possibility and gripped the jar of tea tightly. She had to protect her baby and drink the tea as instructed.

"Oh, and don't worry. There's no caffeine in the drink. I would recommend adding a little honey if you like sweetening to your tea. But nothing wrong with lemon or sugar. Don't add milk, though. For some reason, milk seems to dilute the strength of the magic. In fact, you might want to remove dairy from your diet altogether."

Sarai nodded. "Honey, lemon, or sugar. No milk. Got it." Honey blended with the cinnamon flavor already in the tea sounded nice. She looked up. "Thank you for this. I'd have had no idea about any of this on my own. I never would have guessed something like arthritis."

"It's what family is here for. We're here for you, *motek*. Now, why don't you go sit with the rest of them? I'll be a minute."

Sarai took a deep breath. Marcelle and Setanta would know something was wrong with her now. But she had no reasonable way of avoiding it; she had to go. She hoped it had been too loud with all the very vocal family for them to have heard the details of the conversation.

Sarai went back to the living room and immediately knew she'd been overheard.

"Are you all right?" Marcelle said sympathetically.

Sarai found herself unable to meet her gaze. "Fine. I'm fine." She ignored the look of disbelief on her lover's face. "I got some tea to take home."

Zeinab looked at the jar with confusion in her expression, then realization dawned on her face. "Oh, you and Mazal have the same healer's problem?"

"I guess so, yeah."

"Don't worry, that tea is perfect. Takes away the pain all day long," Zeinab assured her. "I've watched her go from using a cane to running through the park with Yaffa after just one cup."

Using a cane. People with arthritis used canes. The panic that gripped Sarai's chest and caused her heart to race had Marcelle rush to her side as if she were afraid Sarai were about to fall over, and even Setanta looked worried as he leaned forward at the edge of his seat. As she looked at him, she remembered the talk from before of him using a cane due to his eyesight. Seeing him pop out his eye.

Vampires weren't perfect, she thought to herself. They could have physical defects. Her anxiety-riddled mind had run away with itself, and she needed to regain control of it. Marcelle loved her. Even if Setanta didn't love her, he cared for her. She was important to them, and no diagnosis would take her away from them.

"Did you know about this kind of stuff?" she asked him. "With healing magic doing this?"

"I can't say I did," he said. "The healers I've known were more hedge witches, the sort without modern medical knowledge. My own abilities have never caused anything of the sort."

Vampires didn't get arthritis, Sarai realized. Perhaps…if she became a vampire.

How odd that the possibility had never crossed her mind. If Mazal and other healing witches had no cure and she was doomed to a life of increasing chronic pain, perhaps painless undeath was preferable. But that was a conversation for another time. And after she was done having children.

Chapter Eleven

Candles and Cravings

Sarai was exhausted by the time the trio returned to their New York condominium overlooking Central Park. It had gone so well, aside from the arthritis diagnosis. She had such a good family of kind people, loud people, caring people. Her people. Though she did feel sorry for Marcelle.

While Setanta went ahead of them up to their accommodations, citing the need to make a phone call, Marcelle and Sarai lingered, people watching for a little before going up in the elevator.

"Was it too awkward for you?" Sarai asked. "The whole dinner thing, watching us eat food?"

Marcelle shook her head. "I, well. It's been a while since I've had to sit through a full meal with humans, so I can't say I'm used to it. But I knew what to expect. It looked nice. The smells were pleasant if a little overwhelming."

"Do you miss food?"

"You know, I didn't think I did. When I was still alive, most of the food I had access to was nothing special. But seeing so many cuisines I never could have imagined even existed centuries ago, seeing luxury food and easily accessible foods of all sorts."

"Things have changed a lot since the Dark Ages,"

Sarai tried to joke.

"You have no idea. For example, in that market we went to, that wall of spices? I can't get it out of my mind. Do you have any idea how many people kings would kill to have easy access to such a variety of spices like that? I wonder if I might have been better at cooking if I'd had easy access to ingredients like that."

"You could still learn to cook, you know. If it's something you're interested in."

Marcelle scoffed. "So that I can torment myself? No, thank you. Oh, but speaking of torment…let us change the subject. You remember that I do love you?"

"Of course?" Sarai raised a questioning eyebrow.

"Good." Marcelle leaned forward, her hands sliding over Sarai's waist, against her hips, as she whispered in her ear, "Because for the rest of this night, I intend to be cruel to you, and I hope you won't forget."

The elevator dinged and opened to reveal Setanta shirtless in a dark apartment, illuminated by candles surrounding a sort of massage table with cuffs attached to each leg.

Sarai was instantly horny. "There was no phone call," she accused. "You two were plotting."

Marcelle took both of Sarai's hands and held her wrists together behind the witch's back in one hand and buried her free hand's cold fingers in Sarai's thick curls.

"You said you were unsatisfied. So we are going to satisfy your lust for torment tonight, my little witch," Marcelle murmured in her ear before kissing her neck. "Gentle kink, approved after a consultation with a doctor."

Sarai beamed as Marcelle forced her forward toward Setanta.

"We'll be doing something new for you tonight," he said as Sarai's eyes feasted on his toned chest and the beautiful way the woad ink in his blue tattoos contrasted against his pale skin. Suddenly, he drew a dagger from his belt and held the tip under her chin, forcing her to look up as it threatened to pierce her skin. "My eyes are up here," he mused with a crooked grin.

"I'm sure there's a few sets of animal eyes tattooed on your chest, and I know there's that hound a bit down lower. Let me just check again—" As she tried to lower her gaze, he held the dagger firm, forcing her head up enough to strain a little.

"Be good for us tonight, Sarai, and we'll be good to you."

"Mm, listen to that heart racing," Marcelle purred, sliding her hands along Sarai's sides and hips. "You want this too much to be disobedient tonight, don't you?"

Sarai bit her lip and would have nodded if the crook of the dagger wasn't still at her neck.

"Don't move a muscle," Setanta warned. "We wouldn't want my hand to slip."

"I'm going to get you out of these clothes," Marcelle said. "Are you fond of them?"

"This outfit? It's fine, but I'm not attached to it."

"Good."

Marcelle gripped the collar of Sarai's top and ripped it clean in half, and the witch gasped in shock while trying her best not to move. Marcelle proceeded to tear every scrap of clothing until it was a pile around Sarai's feet.

Cold air washed over her skin, and she glanced at the wide walls of windows surrounding them. "Are there blinds?"

"They're tinted so no one can see in, but we can enjoy the views," Setanta assured her, looking at her naked body, nipples pointed from the cold and her own need. He drew the point of the dagger down her skin while she held as still as possible. It slowed at her collarbone, between her breasts, and stopped over her heart.

She reminded herself he wouldn't hurt her. Probably.

"The view is lovely indeed."

"This way, Sarai," said Marcelle as Setanta pulled the dagger away. "Would you like to lie on your back or your side?"

Sarai pondered for a moment, then got onto the massage table and lay on her back. She knew she wasn't supposed to lie on her back for long periods of time once she was past twenty-something weeks along, but she would just make sure not to do it for too long.

"Wrists," Marcelle ordered.

Sarai raised her hands to meet Marcelle's, and comfortable leather cuffs were buckled in place. Not too tight, not too loose. Marcelle knew from practice which notch on the cuffs was the perfect fit for Sarai and always got it right.

Next, Setanta secured her legs so that she was fastened to the massage table. It was quite comfortable. Sarai wasn't even cold with all the candles surrounding them.

"So...what devious plans do you two have for me?" she asked.

Marcelle picked up one of the candles and held it sideways so that the tip was over her opposite palm. Hot wax dripped into her cupped hand, and she revealed it as it hardened, then flexed to cause it to crumble to the floor.

Sarai's breathing quickened. "Does it hurt?" she asked, unsure what answer she wanted.

"It hurts. Would you like to find out for yourself?" Marcelle asked.

Sarai hesitated but nodded.

Marcelle held the candle over Sarai's vulnerable body, and they waited. Air caught in her throat when the first drop of liquid, white wax splashed on the swell of her breasts. It stung a little but didn't burn and was cool within seconds as it hardened. She stared, transfixed as the wax began to drip more liberally. Setanta picked up a candle and began to join the perverse art project on the opposite side of Marcelle. White streams covered Sarai's breasts and encased her tender nipples. Then they poured it over the sensitive undersides of her arms, making her whimper, and even over her belly.

"I think that's enough wax for now. Hold very, very still," Setanta warned. He held up his dagger again, letting the blade shine in the flickering firelight.

Sarai bit her lip but nodded. She trusted him, trusted his skill. Giving him her willing vulnerability was exhilarating.

Slowly, Setanta slid the blade between the wax and her skin, flicking off piece by piece. The cold of the metal was like electricity, and she had never felt so alive.

Marcelle leaned over Sarai's head from above her and kissed her lips as the dagger danced around her breasts. "Don't move, not even an inch," Marcelle whispered. "If you breathe too heavily, he might slice your pretty skin. Draw your sweet blood. We wouldn't want that."

"We wouldn't?" Sarai stared at Marcelle's intoxicating lips and lustful red eyes. She could die drowning in those eyes and be happy about it.

"Mm, no, Sarai. Because your blood is delicious and addictive and I miss it. So let's take care, or I might drain every last drop."

"That warning's no good. You're just turning me on."

Marcelle grinned. "Good. I should see how much it's turning you on, then." The vampire gave Sarai another long, slow kiss that sucked the breath out of her lungs before moving around the table to slide a hand between Sarai's legs. "Oh yes. Very excited. But I need you to remember one thing. No matter how good it is...do not move."

Sarai looked down, nerves fluttering in her chest, watching Setanta's expert dagger movements along her body, then farther down into Marcelle's red eyes. A cold finger slid inside Sarai's sex, and she moaned, fighting her urge to writhe in pleasure. Keeping her torso as still as possible, she pushed her hips up against Marcelle.

The dagger was immediately at her throat.

"She said, do not move," Setanta warned. "Don't disobey again. Understood?"

"Yes," she whimpered. The sharp metal at her throat kept her more still than any teasing threat or effort to hold her down ever had.

Setanta leaned forward, his fangs so close to her lips, the dagger so cold against her neck. "Yes what?"

"Yes..." She hesitated. Marcelle would call him Master, but that didn't feel quite right. Some sort of honorific was missing, though, as he looked at her expectantly. "Yes, sir. My king."

He grinned, evidentially satisfied with her response, and murmured in her ear in a way that made chills run up and down her spine. "Good girl."

Marcelle climbed up onto the massage bed and lowered her mouth.

"Perfectly still," Setanta warned.

Sarai moaned in response, staring up into his eyes as Marcelle's tongue darted against her. The cold of her mouth heightened every sensation to her aching, desperate sex.

It didn't take much. Sarai was so worked up from the need and anticipation of having them give so much erotic attention to her body that the expert swirling sensation coupled with Marcelle's deft fingers had Sarai gasping, clenching, and crying out in climax. Somehow, forcing her body to remain as rigid as possible heightened her excitement through the waves of pleasure.

"You're beautiful," Setanta told her, then released her from under the dagger. "You may move."

The tension drained from her body, and she nearly orgasmed a second time as Marcelle pulled her fingers free. Then she did orgasm a second time when they returned, curled in the sweetest of spots, moving just right to coax every ounce of pleasure from her prone body. The orgasm rolled into a third, and Sarai found herself wondering if she had ever been this sensitive before the pregnancy, or if it was the one good bonus to come from it. Finally, Marcelle released her.

"I hate you both." Sarai moaned in bliss. "I will never get enough of that. You've ruined me."

"Did you want more?" Marcelle teased. "No need to settle for three. We have all night long."

"Maybe in a minute. I need to recover from how good that was."

Setanta picked up a thick pillar candle in a glass container. Something sloshed inside around the flame. "I hope you aren't done yet. I have more I want to do to you."

Sarai strained to get a better look. "What is that?"

"Oil."

She froze. "You're going to pour hot oil on me? I know I heal fast, but—"

"Trust me, Sarai." He used a nearby warm washcloth to wipe away lingering wax crumbs so that her body was once more bare to her lovers. Then he held the oil a few inches above her skin and poured.

It was hot like good bath water. As it spilled, he gathered some on his hands and began to rub over her skin, slowly. It was a massage. A proper massage, with lightly scented jasmine oil. His strong hands rubbed knots of tension out of her arms and chest, as only an expert in human anatomy could. Marcelle joined him, massaging Sarai's legs and sore feet, taking care not to hit pressure points she shouldn't on Sarai's ankles that could affect the pregnancy.

"It's no whips and choking," Setanta mused. "But is it a good substitute for now?"

"This is all amazing."

"Oh, darling, please be more specific so we can do more of what you liked best," Marcelle said.

"All right. The fear, anticipation. The fire. The dagger. A little nervous about the dagger touching me but wow. That was hot."

"Yes, the dagger…" Setanta had it in his hand again, and it was against her skin. Then he pushed down and moved as if to slice open her breast.

Sarai felt her eyes widen in terror as she anticipated pain but felt none. She looked down at where it was against her and realized why. "It's blunt. But it felt so sharp?"

"I had it on ice before you came in. Cold metal can feel sharp if you expect it to be sharp."

She laughed and closed her eyes as her lovers continued to massage her. "You had me there. I thought it was real."

"You're never in real danger with us, my little witch," Marcelle reassured. "But the occasional psychological manipulation to spike your adrenaline and heighten your senses so I can give you mind-blowing orgasms? Well, it's too fun to resist."

Setanta unlatched the cuffs on Sarai's wrists and helped her to sit up. "I can do a sharp dagger for you one day." He smirked at her. "But I would discuss it with you before implementing something of that nature."

"You're both sick bastards, and I love it." She sighed. "But what about you? I'm feeling pretty good, but you know, I could reciprocate a bit."

"This was all about you, Sarai," he said. "We weren't expecting anything but the joy of touching and lightly torturing you."

"Well, lightly torture me with your genitals," she countered. "One of you should put my mouth to use before I start insulting you to get you to shut me up."

Marcelle laughed. "You know, I was going to release your ankles. But if you want more, then let's do more."

And that was how Sarai ended up on her back with her head hanging over the edge of the massage table,

Setanta's member in her throat so deep that she could almost put her parted lips to the tattoo of a hound on his lower abdomen. At the same time, Marcelle wielded a double-ended dildo that connected both women in the sweetest intimacy, slamming deep again and again and again.

Then, barely able to sit up, Sarai was on top of Setanta as he lay on the floor, his hands folded behind his head with a grin as he watched her roll her hips and moan. Marcelle dripped hot wax on both of them from above before taking a turn with the dagger to flick the hard circles off, teasing them both with kisses and caresses as she did until Setanta gripped Sarai's hips and thrust deep into her body to release with a growl of satisfaction, oblivious to the hot splashes of wax, or perhaps excited by them.

The last of the three sated, they curled up together as Sarai reveled in the complete in bliss, illuminated by the candles casting an outline on their naked silhouettes.

"I love you both so much." Marcelle sighed.

Love... Yes, Sarai loved Marcelle. And maybe Setanta too.

"Setanta?" Sarai murmured.

"Yes?"

"Could you tell me a lovely lie?"

He pressed his lips to her forehead. "I love you, Sarai."

Marcelle raised an eyebrow, but Sarai shook her head. She didn't want to explain. "I know it's a lie. Just let me enjoy it."

"I won't say a word," Marcelle reassured. "Enjoy as much as you wish."

"I can't believe how long we've been at this. I

usually pass out by now," Sarai joked.

"Maybe we're going easy on you," he teased.

"I do have one last gift, one grand finale," Marcelle murmured, her red lipstick all smeared from her lips. "If you can stand it."

"Anything, yes," Sarai said.

"I got approval from a doctor for your favorite activity. As long as it's only a little, for sensation, and I'm very careful..." Her pearl-white fangs extended in her mouth. "I can bite you. If you have the strength. Or we can wait until next time."

"Now," Sarai begged. "Fuck, you should have led with that."

"It's my last gift of the night. What better way to end passion than with a tinge of pain?" Marcelle grinned as she pulled Sarai close. "Let me taste you. I miss that powerful, bittersweet taste on my tongue."

Sarai obediently tilted her head to the side and held her breath in anticipation, closing her eyes.

Marcelle brushed the tips of her sharp fangs against Sarai's skin. Every hair stood on end as she waited, craving the feeling.

"Beg," Marcelle commanded. "I want you to beg me to hurt you."

"Please," Sarai whispered. "Please, I need it. I need you." It had been too long, too many months since she'd felt a bite from either of her lovers. The thought was driving her wild, and she was slick down her thighs.

Marcelle's fangs penetrated Sarai's flesh. It was a shallow bite, freeing a little blood, but the sharp sensation followed by slight numbing was exquisite.

Until it wasn't.

Something felt wrong. She needed it to stop.

"Red," Sarai whimpered, but Marcelle had pulled away before the safe word was even uttered.

"Setanta?" Marcelle asked. "It's too strong, I—" Then she gasped. A real gasp, as if filling her lungs with air due to a need to breathe.

Setanta was immediately holding her as she gripped her chest, gasping over and over for air as color flushed her cheeks. He tore into his wrist with his fangs and pressed it to Marcelle's lips. She drank his blood, and the rise and fall of her chest disappeared, as did the pink in her cheeks.

But Sarai barely noticed. She was staring at Setanta's wrist as the wound closed, transfixed by the red droplets that called to her like a siren song.

She could smell it, but more than that, she could feel it in her core. It was more than the feeling of lightning she'd had before. It was…history. She could feel he was the head of his bloodline of vampires. That he had a vampire father and had been born to the life of bloodlust. She could feel misty forests and steep seashore cliffs and rolling wet moorland and fields of barley. And it hurt. She had a growing agony in her mouth and throat, a thirst more intense than anything she had ever known. She couldn't think for the pain and the need.

Then satisfaction. The pain in her mouth, the ache in her gums, was washed away as she drank the most glorious drink.

Strong arms wrapped around her, holding her close, then a chilled hand rested on her back as if to comfort her followed by an embrace from behind. It felt good, and she surrendered to her craving as she was held for a moment that stretched into an eternity of bliss.

As the haze lifted from her mind, she became aware

of what she was doing. She was drinking blood from Setanta's neck. Except he hadn't cut his neck to allow it. She had bitten him.

When she felt satisfied, she pulled her teeth free and looked down at his neck. Two puncture marks healing were evidence of her attack. Puncture marks caused by fangs.

"What just happened?" she whispered. Her tongue ran over her front teeth to discover elongated canines sharp enough to draw blood.

"Something unusual," he murmured as he touched the spot on his neck she had bitten. He gripped her jaw and forced her to open her mouth, analyzing her.

"Did you turn me? Am I turning? You said I was immune, right?" Panic rose in her chest. She couldn't turn. She never asked to be turned, never considered all the implications. Never made the choice. If Setanta had turned her, she would be furious.

"No, I don't think so. You're immune," he said.

She was almost relieved. Except she still had a problem. "Then why the hell do I have *fangs*?"

"Too much magic in your blood, if I had to guess," Marcelle said. "You nearly made me human. Your magic gifts are uncontrolled and must be overwhelmed by the raw power. Our baby needs blood to maintain itself."

"So you grew fangs. But your eyes are still brown. Still mortal," Setanta reassured her. "This is perhaps the most extreme change I've seen a mortal woman take on with a vampire pregnancy, but you're also the strongest, magically speaking. You are powerful, you conceived an impossible child through magic, and your physical form was touched by a demon. You are bursting with magic. I'd hazard a guess that you're as close to being a true half vampire as possible, but I think it will disappear once you're no longer with child."

"Are you sure about that? I'm not going to become a vampire because of your blood?"

"I can sense vampires I've made, to an extent. You aren't among them. And that's how it's always been in the past, the symptoms disappearing after childbirth. Though no one else has grown fangs."

"How do I get them to go away?"

"They should recede on their own when you're satisfied. Retracting them when you're not takes discipline and practice," Marcelle explained. "Do you need more blood?"

Sarai stared, and the realization struck her she had drunk blood. Her insides knotted in horror, and her fangs retracted, returning to normal-sized canine teeth.

"We should set up something regular. I would rather not be your victim of choice since it weakens me, but if I must, I can sometimes," Setanta said. "I'm certain Marcelle would be willing."

"Oh, of course, Sarai. Anything you need," Marcelle said. "Setanta can drink from someone else for a while— I don't think I can feed both of you. Or if you would rather someone else, any vampire would be proud to serve you. Or human, for that matter."

"But…" She sighed. If her need had gotten so intense that she grew fangs and lost her mind to bloodlust, then they were right. "I want to go back to the palace. I think I need to talk to Gedeon Katz."

Chapter Twelve

Disappointment

Back at the palace, Marcelle received notice from Lilly the spymaster that she had news to share with her in the dungeon. Fresh news, in fact, in the form of a Vasi militant captured not hours before Marcelle returned to North Carolina in a rather impressive sting operation performed by Lilly's network of spies.

Marcelle kissed her lovers farewell and went to the dungeon as fast as her vampiric speed could take her. Finally, she could start to get some answers.

The dungeon was a cold place and designed centuries ago to be miserable, with cells for prisoners and two rooms behind locked doors at the end of the hall. One was for interrogations, with a metal ring attached to the floor to chain prisoners to. That room was otherwise empty. The room next to it was for punishments and carrying out sentences for felons, when necessary. That room was much more cruel. The room she wanted was the interrogation room.

She opened the door to find Lilly and Crispin there and a mostly unconscious man chained to the floor, struggling to open his eyes. He smelled of gunpowder and sweat and looked ragged. His black hair was a mess, and dirt caked his tan skin, but he showed no wounds. He had been captured alive and unharmed.

"Impressive," Marcelle said. "Well done, you two."

"When the queen's away, we work." Crispin produced a small bottle of smelling salts from his pocket. "We had to drug him, but I think he's starting to come around. I can rouse him with this."

"Excellent, thank you."

"Which vampires did you take with you to New York?" Lilly asked. "Bear and who else?"

"Bear was with us and Temuulen as our bodyguards," Marcelle replied. "Lochlan too, though he's no vampire of course. Why do you ask?"

"I suppose I find it interesting that we were able to pull off this mission without tipping off the Vasi as you did in the past three attacks."

Marcelle froze. "What are you implying?"

"It could be a coincidence." Lilly's words were simply stated, but the furrow in her brow betrayed that she did not believe them for a moment.

"You don't believe in coincidence, and neither do I," Marcelle retorted.

"I did put much more effort into subterfuge this time around than your teams do. Bear, Temuulen, and Lochlan have all proven themselves many times over. Forget I said anything. We have an interrogation to conduct."

Marcelle certainly would not forget she said anything but had other matters to tend to in the immediate moment.

Crispin waved his smelling salts under the Vasi's nose, and the man jerked up, alert and newly aware of his surroundings as was obvious as his gaze became frantic. He looked every which way around and then up at his vampire captors. He yanked back on his chains, uselessly clanging them against the metal ring that bound him sitting to the floor.

"Shhh." As Marcelle spoke, she adopted a soothing tone as if speaking to a child and she knelt down in front of him. "There, there. Are you hurt?"

He looked confused and shook his head.

"That's good. We wouldn't want that, now would we? Why don't you tell me your name? I'm called Marcelle."

"I'm Theo."

"Theo," she repeated, manufactured kindness in her voice. "We'd like to have a little chat with you. I know you must be uncomfortable. Can we get you something perhaps? Water?"

He stared at her. "You have me chained to the floor in a dungeon. And you want to give me water. What, if I say yes, you'll waterboard me?"

"Not at all, Theo. We're just here to talk. Would you rather be unchained?"

He looked at her with a confused expression.

"Lilly, please, unchain the man for me. Crispin, could you go get him a cup of water?"

"Right away." Crispin bowed to his queen in a show of formal respect and left the room.

Lilly produced the key to his chains from her pocket and unlocked them. He rubbed his wrists. Marcelle smiled warmly at him. She felt good to begin the thrill of a proper interrogation, since it had been a while since she'd had the opportunity. She enjoyed it, learning a new prisoner's personality, getting down to their level on the floor, making herself look and sound kind. Her intentional and deliberate movements and words were all a practiced skill to get someone to open up and spill their secrets. To get them to accept their new reality, to make them trust her. To dangle hope of a better future, and make it seem possible whether it was or was not.

"Perhaps the chains were a little excessive," Marcelle said. "You seem like a reasonable sort. I'm sure they're unnecessary. You have my apologies."

"You're vampires." Hate filled in the word as he spat it from his mouth. "Why aren't I dead? I should be dead."

"Should be? No, Theo, we don't want you dead. In fact, I was wondering if we could talk about the Vasi. It seems to us that you fine folks have been, well, two steps ahead of us. Usually, we're able to get the jump on you, and yet you've been evading us with unprecedented success."

He grinned, then began to laugh. And laugh and laugh. "Yeah, because *fuck* your undead ass. You think you could keep killing us forever? Nah, not anymore. You guys are monsters that belong in storybooks. Legends. And we're gonna wipe you out so that's where you stay. I just wish I could be around to see a vampire-free world."

"I'm sure. Unfortunately, that isn't going to happen anytime soon, so I recommend you make peace with that fact. Vampires and witches are here to stay," Marcelle said. "But we don't need to be enemies, Theo."

"Witches can be useful at least," he said. "Get them contracted, and they'll hunt vampires all night and day. Magic like theirs serves God best when bound to obey their ordained holy human masters. You vampires...undeath is unholy. You're all cursed, and we'll free you of it. Free the world of your blight."

Ah, so he was a religious Vasi fanatic. It had been a

while since she'd encountered one of them, as they'd started to veer toward using science to study magic. Marcelle was almost nostalgic to run into the religious sort once more, reminiscent of their origins being run by churches to hunt the occult all over medieval Europe.

"You know, I was once quite religious," she mused. "A little less so now, but I hold some things sacred. We all serve the divine in our own way." It wasn't true at all. She had become disillusioned with religion the first time she realized how many priests would visit her brothel when she was a human.

"Divine? You're an unholy freak, a monster." He spat at her. "Put me back in chains and spare me this bullshit."

She sighed. "We have all the time in the world here. I'd rather not need to put you back in chains. You're passionate, you have strong convictions, but I don't think that's unreasonable. It makes sense. If anything, I admire you for your drive. You want to make the world better, as do I, even if we might not see eye to eye on how to do that."

"Convictions. Yeah." His eyes flickered with fear.

Marcelle mentally checked her expression. Her eyes felt widened as if in innocence, her eyebrows raised as if in concern for his wellbeing. She hadn't done anything to spike his fear, yet he was afraid. Something was off.

"Yeah, I've got convictions. And I know...I *know* there's something better waiting for me when I die a martyr here."

"We don't intend to kill you, Theo," Marcelle lied with a soft, convincing tone intended to soothe his fear, and chose words with weight he would feel connected to. "Life is sacred, and I would never needlessly waste yours."

He started shaking, staring at her as if searching her face for something. Whatever he was looking for, he didn't seem to find, since his lower lip was still trembling. "You're pretty." He paused before adding, "I guess that's one thing you monsters have. Pretty to look at. No sunset, but it's something." A tear swelled in the corner of his eye.

She supposed that made sense. He was trapped in a rather intense situation from which he would never escape. She reached out slowly, and he recoiled. She hesitated for a moment, keeping her eyes locked on his as she moved her hand forward to caress his cheek, wiping away the tear. The way Theo looked at her told her the little show of kindness worked. He wanted security and comfort, and she would be the source of all that for him until he was no longer useful.

"I'm not here to hurt you," she said. "You won't be harmed. Take a deep breath. Steady yourself. Crispin will be here soon with water for you. That will help."

"Vampires hurt people. You kill people."

"I kill enemy combatants in the field. You are not in the field, so I will not kill you."

He looked down at his lap. "I'm Vasi, and we are mighty," he whispered, as if trying to convince himself. "We are strong."

"You are strong," she agreed. "Theo, no one is saying you aren't. But it takes strength to accept when you've been beaten. To adapt and move forward. We can do that together, you and I. Why don't you tell me about yourself? Do you have family?"

"What, so you can hunt them down?" he snapped.

"Not at all. Though perhaps we can come to an

arrangement. I have many resources. I could help your family. I could help you. What would you like most in your own life, Theo? Healthcare for someone you love? A cure for diseases? Our blood heals most ailments. None of the humans with us ever need to fear cancer. Do you have children you'd like to send to the best schools? We can pay for their education. Work with me, Theo, and this can go well for you."

He paused, staring at her. She could see it was tempting, that it made his resolve falter. The way his eyes flickered when she mentioned disease was a telltale giveaway.

"Is someone you know sick?" Marcelle pressed.

"My sister," he said quietly. He shut his eyes. "Lies. You're lying to me."

"I'm not, Theo. Why do you think so many humans willingly choose to live with us? Because we offer so much in return. Tell me about your sister."

He shook his head. "Death is part of life. Disease is God's plan. I-I have to obey the plan. You're a lying snake. Temptress. Devil. I won't be swayed by your lies. I am Vasi, and we are mighty," he said again, his hands shaking like a leaf.

A strange expression crossed his face. Something between peace, joy, and spite. He clenched his jaw hard, as if biting down on something.

And the back of his head exploded in a shower of brain matter, blood, and skull fragments that coated the floor and wall behind him.

"What the *fuck*?" Lilly shouted in an uncharacteristic burst.

Marcelle took a step back, shocked. She was no stranger to violence or gore, but usually it was more expected.

Crispin opened the door, holding a glass of water, then stared at the corpse. "Why did you have me get him water if you were going to shoot him?"

"I didn't shoot him," Marcelle snapped. "He did this to himself."

"How?"

She leaned over the body and pried his mouth open. A molar in the back of his mouth was blackened. With as much care as she could manage, she yanked it from its roots and found it was a fake tooth, an implant. Etched into the enamel of the tooth was a sigil of some sort that flickered with red magic as if burning from the inside, the kind of sigil witches might use in certain forms of enchantment magic.

"He shot himself with magic," she realized. "Two steps ahead. They keep getting two steps ahead of us. We have to assume they're all doing this now to avoid interrogations. We need to be careful in capturing the next one. Remove the tooth before they can do this."

Lilly nodded. "Yes. I'll make sure everyone knows."

"Good." Marcelle closed her eyes for a moment. The stress of plans going wrong was annoying, but at least they knew what to look out for in the future. She handed the tooth to Lilly. "Test it to see if it reacts to anything. Pressure, poison, sedatives. Have Lochlan take a look at the witchcraft aspect before you give it to Setanta along with your report."

"Yes, my queen. You don't want to do it yourself?"

Marcelle shook her head. She didn't want to explain to Lilly that she needed another break so soon after having come from her break in New York. It felt lazy.

But she needed to step away from the dungeons and the disappointment. Sarai was never disappointing. She would find her co-queen and take another break.

Chapter Thirteen

Pikuach Nefesh

Sarai felt like a fraud. She spoke Hebrew, and she kept some rules from Judaism, but she had fallen to her cravings and drunk blood. Not only drunk it, but she wanted more. After an emergency session with her therapist to calm the anxiety, her need to speak to Gedeon Katz the Jewish vampire was urgent. Luckily, as queen, all she had to do was say the word and he was summoned to the sitting room where she waited for him.

The waiting made her nervous. She'd been to a few human Jewish synagogues but always felt off there. After all, witchcraft was traditionally frowned upon in Judaism. Especially a dark gift like necromancy. And the only Jewish witch coven she knew of wouldn't accept her because of the necromancy that tainted her from her non-Jewish father's side. She had the wrong parent to be allowed in, even if the parent she wanted to emulate and be associated with was Jewish, which should have been enough for the more religious.

She felt that Gedeon would know. The vampire would know Sarai was a fraud somehow. She didn't keep kosher correctly, she made exceptions, and she didn't keep Shabbat right. And she had no idea if she believed in the Abrahamic god at all. All she wanted was to feel close to her dead mother, and her Judaism-lite was a way to do that.

She didn't hear him approach at all before he stood before her with a bow.

"My queen," he said, and she jumped a little. "Apologies, I didn't mean to startle you."

"No, no, I'm fine." Her truth button warmed at her lie. "Thank you for coming to talk to me."

He stood before her, hands clasped behind his back, and it made her feel uncomfortable how professional he looked.

"Would you like to sit?" She gestured to the cushioned chair across from her to offer him the seat.

"Thank you, my queen." He sat, his limbs too stork-like to look comfortable.

"You don't need to be so formal; it's okay." She paused. "I had some questions I was hoping you could answer for me."

"Of course. Is this pertaining to the tryout for the knighthood?"

"Hm? Oh, no. It's about...that." She pointed at his arm where a small string of numbers were half-visible under his sleeve.

"Ah." He smiled a little. "I had wondered when I heard you introduced as Sarai Meir at the Midnight Festival. I recall Reinhart was your last name when you first arrived at the palace."

"Meir is my mother's side." She couldn't help but cringe whenever she had to explain her Reinhart connection. "I didn't get along with my father to put it mildly. So I go by Meir now."

"Understandable. Reinhart would be a difficult name to bear."

"Yeah, it was. But I'd like to talk to you. You are,

well, a Jewish vampire, right?"

"As contradictory as it sounds, or perhaps as maliciously stereotypical according to the propaganda as it sounds, yes."

"I'm so happy to meet you." And she truly meant it. "There aren't a lot, are there? I know there's only a few thousand Jewish witches in the world. We're a minority within a minority. Same with you, right?"

"Yes, very much so. I've met one other living in the Vampire Republic of California, though I'm sure there are a few more."

"For sure. I just, I had so many questions. If I could talk to a rabbi about my questions, that would be great, but human Jewish communities don't know anything about real witches, real vampires, and how it affects us."

"I think the name 'witch' puts them off. If you called yourselves prophets who could see the future, control lightning, and heal the sick, then you're miracle workers," he joked dryly. "Though that would be a little sacrilegious to some. If you want to see magic as holy, though, that's up to you. Or it's a useful tool. Who am I to say?"

"Healing, maybe, but I've also got necromancy. That's as far from holy as you can get to the point that it's explicitly forbidden. And then there's you..."

"The undead bloodthirsty vampire?" He laughed. "That is me. I'm not exactly welcome at *minyan* anymore."

"You have...numbers on your arm. You're a Holocaust survivor?"

"I think calling me a survivor would not fit my current state, but the sentiment is correct. I was at Auschwitz." He rolled up his sleeve to show his number.

"And I'll wear the evidence of that era for eternity."

Sarai exhaled slowly. Something about seeing the numbers up close felt surreal, like she was getting a glimpse of evil inflicted on an innocent's skin. "I'm sorry. I can't begin to imagine what you've been through."

"It wasn't a great time." He sighed and looked down at his arm. "I could cut the tattoo out, let the skin grow back without it. I almost did a few times. But there's too many people who want to erase the proof. This is proof."

"How? If you don't mind talking about it?"

"How did I escape? Get turned? Join the resistance? Learn to be very good at blowing things up?" He smiled. "I don't mind talking about it. I killed a lot of Nazis, and I'm proud of it."

"Yeah, I bet. So yeah, I'd love to know. I mean, I wanted to talk to you about kosher stuff…but wow."

"Oh!" Gedeon slapped his forehead. "*Kashrut*! Here I go, off thinking you want to hear about all that *Shoah* shit; you just want to talk to another Jew."

"No! Well, yes, but your story is really important too."

"Everyone always asks me about the Holocaust and my numbers." He laughed again. "I'm so used to that; I have a whole speech prepared and ready to go."

"No, I'm grateful you're willing to share." She paused, then quickly added, "If you want to?"

"Honestly, it's nice to not talk about it for a change. Maybe, some other time, then, it brings down the mood. I appreciate you wanting to know. Having a queen who cares about such things, a member of the tribe, it's important," he admitted. "But you want to know how I handle kosher laws when I need blood to keep from going insane. We don't have vampire rabbis, so I'm the best you've got. How much about *kashrut* and Jewish law do you know?"

"The basics. You know, don't mix meat and dairy. Don't eat pork and shellfish. Blood is bad. Which is turning out to be a problem because this baby wants me to drink blood. I, well, I bit someone. I thought I could do transfusions, but it's not enough."

"Understood. Answer this—if I hold a gun to your head, give you a strip of bacon, and tell you if you don't eat the bacon, I will shoot you dead, what should you do according to Jewish law?"

"Uh…" Sarai didn't know. "Don't eat bacon?"

"No, wrong. You eat the bacon. Your life, your health, it is always more important than keeping kosher or keeping Shabbat or any other laws or traditions like that. Life is more important than religion. Health is more important than religion. And that is according to the religion. It's called *pikuach nefesh*, the preservation and saving of life. So what would happen if I didn't drink blood?"

"You would go crazy and attack people." Just as she had done to Setanta.

"Yes. Now, what is more important? The lives of the people I would kill when I lose control or me trying not to drink blood because an old book tells me I shouldn't?"

"Their lives. And your life."

"*Kop oif di plaitses.*" He clapped for her as he spoke. "There's a good head on your shoulders. I do try to keep to the spirit of kashrut laws, though. The idea is that you shouldn't let an animal you're going to eat suffer. So I drink from willing donors now, and I do my best not to let them suffer when I take their blood. I always heal them. I think that makes up for not being able to keep kosher anymore. As long as I keep *pikuach nefesh*, I'm happy with that."

"*Kop...* Is that Hebrew?" It didn't sound like it, but she wasn't sure what language it was. "Polish?"

"Yiddish. My Hebrew is conversational, but not the best. Speak any Yiddish? Well, no, I suppose not. You look Sephardic."

She shook her head. "No Yiddish. And yeah, my mother was Sephardic and Mizrahi, Moroccan and Iraqi, specifically. From the Negev Coven."

"Ah, Negev witches. Those are Old Yishuv folks, yes? They've got that ancient temple era magic they pass down."

"New Yishuv witches, in the case of my family," she said with a smile. "But they probably learned stuff. Not that I know any of that."

"Do you speak any Ladino? Judeo-Arabic?"

"Just Hebrew."

"Not 'just' Hebrew. Hebrew's a good language," Gedeon reassured her. "And it's not a common one, so great for speaking secrets in. Lilly's been on my *tuchas* to teach her Yiddish for that. Expect her to come after you for Hebrew, especially if you're going to teach it to your little bun in the oven."

She smiled, rubbing her hand over her pregnant belly. "I guess all languages have some use. I haven't seen you around. You work with Lilly, then?"

"I'm never seen unless I want to be seen." His eyes twinkled as if he were gloating. "And yes. Lilly is my boss. I did work alongside Marcelle's team with Lochlan and Crispin in that Maine mission a few months ago, though that was quite irregular in many ways. It is unusual for someone like me, someone with weak blood and who is young compared to the rest, to make Lilly's team, but she likes that I'm good at blowing shit up and working in codes. So she keeps me around." He leaned forward. "I do have a question for you if it's not too delicate a subject."

"Sure. I asked you enough about delicate stuff."

"You said the fetus makes you crave blood. Do you need a source?"

She bit her lip. "I suppose so."

"Human or undead?"

"Uh, well, I might have…grown fangs and bitten Setanta."

His eyebrows nearly flew off his face with how high he raised them. "Well. That's quite a development. And an impressive appetite. I can't imagine that you need someone as powerful as him, though, especially since we're not meant to bite royals. It's a taboo in vampire culture, you know. Would a human not be enough for you?"

"I figured I'd need a vampire, so I hadn't considered a human." The thought of feeding off someone like Rosaline felt weird. But then another idea popped into her mind, unbidden.

Jackie.

And just like that, her gums began to ache. She pursed her lips together as if she could hide what might happen and prayed that she wouldn't have to deal with fangs in front of Gedeon.

"If you need a vampire's blood, I would be happy to donate. But as you may have noticed in Setanta's choice of almost exclusively drinking from Marcelle, having a source you're attracted to amplifies the experience. I sense no such attraction between us, so you may want to ask Temuulen or someone else you fancy."

Sarai felt her face blush as heat crept into her cheeks in response to him so easily knowing her feelings. Temuulen was an option, and she had a feeling she would enjoy it. But then the image popped into her mind of Jackie's exquisite long neck, her round face, her neck, her delicate fingers, her neck, her soft black hair, her neck... Yes, she wanted to ask Jackie.

She stood, and Gedeon stood with her. He was so lanky and tall, yet so fluid and smooth in his movements. Even watching him do something as simple as stand up was eerie. Regardless of how creepy he seemed to her, he had been kind enough to share so much with her. Not just advice, but his personal story.

"Thank you for talking to me. I really appreciate it."

"It was my honor." He gave her a broad smile that showed maybe a few too many teeth. Then he bowed, took her hand for a light kiss, and straightened himself. "Is that all, then, my queen?"

"Yes, thank you."

As he left, another figure stepped out from the doorway, bowing. It was the interior decorator, Lydia, waiting for her to finish her meeting with Gedeon.

"My queen." The vampiress stepped forward with a bow as she spoke. "I heard you had returned, but didn't wish to interrupt. Might I have a moment of your time?"

"Sure. What's up?"

"Your chambers are finished."

Sarai felt her eyes widen. "Finished? Already? We were barely in New York for a few days."

"Of course. Vampire artisans are efficient. We spend multiple lifetimes perfecting our crafts and move at superior speeds." She smiled. "The only reason it took as long as it did was procuring some international goods that needed to be shipped and inspected. But it's all prepared now. I've already had your things moved so they would be ready for your return. If you could inspect our work and see if there are any changes you would like?"

"Yeah, that sounds fantastic, thank you."

The room was flawless. While Sarai hadn't been sure what to expect in her very general guidelines, she was thrilled with what she got.

The best description was Moroccan sunrise full of vibrant purples, violets, deep pinks, oranges, and golds. Arches were circular, and geometric mandala-like shapes adorned large spots on the walls. Rose curtains graced the windows, plants with vines grew from hanging pots, and the room seemed so *alive.* So fresh. So dramatically contrasted to the rest of the palace. And best of all were the electric ceiling lights. Sarai particularly enjoyed the sight of a sitting space with soft purple pillows facing an actual, brand-new, twenty-seven-inch television perched high enough on the wall no toddler could reach it.

Perhaps the best addition was in the bedroom. Exactly in the center against the back wall sat a beautiful violet bed that matched the decor to precision, but that didn't matter. What mattered was the bassinet next to it, as well as a collection of other baby-related items on shelves and a dresser filled with onesies with each drawer labeled by age. Sarai sat down on her new, soft bed, reached out to touch the bassinet, and ran her fingers across it. Not a single splinter was to be found. It looked sturdy, safe. She rocked it, a hand on her abdomen.

"This is for you," she whispered. "You and me, we're gonna spend a lot of time here. I'm sure your other mom and your dad will want to be here too. All of us together. There are so many people who are going to adore you."

The baby pushed and stretched inside her, causing her stomach to bulge in the corner from a foot or head pressing out as if it wanted to escape. It was unreal. She wasn't sure if it was alien or if it was heartwarming, or some strange intersection of the two.

"I want you out too," she chided. "I'll be honest, little wiggler, I'm getting tired of carrying you around everywhere without being able to put you down. But you have to wait a little longer. Your crib is ready for you now, so don't you rush. You grow those lungs and everything you need. Take all the time you need."

The baby stretched inside her again, and she began to hum to her a familiar melody, the one her mother had sung to her to soothe her whenever she was afraid.

"*Numi numi, yaldati, numi numi nim.*" Her singing voice was soft, and she wondered if her mother had sung those exact words to her in utero. "Can you hear me when you're in there? Can you hear how much I love you? Funny how I can love someone I haven't met."

"Do you like it?" said a voice from the doorway.

Sarai grinned at Marcelle as she entered and pulled herself up to her feet. "It's, pardon my French, fucking amazing."

"That's not even remotely French, *ma petite sorcière*," Marcelle retorted. "But I'm happy to see it turned out so well." She eyed the bed and its violet covers. "We should try it out sometime soon."

Sarai wanted to jump on the opportunity, but a tickle

in her dry throat held her back. "When you get thirsty, do you, well, want specific people?"

"Sometimes. I have suspected your hormonal desires and blood cravings are connected. Do you need blood?"

"Yeah, I think so. What do you mean they're connected?"

"You've been feeling overwhelmed with needs lately, attracted to new people? I think perhaps the people you find yourself attracted to share a blood type, and that's what your body is craving, so it's making you desire them in every way."

"That explains a lot. Like, don't get me wrong, I'm attracted to you and Setanta a lot. But lately I, well. I can't get Temuulen or this source girl Jackie out of my head."

"A new girl? You hadn't mentioned."

"Yeah. I want to ask her to be my source, but it feels so strange to even bring it up."

Marcelle laughed. "Oh, you're too sweet. Another woman? Come then, tell me all about her. What is she like? How is her scent?"

"She's a new source. Jackie. I don't even know if she'd say yes. I don't know much about her; I just think she's cute. And she's been nice to me. I feel like she and I had some sort of connection."

"Well, the best way to get to know a woman is to spend time with her. Why don't we summon her here, and you can make your request?"

Sarai blinked. "Summon her?"

"You're a queen, Sarai. It's simple to ask one of the sources to come speak with us." Marcelle gestured to the interior designer, who had stayed silently behind them.

"Lydia? The source girl by the name of Jackie. Do you mind fetching her for a quick conversation?"

"Of course, my queen." And Lydia disappeared.

"I don't know if that's the best way to get to know someone." Sarai felt butterflies doing full somersaults in her stomach as she spoke. "I don't want her to see me as the queen. I want to be equals."

"Do you want to feed on her?" Marcelle asked bluntly.

"Yes, but—"

"Then ask her, little witch. She'll either say no, in which case you'll be no worse off than you are now, or she'll say yes, and you'll be sated. And if she says yes, I'd like to be here to help you since you don't have much experience in feeding with care."

"Is it wrong to want to feed on her because I think she's cute, though?" Sarai paused to cringe. "It feels manipulative or something."

"Not at all. I do it all the time." Marcelle winked.

"That isn't reassuring. That's the opposite of reassuring. I love you, but you're manipulative as hell."

Marcelle rolled her eyes. "What I mean is, be open about it. Let her know you find her to be a beautiful young woman and it draws you to her, so you would like to establish a feeding relationship and grow from there if she's open to the idea. She's a source. She knows how feeding works."

Sarai paced, her heart racing and her teeth aching with need at the thought of Jackie. "Do you mind letting me talk to her first? I don't want to overwhelm her with two queens, and she's never met you one-on-one before."

"Of course, my love."

Chapter Fourteen

Pomegranate Blood

With Marcelle waiting out of sight on the balcony, Sarai sat down on a cushion- and pillow-covered L-shaped sectional couch and fidgeted with the hem of her shirt. Then she got up and looked at one of the decorative, mosaic-framed mirrors on her wall to check her appearance. She looked well enough. Her hair was thick and full and didn't need a brush at the moment. Something about the pregnancy had made her hair nicer. Her shirt was fine. She'd showered, so she didn't smell bad. But what was she going to say to Jackie? She wished she could have a teleprompter hidden somewhere so she could know what to say without stumbling.

She tried to rehearse a few sentences in her head. Finally, Sarai heard the sound of a knock on the door.

"Come in!" Her voice cracked a tone or two too high with the words.

The door cracked open, and Jackie's big, dark eyes peeked in. The human hesitated, then stepped in, her eyes widening. While Jackie looked at the room, Sarai looked at her. She had on a black robe with a striking red rose pattern, and Sarai couldn't help but openly stare.

"Wow," Jackie said. "This is the queen's apartment, then? This is fancy."

"Yeah, they just did it for me. I asked for a kinda

Middle Eastern thing because my mom's side is Moroccan and Iraqi Israelis."

"That's cool. I'm Indian, but, like, not really. Adopted. I'm about as Indian as chicken tikka masala."

"Oh. That's…cool? Is that the right response?"

"Yeah, I guess. America the melting pot or something, right? There's a place for all of us. Even if my parents are religious nuts."

They stood there in awkward silence.

Fucking hell, Sarai thought. *You're a queen; this shouldn't be so hard.* "Jackie, I—"

"Are you doing okay after everything with your husband? Everything okay with everyone?"

"Oh! Yeah, everything got cleared up, and he apologized to me. And then he and Marcelle were great when we visited New York, and we had a very nice time."

"That vampire you sent, she said you wanted something from me." Jackie stared at the window. Then she did something that shocked Sarai. She dropped her robe to stand there in the nude.

Sarai felt her eyes widen, and her heart raced as her body froze. Jackie was beautiful. Not unnatural perfection like Marcelle, but stunningly human in the most wonderful way. Her brown skin was a good tone or two darker than Sarai's was. Her curves framed by the bright colors of the room looked so sensual. Her breasts looked like they would fit so perfectly into someone's hand, with pointed dark nipples reacting to the cold as if inviting a mouth to warm them.

"This is what you want, right?" Jackie stepped forward out of her fallen robes. "If it is, I'm game."

Sarai was still like a statue as the short woman

leaned in for a kiss. Their lips met, and Sarai inhaled sharply. Jackie's hair had the sweet scent of coconut oil and something floral she couldn't quite place, perhaps hibiscus, and her body was so warm. Warmer than anybody Sarai had touched in a long time. Marcelle was as cold as the grave, and Setanta was closer to room temperature. Jackie was *heat*. Her skin was so soft and giving. Sarai melted in that glorious heat, letting Jackie kiss her slow and needy, until pain shot through her gums, and she stumbled as she pulled herself away.

"Sarai?" Jackie asked.

Sarai covered her mouth, shaking her head as she tried to calm down. "That was, I mean, that wasn't what I wanted to ask you for. But it was really nice!"

Jackie blinked, then looked down at herself. "Oh." She bit her lip. "Is it good, then?"

"Yes! Oh, definitely, yes. But…" She looked around behind Jackie to see Marcelle smirking in the doorway to the balcony where she'd been waiting for the pair to talk before revealing herself. "You might want to put on clothes?"

"Please, don't stop on my account," Marcelle said.

Jackie spun around with a gasp and dove for the robes to hold them against her body so she could hide herself. "Queen Marcelle! I didn't expect—I think I may have had a misunderstanding."

"A little." Marcelle smirked and eyed the pair. "But you're not too far off. Sarai has a request for you, and I'm here to ensure it goes smoothly should you accept. Sarai?"

Sarai lowered her hand and let her lips part enough to reveal the new fangs in her mouth.

"Holy shit, you're a vampire now?" Jackie gasped.

"But you're pregnant."

"It's confusing, I know," Sarai said. "I'm not a vampire. It's a side effect of having the vampire fetus blood in my system. Supposedly, it all goes away after the kid comes out. But I need, well, blood. I need a source."

"Oh." The expression on Jackie's face shifted from one of evident shock to dawning realization. "*Oh.*"

"That's why I wanted to ask you here, to see if you're able? I know you've got something with Artemisia—"

"With *Artemisia*?" Marcelle interjected. "Really? She's a pureblood; she takes from one of my subordinates, Patricia. I've never known her to care for human blood."

Jackie's gaze darted from Sarai's fangs to Marcelle. "I dunno, maybe she changed her tastes? She's been through a lot. It's bound to change a person."

"Do you have any other regulars?"

"N-not yet. I haven't put my name on the lists yet. Artemisia keeps me busy."

"Well then, how fortuitous. Sarai would like to request your services as a source of blood to help her with her new cravings."

Jackie looked like a deer in the headlights as she clutched her robe tightly against her breasts. "You want to feed on me?"

"If you don't want to, it's fine," Sarai blurted. "I just thought of you. And I guess you were thinking of me at least a little."

"Then why are you here, Your Highness?" Jackie asked Marcelle.

"To ensure she doesn't kill you. She's never fed on

a human before, and I have centuries of experience."

Jackie audibly gulped.

Marcelle raised an eyebrow. "Your heart is racing. It's quite enticing, and Sarai's going to notice it soon. Are you willing to be hers? You may need to abstain from any others beyond Artemisia and Sarai. Pureblood thirst can be intense and not good for sharing."

As Marcelle mentioned it, Sarai's gaze fell to Jackie's neck. Yes, her heart was racing. She could see, almost feel even through the distance, the rapid beating of the woman's heart. Sarai's fangs ached with need.

"I guess I don't need to be naked for this," Jackie said.

"I have no complaints either way." Marcelle glanced up and down the human's form as she spoke. "But that's up to the two of you."

Jackie rolled her eyes and looked at Sarai. "You seemed into it."

"Yeah. I mean, I'm not against it. I wanted to ask you here because it's better to pick someone…someone I think is attractive. But you know, you don't have to be naked now if you don't want to. Marcelle's here and all. I've seen vampires bite people before; it can be clean and professional. It doesn't have to be sexy. It can be, but it's up to you."

Jackie glanced back at the vampire queen. She took a deep breath and dropped her robe until it lingered at her fingertips a few moments and fell to the floor, leaving her naked in the cold room again. "This is the kind of thing you like here in this palace, right? You vampires, I mean. I've heard lots of stories."

"And what do you want, Jacqueline?" Marcelle purred, her natural French accent emphasizing the human's name as she stepped forward.

Sarai's heart skipped a beat. And so did Jackie's. Sarai could hear that tantalizing heart pounding, smell sweetness in the air as well as a sharp scent. Something tangy, almost like lemon. No, sharper and more bitter than a lemon.

Marcelle reached out and ran a finger down Jackie's cheek to her neck. "You're afraid."

"A little."

"More than a little. I smell fear oozing out of your pores. If you're this afraid of us, there's no requirement. You can leave anytime you choose."

"No!" Jackie bit her lip, then said with more calm, "No. Please, I need to do this. Don't send me away."

Need. The word set something inside of Sarai on fire. She wanted to drown in Jackie's scent and curves and blood. "I'd never send you away. I just don't want you to be uncomfortable."

"I'll get more comfortable after we do this." Jackie gave her a shaky smile.

Marcelle held out both her hands to the women, who stepped forward close and accepted. "Let me guide you," the vampire said as she led them to the bed. "We'll take it slow. It is Sarai's first time with a human, after all."

They sat down on the bed together.

"Where do you like to be bitten?" Marcelle asked Jackie.

"Oh, um. I guess she can bite my neck?"

Sarai nodded and leaned forward, sliding her fingers against Jackie's waist, around to the small of her back. She was afraid of crossing some line, of being secretly unwanted, but couldn't resist running her fingertips against Jackie's soft skin. "I don't know how to do this,"

Sarai whispered. "Marcelle, what do I do?"

"Touch your fangs to her neck but don't bite yet," Marcelle said. "You want to feel her pulse, find where the best spot is. Rest there for a moment so you don't miss. Living blood will burst when you bite. Be ready for it."

Sarai leaned forward and took a deep breath to steady herself. Jackie's scent clouded her mind, and she opened her mouth as if in a trance, obeying Marcelle's instructions. She touched her new elongated canines to Jackie's throat. There it was, the pulsing. But not only that, goose bumps. Adrenaline. Tiny shivers. The in and out of human breathing. Sarai closed her eyes and focused on the pulse, feeling it under her teeth. Driven by instinct, she bit down. Her fangs slipped through Jackie's skin like twin hot needles dropped through plastic wrap.

The blood burst, just as Marcelle warned it would. It was most akin to an overripe fruit and tasted much like one too. While whatever products Jackie used in her hair or as soap might have been coconut and floral based, her blood didn't taste of either. She tasted like a pomegranate. Rich, tart, sweet, and powerful all at once. The burst of blood was too much for Sarai's unexperienced mouth, and she struggled to drink fast enough to keep it from dribbling out the corners of her mouth.

The moment the pain hit Jackie, the woman tensed. Sarai felt muscle, skin, and vein almost clench around her bite, and tried to keep still to lessen the intensity, but it was difficult to focus on. Jackie's pain was enticing. Sarai wrapped her arms around Jackie, drinking in her body's warmth. The satisfaction was intense, and she didn't want it to end.

"Easy does it, Sarai," Marcelle chided. "That's enough for now. Ease out slowly; you don't want the tips of your fangs to catch and tear the skin."

Sarai wanted a moment longer, just a little more. A little more, and then she could stop.

"Sarai, now."

The authoritative tone in Marcelle's voice snapped Sarai out of her daze, and she pulled free with as much care as she could, her fangs disappearing as she did. Her bloodlust had been satisfied.

Jackie looked shell-shocked. And somehow, that excited Sarai. It made her feel strong.

"Here." Marcelle scratched open her own thumb on a fang and pressed it to Jackie's wounds.

Jackie closed her eyes, moaning as the drug-like blood entered her system and healed her.

"You're so beautiful," Sarai whispered. Her lips and chin were a sticky, bloody mess dripping down to her neck. Part of her wondered how Marcelle and Setanta were so often able to drink without mess. Yet she didn't care. It felt good. "This was amazing."

Jackie opened her eyes, and the two stared at each other. Sarai couldn't quite read the expression on her face. Something between desire and exhaustion, but perhaps confusion.

"I…I'd like to go back to my room for a bit," Jackie said. "That was intense. Good. It was good intense. We can do it again, okay?" She stumbled a little, and Marcelle caught her to hold her up.

"Easy does it, Jacqueline," Marcelle murmured.

"I'm fine," she whispered. She closed her eyes, took a few deep breaths, then got to her own feet and gathered her robes. "I just want to go to sleep in my own bed."

"Oh, okay," Sarai said.

Jackie covered herself and scurried to the door.

"Drink lots of water. Take those iron pills we provide you," Marcelle said. "Do you need help getting back?"

"No, I know the way. I'm fine."

And with that, she scampered out of the room like prey running to hide in a forest. Sarai let the tension flood out of her body and realized she might have frightened Jackie because of how she looked. She needed to clean the blood.

"How on earth do you and Setanta manage to never spill a drop when you feed?" Sarai looked around for a towel or tissue box, but found none. No vampires or healing witches ever got sick, so of course it hadn't been part of her room design.

"Centuries of practice," Marcelle said. "Go clean up."

Sarai washed her face in the bathroom, taking a moment to admire the copper and jewel tones and the large, framed mirror there, as well as the solid granite countertop. When the blood was gone and she was dried off, she returned to Marcelle only to see a perplexed expression of contemplation on the vampire's face.

"What's wrong?" Sarai asked.

"Your Jacqueline has never been bitten before."

"What?"

"That girl, Jackie. She's not feeding Artemisia. I've never known Artemisia to even glance at humans. Something is…off."

"How? And how can you tell she hasn't been bitten before? She's a source, isn't she?"

"She is. Perhaps she was just nervous about you, but that girl had so much fear it stank. The way she reacted to your teeth was like a virgin's response to first penetration. The way she ran when you were done. The way she asked you to bite her neck and not her arm, which is the way most human sources feed us as standard procedure. It's like she got her knowledge of how to feed a vampire from watching Dracula in a moving picture. She has no idea what she's doing."

Sarai frowned. "But that makes no sense."

"No, it doesn't, does it?" Marcelle mused. "I'm not sure what her deal is with Artemisia, but I'll do some digging. I need you to keep an eye on her. Keep feeding on her if you like, you seem to enjoy that, and we don't want to tip her off. Get close to her, but don't let her know that I've told you of her deception. Use your truth-spell button to determine when she lies. She's hiding something. I want to know what."

Chapter Fifteen

Invitation

Sarai chased after Jackie all the way back to the human quarter, Marcelle's words ringing in her head. It was unnerving. Had Jackie told her any lies? She couldn't remember. She didn't remember her truth enchantment going off with a warm warning at any point around Jackie. Could Marcelle be mistaken? No, Marcelle was trained in reading expressions and conducting interrogations. In fact, their very first serious conversation had been an interrogation where Marcelle had pulled out the truth from her, a very reluctant witch with much to hide.

She burst in to find Rosaline relaxing on the couch.

"Where did Jackie go?" she asked before Rosaline had time to say hello.

The human pointed back at the bedroom dorms.

"Thanks." She went back and glanced through a few of the small rooms until she saw Jackie.

She was sitting with some sort of embroidery crumpled in her hands, her legs curled up under her. She looked up at her in shock. "Sarai. Is something wrong?"

Was something wrong? Yes, many things. But none that Sarai could bring up. "You ran off so quickly I was worried. Are you okay?"

"Yeah. It was just a lot. I haven't ever... I wasn't

expecting Marcelle to be there. *You're* cute. *She's* a lot."
She shifted on the bed a little first one way, then the
other, awkward as she tried to scoot around and make
space. "Wanna sit?"

Sarai nodded and sat down, only to be stabbed in the
behind and jump up with a yelp to find a needle strung
with thread stuck through it sticking out of her.

"Oh my gosh, I'm so sorry!" Jackie grabbed the
needle and put it aside on her nightstand. She ran her
hands over the bed, checking for more needles, then
looked up apologetically. "I like to do needlepoint to
relax."

"Well, don't needlepoint my ass," Sarai joked.

"Are you hurt?"

"Nah, I'm a healing witch. No harm done." Already
the sensation had disappeared, though she was surprised
how deep the needle had managed to stick her,
considering the blood on half of the damn thing.

"I'm sorry." Jackie sighed. "I fuck up everything. I
messed up your first time feeding on someone, didn't I?
Marcelle made me so nervous."

"No! No, you're fine. Well, a little, but it's fine. You
were fine. You didn't have to do it if you didn't want to.
I don't want to pressure you." Sarai paused. "I think
maybe it'll be less awkward to do it again if we get to
know each other more. Hang out, you know?"

"Yeah, that might be nice. You're sweet. Compared
to the vampires here, you know? It's weird how nice you
are."

"They're nice too, you just need to take the time to
get to know them."

"Maybe."

"Can I ask you something?"

"Yeah, what?"

Sarai took a deep breath. "Has Artemisia ever bitten you?"

Jackie blinked. "I'm here for Artemisia—"

"Yes, but has she ever fed on you?"

Jackie looked angry. "I know I was awkward just now with you, but you don't have to make me feel bad about it. I was awkward because…because I like you. And it took me by surprise. I didn't think you had fucking fangs when I came to your room."

Sarai frowned. The defensiveness did set off an alarm in her head. But nothing she said was a lie. Still, Jackie hadn't answered the question. Perhaps a direct confrontation was a bad idea. Marcelle had said not to tip the girl off. A different approach was necessary. Let Jackie put her on the defensive for the time being.

"I'm sorry," Sarai said. "I didn't mean anything by it. You were just so nervous. And I felt bad for doing that to you. You tasted amazing, though. Is there anything I can do to make it better? Maybe something Artemisia does to make it easier?"

"Well, I don't *like* Artemisia," Jackie joked.

Sarai couldn't help but smile. Maybe Marcelle was wrong? "I'm a bit focused on my wedding, but after that, maybe we could have a date?"

"Aren't you already married?"

"To Setanta, not to Marcelle. My family's throwing us a wedding. That's two weekends away." Sarai paused. "Do you want to go?"

"To your wedding?"

"Yeah. Rosaline and some of the others will be there. Bunch of vampires. Lots of witches. Some human in-laws of my aunt's. It'll be a fun party. You should come."

Jackie hesitated. "Yes, that could be fun, to hang out with everyone at a party. That's…a good opportunity."

"Yeah, it should be fun. We're doing this henna party thing the night before, not sure who's going to be at that. I think that's gonna be witchy. But everyone's coming to the wedding and the reception. You can too. If you want to."

Jackie nodded, and her expression softened. "That would be nice. Thank you. I'll be there."

****

Marcelle had agreed to the wedding ceremony without much consideration to what it would be like to have a nonroyal non-vampire wedding and found herself gradually more excited as she and Sarai finalized a guest list. Sarai had simple little paper invitations created after a phone call with her aunts to verify details, and Marcelle handed hers out with pride. Bear, and by default Hannah, got an invitation, as did the rest of the elite vampires who served under Marcelle as security, including Temuulen. Lilly the spymaster received one. And of course, Marcelle was happy to present one to Lochlan when they hooked up at his mountain-side cabin for an end-of-night tryst while Setanta occupied Sarai's bed.

To Marcelle's surprise, his face fell. He nodded, put the invitation to the side, and reached to find his pants from the floor, skipping the rest of their aftercare cuddles. "Uh, congrats. I guess. Aren't you already married?"

"Sarai wanted a ceremony for us. Different customs. I'm told henna and a contract are involved, but Sarai's family are handling all the details."

Lochlan stared at the paper as he buckled his belt.

"It's an invitation. You're invited," Marcelle said.

"I get that."

"Well then, why do you look so perplexed?"

"It's gonna be regular folk, right? Witches?"

"I assume. There's a fair amount of humans from one of her aunts' sides, so humans, witches, and some vampires from here. The rest of the knights are going. You get along with them."

"Yeah. But vampires are different. You guys don't give a shit about my stuff." He turned away and stopped, looking in a cheap floor-length mirror hanging from the back of his bedroom door at his half-naked and scar-covered body. "As long as I can hold my own, and I can, they like me. You lot respect me as one of you." His fingers lingered on a blue Celtic triskele tattoo over his collarbone, one given to him by Setanta in recognition of his accomplishments and shared tribal heritage after a particularly intense mission. Then he touched the twin surgical scars on his chest under his pectorals. "Witches and, worse, humans aren't like that. They still see who I used to be, not who I am."

"Is something wrong?" Marcelle came up behind him, still naked, and hugged him as she placed her hands on his chest. "Did someone from the coven say something to you?"

"Not recently. Just...I wish shapeshifting magic wasn't so rare. It's not like the old days when witches were turning into dragons and shit and getting hunted for it. Finding anyone who has the talent and skills to make me right... It feels impossible. And I'm so scared no one's going to fully respect me until I get it all done, you know?"

"Lochlan." She reached out to put a comforting hand

on his shoulder, and he tensed, then relaxed a little. She wasn't sure what to say. She started with the obvious. "You're one of the youngest, most accomplished knights I've ever met. You'll find your way to the body that makes you happy, and whatever that is, wherever life takes you, I'm proud to call you my lover."

He looked up at her, his eyes as vulnerable as a puppy in a way that melted her cold heart. "You call me your lover. Do you love me?"

She paused in thought. Did she? Perhaps yes. She loved Setanta, and she loved Sarai. Love was easy to give freely for her, which she knew wasn't common among vampires. But she couldn't imagine existing for centuries without grabbing love wherever it came from.

"I do, yes," she told him.

"We're so small compared to you, though." Insecurity plagued his expression. "So short lived. How can you?"

She thought for a moment how best to explain how she so easily fell for mortals. "Have you ever had a pet dog?"

He looked at her with exasperation. "And now you killed the moment. I know you're not comparing me to a dog."

"No, not a dog, but think of it this way. You can love a creature that's short lived. Care for it for its whole life. Love it so completely that it is a member of your family. And it dies, and you mourn, and you remember the good things, and you move on. And maybe you have another one day, maybe not, but the memories are special," she explained.

"I guess that makes sense."

"Some of us can't handle the death, the emotional

attachment. We don't seek it out because we know the end is inevitable. But me...I live too much for the moment to go through an immortal life without all the love I can find." She kissed him. The way his lips and body radiated heat made her moan into the kiss, and she slid a hand between his legs to draw a moan from him as well. "And I am so very glad that I have found you."

"All right." He managed to breathe. "Since you love me, and I think I love you, I guess I should go to your wedding?"

"That would make me a very happy bride indeed."

Chapter Sixteen

The Henna Night

Sarai was far more nervous than she'd expected to be for her wedding. Having a wedding, a ceremony, in front of her actual family and the friends she cared about felt unreal. Yet despite the wild butterflies fluttering in her stomach, she loved every moment of the buildup.

The pre-wedding henna party was Sarai's favorite part, taking place the night before the actual wedding. It was more intense than Sarai expected the wedding to be. The venue was Sarai's uncle Ezra and aunt Tzipora's home in the suburbs. It had a large backyard where their five children had plenty of space to run and play, and plenty of space to host a party.

Sarai and Marcelle were separated by the family to get dressed, and Sarai got to wear the beautiful black-and-gold velvet berberisca dress that had come from her grandparents. Luckily, it was enchanted to fit the size of anyone who put it on, so it draped over her pregnant belly with ease. Mazal helped do Sarai's makeup with thick eyeliner she never would have applied on her own, and helped her set the pearl and jewel-encrusted crown in her wild hair before showing her to a sort of palanquin with a cushioned base and a gold canopy supported by two poles, next to which stood her new male relatives waiting for her.

"Uh, what's this?"

"You're a queen, aren't you?" Mazal teased. "So go ahead, act like a queen, and let us carry you out!"

"I'm heavier than I used to be," she warned.

"*Sha, sha,* you let us worry about that. Now get in, *motek.*"

Sarai felt herself blush with heated cheeks as she was lifted in the wedding carriage, gripping the sides as tightly as she could. They took her out of the house, and she saw Marcelle coming to meet her in a similar palanquin carried by amused vampires who must have been roped into participating.

The moment their eyes met, both brides-to-be grinned. Marcelle looked beautiful. She had done her own makeup as usual, that was clear from her signature bright-red lips, but her dress was an elaborate, beaded gold-and-white kaftan borrowed from Sarai's Middle Eastern family.

Music started, with loud ululations shouted in celebration by some of the women in the crowd. Live musicians had been hired, playing lutes, drums, and singing beautiful songs in a Judeo-Arabic dialect. Sarai's family was dancing.

Several held platters of sweets that they uncovered with great flourish. To Sarai's surprise, the marzipan cookies took off from the platters like butterflies, connected by strands of magic. They all held a glow to them, spinning strands of sugary magic in the air and following the crowd as if weaving light through the celebration.

The two were led to a lavish tent warmed by portable firepits to keep out the snowy winter cold, and covered in bright colors like red, violet, burgundy, and gold. Lots and lots of gold, in the form of borders, chairs, and intricate lanterns. Inside was a pair of throne-like, bright-red, cushioned chairs where the pair were helped to sit and everyone gathered around. The guests were everyone invited to the wedding: the witches Sarai knew from the Ellis Coven, the vampires from the New Ulster palace, and Sarai's vast new family members she couldn't keep track of, including all the in-laws, children, spouses, uncles, and aunts. Even friends of the Ali-Meir family Sarai didn't recognize but who shouted welcomes to the family from the crowd were present.

"*Kesemi kadima*! Witches to the front!" Mazal called with a clap of her hands. "Everyone, witches to the front, we will weave spells tonight!"

Sarai looked out at the crowd as Mazal, Ezra, Tzipora, Setanta, Hannah, and Lochlan, as well as all the giggling Meir clan children, made their way to the front as instructed.

"Witches, hold your hands with your neighbor."

The witches all held hands, and the firelight grew brighter in the tent. Mazal snatched two of the flying cookies from the air, and they returned to regular sweets, which she tossed into the flames. Immediately, they burned through a rainbow of color.

Mazal held out her hands and took both Sarai and Marcelle's in hers, then began to sing. Sarai recognized the Hebrew words. They were an opening of magic and a welcome to all present. When Mazal finished her song, the crowd cheered, then grew still.

"We're doing a special combination henna ceremony for you tonight," Mazal explained as she prepared a blend of wet henna paste. "Your grandma is from Morocco, and your grandfather is from Iraq where he escaped the Farhud pogrom and made his way to the Negev Coven. But we manage to bring our traditions and our magic no matter what outsiders do to us, and that's the birthright I give you now. This henna I'm going to give your palms is for your grandma's side, to protect you from the evil eye, to bless your marriage so that you'll always have prosperity and good luck."

Mazal spooned a large amount of henna paste out of a golden bowl and into Sarai's palm and pressed a gold coin in the center, then wrapped a satin ribbon around it and bound her hand with a decorative fabric flower in her palm with help from Zeinab.

"Your mother should have been able to do this." Mazal wiped a tear from the corner of her eye. "It's such an honor to do this for you. To be here for her, for you."

Sarai's throat closed with emotion, and she didn't reply with more than a nod. The henna felt cold and moist, almost like mud but important. It was a gift from her family. Marcelle received the same treatment, henna and gold tied to her palms.

"This henna is Iraqi from your *saba*, your grandfather. These specific designs are more than fun. These are spells, *brachas*. This pomegranate means fertility, not that you need help there, and these eyes watch over you. I put magic passed on from our family in the henna to shield you from harm as long as the henna lasts, blessed under the stars of the *rosh chodesh*, the new moon. It goes on all your fingertips, and we wrap them," Mazal said with a smile as she applied the paste in circles and designs to Sarai's fingertips, again with Zeinab's help. "Humans do this too, but ours are magic because we have the blessing in our veins. We are *kesemi*; we are magical. Always remember you are *kesemi*." With a loving kiss to Sarai's covered hands, she moved on to Marcelle's fingers.

"I must admit, I never thought any marriage preparations I'd go through would look quite like this. I was raised Catholic, and I spent much of my human life near Notre Dame. This is, well, quite different," Marcelle murmured as her fingertips were decorated and covered.

Mazal once more began a song, and a thread of magic glowed through the tent, drawing power from each of the witches present, passing through Mazal and through her hands. It twisted like embroidery from her palms and into Sarai and Marcelle's henna. It was love. Warm, comforting, and safe, like a hug. Sarai closed her eyes and felt her family's love all around her, passing over and through her. A protection spell indeed, and a powerful one. She felt it not just in her henna, but joining a chorus of generations past in the embroidery of her dress.

Mazal pulled the wraps off Sarai and Marcelle's fingertips when she was done with the spell, and the henna had dried and dyed them faster due to the magic. Shapes like eyes, fruits, and flowers bloomed and shifted under their skin, evermoving with the power of magic.

And then the night sky invaded Sarai's mind. She fell back into her chair, and when she opened her eyes, she was somewhere else, Marcelle in front of her looking just as confused. Below them was a lake with a surface like glass. It reflected what looked like the entire universe in the night sky above them, all the way out to a golden line of a horizon that surrounded them.

"What is this?" There was a slight nervousness to Marcelle's voice.

"I'm not sure," Sarai said.

"*Bruchim ha'baim*, welcome," said a familiar voice.

A figure took form before them. It was Liora. Her mother. Except unlike the ghostly apparition she remembered her as, she seemed as solid as any living person. Sarai threw her arms around Liora and could feel her warmth.

"Mom," she whispered. "Mom, you're here? I never thought I would see you again."

"Of course." Liora wiped away Sarai's tear. "Mazal called on your Meir ancestors to welcome a new member into the family and rejoice in your marriage." She looked at Marcelle, who bowed her head. "You're marrying the vampire, then?"

"I love her."

"Then we will love her too. Marcelle, you are going to become family tomorrow. You are one of us, and we will be here to protect you, to protect Sarai, and to protect your daughter."

Sarai felt her eyes widen. "Our daughter?"

Liora kissed Sarai's head, then stepped back as more figures appeared. They all looked similar, with Middle Eastern features, but their clothing was different. Each new person who appeared had an outfit that looked older and older, from modern clothes all the way to ancient sudras and robes. She could see hundreds of people, more even. Thousands. All of them were her ancestors. Somehow, she could feel that more than just the spell Mazal had cast was calling them forward. Her own necromantic power strummed inside her and was responsible for bringing forward so many apparitions so vibrantly.

As Sarai watched, they all closed their eyes, covered them with one hand, then held out the left hand. In the center of their palms, an eye appeared.

"We will watch over you," Liora promised. "If you carry our talismans or if you wear the henna designs on your hands, we will love you from afar and protect you from harm when we can. *Mazal tov*, my daughters."

She heard a chorus of "*mazal tov*" congratulations from the ancestors before they faded away, and Sarai found herself holding Marcelle's hand back in the tent. They stared at each other, and Sarai broke into a grin.

"That was amazing," she whispered.

"It was," Marcelle agreed.

"Our brides!" Mazal called out and ululated with joy to the response of many others.

The witch circle was broken, and the party began in earnest. Guests decorated each other's hands with beautiful henna designs, some with magic that moved patterns over their skin just like Sarai's fingers. They feasted from platters of food: tajines, couscous, dolmas, pitas, falafels, and all sorts of delicious homemade sweets like marzipan cookies and hadji bada almond cookies wrapped in platters that people threw into the air where they fluttered about until eaten. The music was loud, perhaps too loud for the comfort of some vampires, and the joy was palpable. Nothing was stiff or choreographed about the party, the way Setanta's coronation and the Midnight Festival had been. That had been regal, aloof, and calculating. Every moment had been layered in politics. The henna party was…fun. Just pure, unbridled fun.

Sarai and Marcelle danced together, not to perform to a court or to seduce, but to enjoy each other, overwhelmed constantly by family and friends congratulating them, telling them what a beautiful couple

169

they were.

When Sarai needed a water break, Mazal pulled them aside to introduce the brides to someone, a brown-haired, light-skinned woman wearing an embroidered kippah and a large smile from ear to ear.

"Sarai, Marcelle, this is Rabbi Jennifer Goss," she said. "She's going to be doing your wedding ceremony tomorrow."

"It's my honor," Rabbi Jennifer said with a thick Brooklyn accent. "Jewish witches getting married, there's not many of us, not at all. And a vampire too? Oof, my mother would *plotz*."

"You're okay with marrying an interfaith witch and a vampire queer couple, then?" Sarai couldn't help but be amused at how strange their label was. "I know my aunts said they knew someone, but I figured something in that list of differences would keep any real rabbis away."

"Oh, most, yes, but I've already had enough scandal in my family after my second cousin brought a very sexy and very naked golem to life and married him, so what's an interfaith witch-vampire queer couple compared to a clay monster?" Rabbi Jennifer laughed, and Sarai found it infectious, joining in the joke.

"Thank you," Marcelle said, her smile one of the most genuine Sarai remembered seeing. "All this feels so welcoming. I hadn't expected it."

"You're marrying into our tribe, so of course we welcome you," Rabbi Jennifer said. "You two are such a beautiful couple. I'm looking forward to tomorrow. I promise that it's going to be perfect. The synagogue is small, but it's warded. You and all the guests you gave your invitations to are invited in, of course, so just warded against outsiders. No Vasi interruptions, no witchy *mishegas*. I'm going to give you the best wedding in the tristate area. I set up the ballroom for the reception party too. I've done some DJing before, so we're gonna have a blast."

Rested, Sarai was eager to return to the dance party with Marcelle and Setanta as well. There was no tango, just grins and fun.

Bear bounded up to them with Hannah in tow, and the couple flashed their palms. "We did the henna thing!" he said, then wrapped up Sarai in an oppressive hug that lifted her up off her feet. "This is so much better than all those stiff vampire rituals at the palace. Congratulations. This party is amazing, and you two look like proper brides."

"They didn't at our wedding?" Setanta asked.

Bear rolled his eyes. "They looked too important at your wedding. Queenly and all that regal bullshit. Here, they look happy."

Setanta laughed. "I suppose that's true." He looked at their covered, henna hands. "You know, I was thinking of getting a real tattoo, a woad one, to commemorate our relationship and marriage."

"Really?" Sarai asked in shock.

"It would be nice, and I already have a small fleur-de-lis for Marcelle. Is there a design you'd like me to associate with you?"

She pursed her lips a little. Getting a tattoo, a real one that was permanent, was different from temporary henna, and she wasn't sure how she felt about it being associated with her. "I think I'd rather you leave a spot blank for me."

Setanta smiled. "I think I can do that. What spot?"

Sarai looked down at her hands, then held them up with a grin. "Your hands. I'll get mine dyed, and you leave yours uninked. Forever."

Setanta chuckled and took her hand, then lifted it to his lips to lay a kiss on her palm and then her hennaed fingertips. "As you wish, *mo chailín álainn.*"

****

Marcelle was overwhelmed by the henna party, and she could tell she wasn't the only one. All the vampires experienced some culture shock, and she knew why—the noise level. She asked the musicians to lower the volume of the speakers, but even the few notches turned down didn't quite do it enough, and she didn't want to ruin the fun of the throngs of warm-blooded witches and humans having a party, eating their confections out of the air. After a while of dancing and enjoying her time as a bride-to-be with Sarai, she needed a little space. She excused herself with a kiss, making an excuse that she needed a little break from the noise, and left Sarai dancing in a circle with her aunts.

Outside was much more suitable for a vampire. Some light snowflakes drifted down from a clouded sky, and a sweet, silent blanket of the white powder covered the trees and ground. The sound outside the tent was so much better. She sighed in relief and darted into the woods behind the house to rest there in the trees. To her surprise, she wasn't alone. Bear had Hannah pressed up against a tree, kissing her neck. No...not kissing. The scent of witch blood was unmistakable.

Marcelle was about to walk away when Hannah gasped at the sight of her and demanded Bear stop. He did, pulling away with care so that his fangs wouldn't tear her delicate skin.

"I'm sorry, I didn't mean to interrupt," Marcelle apologized. "I was just getting away from the noise for a bit."

"It's fine." Hannah was breathing heavily. "Don't tell Danior, please?"

Marcelle stifled a laugh. "If you insist. This is becoming a habit, isn't it? Catching you two lovebirds sneaking away from parties to do naughty things."

Bear scoffed as he scratched open his fingertip and pressed it against the wounds in Hannah's neck so that she could heal.

"Honestly, I don't know how it keeps happening." Hannah closed her eyes in clear relief as the healing took effect. "I'm not a spry young twenty-something anymore, yet I find myself in more and more situations suited for one. I still don't know what he sees in me."

"You're beautiful," Bear said. "Mind, body, soul."

"Mind and soul, maybe," she said.

"You are everything I can never achieve. You're beyond my reach. You're better than all of us who failed at living and died young getting stuck in time," he told her, then kissed her lips. "That's why you're so beautiful to me. You're everything I wish I could have had, and I admire you for it."

"And yet as I grow older, I'm envious of all the many years you have ahead of you," Hannah murmured. "Years I don't have."

"Years you could have, perhaps. With the right gift," Bear said.

Marcelle's eyebrows nearly leapt off her face. "Bear…" she said warningly.

Hannah seemed just as shocked as Marcelle. "Are you making a joke?"

"I… No, no, I'm not. I'd give it to you if you asked."

"You can't," Marcelle interjected. "I'm sorry, I know this is a moment, but he is incapable of it."

Bear glared at her.

"What? It's the truth," she snapped at him.

"What do you mean?" Hannah asked.

"I mean that he's not of an Ulster bloodline. He wasn't turned into a vampire by someone from King Setanta's family; he was turned by a Norse vampire. It is very rare for a vampire to work for a kingdom that isn't their bloodline because outside purebloods could compel him and force him to harm us or spy on us. But Bear wanted to stay here because it's his homeland, and he's not a fan of the Norse. So we worked out a deal. As part of that deal, one of them, under our supervision, compelled him to never sire a new vampire as long as he remains a citizen of New Ulster. Bear cannot offer you a gift."

"Fine, I can't turn her myself," he snapped. "But there's loopholes. I can petition Setanta for a favor. Hannah, if you want to be with me for eternity, or at least, if you want to have all the time in the world for whatever you want, just say the word. You can be an eternal testament to our cultures. You can learn new languages, learn new crafts. Watch the world grow in ways you could never imagine. Say the word, and I'll find a way. I'll give you everything. I love you, Hannah. *Mičík'ala čhetaŋ*."

Hannah stared at him, breathing heavily, then kissed him with more passion than Marcelle had ever seen someone of her physical age kiss anyone. "I love you. But I need to think about this. Give me a little time. Is that all right?"

"Yes, of course." He looked at her with love in his eyes.

"Let's go back to the warmth. The privacy was good, but I think I need to be back around a nice fire." Hannah nodded her head to Marcelle. "You are a beautiful bride. I'm looking forward to the ceremony tomorrow."

Marcelle nodded back respectfully and sat down in the snow as she stared up at the drifting flurries coming down from the sky. They did not melt as they landed on her as they would have on a human, since she had no body heat to melt them, and soon a light coating of snow had fallen over her skin and dress.

Everything about the night was so strange. Bear being so enamored with his girlfriend in a way she'd never seen before, and such a statement of devotion happening at her pre-wedding party. A wedding that was hers.

She looked down at the white-and-gold kaftan she'd been given to wear and felt uncomfortable. She supposed they were kind to include her in their culture, but she was looking forward to wearing something a bit more her style. She'd worked with her dressmaker on the design for her wedding outfit, perfecting every detail, and was excited to show it off in front of everyone the next day. Especially, she looked forward to showing Sarai and impressing her wife all over again.

Chapter Seventeen

Brides

The next day, Sarai felt as if she were floating in a cloud as she stood in her bridal berberisca dress at the door to the sanctuary of the only Jewish witch synagogue in the tristate area.

"Nervous?" Zeinab asked, patting her hand.

"A little," Sarai said.

"It'll be wonderful," Mazal promised. "Are you ready?"

Sarai gave a nod, and they opened the doors.

The sanctuary was small but beautiful. It was decorated with stained-glass windows, and at the raised *bimah* altar area at the front was a closed glass-door cabinet where Torah scrolls were kept. Above the *bimah* was a flickering magical oil lamp that never extinguished. And in the middle of the *bimah* was a *chuppah* canopy as well as Rabbi Jennifer and...Marcelle.

Sarai forgot how to breathe as she laid eyes on Marcelle as her bride. She wore an exquisite pure-white pantsuit with a back like a long cape, and the front neckline plunged to her waist. It was borderline disrespectful in how obscene it was, but Sarai didn't care. All she could think was this stunning woman was *hers*. She'd seen it just a little before when they'd signed the marriage contract, the *ketubah*, together, but seeing Marcelle waiting at the end of the aisle was like taking her in for the first time all over again.

Sarai walked down halfway, and Marcelle descended to meet her.

"You're so beautiful," Sarai whispered, and Marcelle grinned.

"For you, *ma petite sorcière*." She pulled the veil down from Sarai's head to cover her face and took her away from her aunts up the aisle to the rabbi with her.

Sarai tried to pay attention to the ceremony. To the importance of ritual moments like walking in circles seven times or drinking grape juice from a cup of wine, which Marcelle could not do but Sarai did. All she could think the whole time was how lucky she was. How happy she was. She was lost in and drunk on joy. The couple was given a new *tallit*, a prayer shawl, to cover their shoulders in and drape them in something symbolic of their new life together, of building a home together for their child. They exchanged simple gold rings to symbolize their promise.

At the end of the ceremony, a wineglass was put into a cloth bag and placed on the floor. Marcelle stomped on it as Rabbi Jennifer instructed, shattering the glass, and a chorus of *mazal tovs* and cheers erupted from the crowd.

Marcelle grabbed Sarai, and the two kissed. Sarai ignored everyone and completely melted into the moment, inhaling her new wife's sweet rosewater scent and losing herself to those soft lips. At least, until a rain of wrapped candies was thrown at them. Struck in the face, Sarai couldn't resist laughing, and Marcelle joined in, though looked confused and snatched one out of the air before it could hit her on the nose.

"What is this?"

"Candy, for sweetness," Rabbi Jennifer explained. "Go, go ahead, you lovebirds!"

The brides made their way through the congratulatory crowd and were led away to a private room where they could sit in quiet for a moment, just the two of them together, married and alone for the first time.

"I can't believe how much I love you," Sarai whispered, holding Marcelle's hands.

"And I love you too." The vampire woman kissed her tenderly.

It was a moment of reprieve from the crowd, and they relished it together but soon had to leave and find their husband. The three shared kisses and an embrace.

"I think Bear might be right about this being better than our stiff political vampire court wedding," Setanta mused. "I won't lie that I'm a little jealous. You're both beautiful."

"You snooze, you lose," Sarai teased and stood on her tiptoes to flick his nose with a giggle.

He kissed her forehead.

"Come on, let's go to the reception. I want to dance."

They were the last ones into the reception hall.

"And here come the happy throuple," said Rabbi Jennifer, now DJ Jennifer, on a microphone. "Give it up for Sarai, Marcelle, and Setanta!"

The doors opened as music blasted, and Sarai danced to the center of the dance floor where everyone had made a circle, dragging her spouses along behind her and unable to stop smiling.

A *hora* dance began as everyone formed circles in alternating directions, singing and laughing and dancing for joy. It was much like the dancing at the henna party—just fun. Not sexual, not political, not seductive. Just fun. Even Artemisia, who had attended without her father and Sarai had rarely seen out of the shadow of her mother's skirts, seemed to be enjoying herself, holding hands and dancing around with the other children present.

"All right, we need four strong men in the middle of the circle with a chair and a bride!" called DJ Rabbi Jennifer from her booth. "Four strong men, I know we have them!"

Sarai doubted it would take four men, given half the guests were vampires. She was pulled to the middle by Bear, who had a chair in his free hand.

"I got this!" he shouted back at the rabbi DJ.

Sarai found herself in the chair, people clapping and dancing around her. Bear scooped the chair up with ease in both hands, and she yelped, gripping the edge of the seat tightly to avoid a fall. She couldn't keep a wide grin off her face.

"Oh wow, we have a strongman in the *shul*!" Rabbi Jennifer laughed.

Setanta pulled Marcelle to the middle with another chair as she laughed, shaking her head. Despite the half-hearted protest, he had her in a second chair hoisted up above his head moments later, dancing alongside Bear so that Sarai and Marcelle were next to each other in the air. Marcelle laughed, her eyes bright with joy. Setanta and Bear held them both aloft, circling with the flow of the hora dancers as Sarai squealed. Marcelle reached out her hand for a high five, and Sarai managed to connect, her other hand holding on with a white-knuckled grasp so that she wouldn't slip.

The two were put back on their feet and greeted with

hugs, then Sarai found herself embracing Marcelle. Sarai could not stop smiling and, from the look of her, neither could Marcelle.

When the *hora* was over, Sarai excused herself from the vampires to make her way to the refreshment buffet table. With the wedding ceremony over, she was famished. And luckily, since it wasn't a strictly vampire affair, other people milled around the buffet. The humans she had invited, led by Rosaline, were there. But as she looked, she saw several were missing. In particular, Jackie was.

"Where's Jackie?" Sarai asked. "And Will? Nadine?"

"We've got a flu going around," Rosaline said. "It was so weird, like half of us had it. Usually, vampire blood keeps away everything except seasonal allergies. I had it a few days ago but got better in time for this, thank goodness. I'm so happy for you."

Someone tapped her on her shoulder, and Sarai turned around to see Temuulen standing there in a fancy suit and his black knitted ski cap.

"*Mazal tov*, is that the right phrase?" he asked.

She smiled and gave him a hug. "Yup, you got it right." She inhaled and had to hold her breath as his scent overwhelmed her. He smelled better than the buffet. Somewhere between basil or mint. Savory, refreshing. Her fangs grew.

He raised his eyebrow. "Well, would you look at that? I heard the rumor, but that is something else to see in person. Did you see something you want a taste of?"

She felt her cheeks burn as she blushed. "Quit teasing me."

"Oh, it's no tease, my queen. I'll give you my blood

if you want it."

Sarai's throat burned at the thought, and she looked around. "I feel like it's a bit disrespectful to do it in a synagogue." But she wanted it. She needed it.

She took his hand and pulled him way from the reception hall, nearly trampling over Lochlan in her rush, and over to an alcove where water fountains jutted out of the wall near a vending machine and the bathrooms. Across from them in the lobby was a glass case with a very old Torah scroll preserved there, one with a large memorial plaque identifying it as a rescued Holocaust scroll. Feeling as if what she was planning to do was too perverse to do in the presence of an item like that even if it technically followed the rules of preserving her health, she ran to close the doors to the main lobby and turned her attention back to Temuulen to eagerly press her body against his.

"My, so forceful," he teased. "You know, if you find your wedding-night plans lacking…three is a crowd—four is a party."

She bit her lip. Marcelle and Setanta would no doubt be interested. Setanta had all but claimed him, and Marcelle was a known flirt. But, Sarai wasn't sure she wanted to introduce a new partner in bed for her wedding night.

"Not tonight. We had plans already. But I think I would like that another night?"

"I can wait for you. Whenever you're ready, I'll be ready." He brushed a lock of hair behind her ear. "Just give me enough advance notice to have some blood first."

"I'm not that intense," she joked. "Though that's fair; Marcelle and Setanta are. But you shouldn't need anything extra for healing or a boost. We'll have that covered."

He frowned. "No, not for… Have you been with any vampire men before?"

"I think it's pretty public knowledge who I'm married to."

"No, not like Setanta. He's alive. I mean someone like me. An undead vampire man."

Sarai shook her head. "No, but I know a bit what to expect. Marcelle's like you. I know you're cold and all that."

"It's not that. Made men like me need to have fed recently to perform well. And for another reason." Temuulen laughed a little. "You understand we can't change, physically. Undead can't have kids because we're dead. I can't shoot off into a human woman and make a half-vampire baby because I can't make the materials you'd need."

"Um, oh. Okay. What would that mean then?"

"It means it's not white. It's red."

"What's red? You mean…"

"I mean I shoot bloody blanks. I ejaculate blood."

Sarai stared in shock; her mind flooded with the image of what that might look like. Perhaps a normal person would have been put off, but all the thought did was make her gums ache with vampiric desire. "Oh. Okay."

"I didn't want you to be surprised by it. You can imagine it was pretty shocking to me when I found out."

"Yeah, I bet." She laughed a little. "Is it like regular vampire blood, then?"

"Oh yeah. It'll get you high." He winked at her. "And it feels good. Like a tingling sensation in all the right places. Or extra fun if you like to swallow."

Her fangs couldn't be held back any longer, and they erupted in her mouth, visible through her parted lips.

Temuulen chuckled and gripped her chin so he could look at them. "I see that's not a problem for you."

"Maybe I want a sample. Where do you want me to bite? Wrist?"

"Nah, let's make this intimate." He leaned against the wall to slide down a little to her height, then tilted his head to the side. "Don't be shy, pretty bride. I can take it."

Sarai believed him. She rested her fangs against his throat and felt no pulse. Of course not, he was undead. Regardless, she bit down, moaning into the sensation. It felt so taboo. She'd tried to avoid blood for so long, and now she drank blood in a synagogue. The taboo made it more fun. And he tasted so good, savory as she had expected but refreshing. She found herself having to suck harder on the wound rather than letting a living heart beat the blood into her mouth. But it was no trouble. She loved it.

"Fuck yes." He groaned.

Apparently, he loved it too.

When her craving was satisfied, her fetus doing flips in her belly, she pulled away to watch the wound close.

"Was it as good for you as it was for me?" Temuulen asked.

Sarai smiled. "I think it was. Did I do it right? I'm still learning."

He pulled a handkerchief from his pocket and dabbed her mouth. She'd made less of a mess than her last attempt at feeding but still needed more practice. "You are perfect."

She placed a hand on his chest and let healing magic flow through him to rejuvenate him at least a little.

"That's a new sensation. I like it." He looked down at her, then pressed his lips to hers.

She closed her eyes. His facial hair tickled a little, but it was nice. Different. She kissed him back, flicking her tongue against his.

"Oh, come on, seriously? It is your *wedding*."

She pushed apart from her bodyguard to see Lochlan emerging from the men's bathroom with a mildly judgmental smirk. Her cheeks burned as she blushed. "I was just…" She paused. "What are you doing here?"

Lochlan gestured to the bathroom. "Uh, I think that's obvious?"

"No, not— I saw you just now in the party. We bumped into you on the way here."

"No, you didn't."

Temuulen gripped Sarai's hand tightly and pulled her behind him. He inhaled, then gave a nod. "This one smells right. It's Lochlan. Look out there." He gestured with his chin toward the dark windows. Out in the parking lot, black vans had pulled up, disturbing what remained of a swirling pile of dust where a vampire guard had been posted, and people in body armor and guns.

Sarai inhaled sharply. "There are kids here. We need to warn everyone. Now."

The three raced back and found Marcelle and Setanta doing some sort of disco dancing together.

"Your Highnesses, we have a problem," Temuulen said. "Armed men outside. There was dust. I believe Patricia's down."

"There he is," Lochlan snapped, pointing into the

crowd.

There, the doppelganger stood, identical in every way to Lochlan, and no doubt how he'd managed to trick his way into the synagogue and past the wards. They were eerily alike except for his eyes. The doppelganger's eyes looked dead to the world as if the light inside had gone out.

The doppelganger's skin shifted like a ripple in a still pond. Hair disappeared, leaving him bald, and his body grew.

The dancing stopped, people stepped back, and the music came to a halt.

"Get her out of here. Now," Setanta said, stepping in front of Sarai.

Marcelle gripped Sarai's shoulders, holding her close.

A wave of cold air blasted through the room as if all the heat had been sucked in by the vortex of shifting flesh that had become the doppelganger. It crunched and tore itself with a high-pitched, agonized scream that soon morphed into a deep roar that shook the walls and the ceiling. No more was the shape humanoid.

Instead, there was a dragon.

"What the—" Sarai couldn't find the words to relay her absolute shock. A dragon. A real dragon. Complete with shining white scales, violet eyes, sharp talons, and many, many teeth the size of her arm.

"Shapeshifter." Marcelle gasped, her eyes wide. "I thought they were extinct. So much for an albino dinosaur."

"Vasi slave." Setanta snarled.

Sarai's heart caught in her throat. The dragon took a deep breath, and flames shot forward from its mouth at the panicked party guests.

The real Lochlan leapt forward, his hands out, and caught the fire to twist it back at the monster. It looked surprised, or as surprised as a dragon could look, then exhaled again. This time the flames pushed forward farther, but Lochlan kept it at bay with a determined scream. The heat seared the air all through the room, and Lochlan was shouting as the flames reached his arms and burns scorched them.

He stumbled back with a look of obvious shock, staring at his hands as if the thought had never occurred to him that fire could be hot.

"Everyone, exits, now!" Marcelle shrieked at the crowd.

"No, wait, Marcelle—" Sarai started to say, but it was no use.

They all began to run in a frenzy, clutching children, while the vampires and witches with offensive gifts fortified the rear. Marcelle started to pull Sarai toward the exit, steeling them against being trampled by the crowd, when gunfire rang out and people screamed from the front, pulling back in.

"Vasi bastards," Marcelle hissed.

Sarai strained her neck to look out the window to see a group of armed Vasi were outside to keep anyone from escaping the dragon's fire. They wanted to kill them all, to see the witches and vampires all burned alive, eaten, or shot. If they couldn't storm the synagogue with its wards, they would make it a death trap.

Sarai saw her aunts, clutching their terrified and sobbing daughter. Family members she had only just learned of, now targets of the Vasi. Had she led them there? The reception hall was full of witches and vampires and family, all people she cared for. The only one of them who'd ever been captured by Vasi was Sarai, and they had wanted her to use her abilities to fight her own people and possibly cure vampirism. Well, Artemisia had also been captured and rescued, but Sarai doubted the Vasi were after her. Though the creepy child was unusually calm.

"Leave them alone!" Sarai shouted at the dragon. "I'll go with you if you leave them all alone!"

"Sarai, get down—" Setanta began, then stopped.

The dragon focused on Sarai and readied a breath. Before it could immolate her, wings burst from Setanta's back through his clothes and he shot up into the air with both her and Marcelle in his arms, landing well away from the stream of fire.

"I don't think they're here to capture you, but that was a valiant effort," Marcelle mused as she pulled up her pant sleeve to reveal a small gun strapped to her inner thigh.

"You married me with a gun under your clothes?" Sarai asked.

Marcelle pulled out the weapon and took aim. "I always have a gun under my clothes."

The dragon seemed to have lost sight of them and refocused on Lochlan, still nursing his burnt hands.

"Hey!" Marcelle shouted, jumping forward and taking aim. She fired several rounds into its snout, then pulled out a new clip from the strap on her thigh. Instinct seized Sarai, and she held out her hands, flooding her healing powers forward. But not only her own. She could feel the strength of a thousand ancestors surging in the moving henna that dyed her skin. The flesh of her one good palm shifted, and she looked down to see an eye in the center. It was brown, like her own. Like her mother's.

Sarai knew she could keep Marcelle healed at a distance. She held out her good hand, overflowing with protection from her ancestors' spirits, and healing magic spilled forth.

It worked as the dragon exhaled its fire again and Marcelle ducked down in a ball. She screamed, perhaps in fear. Her wedding outfit was burned to cinders at her feet, but her skin was untouched, her henna markings glowing gold and growing like vines across the entirety of her arms.

Lochlan stepped in and bent the flames back at the dragon while Setanta leapt forward once more.

The moment the dragon saw Setanta, its eyes narrowed, and it snarled, as if it had found its prey. It snapped forward with its massive maw, and Setanta grunted as he caught the jaws, gripping teeth to force it back with his bare hands. Despite his supernatural strength, it was an obvious strain.

Sarai focused her intent, her darkness, reaching into the pool of necrotic necromancy that welled deep in her soul and let it out in a single bolt, striking the dragon's open mouth. It roared and pulled back, withering flesh spreading across half its face.

Then it healed. And it lashed out again at Setanta, who caught it again, trying to twist the head to snap the neck but was unable. Light grew, glowing deep from inside the dragon's open throat. Lochlan stepped forward with his burnt hands and twisted the fire back into the creature as Setanta managed to throw it off.

The fire seemed to choke the great beast, and it coughed, struggling on the smoke and clawing at its own throat. It growled, then unfurled its wings and flew up through the ceiling, tearing apart the roof as it escaped.

"Marcelle, Temuulen," Setanta snapped. "Bear. With me. We'll take on the Vasi in the front, a quick ambush. Lochlan, Hannah, Sarai, get the humans and witches into the sanctuary. There are protective magics there. Heal any injured."

He didn't wait for an affirmation, simply darted off into the night with Marcelle and Temuulen while other vampires saw them and followed suit.

"Everyone, into the sanctuary," Sarai shouted.

Rosaline and the other human sources present helped herd the families and vulnerable mortals away from the fighting as bullets and shouts rang outside in the snow, while Lochlan put out fires with a wave of his hand.

Rabbi Jennifer put her shaking hand on the floor. Muck and clay bubbled up from the ground and took shape into a lumbering giant, a golem, with the Hebrew word *emet* written in Paleo-Hebrew script on its forehead.

"Help them, protect us. Protect this temple and her people," she ordered it, and it stomped toward the fighting as she locked the sanctuary door behind it.

Sarai and Mazal got to work healing. Some few people had bullet wounds and burns, but no one was dead.

"To be so brazen," Mazal whispered as she healed her mother-in-law's burnt hand. "To attack us here. Why?"

"The Vasi have never been bound by morality," Sarai said dryly. She looked at Lochlan's hands. "I didn't think you could get burned."

"I didn't think I could either." He winced as she put

her hand over his wounds to heal them. "I didn't think heat could hurt. I've never felt heat like that. Fire that wasn't mine. How the hell did the Vasi get their hands on a shapeshifter?"

"Probably young, if I had to guess," Mazal said. "One of that power... I'm shocked to see such a thing. Sarai, *motek*, I'm so sorry this happened at your wedding."

Sarai shook her head. "It was nice while it lasted. I'm sorry everyone is in danger." She looked down at the eye in her palm. It blinked at her. "Is this normal?" She held it up to show Mazal.

Mazal yelped in a clear expression of what could only be total shock, then leaned in closer, taking Sarai's hand and examining the eye. "I can't say I've ever seen protective henna magic work like this before. That looks like a *hamsa*. Perhaps it's because your necromancy strengthened your bond with our ancestors?"

"Maybe. How long do you think it'll last?"

"I don't know. I've never seen it manifest so physically."

Sarai heard the sound of a knock on the door to the sanctuary.

"It's us, let us in," Marcelle called.

Sarai started to move forward, but the rabbi grabbed her shoulder to stop her.

"There was a shapeshifter. Tell us something they wouldn't know," Rabbi Jennifer said.

"Sarai, are you there listening?" Marcelle asked.

"Yeah, I'm here."

"I almost kissed you for the first time in the women's bathroom at the mall when we went to have your dress designed. I told you my eyes turning red meant nothing, but it wasn't nothing. I was falling for you before I knew what to do with myself."

Sarai smiled at the memory. "That's her. Let them in."

Rabbi Jennifer unlocked the door, and the vampires returned, blood on their mouths and hands. Marcelle was still naked, and those with children covered their eyes.

The rabbi pulled off her burgundy suit jacket and handed it to Marcelle, who accepted with thanks. Mazal rushed forward with a *tallit* prayer shawl and wrapped it around Marcelle's waist like a skirt.

"Is everyone here unharmed?" Marcelle asked.

"Superficial wounds, all healed," Sarai said. "What about our side?"

"We killed the Vasi outside, lost two of our own," Setanta said. "Your golem was most impressive, it's still outside in a defensive position, so we have a little time. But the dragon may circle back. We need to leave this place. Now."

"There's a teleportation arch that leads to the Ellis Coven," Rabbi Jennifer said. "It should be sufficiently charged for a large group. Children, parents, and elderly first."

As they spoke, Laila shuffled to them. "This is more than we expected even from magic folk. Are we safe now?"

"For the moment," Setanta said. "But you will not be if you stay. Whatever your feelings regarding magic, you need to use the portal to preserve your lives."

Her eyes narrowed on him. "You. You and the ones who move fast, who can hold a dragon by the teeth. Are you djinn? Ifrit? What haven't Zeinab and Mazal told me? You're not part of her *kesemi* people; you're all something else."

Setanta shook his head. "We are not from Arabian legends," he reassured her.

"I'll explain later," Mazal promised her mother-in-law, who huffed.

"You had better."

"Right now, we're going to get everyone out before the dragon comes back," Marcelle said. "Rabbi, where is the arch?"

Rabbi Jennifer gestured for everyone to follow her up to the *bimah*, where she pulled the Torah scrolls out of their ark and handed them to nearby adults. She took a *yad*, a golden stick with a small hand pointing at the end traditionally used for reading from the Torah scrolls, from her pocket, and Sarai recognized it as the witch's magical focus item. She used the *yad* to trace Hebrew words that shimmered in the air like effervescent gold all around the doors to the ark where the Torahs were stored. When she opened the doors, the air flickered, and instead of opening to the ark, the doorway led to the main hall in the witch's pocket dimension on Ellis Island.

"Everyone here, you're invited to the Ellis Coven," Rabbi Jennifer said.

The wedding guests streamed through, but Laila and her husband stopped, and the old woman took Sarai's hand, looking solemnly at the eye in her palm as it blinked up at her. "Fatima," she murmured, though Sarai didn't understand the significance of the name and thought the eye looked like her mother's, Liora. "I trust your protection. Keep us safe, *kesemi*."

Sarai gave her a reassuring smile. "I will. You're my family."

Laila nodded and walked through.

Last, the only people left were Rabbi Jennifer, Sarai, Marcelle, and Setanta. Something roared outside.

"The Holocaust scroll," Rabbi Jennifer whispered. "You go ahead. I need to get something."

She began to run forward, but Sarai immediately chased after and grabbed her arm.

"Let go!"

"Are you nuts? That's a dragon."

"The Holocaust Torah, I need—"

"It's not worth your life." She tried to remember the words the vampire Gedeon had told her, the rule of saving a life above all else. *"Pikuach nefesh."*

Tears swelled in the rabbi's eyes. Then the ceiling collapsed in a ball of flame above the pair. Sarai couldn't make sense of what had happened between the smoke and dust and screaming and fire but knew that she had just barely avoided being crushed.

Marcelle and Setanta darted into the mess, and the dragon appeared out of the settling clouds, larger than before. Everyone froze except for Rabbi Jennifer, half crushed and screaming under the dragon's massive front talon.

Marcelle was by her side, struggling to pull off the dragon's claw. It either did not notice or did not care, instead fixing its gaze on Setanta, snarling and growling as light grew beyond its teeth.

"It's me you're after, isn't it?" he called to the monster. "Well, come, then, come forward and face me. I am the hound of Ulster, trained by Scathach the battle witch to defeat entire armies. I am the king of New Ulster. I am an ancient vampire, and I have killed more people than you have scales on your body. If it's me you want, take that step and let us see which of us fears death more."

The dragon did as he said, stepping forward and releasing Rabbi Jennifer from its grasp. Marcelle scooped up the woman and darted to Sarai's side.

"Setanta!" Marcelle shouted.

The golem from before stomped into the room, dwarfed by the dragon and soundless except for its footsteps. It swung at the dragon, its fist shattering against scales and reconstituting for a second attack.

Setanta grinned at the dragon. "I'll tell you a secret. I fear death. And I know when I'm outmatched." With that, he flew back in retreat, heat of blooming flames billowing behind him and a golem vs dragon fight in full swing as he wrapped Sarai in his arms and they all tumbled through the portal. It closed behind them.

Sarai lay there for a moment in shock. Then she heard a shriek. Someone was screaming, screaming Jennifer's name. And wailing like Sarai had never heard before.

"Heal her," Marcelle said, heaving the limp body toward Sarai.

She nodded and put her hands on Rabbi Jennifer's shoulders to flood her with healing magic. But her life was so faint healing was a struggle.

Her *kesemi* family, the Jewish witches, sat around her, and she felt hands on her shoulders and arms. They began to sing again, singing a prayer. *"Shma Yisrael."*

The rabbi was dead, but the healing power of Sarai's ancestors, her family, and her own necromantic power swirled inside her, beating like a thousand hearts. She could see Rabbi Jennifer's soul, so close.

"Not yet," Sarai whispered. *"Shma koleinu." Hear our voice.* And the rabbi heard them. Gold, healing light swimming with darkness of necromancy magic flowed from Sarai's good hand. The broken body crunched and clicked and looked much like a deflated balloon filling with air as it reformed itself. Finally, Rabbi Jennifer opened her eyes, gasping for air.

Sarai had defeated death. And as the power released her, exhaustion forced her into blissful unconsciousness.

Chapter Eighteen

The Elderly

Marcelle was furious. Furious with the Vasi. Furious with her security team. Furious with herself.

After working with the Ellis Coven to set up all their wedding guests in appropriate accommodations, she and her spouses made their way to their condominium overlooking Central Park. It was dawn, and they were all exhausted.

"This was an intelligence failure," Marcelle said, once they were inside and the three of them were alone in the silence and Sarai had woken. "I knew something was off with the Vasi. I knew they were being tipped off somehow. Two steps ahead of us. They're even implanting suicide sigils they can activate on their teeth to avoid interrogation and capture. I spoke to Lilly, but I should have pushed my ground teams harder."

Setanta didn't look at her, confirming her belief. This was her failure.

"I failed you." The words felt like stones in the pit of her stomach. "Sire, *mon amour. Je suis désolé.*"

"Yes. You failed," he agreed. "And some of our people are dead now. But any failure of yours is a failure of mine. The responsibility is on my shoulders."

"Oh, shut up, both of you," Sarai said.

Marcelle blinked. "*Pardon?*"

"You didn't do anything wrong. Either of you. Fucking hell, we faced down a dragon tonight. A dragon. And only two vampires died protecting a crowd full of easy targets who all made it out. You took a blast of dragon fire to the face, Marcelle, and you survived without a scratch. This could have gone so much worse." Sarai fell onto the couch and looked out at the rising sun. "Let's not do it again, though. I'm still so damn tired. I don't even know if I could do that again."

"Do you need blood?" Marcelle asked.

"No, I had some earlier. Temuulen."

Well, that was amusing. Marcelle supposed it was a matter of time before Temuulen made a move on Sarai. Though, knowing what Marcelle did of the witch, she mused that Sarai was just as likely to have been the one to make the move.

"This is the worst wedding night in the history of wedding nights, isn't it?" Sarai sighed. "I was looking forward to so much with you two tonight, but…no, not now."

"You mean sex?" Marcelle asked. "Another night, yes. I agree. We'll make plans for another night when we're not so riled."

"My birthday's coming up. March first. We should do something then. Make a nice night out of it, enjoy things," Sarai said. "But not tonight. I wish I could focus on anything else. Rabbi Jennifer…"

"That was a very impressive use of your necromancy and healing," Setanta murmured. "Not many could bring even a recently departed soul back to a body."

"Just don't make me do it again. It took literally everyone there and my ancestors and all my strength."

Sarai sighed. "That much power is way too much. I don't even want to think about the headache."

"Do you want a topic for distraction?" Marcelle asked. "Or do you want to process it?"

"A distraction," Sarai said. "Everything was going so nicely before the dragon. You guys were dancing, and Temuulen let me bite him. It was nice."

"We could invite your new beau," Setanta mused. "I'm sure he would be happy to join your birthday celebration."

She blushed. "I, uh, I would be okay with that. As long as he doesn't mind it. And you don't mind it."

"I think you know full well that I do not mind it at all." His lips curled into a smirk. "In fact, if you want more, we can always do more. It will be your birthday after all, and you deserve something enjoyable after enduring all that you have. We should have some revelry."

She raised an eyebrow. "What did you have in mind?"

He exchanged looks with Marcelle. "Who do you think would be a good fit? Maybe Dhana in Boston. She's about the same age as you but Moorish. Do you remember her?"

"We've met a few times," Marcelle said. "And played some, but it's been a while."

"She and her wife, Amanda, they're always a good time when they're around," he reminisced. "I think Sarai would enjoy their dynamic. That is, if she's open to some new people."

Sarai bit her lip, then nodded. "You want to plan a birthday orgy for me? And for me to just have sex with someone I meet that night?"

"If it's something you think you'd enjoy," Marcelle said. "We can meet them earlier if you prefer. Dhana doesn't date outside of Amanda, though. There is something tantalizing to the thrill of meeting someone new and falling into bed with them." She watched the wheels turning in Sarai's head and found it rather cute. Marcelle knew accepting an experience such as a tryst with a new couple was a big step into a new level of self-confidence that allowed for her to admit interest in such casual fun.

"Well, when you put it that way," Sarai murmured. She paused another moment. "Yeah, that does sound fun. Sure, why not? The more the merrier, that's how you guys see it?" She frowned and looked down at her good hand. "Well, generally speaking."

"What is it?" Marcelle asked.

Sarai showed Marcelle the palm of her good hand where an eye blinked back at them. "You don't think it's permanent, do you?"

"Let me see." Setanta took her hand. "I've never seen a protective enchantment quite like this before. It's quite a bit more advanced than rudimentary lines of salt at doorways or red strings."

"That's great, but I've had to pee for hours now, and I don't want to with my ancestors staring at me out of my hand."

As if on cue, the eye closed and turned into a spot of henna in her palm, now vaguely eye shaped.

Sarai breathed in a sigh of evident relief. "Well, if you'll excuse me, I'm going to go take care of mortal business," she said and left the common area. With her left the scents of adrenaline and power, as well as any feeling of positivity.

Marcelle's entire body slumped. "Setanta, I—"

"Don't," he said. "Sarai's right. We faced a dragon. All considered, we were fortunate. I didn't think power like that still existed. The Vasi outwitted us this time, but we'll have them next. I'll include myself in your meetings with Lilly to plan our next steps."

"There's a leak somewhere. This could have been anyone telling the Vasi where we are, and there's one of the new humans in the palace who rubs me the wrong way even if she wasn't there tonight, but other things…anticipating our raids on their compounds. That requires someone with access. Someone listening in on important conversations. It couldn't have been a mortal. Well, I suppose Lochlan. But I trust him, and he fought the dragon with us."

"Do you think a vampire would betray New Ulster?"

"No. But I can't think of an alternative."

He gave a solemn nod. "I'll go through everyone of my blood and compel the truth. For those not of my blood…"

"Bear wouldn't team up with the Vasi," she said forcefully. "He was there helping us tonight. And the Norse would have no interest in compelling him to betray us right now; our countries are stable diplomatically."

"They have an expansionist past. And it is possible for them to force him to betray us and also force him to forget he did so with a compulsion. His memory is already in a frayed state when it comes to the far past. It would be easy." He paused as Marcelle watched the gears turning in his mind. "He's had a lot more leave time lately, to come up to New York to be with that witch, Hannah. Much more opportunity to be confronted by a Norse pureblood and compelled. We may need to quarantine him for observation just for a little while until we sort out everything. But don't let him know until we return to the palace. We don't want to risk triggering some compulsion to run from us before we can lock him away."

The logic was sound. Marcelle hoped the leak wasn't Bear. The thought of such a good soul being forced to turn against his chosen country was nauseating, not to mention it could spark fighting between the vampiric northern Nordic clans and New Ulster if it turned out to be true.

"I hope it's not him. He's a good friend," she said.

"Agreed."

Returning to the palace felt solemn. The vampires chartered a flight and took themselves and their human sources back to North Carolina. Strangely, no cars were there to greet them. It worried Marcelle. Something felt off. There should have been transportation ready.

She exchanged glances with Setanta before turning to give orders. "Sarai, stay with Temuulen. Lochlan, Bear, you too. Stay with the sources and Artemisia and protect them. Rent something and go to a safe house," she commanded.

"Why?" Sarai asked.

"Just a precaution. There should have been cars here to meet us."

Sarai bit her lip, her hands running over her baby bump. "You don't think... The dragon couldn't have found the palace, right? You guys have lots of wards."

"In theory, yes," Setanta said. "But they shouldn't have known where the wedding was either. Marcelle and I will scout ahead."

Instead of driving, they walked away from the busy airport crowds, and Setanta removed his shirt so that he could grow his wings.

"You should consider a halter top," Marcelle joked with him. "Not that I'm complaining about the view."

He chuckled as he held her close, his arms secure around her waist. "Ready?"

She nodded, and they were airborne, flying through the moonlit clouds at speeds too fast for humans to notice them. The palace wasn't too far of a flight, though they still took a little time to reach and circle above it. To Marcelle's great relief, she could see no evidence of a dragon attack. The building was in one piece and unscathed.

"It looks fine from up here," she said.

"It does. Then why was there no one to drive us at the airport?" He circled the building twice more before landing at the front door and pushing it open.

At first, Marcelle wasn't sure what she was looking at, then the sickly-sweet smell of corpse rot hit her. Bodies filled the floors of the main hall, strewn about in chaos, limp and face down. All had silver hair or no hair. At the main staircase stumbled someone familiar—Lilly.

And Marcelle could hear her heart racing.

"My king," Lilly rasped, then vomited, blood drenching her front.

Both vampires darted forward to hold her up as she gasped for air. As Marcelle watched in complete horror, a streak of white grew through her hair.

"What happened to you?" Marcelle whispered. "You're…human."

"Please, don't let me die like them." She gripped Setanta's arm with frail, human fingers as she begged.

"Please. Help me."

He wasted no time. His fangs grew, and he bit deep into his wrist to offer his blood.

Lilly latched on with what Marcelle recognized as obvious desperation, drinking mouthful after mouthful until the wound healed and she could drink no more. A flicker of pain crossed her expression, and before she could cry out, Marcelle snapped her neck.

"Rest, my friend," she whispered, cradling the changing body. "We're here for you."

Setanta stood. "Leave her. She'll rise in due time when the change is complete. We need to see if there are others." He marched to the row of bodies and pushed one over to reveal elderly humans. One in particular caught Marcelle's attention.

"That's Crispin." She gently laid Lilly on the floor so she could get a closer look. Her heart broke to see him, but she couldn't dwell on the pain. She pushed her emotions to the side and focused solely on facts. "That one, with the eye patch and the fake leg. But he's old. And human. And this one..." She knelt next to the tall body of an elderly man and looked at his arm. A string of numbers was tattooed there, the remnants of a concentration camp. Strangely, the expression on his face held a slight smile. She wondered if he was happy to have been able to die of old age, something that she knew he'd felt robbed of. She never related to that sentiment, but knew many did. "This is Gedeon Katz. The rest of these...I'm not sure. I've never seen them old before."

"You saw the way Lilly's hair changed just now, how quickly it happened. They must have aged to death rapidly."

"Have you ever seen anything like this before?"

"No. No, I have not. And I do not like it." He stood, closed his eyes, and listened. "There are more heartbeats. There may be some still alive. We should split up. I know you haven't turned many people on your own, Marcelle, but do you think you can if you find them in Lilly's state?"

She shifted a little uncomfortably. "Yes. Drain their blood, give them mine. Just, more."

"Don't drain their blood by drinking," Setanta ordered. "There's a scent, a feeling, something magic in it. I fear if you drank their blood, you would meet their fate. In fact, I don't doubt that happened to some of our poor friends here. Cut an artery and let them bleed out to the edge of death, then give your blood as much as you are able. We'll bring any other survivors back here."

"Understood, sire."

Through the mansion, Marcelle turned three vomiting humans back into vampires. They had several new wrinkles, a little touch of gray hair, but none as far gone as the corpses in the main hall. At the fourth, she felt drained and was glad to see a human source holding up the ailing former vampire in a reserved feeding room on the couches.

"Queen Marcelle!" Will gasped, trying to stem the bleeding from his own wrist. "Oh, thank fuck, I mean, thank goodness. Please, you gotta help. It's all over. I don't know what happened. Rosa was just feeding on me like normal, and I don't know what happened. Her fangs are gone. She's *breathing*."

"She's human. She was feeding from you, and it just happened?"

Rosa whimpered and reached her arms up toward

Marcelle, who pulled out her dagger and cut the vein at her neck. Blood spurt over them all, causing Will to yelp and stumble back off the couch with a shout.

"Relax, boy. I'm helping." She bit into her wrist for the fourth time that day and offered Rosa her blood. With how much she had already given, she wasn't sure she would be able to do another. Setanta only needed to give a few drops to turn someone, but it took more energy from Marcelle. Not being able to replenish herself on the humans being turned did not help matters.

She looked at Will, for a moment considering feeding on him. But she knew better. "It's you humans. You poisoned us."

"What?"

"I can smell it now, the similarity between Rosa's blood and yours."

Rosa began to shriek and scratch at her throat from the pain of every cell in her body screaming for blood, a pain that Marcelle knew intimately and could never forget even over five centuries after her own experience.

She snapped Rosa's neck and laid her out, dead, to rise later. Then she rounded on Will. "You poisoned us."

"I-I swear," he stammered. "I wouldn't. I don't know how this happened."

Marcelle bared her fangs.

"Please," he whispered, tears in his eyes. "Please don't kill me. I swear, I don't know."

"Come," she snapped, grabbing him by his neck and dragging him with her. "I am going to round up every poisoned source in this palace. If you're responsible or not, we'll learn soon enough."

Fortunately, only half the vampires in the palace had been affected by the poisoned blood. Marcelle soon began to run into some who had been running around trying to help their comrades, and ordered them to collect all the human sources and keep them locked under guard in their quarters. She also ran into the former king and Setanta's father, Lugh, who had been going through those he had found and turning the survivors back as well. He looked exhausted, considering how close he physically had allowed himself to age to death, and Marcelle insisted she, Setanta, and the rest could manage without him, so he went back to his room to recover.

When she saw Setanta again, they were both paler and weaker from helping so many.

"The sources—" she began.

"I know. No one is to drink blood from sources here, only stored blood in our reserves until we have an antidote."

"This has to be the Vasi, same as the shifter attack. Perfectly coordinated. They tried to take out the pureblood royals with a dragon and our best knights at our capital at the same time. If it wasn't so damn devastating, I'd be impressed."

"Indeed. Call the safe house, let the others know what's happened. Tell them not to feed on the sources, just to be cautious. We don't know how many are infected with this aging rot of a poison."

"Yes, sire." She took a step to dart to his office where she knew she could find a phone, then stopped, swaying on the spot. Her throat burned with need. "I need blood, Setanta. I turned four. I can't..."

He bit into his wrist and offered it to her, which she drank with relief.

"It's ironic," he murmured, stroking her hair as she took his blood and relished in the high it gave her. "We lost many, but the ones we saved are now all first- and second-generation vampires, turned by us. In this attack, we've grown stronger."

She pulled away, sighing with relief at the sensation of strength that flooded her body. "You make us stronger, my king."

He kissed her lips. "Go. We have work to do."

Chapter Nineteen

Uncovered

Sarai felt numb as she walked into the palace alongside the rest of the wedding guests who had been at the safe house. Bodies had been lined up on the side, covered with sheets. It was all so wrong. Her home was full of death, and it felt so much more devastating than the dragon attack. She rested at the first body and tried to summon the power she'd used to save Rabbi Jennifer, but it was pointless. She didn't have the strength of her family backing her magic, and they had been dead for too long. Sarai had nothing to heal.

Rosaline and the other humans were led away by Lilly, who wore a stern, hateful mask of an expression and now had a streak of gray in her braided hair, while Sarai just stood in the grand entrance, trying to find the right response to all the death. The shock hadn't left her system yet, and she was too overwhelmed to cry.

Her tutor was dead. As was Crispin, whom she knew in passing and knew that Rosaline would mourn as she'd had a fling with him a few times. Gedeon was dead as well, after he had been so kind in speaking with her and survived so much, a testament to perseverance. Lochlan was devastated, having lost so many of his comrades in arms, and his furious grief caused ripples of heat to surround his body, barely contained.

It wasn't right. Everything was wrong. She was grateful Temuulen and Bear had been at her wedding away from the catastrophe when it struck, and glad that it hadn't happened at a time when Marcelle might have been a victim. She felt selfish in that little joy when so many had been lost, but she couldn't help herself. At least the ones she cared for the most were safe.

Marcelle appeared at the bottom of the stairs, then darted to Sarai's side to embrace her. "I needed to see you." She pressed their foreheads together.

Sarai closed her eyes, focused on the cool sensation of Marcelle's pallid skin.

"We haven't had anything this bad, well, ever."

"Do you know what happened?" Sarai asked. "How could anyone do this?"

"It must have been witchcraft of some kind. We have a suspect." Marcelle looked up at Bear. "I'm sorry about this."

He frowned, then gasped with an expression of pain when a vampire darted next to him and stuck his arm with a silver needle, robbing him of his strength and speed. Bear looked at the wound, then at Marcelle. "Are you serious?" he demanded. "You think… Are you insane?"

"Marcelle," Sarai whispered. "No, that's wrong. Bear was with us. And he's kind. He's dedicated to everyone here; even I can see it."

"I know," Marcelle said. "Bear, you've been away from the palace a lot visiting Hannah. A Nordic pureblood could have caught you while you were gone, compelled you to betray us, then compelled you to forget. Until we rule it out, we need to confine you."

Bear glared at her, a snarl threatening at the corner

of his mouth. "Fine," he snapped. "I should be helping right now, but lock me up. If it makes you feel better. I haven't done a damn thing. How are you going to determine if I'm being mind controlled or not?"

"Setanta will examine your mind when he's finished managing the damage," Marcelle replied.

"Invade my mind, you mean. Fuck." He looked back down at the needle in his arm. "Just put shackles on me, Marcelle. I don't want this thing in my arm."

"As you wish. We needed to take you by surprise, just in case."

"Consider me surprised." He held out his wrists. A set of silver manacles was locked in place, hissing and burning his flesh, and the needle was removed. "Are you going to keep me in the dungeon like Vasi trash?"

"I think that would be extreme. Rosa will escort you to wait in Setanta's office. He'll be there when he's able, and we can have this mess sorted."

"And if I'm being controlled, what happens to me?"

Marcelle pursed her lips. "Let's hope it doesn't come to that. We care about you here, Bear. I'm sorry about this."

"Yeah. Sure."

The vampire Rosa put a hand on his shoulder to lead him, but he jerked away.

"I know how to get there. Pick me up to take me there, and when I get out, I'll break your arms," he snarled at her and started walking, his chains clanking with each step.

"You don't believe it could be Bear, do you? Not really?" Sarai whispered as she watched him be led away. It was unthinkable.

"We need to rule out the possibility. There's a leak

to the Vasi. Someone tells them when we're about to do a raid. Someone told them about our wedding. Someone snuck magical poison that did…this…to us into our home. They need to have access to our conversations, and they need to have access to witchcraft. If Bear is being controlled by a foreign pureblood using the Vasi to sabotage us, that would explain it. He's been at all those events, had access to all those spaces."

Sarai shook her head. "I met someone from the Nordic Clans at the Midnight Festival. Yrsa, she danced with me. She seemed so nice."

"Most royal lines are vicious, backstabbing, power-hungry bastards. The Norse are no exception. The Norse used to do horrific mass turnings to build their invading forces and massacre people. Yrsa wouldn't blink twice about doing something like this. But enough of that… We need to inspect the humans. Lochlan, Sarai, you're witches. Do you think either of you can tell whose blood is poisoned and whose isn't without me having to spill it?"

"Yeah." Lochlan wiped tears away with a closed fist and composed himself. "I'm not great at spells, but I can do that."

"Good. Then we go to meet the humans." Marcelle paused. "If this is the Vasi, there may be misdirection. Whoever is blamed, I don't want you to interfere. Don't reveal anything in front of them. Don't let them know you can see if they're lying or not. There's something deeper going on here, and I intend to play this game to win."

****

Marcelle threw open the door to the human quarters where everyone was gathered, making them jump.

Rosaline stood up, her gaze darting back and forth between all the uniformed vampires and Lochlan until she landed on Sarai. "Is Crispin okay?"

Sarai looked away and shook her head. "He's dead."

Gasps rippled through the room. She wanted to reach out and hug Rosaline but couldn't. The difference in social status and her position as someone who needed to drink their blood created too much space between herself and these humans. These suspects.

"Yes, he is dead," Marcelle said. "From drinking source blood. Twenty-four other vampires are also dead now, transformed into humans and crumbled into old age. Because of your blood. You, whom we treat fairly and with respect, whom we rely on for our lives to keep us from becoming true monsters. You have betrayed us."

Rosaline shook her head. "We didn't know. I wasn't even here. Whatever you need, you can have. We want this fixed too. What do you need from us?"

"Your belongings will be searched, and Lochlan will be performing a magical assessment on each of you. If we find nothing, we will move to individual interrogations." Marcelle snapped her fingers and pointed forward.

A vampire knight named Geoffry nodded and led the others to begin ransacking the place. Drawers of utensils were spilled. Furniture pushed aside. Cabinets flung open. All while the humans stood huddled together and guarded by Marcelle as if they were criminals.

Lochlan went through each human, adjusting his glasses as if they let him see something more, holding each hand and moving through the crowd.

"That's your focus, isn't it?" Sarai asked as she watched him work. "I always thought it was the bow."

"Nah, too conspicuous. I just like archery. These specs let me see body heat so I could find vampires easy. And I can see magic with the right setting." He tapped them and looked over another human. "They're all poisoned." He looked around the room and to the kitchen where a platter of breakfast muffins sat on the counter. "There."

Marcelle picked one up and sniffed. "Who made these?"

One of the boys, Will, raised his shaking hand. "I did, but I didn't do anything bad. I make those all the time; everyone loves them. They're just breakfast."

He was telling the truth. The button in the cuff of her glove didn't change to alert her of any lie. She exchanged glances with Marcelle, who gave a short nod of acknowledgment.

Someone must have slipped something into the batter. One of the humans might have done it. She couldn't imagine that Bear would be able to slip in and out of the human kitchen unnoticed.

"Was anyone unusual around while you were baking? Any vampires come into the kitchen?" Sarai asked.

"No, that's our space," Will said. "Vampires don't come here. And everyone uses the kitchen. I don't know."

Sarai finally landed her gaze on Jackie, the human Marcelle had warned her was hiding something. It wasn't this, surely. Except who else could it be? Something about the wide-eyed and frightened doe-like expression on her face looked so...rehearsed.

Sarai heard more commotion in the bedrooms as each one was systematically thrown apart in search of some clue. Then Geoffry emerged, holding a glass bottle with what looked like a few drops of a glowing potion inside.

He marched forward and handed it to Sarai. She inhaled. She noticed a certain humanity to the scent and a twinge of something bittersweet like dark chocolate but magic as well. Other scents wafted from the bottle, ones of poisonous plants, and she knew it had to be the culprit.

Still, that bittersweet scent was so familiar. But it was so buried under other scents of plant matter that it was difficult to place.

"This is it." Sarai passed it to Marcelle. "It's a magical poison."

"Where did you find it?" Marcelle demanded.

Geoffry's expression softened for a moment, then he looked into the crowd of trembling humans. "Rosaline's mattress."

Sarai felt like she'd been punched in the gut. Rosaline... No, it couldn't be. Yet Rosaline did have a history of being close to Bear. If anyone would do whatever he asked, it was Rosaline.

"What?" Rosaline laughed a little. "That's... No. No. Is this your idea of a sick joke?"

"Rosaline..." Sarai whispered.

"I wouldn't!" The human rushed forward and threw herself at Sarai. "Please, you need to believe me. I wouldn't."

Sarai shut her eyes, struggling with the desperation of Rosaline's plea. But she felt glad to hear her say she hadn't done it, and to verify that it was the truth. Still, she had to try to stay detached. She couldn't interfere with Marcelle's plans.

"Please!" Rosaline begged, her voice anguished.

"Take her," Marcelle ordered.

Rosaline fell silent as Geoffry gripped her shoulder and steered her out of the room, no doubt descending down and to the dungeon.

"She's my friend," Sarai whispered. "I don't want to treat her badly."

"I know," Marcelle said. "Then let us go to her together about this matter."

Sarai didn't look at the other humans as she left. She felt almost like a traitor. Sure, she wasn't exactly human herself, but she was mortal, and they'd accepted her as one of them. She didn't know what they would think of seeing her in such an authoritarian role with such power over their lives.

Sarai followed Marcelle down to the dungeon, listening to Rosaline pleading with Geoffry from up ahead of them the whole way.

When they got to the cold, dark dungeon, they were illuminated by no light but for flickering torches. While the upper palace was grand and beautiful, reminiscent of the renaissance in its glory, the dungeon was medieval. And it was meant to be, to evoke fear in anyone unfortunate enough to find themselves imprisoned there.

Rosaline's crying could be heard from the interrogation room, a stark and empty place. Sarai was grateful when she entered to see that Rosaline had been spared chains.

"Please," she whimpered. "Please, you have to believe me. Sarai, you're my friend. You know I wouldn't. Marcelle, Your Highnesses, my queens. Please. I owe this kingdom everything; I'd never do anything to hurt anyone here."

"Be at ease, Rosaline," Marcelle said. "I apologize

for the theatrics. We know it wasn't you."

Rosaline blinked, took a few deep breaths, then began to laugh in what appeared to be manic relief, leaning against the wall and sinking to the floor. "Oh my goodness. You have no idea how scared I was. Holy fuck." She took several deep breaths, then exploded into more laughter.

Sarai rushed forward and hugged her friend. Tears soaked her sleeve as they held each other.

"I'm so sorry," she said. "I didn't know it would be like that, but Marcelle told me not to give anything away. Honestly, I'm half in the dark about most of this stuff, but I'm here for you. I didn't want them to drag you off to a dungeon and not be here for you."

"I guess I appreciate that? Okay." Rosaline took several more deep breaths and wiped the salt water from her eyes. "Why did you do this? If you know it wasn't me."

"Because I wanted the person who framed you to believe their ruse worked," Marcelle said. "I believe, somehow, Jacqueline Pine is working for the Vasi, though we don't have direct proof or knowledge as to how she's managing to inflict so much damage."

Something in Sarai's mind clicked. "Bittersweet…like dark chocolate. That was part of the scents in the bottle of poison, right?"

"It was," Marcelle said.

"Like my blood. That's how you and Setanta always describe my taste. And with what happened last time you tried to drink my blood…holy shit." Sarai shook her head. "I sat on a sewing needle in Jackie's room last time I saw her. There was blood. She got my blood. She's not a witch, I'd know if she was, but she got my blood, and someone used it in a poison to turn vampires into dying humans."

"Holy shit." Rosaline breathed. "Jackie? She's always so nice, though. She helps with the cooking and... Holy fuck, she helped with the cooking. What are you waiting for? She should be down here, right?"

Marcelle shook her head. "There's a reason I didn't confront her despite my suspicions. The last few Vasi we've caught had explosive sigils on their teeth to avoid interrogation. They blow out their own skulls. If we confront Jackie, I suspect she might have something similar. We can't slip something into her food to render her unconscious, unfortunately, as we discovered most ingested sedatives and poisons trigger the sigil. Trying to remove it while they are unconscious triggers it. Any attempt to take her into custody, and she could activate it. We would lose the opportunity to learn from her. We need her to believe we've fallen for her trick so that we might devise a method of disarming her first. Then we can interrogate her."

"What can I do to help?" Rosaline asked.

"We'll smuggle you out of the palace for now. You can stay with Lochlan at his cabin. You'll be comfortable enough there, well-fed, cared for. It was not my intention to cause you extended discomfort or stress, but I needed your authentic reaction for this to be believable. I also had no idea which human might be framed. It's luck it was you and not someone else."

Rosaline nodded. "Okay. Yeah, so just chill at Lochlan's until you guys figure things out?"

"That's all we need from you, yes. And I do appreciate your understanding. We can increase your salary if you would like monetary compensation for the trouble."

Rosaline waved her hand dismissively, then stopped. "Any chance of asking to be turned?"

Marcelle shook her head. "You know the rules. Former addicts make for dangerous vampires."

Rosaline shrugged. "Worth a shot. I guess, yeah, I wouldn't mind a little extra pay, hit me up with that bonus."

"Of course, Rosaline."

"Can I ask, do you have a plan yet?"

"I have an idea," Sarai said slowly.

"I'm listening," Marcelle said.

"She, well, she's been working hard trying to keep me seduced, right? So she'd have to keep that up. I'll go on a date with her, all upset about my best friend betraying us. Maybe I can get something out of it, get her trust and figure out how to disarm her."

Marcelle leaned forward and gave a kiss to Sarai. "I knew I loved your mind for a reason. Yes, that plan could work. But be careful. We don't know what else she might be capable of."

****

Marcelle was restless as dawn began to break and illuminate the thin line under her curtains. It was time to sleep, but she had too much on her mind. Something nagged at her mind that she couldn't quite put her finger on, something she was missing. She had to think it through and figure out what that thing could be.

Jacqueline was almost certainly responsible for the poisoning and a likely Vasi spy—of that Marcelle had little doubt. But she couldn't do it alone with clear witchcraft involved in the poison. Vasi were known to work with enslaved witches, of course, so that wasn't a surprise. She didn't think Jackie would have a chance to smuggle in magic from outside the palace since a close eye was often kept on sources' movements.

But then the palace didn't have many witches. Sarai and Lochlan were loyal to New Ulster. Despite Lochlan's once raging hatred of vampires, the man he had grown into was understanding of vampires and viewed them as his comrades. He would never kill his comrades. Sarai was a queen; she had no reason to ever betray her own kingdom.

The only other witches were the pureblood royal family. Setanta, his father Lugh, and Artemisia. Giovanna, perhaps, but she had been banished from the kingdom.

Lugh was too tired and preoccupied with allowing himself to die by aging to care about made vampires or anything to do with the kingdom other than the welfare of his son.

Artemisia was too young to...

Artemisia.

Marcelle sat up sharply from her bed. Artemisia had been held captive by Vasi once. They'd had the chance to force her to submit to a contract, and Marcelle had never considered it might have happened at the time of the rescue because Artemisia had so eagerly killed Vasi that day. Yet the rescue had been rather easy, all considered. Perhaps too easy.

Perhaps it was all a trap.

Marcelle jumped to put on a robe and open the door, needing to alert Setanta of her suspicions, to find Artemisia standing there in the doorway, blinking up at her with unnervingly young red eyes.

"Time for another chat," Artemisia said. "Come on,

sit down on the bed, and let's be quiet now."

Marcelle's mouth snapped shut from the compulsion as she felt her blood command her to sit down as instructed.

"Tell me, are there any more plans you know about to do any raids? I know Lilly went and caught someone. They're dead now, right?"

"Yes." The word tore from her mouth against her will.

Oh fuck.

Marcelle was the leak. They knew everything she knew; that was how they planned around her raids.

"We have no plans for a raid. Artemisia, you don't need to do this. We can help you. Talk to Setanta."

Artemisia sighed. "I hate this, you know. Every time we talk, you say the same things. I've told you a hundred times I can't talk to Setanta. They won't let me speak to him, and he never cares to speak to me. Why would he? He hates my mother. I thought with her gone he'd pay some attention and notice, but he hasn't. He's too busy to care about me. I am just the last in a very long line of siblings he never loved."

"Artemisia, I…" Marcelle didn't know what to say. She wasn't wrong. Setanta viewed his little sister as a spoiled annoyance. He had to know that she had potential once she grew up and matured, but that meant little to a child.

The girl looked up with tears in her eyes. "I didn't mean for them to die. It didn't work right. I wish you would remember I didn't mean to kill them."

"We can do something, anything. Artemisia—"

"No. We can't. All you can do is…forget."

Chapter Twenty

A Favor

Setanta was not looking forward to confronting the prisoner in his study. He had taken all night to manage everything he needed to, and felt bad for keeping Bear waiting in silver. He admired Bear, and as they were both some of the very few remaining vampires in the world with an age that was counted in four digits, he related to him. They both knew what it was to watch the world change and become unrecognizable. To have to adapt to new societies and customs that didn't always welcome them for arbitrary and hateful reasons. He felt a kinship to Bear. Opening the intricately carved wooden doors to his office to see Bear standing in the middle, his wrists burned by silver, was not a sight he enjoyed.

"Rosa, thank you. I'll take the key, and you may leave," he told the other vampire in the room.

Rosa handed over the keys to Bear's chains and gave a small bow before leaving them alone.

"This was necessary?" Bear snapped, shaking his wrists.

"You know full well that compulsion could make you a threat. It isn't personal."

"Yeah. But it sure feels personal. Let's get this over with. What do I need to do to prove that I'm in full control of all my actions and I'm not responsible for any of this shit?"

"Please, have a seat."

Bear looked at the seats in front of the desk, scoffed, and walked around the desk to sit in Setanta's chair.

Setanta raised an eyebrow.

"If you're gonna chain me up, I get your chair," Bear said. "You're my king, yes, but I see us on more equal footing no matter what your powers are or what fancy fucking titles you have. I see you as a friend I choose to associate with. There aren't a lot of people like us. Old like us. I thought you saw me the same way. And this is fucking offensive, Setanta. This is an insult to every choice I've ever made. Do you really think I'd let one of those Viking nutjobs get one over on me?"

"I don't think you'd let it happen, no. I'm more concerned about what might have been forced on you than what might have been allowed."

"Yeah." Bear's shoulders slumped. "You know, I really hate how all this works. Purebloods. Bloodlines. This control you guys have over us so-called lesser vampires. I hate it."

"Unfortunately, there's nothing I can do to change how it works." Setanta retrieved his magical focus from a glass case in the office. "This should be easy and quick. I'll cast a spell to see if your mind is your own, and it'll be done."

"Do it, then."

Setanta cut himself on the spear and focused his thin magic, wrapping the threads of it through Bear's mind and strumming at it carefully. The vibrations through the magic brought thoughts forward but no magic. No control. No imprint of a compulsion at all, other than the ones he knew of that were part of the deal they'd made with the Norse to allow Bear to serve New Ulster instead of them.

Setanta pulled his magic back and returned the spear to the case. "You have my most sincere apologies." He unlocked Bear's shackles.

Bear let them drop with a loud thud on Setanta's desk. "I'm dedicated. Through and through, I'm your man."

"You know it wasn't personal or about any choice you would consciously make."

Bear shut his eyes and sighed. "Yeah. I know. Maybe it just freaked me out that you might have been right." He opened his eyes and looked at Setanta with a strange expression.

"Is there something you have to say?"

"Yeah. Yeah, actually." Bear sat up. "I wanna petition you for a favor."

"A favor?" Setanta mused.

"A favor."

"Well then, perhaps a better way to ask for a favor would be to get out of my chair."

Bear chuckled. "All right. Get your spot back." He got up, and they changed places.

"What favor do you wish to petition me for?"

"Your blood." Bear paused. "I want to turn Hannah. She's retiring from the Ellis Coven leadership. We love each other. But you've seen her; she's old. We don't have much time left together. I can't lose her, but I can't do it myself because of the rules, because I'm not your bloodline. I want her to have your blood. And besides, your line doesn't have memory issues. That would be better for her."

Setanta leaned back in his chair as he pondered the

request. "That's interesting. Have you spoken to her about this?"

"I brought it up. She's interested."

Setanta thought about it. Hannah had helped them in the past and had a formidable spell-crafting ability as well as the useful gift of astral projection. As a vampire, she would be an asset. Especially after a few years or decades to form a bond of loyalty to her sire's kingdom, if Setanta was her sire. And giving Bear his lady love would help mend their current rift.

"I suppose," Setanta said. "We need more vampires in our kingdom now with this latest attack. A little repopulation and recruitment is due. Tell me when the date is set, and I'll give you a vial of my blood. You can have some privacy between the two of you for the turning. I wouldn't want to intrude on something as intimate as death."

Bear lit up with visible joy. "Yes! Yes, thank you. I'll go help with everything going on for now, and I'll bring her as soon she's ready. Mind if I use your phone to give her a ring?"

Setanta gestured to the office phone at the end of his desk. "Please, help yourself."

Bear snatched it up, dialed, and twirled the cord in his finger while he waited for the ringing to end. "Hannah, it's me," he said as soon as someone answered on the other end. "I need you to come to North Carolina. Setanta's agreed."

"I'll let you talk," Setanta said as he left. "Come out when you're finished. There's much to be done."

The rest of the night was spent making plans for funerals. Vampires didn't have funerals for each other as the undead turned to dust and were blown away by the wind. But with so many human bodies, something needed to be done with them. Pyres were built except for a handful who were buried in a fashion fitting their respective cultures of origin. Once the burials were finished, Setanta walked from pyre to pyre with a torch, lighting them. It was a solemn occasion for which even his father had come out of his rooms.

"You retain your respect for the dead," Lugh said in ancient Irish to his son.

"Of course," Setanta replied in the same tongue. "They were mine to protect, and I failed them. Honoring their sacrifice is the least I can do."

"Will you build my pyre with your own hands?" Lugh requested in a casual yet tired tone.

The words stung. Setanta hated seeing how his father had chosen to age, to meet death. But he was glad it was happening on the man's own terms. There didn't exist many ways for a vampire to die, and the kindest one for a pureblood was to age and pass away peacefully.

"Yes," Setanta promised. "It will be my great honor to build you a grand pyre by hand."

"I should like it on a mountain top," Lugh said. "Open to the sky and the ravens."

"Then I swear to you on my honor it will be done for you."

Chapter Twenty-One

The Starlit Fountain

Sarai let Marcelle dress her for her date with Jackie. Everything had to be just right. Casual but cute. Hot but not too over-the-top. Like she was trying to be seductive without going too far in a way she wouldn't normally. Light makeup. Warm leggings and a cute winter coat for the cold. A maternity shirt that was actually flattering to her bust despite the eight-month swell of pregnancy under it. Sarai would have liked a simple restaurant date, but Marcelle advised against leaving the palace with a suspect. The best policy was to keep her an unknowing prisoner away from excursions where she might have an opportunity to contact other hunters. So Sarai had planned a romantic dinner date in the gardens behind the palace.

"I look like a ridiculous hippopotamus," Sarai said to Marcelle.

"You look *hot*."

"That's a funny way to pronounce a ridiculous hippopotamus." Sarai tugged at her curls. "What if I screw this up? I haven't done anything like this before."

"I'll be eavesdropping just out of sight. If anything goes wrong, I'll be there to help. You do like her, yes?"

"I mean, I did until I figured out she's playing us all," Sarai said.

"Understandable. But forget about that. Lean into that natural attraction. The best lies are true."

"That makes no sense."

"It will." Marcelle kissed her. "Ask her about herself and her history. Any bits of information you can get. She knows that you have that lie detection trinket, yes?"

Sarai nodded.

"Then she'll be careful not to tell you any direct lies. I suspect that's how she flew under your radar as long as she did in the first place. She'll tell you the truth in ways that don't incriminate her. Let her and get every grain of truth you can."

"Okay. Just a date. A regular girly date." Sarai exhaled. "I've got this."

She went out to a beautiful spot in the middle of the curated palace gardens. While most of the outdoors was the wild forests of Appalachia, a fraction of the space outside the palace was designed like the gardens of the palace in Versailles in France. She suspected Marcelle had played a hand in that design choice, and Setanta had given it to her as a grand gift. The thought crossed her mind that she could ask him for a plot of land for a witch's garden to expand her potion-making ability beyond the kitchen pantry of spices. She could grow her own unique poisonous plants or even use magic to create the right temperature to grow species not found in a temperate climate. Though she would pass on growing belladonna out of respect for Setanta.

After walking through the cold all the way out to the center of the gardens, Sarai reached a beautiful fountain full of chemically clean, crystal-clear water. And in front of that fountain was a table for two with a candlelight dinner on two covered plates. Surrounding the scene was a line of pebbles she'd requested from Lochlan, imbued with just enough of his power to warm the space comfortably so that, despite the winter air, it felt like summer. She pulled off her winter coat and hung it on the chair, then began to pace.

Should she sit? No, she was too anxious to sit. But then pacing didn't help.

She sat down. Her foot bounced. The sitting did help take the pressure off her knees, at least. The tea that Mazal had given her for the arthritis helped, but she still experienced a discomforting sensation to standing for too long. Sitting did help to also take pressure off her back. Her swollen abdomen had gotten to a size that put significant pressure on her, and it occurred to her…what if Jackie had no real interest in her? What if she secretly found the pregnancy grotesque? The idea that it was all an act horrified her. Yet she had an easy solution. She could somehow ask for Jackie's thoughts in their conversation, and she'd learn if Jackie's supposed attraction to Sarai was the truth of how she felt or a very convincing lie.

Sarai saw Jackie walking up from afar, bundled up in a winter coat to protect against the cold. Her breath was white until she stepped into the circle and paused, looking around.

"Oh wow," Jackie said. "That's nifty." She stepped back out, then in, out, then in again.

"Yeah, I thought it would be romantic? You know, enjoy the outdoors but also be warm."

"No, it's nice." Jackie bit her lip. "So an actual date?"

"Yeah. I wanted, you know, something nice. It's been a lot lately. Rosaline…" Sarai shook her head. "I just want something enjoyable. And I thought maybe you would like it too. I was sad you weren't at the wedding, but considering how it went, that's for the best."

"Yeah, I got sick. It must have been from those muffins."

No lie there. She must have eaten it along with everyone to avoid suspicion. To be safe, Sarai decided her best course of action was to not drink her blood.

"But I heard. It's so wild. I mean, a real dragon? How many people can say they've seen one of those?" Jackie said.

"Yeah. Technically it's not a dragon; it's a shapeshifter witch. But yeah, supposedly shapeshifting lines were extinct. I have no idea how they managed to find one, let alone enslave one." She pursed her lips. This was possibly an enslaver in front of her, but she had to put that out of her mind. "Do you want to eat? I'm hungry."

"Yeah, sure." Jackie sat down. "You, uh, you just picked something for me?"

"Remember when we first met, you said your favorite dinner is chicken alfredo?"

Jackie's eyes widened, and she blushed as she uncovered her plate to reveal a bowl of chicken alfredo with a side of garlic bread. "Oh wow. You were paying attention to me?"

"Well, yeah. You're cute. I liked listening to what you like." It was Sarai's turn to blush as she uncovered her own meal, also an alfredo dish but without the chicken, and more garlic bread. She also picked up a bottle of white wine and poured one glass for Jackie. She poured water for herself. She wasn't usually one for alcohol, and the pregnancy gave her the perfect excuse to use the libation to loosen Jackie's tongue without indulging in it herself. "The kitchen did not like that I asked for garlic bread. Marcelle and Setanta will probably not appreciate it later."

Jackie giggled. "Wait, that's not true, is it? About vampires and garlic?"

"I mean, they have a heightened sense of smell. A lot of garlic, or onions, is a bit off-putting." Sarai laughed.

"Well, I appreciate you making them miserable on my behalf." Jackie smirked and dug into her meal.

"So, um, we're supposed to talk to each other about stuff? I'm sorry. I haven't been on a lot of dates. I guess, tell me something about you?"

"Well, you're doing great. Something about me?"

"Yeah, like, where did you grow up? You said you were adopted."

"Oh, sure. Yeah. Um, as a baby. My adopted family were religious. They homeschooled me. I didn't get out much. PE was rough. They were big believers of physical discipline. If I flunked their version of history assignments, I had to go run laps, do a hundred push-ups, all that sort of thing."

That tracked. Sarai knew a lot of Vasi got involved in the organization due to religious convictions, though she hadn't thought about how they would raise their children into the organization. They had always been terrifying masked men with guns, to her mind. Yet to hear Jackie tell her truths was unsettling somehow.

"I kinda got homeschooled too," Sarai said. "A lot of witches do. It's hard to keep kids from using magic in front of humans in first grade, you know?"

"I can't say that I do."

Sarai put her fork down and looked at Jackie, put off by her dismissive tone, the way it seemed to be covering up disgust. "You don't like magic much, do you?"

"I mean, it's fine enough. It's a little weird to me since, you know, I'm just human. No offense, though! It's useful, I'm sure."

"It can be beautiful." Sarai smiled. "Could I show you something?"

Jackie also put down her fork. "I guess?"

This was a Vasi. If Sarai could convince her somehow that magic had beauty, that vampire society was as valid in its existence as human society, and that witchcraft was an artform, maybe she could convince Jackie to switch sides. Maybe they could have something genuine between them. It wasn't the direction that Marcelle had told her to take the date in, but Marcelle wasn't on the date. Sarai was. She would do things her way.

Sarai straightened out her blue, fingerless glove and focused her intention. "*Or ha'kochavim le'yadi*," she whispered in Hebrew, her preferred language for spellcraft. *Light of the stars, come to my hand.*

A bright orb of white light grew in her palm, and she flicked it out around them. Then another and another until their shared space was glowing with beautiful starlight drifting all around them.

Jackie's face lit up with an almost childlike wonder. "I didn't know you could use magic like that."

"Magic is just a witch's intent," Sarai said softly. "When Vasi witches use their spellcraft, it gets twisted. It's not their intent; it's intent that's forced on them. Everything they enchant has a cruel edge because they're slaves. It's a perversion. That's why we're so afraid of them and of becoming them. When witches are free, the sky's the limit. What I'm doing now, I'm borrowing starlight and making it dance. Not a protection spell or an offensive spell. Just…for beauty." She tossed a few to circle around Jackie's head like a slow halo.

Jackie looked up at Sarai, bathed in the gentle light, and she looked like an angel.

"You're beautiful."

Jackie's expression softened as her wide, brown eyes darted between the orbs of starlight. "When you do it, witchcraft doesn't look scary."

"It's not. I mean, it can be. But something like martial arts can be scary too. Or it can be a kick-ass performance. Or tai chi or something. Just because something can be scary doesn't mean that's all it is."

Jackie stood, the lights dancing around her as she spun around. Her skirt flared up, and Sarai directed the light to land on her clothes like fairy lights. She was angelic, the way she smiled with delight. She stumbled slightly but caught herself, giggling as she looked at the fountain.

"Almost fell in, that would suck in the cold. Although…" Jackie stopped and looked down at the ring of warm pebbles. She snatched her food cover and scooped some of the stones up, then tossed them into the fountain. The water began to bubble and steam. "Instant hot tub?"

Sarai couldn't help but grin as she watched Jackie pull off her clothes and step into the water. Though she did think perhaps Jackie's rush to get naked in front of her was suspicious. She didn't want to let it distract her from her purpose. But it was very distracting.

"Well?" Jackie asked. "Aren't you going to join

me?"

"I'm not sure. I'm not supposed to take baths that are too hot." Sarai stood. "Do you…mind the way I look? Being pregnant."

"Sarai, shut up, you're gorgeous. Get in the water with me. It's lukewarm with how cold it was before, so you're fine."

Her button charm detected no hint of a lie, and Sarai's confidence surged. She stripped off her clothes and her shoes and looked down at her prosthetic hand. She always took it off before getting into a bath so that she could clean the skin under it. But it was magical, so it wouldn't be ruined by water. She decided to keep it on.

She tried to step over the edge of the fountain, but her center of gravity caused her to wobble. Jackie reached out for her hand to help her. The touch was like a spark. Sarai looked down at their hands and locked their fingers together.

"You really are gorgeous, you know," Jackie said. "I mean it."

They eased into the warm water. It was comfortable but not too hot to be a concern. Sarai curled up against Jackie's naked form as she wrapped an arm around her.

"You're beautiful too," Sarai said. She closed her eyes, listening to Jackie's heart pounding and enjoying the scent of her pomegranate blood. But it wasn't time for blood. She was meant to be on a mission. She turned to look at Jackie and opened her mouth to speak, but the human leaned forward to press their lips together. Sarai promptly forgot what she was going to say. Jackie's lips and tongue tasted like wine, and Sarai wanted to lick every drop of indulgence from her skin.

Hands shifted against soft curves under the water.

Sarai's mouth found Jackie's breasts, and her tongue swirled against her pointed nipples. Her star lights swirled around them in spirals along with steam from the fountain. Jackie's moans filled the air, and Sarai felt starved for her body. Her lips and tongue hungrily explored every part of Jackie's breasts and collarbone and neck. She nipped against Jackie's ear, bracing herself up with her good hand, finding Jackie's mouth again.

It was so different from Marcelle or Setanta, Sarai found herself thinking. Her vampire lovers had an innate power over Sarai, but Jackie didn't have that pull. Instead, they were pulling at each other, almost desperate in their kisses and need.

Fangs slid free from Sarai's gums, and she jerked away. "Sorry." She gasped.

"Don't be sorry. Is that...what you want?"

Sarai shook her head. "It's just a reaction. I'm good, really. But I shouldn't go down on you with these, though. I, uh, I haven't tried that before since they started appearing, and I shouldn't risk hurting you."

"Then use your fingers," Jackie insisted. "Or just a little tongue. Please, I want you so bad."

Sarai nodded and leaned back to put her weight on her kneeling legs. Her knees hurt, but she didn't care. Jackie spread her legs apart, and Sarai could see beautiful pink flesh beckoning from between them. She trailed a hand down Jackie's dark skin, admiring the way the starlight glistened like diamonds in droplets on her. She slipped her hand under the surface of the water to that sweet spot to tease her entrance.

"Please," Jackie whimpered.

It was so warm, her body. The way she gripped

Sarai's finger with powerful need. The water wasn't conducive to friction, but Jackie was wet enough with her own slick nectar that it wasn't a problem as long as Sarai kept her finger mostly inside as she rocked her hand back and forth. Encouraged by Jackie's groans, she added a second finger, the pair of them curling inside the warmth just right, caressing as deep within as she could, and used her thumb to trace circles around the sweet button that gave the most pleasure.

"You're good at that." Jackie breathed.

"I practice."

"More, please... More."

Sarai complied, adding another finger. She found herself surprised and excited by how easily it went in, how much Jackie's arousal allowed for, and realized the possibility existed for her to slip her pinkie in. Her hand was just small enough, her fingers so narrow, and she could feel Jackie clenching tight against her with new urgency.

"Yes, yes, yes," Jackie whimpered, holding her legs apart as wide as they could be held.

Sarai stared at Jackie's sex. She had soft black curls, bright-pink folds, and streams of water dripping down that beautiful skin as it pooled around her seat.

"You're so beautiful," Sarai whispered.

"Stop staring and keep going." Jackie paused then added, "Please."

Sarai nodded and pressed her fingers forward into Jackie's sex, watching her body take it as deep as she could push with a loud moan from the human. Jackie gripped the fountain ledge in such a vice that if she'd been a vampire, the stone would have crumbled under her.

"Please, yes, please, yes," Jackie kept begging.

Sarai couldn't resist. She lowered her head and flicked out her tongue, just her tongue, being sure to keep her fangs away from any sensitive parts. Jackie's body seized, her sex pulling and pulsing around Sarai's hand as she orgasmed.

And as Jackie orgasmed, she threw her head back with a cry. What Sarai saw caused her to feel cold.

Engraved in the enamel of a black tooth was a shimmering sigil at the back of her mouth, only just visible from the angle they were sitting.

As Jackie relaxed from the pleasure, staring up at the sky, she seemed to be oblivious to the proof she'd just provided Sarai and smiled. Sarai smiled back but said nothing. Marcelle had been right, and they had to figure out a way to stop Jackie from blowing out her own brains if confronted with her subterfuge. But she didn't know how. Sarai had to figure out how if she wanted any hope of changing Jackie's mind and convincing her to switch sides.

Jackie looked down. "Do you want me to give you a turn?"

If she hadn't just seen the blackened tooth, Sarai would have said yes. But now her desire was dry. "I'm just happy to see you enjoy yourself. And I've been feeling a little off down there with the pregnancy, so don't push yourself. Come cuddle with me. I just want to feel a warm body."

Jackie slid back into the pool and wrapped her arms around Sarai to guide her to lean back against her. They watched the starlight orbs Sarai had made drift like light feathers down from the air around them and land in the water where they dimmed until they were extinguished.

The witch and the Vasi were alone under the dark night sky. And Sarai had never felt so empty.

"You should leave all this," Jackie said suddenly.

Sarai blinked. "What?"

"All of this. I'm just here because I ended up feeling like I don't have a choice, Sarai. You know, blood for pay. It's not a terrible deal. But you have a choice. You should live with the rest of society. We could go on real dates, see a movie. Do normal things."

"I'm the queen here," Sarai reminded her. "And I love it. I love Marcelle. Maybe I even love Setanta. I don't know."

"But they're so much older than you. Don't you think that's weird?"

"A bit. But I'm not normal, so I fit in. I've got a place here. They're kind to me. They need me. And I'm not sure if you've noticed, but Marcelle and Setanta are hot. Very difficult to resist."

"Okay, yes. But maybe take a break for a little while. A vacation while you're pregnant, away from the palace. See what it's like to have a more normal life. I could come with you."

Sarai didn't reply. Then a thought crossed her mind. They needed to get Jackie into restraints so that they could remove the exploding tooth before it could be activated. They had to do it while she was awake. They couldn't put her in restraints without her knowing they were onto her. Unless...

"You think they're hot too?" Sarai said with a smile she felt was stolen right off Marcelle's face. Teasing, flirty. Manipulative.

Jackie laughed a little, shaking her head. "Fine, okay. Yes, they're objectively hot."

"I'm having a birthday party coming up." Sarai thought carefully as she chose her next words. "They said they'd plan something, well, fun. To make up for my wedding night being ruined. They'll be there, Temuulen will be there, and I think they're talking about a duchess from Boston and her wife joining us."

"Oh. Oh, this is a sex party." Jackie's eyes widened as she spoke.

"Would you want to come to the party? We can get a little kinky sometimes. If that's okay."

Jackie blushed. "Yeah, I did like that. Maybe I can just watch if it gets too intense. Do you want me there?"

"Yeah. I'd like you there." Sarai did her best to channel Marcelle and Setanta's attitude as she added, "If you'd like it, I wouldn't mind seeing you in some rope or handcuffs."

Jackie bit her lip, a flicker of fear in her eyes. "When you say it like that, how could I ever say no?"

Chapter Twenty-Two

The New York Style Cheesecake

Sarai thought Marcelle would have been proud of her fast thinking in inviting Jackie to the upcoming sex party. She had been wrong.

"You invited the Vasi spy to an orgy?" Marcelle asked incredulously.

"Yeah."

"I'm sorry, but have you lost your mind? I know all the blood is in your womb, but you should have at least a few brain cells still working."

Sarai rolled her eyes. "Look, I saw the tooth. She has it, one hundred percent. She's one of them. But I don't think she wants to be, not from the way she was talking. She really does like me. So we need to get the tooth out. We need to get her into restraints so we can get the tooth out. But if you force it, she'll blow herself up because she'll know she's been caught."

"And your thinking is…"

"We convince her to put herself into restraints. I even mentioned it to flirt a little. She's down. She'll do it for me. Either because she likes me or to keep up her act. Then you have her disarmed and vulnerable. Get her to open her mouth, use your speed to yank the tooth, and presto! You don't have to worry about losing her. She won't be able to do anything but talk with us, and I'll be able to tell if she's lying. Not that you guys can't, but I've got that enchantment. What do you think?"

Marcelle paused. "I'll admit, it's not the worst idea I've ever heard. But I wouldn't want to ruin your birthday celebration by ending on such a sour note as revealing a Vasi spy. You realize if it goes wrong, we might end up with her brains painting the wall."

"It was my idea. Catching her and making her take responsibility for what she's done to us is not a sour note. In fact, I think it'll be the best birthday present I've ever had. You know, assuming no brains on the wall. I believe in you and Setanta being fast enough to do it without setting the thing off."

Still, Sarai found it nerve-wracking to plan such a plot. Jackie was right about one thing. Getting away from it all and having a vacation, even for a little while, would do wonders for her stress levels. So the next time Marcelle decided to visit Lochlan, Sarai tagged along so that she could visit Rosaline in her temporary exile. And one more unusual event was taking place at Lochlan's cabin. They had a special feast prepared with samples of all sorts of foods imaginable for the guest of honor, Hannah Little Hawk.

It was officially Hannah's last night alive, and they were celebrating her life. Sarai felt a little awkward about the small crowd but at the same time vindicated. Hannah had shown very clear disapproval for Sarai's choice to marry Setanta specifically and to have children with him and Marcelle. The hypocrisy when Hannah herself was so head-over-heels involved with Bear tickled Sarai's amusement.

She got to Lochlan's with Marcelle before the couple of honor arrived. The house itself wasn't large, but the two-bedroom, two-bath home was plenty for one person, positioned on a mountain slope so that it had a beautiful view of the scenery. Outside, it was made of old stone with a brand-new bright-red sports car in the gravel driveway. Inside, Lochlan had given the walls a fresh coat of steel-blue paint and bought all new furniture all in black to put on cheap rugs over the original hardwood floors. A fire burned bright in a stone fireplace, filling the space with heat, and a pride flag was draped on the mantel above it. Other than that, Lochlan's home had almost no decorations unless one counted a handful of herbs growing in pots by the window.

As Sarai stepped inside, the most notable thing about the house was an absolute cacophony of scents blasting her senses. "Wow. It smells like everything."

"Yeah, come on in, make yourselves at home," Lochlan said. "We're still setting up. I ordered every kind of takeout I could. Rural North Carolina options are seriously limited compared to New York City, let me tell you. But there was this one bakery that's actually good. New York style cheesecake. I tested it; it's legit."

"I helped test it," Rosaline called from inside and ran to give Sarai a hug. "Sup, girlies!"

"How are you holding up here?" Sarai asked.

"This house is so warm." Rosaline groaned as if in pleasure. "The palace doesn't heat up like this."

"Another point why I will never live there," Lochlan joked as he got paper plates out of a pantry and cracked open a beer he pulled from the fridge. "Anyone else want one?"

Rosaline made a face. "Got anything that doesn't taste like cheap piss?"

"As opposed to expensive piss? Why do you know

what cheap piss tastes like?" he countered.

Sarai suppressed a laugh that turned into an unattractive snort.

"Ugh, just answer the question."

Lochlan took a long sip, then nodded. "Yeah, I got some vodka and mixers. And margarita mix. Fridge and bottom shelf in the cabinet. I kinda wanna see what kind of drunk Hannah is before she goes all..." He put two fingers up to his mouth to imitate fangs and pretended to gnash his teeth. "Though I don't think she really drinks much."

"You have no idea how spoiled for choice you are." Marcelle sighed. "All I had was wine back when I was alive. And I didn't even get the good wine. Taverns would put water in their barrels most of the time, you know. And all the vintages you have now? I never could have imagined it all."

"You get drunk if you drink a drunk human's blood, right?" Rosaline asked. "Is there any flavor difference for you if it's a margarita or a beer?"

"Higher sugar content makes a difference," Marcelle said. "Other than that, not really."

"You know, come to think of it, I don't think you've ever fed from me before, have you?" Rosaline pulled the drinks out and set the table with red plastic cups as she spoke.

"No, I'm partial to Nadine."

"Well, I got the antidote for the poison, so I'm safe now. If you wanna get drunk with us, I'm down," Rosaline offered.

Marcelle smiled. "Thank you. We'll see how the night goes."

Sarai heard the sound of a knock on the door.

Lochlan soon invited in Bear and welcomed Hannah into the cabin.

"It's so kind of you to host this," Hannah said.

"Yeah, no problem, Councilwoman."

"Please, you don't need to call me that anymore. I resigned, you know," Hannah said. "They'll be holding elections within the month, I'm sure."

"That's giving up a lot. I thought you'd be on that board forever," Lochlan said. "You've been there my whole life, at least. And giving it up for this…"

Hannah locked her fingers with Bear's. "I know it isn't what you might have expected from me."

"You don't owe anyone an explanation," Marcelle interjected. "You're making a choice for yourself. For your happiness. Don't make excuses for that."

Hannah gave a close-lipped smile. "Thank you. I appreciate that." She froze a little when her gaze met Rosaline's, who gave a polite smile.

"Hey," Rosaline said awkwardly. "I know we didn't get off on the right foot. I've gotta stay here because they're running some sting operation on some Vasi spy and I got framed for some stuff. Hope you don't mind. But I'm happy for you. Really. And I'm glad that you and Bear make each other happy. I helped Lochlan bake you some brownies."

"Brownies?" Hannah asked.

"We have so much food for you," Lochlan said. "Anything I could get my hands on. We've got Chinese takeout, pizza, sandwich station, wings, mashed potatoes, corn on the cob, burgers. Salad if you're into that. I found a place nearby that had bison burgers on the menu. Can you believe that? I picked up those, thought you might like them. And I've got some steak I cook up for you; I've gotten good at those. Filet. Oh, and salmon, I can make salmon. Then there's desserts. We made brownies. There's cake, ice cream, and New York style cheesecake. We tested that out. It's legit just like home. Oh, and we've got alcohol."

"Goodness." Hannah covered her mouth as she laughed. "All this for me?"

"Yeah. Honestly, I wasn't sure what kind of food you'd want. If you want something else, just say it and we'll figure out how to get it here." Lochlan beamed as he spoke. "I can drive to get it. I've got a car now."

"I saw it in the driveway," Hannah said. "They must be paying you well."

"We wouldn't ask for service without fair compensation," Marcelle said.

Hannah walked to the kitchen to look at the spread of food. "Would you mind if I added one thing? I'll need sugar, baking powder, flour, salt, water, and oil. Plenty of oil."

Lochlan got all the ingredients together, and soon Hannah was instructing everyone in making fry bread. It was rather fun and easy to do, though Sarai had never done much cooking. Hannah made it look easy, and she appreciated that.

"I ate this all the time as a little girl," Hannah said. "I wish you could taste it, Bear."

"It smells great," he said supportively.

Hannah had Lochlan cook up the fish and steak, making comments about how much she appreciated home-cooked food over takeout, though the thought was kind of everyone. Sarai thought it a little passive-aggressive, but it was Hannah's night. Her last night. She was entitled to whatever food she wanted. Not all the takeout was ignored, though. Hannah happily pulled apart the bison burger meat and mixed it with some spices and onions from Lochlan's cabinet to make a spread for the fry bread.

"No offense, Ms. Little Hawk, but my nails are terrible for this." Rosaline pouted. "I had them done just a few days ago, and they are not good for cooking."

Marcelle looked at Rosaline's hands. "Those look so nice," she said wistfully.

"Hey, how come I never see you with painted nails? You seem like you'd be into girly nail stuff."

"Oh, no. My nails are too short, and they never grow. Painting them makes my hands look childish," Marcelle dismissed.

"Why don't you just get acrylics?"

"A what now?"

"You know, where they put a fake nail on top of the real nail to make it longer and paint it up pretty." Rosaline held up her hands to show off her purple fingertips. "Acrylics?"

Marcelle's mouth gaped open as she stared. "You mean you didn't grow those to that length naturally?"

"Oh, definitely not."

"You are my new best friend, and when all this Vasi business is done with, you are introducing me to wherever I can get these acrylics," Marcelle said with an intensity that made Sarai laugh.

As they finished their cooking, Sarai felt a connection had been made between them all, laughing and smiling, making a mess of flour. It was fun. And somehow, it was bonding. Was it something that regular people felt when they were close to each other, or if there was real magic involved, since there were three witches present?

"Is this magic?" Sarai asked as she looked at the food they'd made together. "I know kitchen witches are a thing."

"When you cook, you take many different ingredients that alone would be nothing special, then turn them into a feast," Hannah said. "In that sense, it is magic. A mundane magic accessible to witches and non-witches alike. We've created something wonderful together. Thank you all, so much, for all of this."

They all sat down to eat together, and Bear and Marcelle joined the mortals at the table. The tension between Rosaline and Hannah melted away as they drank, and Sarai found herself in the unique position of joining Bear and Marcelle as the sober half of the room, while Lochlan performed fire tricks by spitting alcohol in a stream into the air and igniting it with his fire to a round of cheers.

"Who's going to be your first?" Rosaline asked after her second margarita.

"Hm?" Hannah said.

"Who are you gonna bite first? You gotta have someone picked out before you turn."

"Oh. No, I hadn't thought through that part." She glanced at Bear. "How are we handling that?"

"I had a blood bag I was going to give her," Bear said. "Start her off easy without needing to deal with self-control the first time. O positive, vegetarian. You know, premium stuff for a bag."

"Oh, she's a grown-ass woman. She can handle herself," Rosaline dismissed. "Come on, give her the good stuff."

"I mean, I would, except she'll be stronger than me,"

Bear said. "We're giving her Setanta's blood. If she goes nuts, it would be hard for me to stop her in the middle of feeding without also hurting whoever she was fixated on."

"I could," Marcelle said. "I'll be at the same strength as her, and I have enough experience to manage it. Hannah, do you want a human source to start with after you turn?"

Hannah took a long drink of the cocktail in her hand and gave her head a shake. "What a question. My. I'm not sure how I want to handle that. I know it's quite necessary for the life I'm joining, but it does make me uncomfortable."

"You'll get used to it," Marcelle dismissed. "Rosaline, are you offering?"

"I could, yeah," Rosaline said. "I've been at this for a while, so I know the routine."

Hannah looked uncomfortable.

"It's not so bad," Bear said. "With a source like Rosaline, it can be professional. You know it's not too bad when I do it to you. Just stick to her wrist, not the neck bites we do."

Lochlan choked on his beer. "Fuck. That's an image I guess."

"Language, young man," Hannah chided him. "And you're hardly one to talk. You and Marcelle. And who knows who else."

"What's that supposed to mean?" Lochlan asked.

Hannah pursed her lips. "I only meant these vampires are very…free. Marcelle in particular."

"We are that," Marcelle murmured.

"Yeah, but I'm not a vampire," Lochlan said. "It's just Marcelle for me. Not sure exactly what that is, but that's all for me right now."

"I didn't mean any offense," Hannah said.

Lochlan finished off his beer. "Getting another. Anyone else? Rosaline?"

"I'm good," Rosaline said, holding up her drink.

Sarai enviously wished she could be just a little buzzed if Hannah and the others were going to keep trading barbs. After the pregnancy was done, she was looking forward to being allowed something alcoholic.

She scooted her chair closer to Marcelle. "Is this what it's usually like when someone decides to turn?"

"Honestly, it's rarely this pleasant," Marcelle said. "I'm jealous."

"What was it like for you?" Hannah asked.

Marcelle shook her head.

"Is it too much?"

Marcelle sighed. "I'll tell you since we're to be blood sisters soon. I'd known Setanta when I was human, when I worked at a brothel. He would feed on my blood for the enjoyment of the warmth. That's all he took, nothing else, and paid me well for it. Then I got sick with consumption... Sorry, I believe it's called tuberculosis now? There's cures with your modern medicine, but then it was near certain death. I was kicked to the streets, and that's where Setanta found me. He brought me to his home, held me in an empty bath, and cut my thighs to bleed me out before he gave me his blood. Normally, he would have bitten me, but with the sickness, the taste would have been wrong. I didn't have good food and drink like this. I don't know what my last meal might have been. Bread, perhaps. Dirty rainwater. Then his blood was—" She stopped. "You'll see soon enough. When the change began, it was the most horrible and yet most wonderful I've ever experienced. Like childbirth, but you're birthing your own soul. Your body tearing itself apart from the inside to transform you into something new. He broke my neck before I could feel the worst of it. When I awoke, I was something eternal. Then the world was open, and everything was mine."

"That's...intense," Hannah said.

Marcelle put her hand on Bear's. "Why don't you tell her yours?"

"Because I would need to be drunk to think about it," he muttered.

"Do you remember it?" she asked.

"I remember it better than I remember my own children's faces," he retorted. "It's all a blur from back then, except that. I know I had a life before, but it's like that night was my first memory."

Hannah leaned closer. "You never talk about it."

He shrugged and looked around at the expectant faces. "You really want to hear?"

"I want to know all I can about you," Hannah said.

"You two are so cute together it's nauseating," Lochlan muttered.

Rosaline smacked his arm.

"Ow."

"Grow up," the human told him.

"Sorry. Sorry, I'll lay off the beer."

Rosaline ignored him. "Come on, Bear. I really wanna hear this."

"Fine, fine. Since I have an audience." Bear paused. "I don't know what year it was on the modern calendar. But white men hadn't fucked up the continent yet, so make your guesses. We were the Mi'kmaq, and I was a good hunter. I had a wife. Three daughters. Don't ask me their names—I can't remember. But I remember hunting in the forest and realizing for a split second that I was being hunted too. It was like a feeling at the back of my neck, the feeling of being watched. I thought maybe something big was nearby. A mountain lion. Wolves. A bear. No such luck. It was a person but not a person. Cold like snow in winter, red eyes like coals in the middle of a face as empty as ice. Hair like the sun on his head and in a braided beard. Teeth like an animal. He spoke a language I didn't know, but I learned from him later that he'd been impressed by me and that's why he wanted to make me like him. I fought him. Of course, that was useless. He toyed with me like a cat with a mouse. Let me think I had a chance, then stole the chance before he bit me and forced his blood down my throat. He didn't break my neck like Setanta did to you, Marcelle. He made me feel it. I don't know how long, maybe minutes, maybe hours, screaming there on the forest floor, trying to rip out my veins while he watched. You're right about one thing; it does feel like your body is tearing itself apart. Like something primal clawing its way through every shred of muscle and bone. Turning your veins inside out." He smiled. "Yadda, yadda, yadda, long story short, I killed my sire, made a deal to live in New Ulster, I met Hannah, and I'm happy now."

Sarai's mouth felt dry. She knew that Bear hadn't been turned willingly, but to hear him tell such a brutal tale drove home the horror. She was glad he'd killed the man who turned him. It was just even if it would never undo the pain Bear had endured. The thought of being alone in the forest and hunted by a vampire was terrifying.

Hannah got up and threw her arms around Bear. "He

250

shouldn't have done that to you. It's wrong, and you didn't deserve that."

"Hey," he said. "Don't worry. I won't let that happen to you. The Norse, they're weird about their rites of passage and feats of strength. But I wouldn't let you endure that. You won't feel a thing."

They kissed, and Sarai looked down at her soda.

"Do you think you want it?" Lochlan asked Sarai as he came back to his seat. "To be a vampire one day."

Did she? It had crossed her mind more than once. It would rid her of the chronic illness growing in her joints and give her a potential eternity with the people she cared for the most. Yet it was such a massive change and one she could never take back. "I'm not sure. It's a lot to consider. What about you?"

"Mm, yes, I'm curious to know the answer to that," Marcelle said.

Lochlan shook his head. "I don't think I could do it. No offense. I like food. Liquid diet isn't my deal. Plus, getting stuck in my body the way it is now would be literally my worst nightmare."

"You look fine?" Sarai was confused by the distaste on his face.

"Eh," was all he said in reply. "Marcelle knows what I mean."

Oh, he meant he hadn't finished transitioning yet. She felt slow on the uptake for not realizing it sooner.

"I'll ask you again in ten or twenty years," Marcelle teased. "We'll see what you think then when your body is how you want it and you're facing your first gray hairs."

"Shoot your shot, girl, but I don't think the answer's gonna change."

Hannah leaned back against Bear. "I don't think I can eat another bite." She fished in her purse for something and pulled out a small vial of a potion. "I should be sober to do this, right?"

"Doesn't matter either way. But if you'd rather be sober, that's fine," Bear said.

"Perhaps a little tipsy wouldn't be so bad. I find myself fearful."

"I'll take it," Rosaline said. "If you want me to be your source, I shouldn't be getting you more wasted."

Hannah offered it, and Rosaline downed the potion like a shot before instantly coughing on it.

"That is the nastiest taste I've ever put in my mouth." She groaned.

"Yes, it's quite sobering. I haven't much need of it myself, but Tobias back at the coven always has some around, and watching him take a dose is quite entertaining." Amusement sparked in her eyes. She turned to Bear. "Will we be doing this here? Or back at the palace?"

"We can't bring Rosaline back to the palace just now," Bear said. "Lochlan, is it okay if we do this here?"

Lochlan let out a long, slow breath. "Yeah. Yeah, sure, man. I've got a guest bedroom. I just don't want to see it, okay?"

Hannah pulled a small jar from her purse with a slow-moving, thick, red liquid inside. She looked at Bear. "I'm ready."

He scooped her up into his arms like a bride, carried her over the threshold of the guest bedroom, and closed the door behind them. The remaining four sat in silence, waiting. At one point, Sarai was certain she heard something like the faint sound of wood breaking, but no screaming and no calls of pain. She was glad for that. Hannah didn't deserve the cruelty of being allowed to suffer.

After some time, Bear opened the door a crack. "Marcelle, Rosaline. You're up."

"Ready?" Marcelle asked.

"As ready as I'll ever be," Rosaline said. "This is not even a little the kind of threesome I imagined having with Bear."

Lochlan snorted and shook his head.

"Lochlan, why don't you and Sarai go for a walk outside?" Marcelle suggested. "Witches are, well, more enticing. We don't need her getting distracted by your scents."

Lochlan and Sarai put on their coats and made their way outdoors into the night.

"Hey, I had a question for you," Lochlan said.

"Okay. What's up?"

"I know you've got healing magic. Do you think that, I dunno, you could use that to help me somehow? To make my body...right? Right for me, I mean. I was going to wait to ask you after the pregnancy, but I guess it's just on my mind."

"Oh." She blinked. "I, well, I'd love to. I'm not sure where to start with that. Magic surgery isn't my area of expertise. But I could look into it. No promises, though."

He smiled. "That's all I can ask for. Thanks. You know, it really means a lot to me that you'd even be willing to look into it."

They walked a few more steps out into the cold air until he once more broke the silence. "It's wild. Hannah's a vampire, just like that."

"Just like that. Are you doing okay with it?"

"Yeah. It's just going to take some getting used to. I'm okay with vampires now. Working with them's been everything I could have ever wanted in life. With Crispin and Gedeon…" He shut his eyes. "That hit me hard. I didn't realize how used to them I was 'til I saw them… We had a mission in Maine together, you know, just the three of us. We've seen some shit, and they were there for me. I didn't expect to outlive both of them."

Of course. Sarai had only known them in passing, but Lochlan had worked with Crispin every day and had done missions with Gedeon. "I'm sorry," was all she could think to say.

"Thanks. Guess Setanta wants to fill the ranks back up, and Hannah was down for it. It'll be weird to see the before and after. But I'm okay with it." He shook his head. "I never knew her well. It's not like we were buddies back in the Ellis Coven. She was always very involved in everything, always doing things for other people. She was like everyone's grandma but a distant and judgy grandma. I guess it would make sense she'd want some do-over time now that she's old, focus on herself. Still fuckin' weird."

"She was so mad when I said I was marrying Setanta." Sarai laughed. "But yeah, it does feel weird. I'm happy for her, though. She and Bear are a cute couple."

"I guess. Hey, whatever else…it was a killer party, am I right?"

They looked at each other and burst into laughter. Hannah Little Hawk was dead at the hands of her lover Bear. It had indeed been a killer party.

Chapter Twenty-Three

The Pianist

Sarai had expected her birthday celebration to take place in Setanta's rooms, given the restraints already connected to his bed. But she was surprised to be led by her lovers to a new room in the palace she'd never visited before. It was one of the locked bedrooms, which Setanta opened with a key. Inside was decadent debauchery. Sarai had no other word for it.

The walls were black with gold detailing painted on the crown molding and red curtains framing large mirrors that hung on the walls. The furniture consisted of several different padded benches, two different types of person-sized cages, and a bed larger than any she'd ever seen. Chains hung from hooks on the ceiling, as did a sex swing. At the end of the room was a warm, roaring fireplace that illuminated and heated the space and, perhaps more confusingly, a shiny black baby grand piano.

An assortment of impact implements ranging from intense barbed floggers that looked like only a vampire could take their lash to mild, cushioned paddles. Bins were full of various ropes and restraints. One was labeled *silver*.

"Welcome," Setanta purred in her ear. "See anything you like?"

"How did I not know you guys had this yet absolutely I knew you had this?" Sarai joked as she walked into the room. She was glad she'd let Marcelle dress her in a black, lacy babydoll lingerie outfit. Wearing regular pajamas such as an oversized shirt would have been ridiculous.

Marcelle stripped off her outer jacket to reveal a floor-length black skirt with a long slit and a cupless black corset before lounging on the bed, her reflection paralleled by the mirror attached to the ceiling above said bed.

"Wow." Sarai glanced at Setanta wearing black pants and a black button-down shirt. "You're underdressed compared to us, you know. Or maybe overdressed."

"I make it work," he retorted. "We do have something for you. Unrelated to all of this."

"Yeah?" she asked with a raised eyebrow.

"Oh, yes!" Marcelle jumped up from the bed and thrust her hand into a pocket in her skirt. She produced a small jewelry box. "A little birthday present. If it's not to your liking, that's fine. We can come up with a different design together, and we won't have any hard feelings."

Sarai flipped open the box and felt her eyes widen. Inside was a golden ring with a seal depicting a delicate pomegranate in the middle. "Oh wow. This is beautiful."

"I thought you might like to adopt it as your symbol of authority. You need one since you're queen, and we overlooked doing that," Marcelle said. "I noticed pomegranate designs in the henna we did and thought it might make a good ring. But if you want something else, then just consider it a nice birthday gift and we'll design something different."

"It's perfect." Sarai slipped it onto the ring finger of her right hand. It fit comfortably there, as it was made to do. She smiled. "So we're a fleur-de-lis, a pomegranate, and a hound, the three of us together?"

"Not connected symbols on their own, but we wear them well," Setanta said.

"Happy birthday, my love," Marcelle said and kissed Sarai. "The rest of your present should be here soon."

"The rest?"

Marcelle smirked.

"Oh, right. The sexy people." Sarai laughed to hide her nerves. "Who's this couple you invited?"

"Dhana Medina and her wife Amanda Harper," Setanta said. "Dhana's the Duchess of Massachusetts, and Amanda is a human. She used to work as a source, but we paid for her education as part of her arrangement with us, and she's moved on to concert pianist."

"Oh, okay, now I understand the piano." Sarai laughed. "She's going to, what, play mood music for us?"

"Hopefully," Marcelle said. "I've been to two of her concerts; she's wonderful."

"But she's also a mortal from whom it's safe for us to feed," Setanta mused. "Given there will be four vampires and your situation, I thought it might be a good idea."

Sarai raised an eyebrow questioningly. "She's okay with five of us feeding from her? Personally speaking, two is a lot, and that's with my healing factor."

"More than okay," Marcelle said. "She was excited."

Sarai heard the sound of a knock on the door, and Setanta opened it to reveal Temuulen, looking amazing with his leather jacket and knitted black cap.

He grinned when his gaze landed on Setanta. "Everyone can enjoy themselves now; I've arrived." He paused. "Not that you aren't a dream to look at, but where's the birthday girl?"

"Hey." She was nervous but excited to see him and found herself unsure of what to say. Her gaze drifted up to his ski cap, and she chose to break the awkward moment with humor. "Are you seriously going to keep that hat on for this?"

He winced. "Yeah. Trust me, my hairstyle did not age well."

"Now I want to see," Sarai teased.

He sighed. "It's supposed to keep your head from overheating in a helmet, but it's also about your tribe, distinguishes you from other tribes. Indicated your class, that sort of thing. Go to the wrong place with the wrong haircut and someone might try to kill you." He pulled off his cap, and Sarai felt her eyes widen at the shaved parts of the top of his head, reminiscent a little of stereotypical Christian monks if they let the sides and back grow long, but with braided loops to the back and a stripe of a fringe down the front middle part of his head.

"I think only the threat of literal death would convince me to have that hairstyle." Marcelle chuckled.

"Yeah, well, that's what convinced me," Temuulen joked. "It was very fashionable once, you know. Then there was another time period it was forbidden. People used to be weird about hair. But I used to love it."

"It's not so bad," Sarai tried to reassure him. "I mean, it's cultural. That's not a bad thing."

"It is a bad thing when you're trying to blend in with modern society." He put his cap back on as he spoke. "Not all that unlike your hair, then, Marcelle?"

Marcelle rolled her eyes. "All right, that's fair. *Touché*, Temuulen. *Touché*."

New figures appeared in the doorway, capturing Sarai's attention.

"Good evening," said a voice like silk, thick with a Spanish accent.

Sarai gasped a little as a vampire woman with dark skin and a long flowing robe entered the room, a petite pale human girl with pixie-cut blonde hair and red lace lingerie smiling behind her.

The vampire woman wore nothing but the color gold except for a black mini-skirt and tube top under her robe. Even that was covered in intricate golden embroidery of floral designs. Her high-heeled shoes were gold, the body jewelry draped over her shoulders and chest, and the heavy earrings that hung from her ears.

Marcelle rushed forward and pressed her lips to Dhana's first, then to Amanda's. "Come, please. This is my wife, Sarai."

"Hi—" Sarai was cut off as Dhana stepped close and kissed both of her cheeks.

"*Encantada, mi reina*. Oh my," she murmured. "You must invite me back when you're no longer expecting if you'd be permissive of granting me a taste. You smell divine, Sarai."

"Lately I've been the one doing the tasting," Sarai said.

"Really? Intriguing…" Dhana's fangs shot from her mouth, and she pierced the tip of her finger with one before touching it to Sarai's lips as if painting them.

259

"And how is the taste?"

Saffron and orange citrus danced on Sarai's tongue as she licked the liquid, and her gums ached as fangs grew, eager for more.

Dhana's gold-and-black-lined eyes widened. "Fascinating. You seem to have more in common with Setanta now than with my dear Amanda."

"Temporarily," Sarai said. "He says it'll go away once the baby's out. Like gestational diabetes."

"How sweet," Dhana joked. "Then we can share my Amanda tonight."

Sarai looked at Amanda, at her pretty green eyes and...her delicate steel collar with a D-shaped link dangling from the front. Well, that was a quick summation of that relationship.

"You can drink from me as much as you like, my queen." Amanda curtsied.

"Amanda, just who I was looking forward to seeing." Marcelle looped a finger in the collar and pulled Amanda toward the piano where she sat her down at the bench.

The human laughed. "If there's one thing I like about you vampires, it's that you all have an appreciation for live music."

"We do indeed. Are your safe words still the same?" Setanta said as he retrieved a length of red nylon rope. He let it touch against Amanda's skin.

She tensed, biting her lip with visible anticipation. "Cinnamon." Amanda breathed. "Still cinnamon."

"Good. Play something for us while I tie you."

She played a few notes, and Sarai recognized the classical piece. So did the other vampires, as was evident by the way they all burst into laughter.

"Is that Dracula's theme song?" Sarai snickered.

"Toccata and Fugue in D minor, by Johann Sebastian Bach," Amanda boasted and played the next few measures of the song. "Unless anyone has some requests?"

"Mm," Setanta mused as he wove red rope around her legs, tying them to the piano pedals. "How about something iconic in a less gothic manner. Tchaikovsky's Swan Lake, Opus 20a-I, do you know it?"

"The Swan Theme? Of course, Sir."

And so Amanda began the song as Setanta continued to spin the rope and knot it into an elaborate restraint. The music was like magic, and Sarai felt entranced.

"Focus on your notes," Setanta murmured a warning in Amanda's ear. "I'll know if you slip. You don't want to displease me."

"Yes, Sir," she whispered.

Sarai walked forward as if the music beckoned her.

Marcelle smirked a little, got up from the piano bench next to Amanda, and embraced Sarai at the center of the room. "Look at you, so bold. So beautiful. So much more confident than the little witch I once took to my bed. I want you to have fun tonight, *ma petite sorcière*. Everyone here, we're here for you. Anything you want. Blood, pleasure, pain, men, women. Everything and anything you want is yours tonight." She smiled. "Do you want her?"

"Yes," Sarai whispered.

"Then she's yours," Marcelle said, leading Sarai to sit on the piano bench next to Amanda while she went to cuddle on a couch between Dhana and Temuulen.

Sarai watched the pianist's slender fingers work

magic on the ivory piano keys. They were so delicate, the nails trimmed so short. Yet they were so long and elegant, dancing like strange pale spiders across the instrument.

So close, Sarai could smell floral notes from Amanda's shampoo and soap. Lavender. It masked her natural scent a little, so Sarai wasn't sure what her blood might taste like. Yet that gentle pulse in her neck called to her like a siren.

"May I touch you?" Sarai asked.

"However you wish," Amanda replied. "I'm here to serve."

"You are, are you?"

"Oh yes." Her eyes never strayed from their intense focus on the piano. "However you wish."

Sarai blushed as she ran her fingertips up Amanda's arms and across her collarbone, against her neck. "I'm not a demanding type."

"Would you like demands to be made of you?" Setanta asked, flicking the rope around Amanda's waist and the piano bench and pulling it tight.

"Maybe. You know the kind of stuff I like."

"I do." He smirked a little. "Sarai is—let's see if I remember the modern term—a brat."

Amanda snorted but didn't miss a note.

Sarai raised an eyebrow. "Oh, is that what it's called?"

"When you challenge us to dominate you while arguing every step of the way? Yes. Though you have been more compliant and needy in these later pregnancy days," he said. "I wholly approve."

Sarai rolled her eyes and leaned forward a little closer to Amanda and pressed her lips to warm skin.

Blood rushed through Amanda's arteries and veins, beating faster as Sarai kissed her again and again in the sweet spot between her neck and shoulders. She wanted to bite down but was enjoying the music and didn't want to distract.

"That's one note," Setanta chided Amanda and gave a tug on the rope before finishing the harness. "Is my wife too distracting?"

"No, Sir," Amanda whimpered.

"Good. Keep playing for us. And we'll play with you. Do you think you can play through a bite? Or would you prefer to start with a beating?"

"I'd like the biting later, Sir," Amanda said.

"As you wish." He retrieved a pair of easy floggers in his hands, ones with wide and soft leather strips rather than something more barbaric unfit for human flesh.

Sarai eyed them. He'd used similar ones on her a few times, and it wasn't something she considered too intense. The instrument caused a stinging sensation in a pleasant manner and, when done in a light way, felt closer to a massage than a beating.

"Sarai, be a dear and take off her top for me."

Sarai slid her hand up Amanda's back and unlatched the bra so that her bare back was exposed without interrupting her piano playing.

"And now your own."

Sarai looked up, her face flushing with heat as she blushed but agreed. She pulled off her top and dropped it to the floor next to the piano bench before sitting there, straight-backed and waiting for what she wanted in only her black lace panties.

With one flogger in each hand, Setanta spent the rest of the song hitting both women. It was done just right as usual. Sarai closed her eyes, moaning into the sensations and resting a hand on Amanda's bound thigh as they both endured together.

"You can hit me harder, you know," Sarai said as the song ended.

"I will most certainly not," Setanta retorted. "Not tonight. Another night when your situation is less delicate."

"What, you don't want to beat a pregnant lady? Coward," she taunted him.

Temuulen and Dhana burst into laughter, while Marcelle smirked.

"My goodness, are you going to let her get away with that?" Dhana snickered.

"Of course not." Setanta grabbed Sarai's hair in a fist and twisted it as he pulled her up to her feet, causing her to gasp. "The little queen wants attention, and I think we have enough skill here tonight to satisfy her. Would you like to be thrown to the wolves tonight, Sarai? There are three vicious vampires watching and waiting for you."

She whimpered.

He grinned and dragged her over to the three, all of whom had irises flushed crimson. "I warmed her up for you. Go on, have your fun. I have a pianist to untie." He pushed her at them.

Temuulen caught her, nuzzling against her hair. "It will be my pleasure," he murmured and pulled her to straddle him as he sat back on the couch.

She felt a half-hard erection pressing up against her through his leather pants and rotated her hips, wanting to coax it into further growth.

A cold hand slid down Sarai's side, belonging to

Dhana.

"We might not be biting you tonight," she whispered in Sarai's ear, causing chills to run up and down her spine. "But we will drown you in so much pleasure you'll beg us to stop."

"And fangs or no fangs, I will be penetrating you." Temuulen grabbed her hips and held her down tight against him as he thrust up against her to punctuate his words. His hands were strong as stone, completely immovable.

She tried to pull away, grinning as she found herself unable to. "Stop talking about it and do it, then. Just watch out for my knees; they're a little weak."

"That's my good little witch," Marcelle chided. "So impatient." She slipped a hand between Sarai's legs. "So wet. You've soaked your panties. I love it."

Sarai's face burned. "Do something about it."

Marcelle tore the panties from Sarai's body, causing her to yelp. Then she stuffed the panties into Sarai's mouth so that she could taste herself on them.

"Oh, I was going to use that mouth." Dhana sighed.

"You still can. Patience," Marcelle teased. "I have some very fun ideas for tonight." She glanced over at Setanta, who had now finished untying Amanda. "To the bed?"

Chapter Twenty-Four

Bloody Hedonism

Sarai was brought face-to-face with a now naked Amanda on the massive bed. Setanta and Dhana held one of each of her arms, while Marcelle and Temuulen held Sarai in place.

"Two toys to play with," Dhana said. "We are spoiled tonight, aren't we, my pet?"

"Yes, Mistress," Amanda said.

"Let's have you serve your queen," Marcelle recommended and helped Sarai to lean back while Temuulen held one of her legs to spread them apart.

Dhana pushed a very happy Amanda down. Sarai couldn't see her over her pregnant form but gasped when she felt a talented warm tongue trail up her slick sex before stopping at that delightful button of pleasure and swirling, sucking, kissing, and teasing it with her mouth.

Sarai gripped Marcelle's hand, but the vampire just smiled and pulled away so that Dhana could take her place. "Are you enjoying my wife?" she purred, then leaned down to pull the panties out of Sarai's mouth and give her a demanding, needful kiss. Sarai's tongue flicked against fangs, careful not to cut herself, making the vampire moan before she pulled away and began to take off what little clothes she wore, but not her gold jewelry. "Do you think you can focus on two women at once?"

"We can find out." Sarai breathed. "Just don't leave me on my back for too long."

Dhana grinned, showing off her fangs as she pushed Sarai all the way back onto the bed and stood over her. She was stunning. Pink and lovely and…glinting with a gold stud on the hood of her clitoris.

"I didn't know vampires could get piercings," Sarai said.

"It was quite painful," Dhana mused. "I had to silver myself to be able to apply it. If I remove the gold, then it heals, and I need to pierce it all over again. Do you like it?"

"It's beautiful." Though not beautiful enough that Sarai would ever consider enduring such an intimate pain herself. Still, she couldn't deny the entertainment value when she sucked it into her mouth and played with it using her tongue. She liked the way the hard gold contrasted against the soft and sweet flesh, the way it felt to toy with. Dhana groaned in clear pleasure, squeezing Sarai's head between her thighs. The realization occurred to Sarai at that moment that the vampire woman could crush her skull with her thighs as easily as squishing a grape. But since Dhana had a human wife who was still in one piece, she put the thought out of her mind.

Amanda's warm mouth was gone, and Sarai looked up at Dhana pitifully, trying to communicate with her eyes that she wanted more, that she hadn't reached a climax yet, but the vampire was apparently too busy enjoying herself to care. Luckily, someone else had noticed enough to slide cold fingers inside her. She groaned against Dhana as they curled, and tried to figure out whose they were. Marcelle's were smaller, more slender and familiar. Setanta was warmer. It had to be Temuulen.

Yes, she thought, moaning louder as he moved slowly and steadily to caress her insides.

"You are so warm," he murmured.

"Has it been a while since you've slept with a mortal?" Marcelle asked.

"A bit, yes. I still remember how, don't worry. I won't break her."

"I should hope not," Setanta told him, and Sarai heard a gasp from Temuulen, though she couldn't see what had caused it as Setanta continued to speak. "Anything you do to her, I might have to do to you."

"Promises, promises," Temuulen said.

Sarai looked up at the mirror in its gold frame on the ceiling and watched, transfixed, as he pulled his fingers from Sarai and Setanta licked them clean of their smokey coating of arousal. Fangs elongated in Setanta's mouth, and he scratched open the length of Temuulen's finger. The made vampire exhaled sharply from the pain as Setanta's tongue ran the length of the wound to catch the blood.

"You can keep pleasuring my wife, you know. You have two hands. Just because I'm feeding from one doesn't mean the other should be idle," Setanta told him. "She's empty. Fill her."

Immediately, Sarai had the satisfaction of fingers inside her again, this time more aggressive as they rocked back and forth against her, as if Setanta feeding were fueling Temuulen's movements, which in turn fueled Sarai's oral movements and Dhana's pleasured moans. All the while, Marcelle held Amanda close, running her hands over the human's body and scratching at her pear-shaped curves with her fingernails. She didn't draw blood, but red lines rose to the surface of Amanda's pale skin.

"I adore you, Sarai, but I must admit it is nice to practice my art on a canvas that doesn't heal the way you do. You, sweet Amanda, are going to go home bruised and battered. Marks from everyone's mouths are going to be carved all over that pretty skin," Marcelle reassured Amanda, who giggled, then yelped in response to a loud smack.

"I think Sarai's ready for more," Temuulen said. "Amanda, sweetheart, mind sparing a few drops so I can give the queen proper attention?"

Amanda held out her arm, and Temuulen bit down. The human didn't flinch but moaned in pleasure. After he'd drunk enough of her blood and Marcelle tended to healing her, Temuulen turned his attention back to Sarai.

"Let's switch this up a little," he told Dhana. "You sit over there so I can put her on her hands and knees. I think that'll be an easier position for her in her condition."

"Mm, as long as she keeps going, I don't care," Dhana replied and stood up, allowing Sarai to gasp for air, the lower half of her face drenched. Sarai found herself flipped over by Temuulen. One of the vampires pushed a pillow under her, and her hair was grabbed by Dhana so she could be pushed back to tongue that pretty golden stud. She tried to focus on doing well for the vampire woman, but Temuulen spreading her legs by parting them with a swift kick from his knee made focusing an increasingly more difficult task for her. She could hear his belt buckle being undone and the click of metal, and the thud of it being discarded to the floor followed by his pants and top served to heighten her need.

Sarai glanced back, wanting a look at him naked. He had a slightly stocky build in a muscular way. The half-hard erection from before had grown to full length, to Sarai's delight. Amanda's blood had taken an immediate effect as it flowed through him.

He grinned as he caught her gaze and stroked himself as she watched. "You look good on all fours." He reached forward, grabbed her hair, and pulled her into an arch as he slowly speared her body with his.

Sarai gasped as he parted her lips and pressed forward, stretching her in the most pleasurable way. It was different from the way Setanta felt. Setanta's body had a living, if reduced, warmth. Temuulen had no warmth. He was hard, cold, and thick, like a rounded icicle penetrating her warmth without melting, and the cold heightened her to new sensations and sensitivity.

Sarai longed to see the expression on his face as he groaned, but couldn't from where she was. She turned her head and caught sight of them on the ceiling, in the large mirror. It was beautiful and more erotic an image than anything she could have imagined. She could see a perfect view from above of Dhana's firm breasts, of Temuulen entering her from behind. Of her back that made her look almost slender from the angle. Of Marcelle teasing Amanda. And...of Setanta's hand sliding down Temuulen's lower back, a bottle of lubricant put to the side near him. Temuulen thrust forward, hard, causing Sarai to cry out, as Setanta's hand disappeared below him.

"Do you like the show up there?" Dhana teased,

meeting her gaze in their reflections.

Setanta looked up at them as well and grinned, giving Sarai a wink as he began to unbutton his shirt with his free hand, revealing his many blue tattoos and lean, muscular chest. "How strong are you, Temuulen?" He unbuckled his belt, which soon clinked against Temuulen's on the floor. "Are you warm enough yet for me?"

"I'm strong enough to take whatever you can do to me."

"You may regret that."

"Oh, I've no doubt. Just remember I'm connected to your very mortal wife, so take some care."

Temuulen thrust forward again, hard, and Sarai cried out, twisting her fingers in the bedsheets under her.

Setanta chuckled. "Of course. I'll start gently for the mortal's sake." He removed his fingers, cleaned his hand on a nearby washcloth, then gripped Temuulen's hips.

As he pushed forward, Sarai felt Temuulen push forward, and both of them moaned in response to Setanta's movements as Sarai's twisting fingers now threatened to tear holes in the bedsheets.

"You take it well." Setanta breathed. "But I want more. I will have more."

Setanta bared his teeth and bit down into Temuulen's neck, causing the man to shout as he was penetrated in two ways, his member throbbing and swelling inside of Sarai in response, in turn causing her to gasp.

The unison thrusting from both became more intense, faster. Then too fast. Sarai was afraid she might be pressed down through the bed, that they might break it with the force they were using. Yet she knew how restrained it was for them. How much more violent they could be. For a moment, she wanted to be turned. Wanted to be a vampire like them so she could feel the true intensity of everything they could offer her. But she couldn't voice any of it. She could only cry out in pleasure again and again.

"Have you had enough looking?" Dhana said. "I'm feeling neglected."

Sarai whimpered and looked back at the vampire woman's spread legs. Temuulen gripped her by the hair and forced her to arch her back once more. She gasped.

"Did you stop just because we distracted you?" he managed to growl. "No one told you to stop. Get back down there."

Sarai didn't have a chance to respond before he pushed her head back down, holding her trapped in place between his thrusts and Dhana's sex.

Sarai was nearing tears from the intensity and eagerly allowed her mouth to be used, plunging her tongue between the vampire's labia, licking up and teasing the pierced source of pleasure again.

"You're so close," Dhana coaxed. "Just right there, keep playing with it just like that."

The sensations were building for everyone, it seemed. The first was Dhana as she threw back her head and shrieked, her body seizing with pleasure. Clear liquid gushed from her to soak Sarai's chin and drench a puddle under the vampire's hips. Sarai blinked. She'd never seen a woman's orgasm quite like that before, but she liked it.

The intensity of Dhana's orgasm triggered some deep need inside Sarai, and she found the desire building, clenching and tensing around the intrusion inside her until bursting. She cried out, convulsing with pleasure of her own against the borderline violent fucking from Temuulen and Setanta.

"Should I let you?" Setanta asked Temuulen.

"I can recharge and go again with another bite of Amanda, if you want that." He gasped. "I'm close."

"Don't you *fucking* dare. Not yet," Setanta snarled.

Sarai recognized the tone of his voice. It was a magical compulsion. Temuulen groaned but was forced to obey. Sarai felt so sensitive after her orgasm that tears flowed from her eyes. She wanted to lie down and breathe. And yet it didn't stop. Everything was intense pleasure, more and more and more.

"Please," she found herself begging. But what exactly she was begging for, she wasn't even sure. More, less? Pleasure was pain, pain was pleasure. Her body was limp.

"You have permission, Temuulen. Come for me now," Setanta ordered, forcing the orgasm with his compulsion.

Temuulen's fingers dug into Sarai's hip bones, so hard she feared he would fracture them, and he grunted as liquid burst inside her body. It set her off again, though less intense than the previous climax, and left her gasping on the bed, shaking.

As she lay there, she remembered what he'd told her the night of her wedding, about undead vampire men. Her sex tingled just as he'd promised, as if he'd shot her full of sexual stimulants. She moaned and closed her eyes, touching herself with her hand and bringing her dark-red fingertip to her lips. It tasted like him, and she craved him. She wanted his essence in her core as deep as it could get, wanted it dripping down her thighs, throat, and chin in red streams that made her fangs hurt with want.

But Sarai wasn't the only one who wanted a taste. Amanda leaned forward with her gaze transfixed between Sarai's legs. "May I?"

"You may," Setanta said. He gripped Sarai's leg and lifted it up as she lay on her side, resting it on his shoulder while he cleaned himself off. Amanda's warm mouth was once more attending to her, licking Sarai's body clean starting with her thighs and up to her sex. It was almost relaxing compared to before, and the pleasure rolled on, though less intense than before. The focus was less on building pleasure and more on the slow sensations. It led to an orgasm that felt like a true release, one that let her lay and twitch and surrender completely.

When Amanda finished, Marcelle pulled her away from Sarai and kissed her, licking her lips clean. "Not too much now," she teased.

"It makes me feel like the world is spinning in both directions at the same time. It's so good," the human whined.

"Amanda." Setanta offered her a hand. "Do you feel strong enough for more?"

She giggled and took his hand, letting him pull her close as the other three vampires closed in around her. "I feel great."

"How many fangs do you want to take?"

Sarai's heart skipped a beat. Yes. That was what she wanted after her ravaging and her orgasms. She wanted an energy boost. She wanted human blood. She sat up to join the circling vampires, fangs as natural in her mouth as her other teeth. She had embraced the bloodlust.

Amanda looked around her, the rise and fall of her

chest increasing as she breathed heavier in what could only be aroused anticipation. "I can take it," she whispered. "Do anything you want to me."

Marcelle made room for Sarai at Amanda's back where they each had access to one side of her neck. Temuulen took one of her wrists while Dhana took another.

"My little pet," Dhana purred. "This is going to bring you quite close to death. But you're safe. I have you. We'll bring you to the brink and nothing more."

"Thank you, Mistress." Amanda's body began to tremble as she spoke those words.

"Sarai," Marcelle said. "You'll use your healing abilities when we stop. No one give her more blood. We don't need her turning."

Setanta pulled her legs apart and kissed her inner thigh, then slid a finger inside her, slow and steady, causing her to whimper. "Ready?"

She bit her lip. "Could you…"

He grinned. "Ask for what you want." He thrust his hand harder against her, and she yelped.

"Please fuck me," she whimpered. "Fuck me and bite me."

He licked his fingers, then gripped her thighs to force them apart. "Marcelle, Sarai? Hold her for me."

The two obeyed, each taking hold of one of Amanda's legs to keep them spread. He thrust forward, causing her to cry out. Her mortal, weak body arched and trembled, and Sarai felt such a lust in her at the sight.

Setanta pulled out, then thrust forward until he filled her with every inch he could offer, holding himself there as he looked down at Amanda, his fangs exposed. "Drink your fill of her," he told all present.

The vampires struck like vipers, and Sarai along with them. The human screamed but held still, allowing them to drink. Amanda's skin on her thigh punctured like the peel of a nectarine, and her blood was just as sweet. It felt like hot honey as it gushed down Sarai's throat, a flavor she knew to be pure pleasure caused by the endorphins flooding Amanda's system.

As they drank, her body rocked with slight movements, and her vocalizations betrayed her experience. Setanta's thrusts worked their skill, and Amanda was soon shouting, her body jolting with each wave of her climax. It was heaven in her bloodstream. But Sarai could feel the pulse in the blood begin to struggle, to slow. Amanda was dying.

Though she wanted more of the amazing flavor, Sarai along with the other vampires all released their bites. Blood trickled from assorted sets of bite marks and down Sarai's chin. She noticed everyone but her had managed neat bites without making a mess of themselves. The poor human's eyes fluttered, and she seemed close to unconscious as she looked around at the vampires and witch surrounding her.

"Sarai, use your healing gift," Marcelle instructed.

Sarai complied, flooding Amanda with golden healing light. The wounds closed, and she stirred.

"Cinnamon. I think I'm done," she whispered, her voice hoarse.

Dhana scooped her up in her arms and cuddled against her at the side of the bed against the wall. "Rest well. You've more than earned it. I'm so proud of how well you did."

Setanta looked over to Marcelle. "Did you want attention?" He offered her his hand, and she licked his fingers of Amanda's nectar.

"Mm, maybe just a quick orgasm," she said with a grin. "If you order it."

Setanta smirked. "Embrace bliss. Three times."

With the code words to her long-standing compulsion spoken, Marcelle fell to the bed, undulating in pleasure as she gripped the bedsheets. Her eyes rolled back as the first orgasm rolled into a second, then a third. "*Je t'aime, je t'aime, je t'aime*," the French vampire cried again and again as Setanta's magic forced her to endure.

"Damn," Temuulen murmured. "I would have come to the palace years ago if I knew compulsion extended to pleasure. It seems, though, my king, that everyone's had their moment except for you." He looked pointedly at the erection standing tall between Setanta's legs. "Honestly, man to man, I'm impressed you waited this long for all of us."

"I am a master of control," Setanta flirted. He looked around at his options, then beckoned to Sarai and Temuulen to join him as he leaned back on pillows. "Together, then. Mind your fangs."

Eager to please her husband but too nervous about scratching him with her fangs, Sarai used only her tongue up and down his length to taste Amanda's flavor on him, then below to lick the source of her child. Temuulen mirrored her on the other side, then when she went below, he retracted his fangs and took the full length down his throat with the practice of experience.

"Very good, you two," Setanta praised. "Keep going."

Sarai was happy to let Temuulen be the primary source of pleasure, and he seemed happy with it as well.

Their tongues worked in tandem, their mouths open and giving.

"Kiss the hound," Setanta murmured, tapping the tattoo inked into his abdomen just above his member, and Temuulen complied. He took the entire length, every inch so that his lips were pressed to the base of Setanta's body, to the hound tattoo. Setanta held Temuulen's head in place as he released into the man's throat with a groan.

"I think I like having you around, Temuulen." Setanta sighed. "The pair of you make a wonderful team."

Sarai couldn't resist a grin, to reveal her still extended fangs, which caught Setanta's gaze.

"Do you need more blood?" he asked.

Temuulen started to pull away, but Setanta held him in place, causing him to grunt.

"Maybe. Amanda was running a bit dry, and you let Temuulen get the good stuff. I'm still thirsty."

"Then come here, Sarai. Would you like to share him with me?" Setanta asked.

Sarai nodded as she rolled over, and Temuulen was released from the king's hand.

"Slowly," Setanta instructed. "Don't spill."

Temuulen's mouth and tongue caught every drop as he pulled free.

Sarai's throat felt dry as she stared at Temuulen there on his knees, remembering the taste she'd taken from him already. How refreshing he was. Sarai craved more.

"Do it." Temuulen pulled his hair back away from his neck as he spoke. "I'm strong enough. I can take you both."

"I have no doubt you can." Setanta pulled him up

close and beckoned Sarai forward.

But she hesitated. Self-consciousness burned in her cheeks. "I'm not as good at it as you. I'll make a mess."

"Then let's make a mess of him. Together."

Setanta bit down into Temuulen's neck, making no effort to be neat about his attack. Dark-red blood like violent rubies dripped down flesh as Temuulen groaned. Sarai couldn't resist. She was overwhelmed by the bone-deep exhaustion in her from so much activity, and that exhaustion had her craving what he had.

Setanta pulled his teeth free and tapped the opposite side of his victim's neck with two fingers. "Right here."

Sarai bit down as Temuulen groaned then screamed when Setanta bit him a second time. It was perfect. Cool, savory, sweet. Basil and mint. She sucked at the wound until Temuulen felt limp against them both, then pulled out her teeth to see Setanta watching her intently, his mouth red.

"What?" she asked.

"You are an exquisite beauty. My vampiric witch queen." He leaned forward and kissed her, the taste of blood fresh on his tongue. He felt so warm compared to Temuulen.

When they parted, Sarai looked down at Temuulen between them and let healing magic flow from her hands into his body, for which he murmured a thanks.

"Happy birthday, Sarai," Setanta said. "And may we have many, many more celebrated in such hedonistic pleasure."

Chapter Twenty-Five

Restrained

Sarai was glad they'd had the enjoyment first before sending someone to bring Jackie to the sex dungeon. It was like a pressure release and a confidence booster at once, both of which she needed to mentally handle a Vasi spy.

They all had a quick shower and bid farewell to Dhana and Amanda for the night since they were not needed for the interrogation. The pair promised to meet up again in the future for further enjoyment. Temuulen was allowed to stay as he was a knight, and everyone put their clothes or new untorn clothes back on before Jackie arrived, as if to reset the room.

"This is pretty devious," Temuulen told Sarai. "This whole reverse honeypot scheme. You came up with it?"

"Yeah." She sighed. "I feel a little bad." And it was true. She hoped that once the tooth problem was gone, Jackie could be convinced to change sides. Or perhaps she would even consider them saviors from the suicidal explosion implanted in her mouth.

Temuulen scoffed. "Don't. She'd do the same to you or worse."

"Maybe. That doesn't make it feel good."

Sarai heard the sound of a knock on the door, and Setanta opened it. Jackie stood there, wearing tight leggings and a shirt that a lacy bra peeked out from under at the cleavage. The smile on her face faltered when she looked up at Setanta.

"Good evening." He held the door open wider as he spoke. "Please, come in."

She did, and he closed the door behind her.

Jackie looked around the room, a falter in her forced smile. "Wow. This place, wow. Luxury in a sex dungeon. I guess that makes sense for you guys."

Sarai took a deep breath, then walked up to Jackie and kissed her as convincingly as she could. "I'm so glad you could make it." She ran her hands over Jackie's waist, then up her body and down her arms. Her grip encircled Jackie's wrists. As close as she was, she noticed something about Jackie's scent. It was...off. Sarai couldn't put her finger on what was off about it, but it had changed. Sarai didn't trust it, but she kept a smile on her face. "Nervous?" she teased.

"A little, to be honest." Jackie's gaze darted back to the others in the room. "But I want to do this. And I...I want it to get intense, you know?"

"I want that too." Sarai was hyper aware of all the vampires watching them, giving them space. It was space for Sarai to take charge, to manipulate Jackie to where they needed her to be. "I'd really like to show you what I like."

"Hey, if it's anything like our fountain date, I'm down." Jackie grinned. "I had so much fun with that."

Sarai took a few deep breaths. She didn't want to drag this out more. She needed to get it done. "Are restraints still okay?" She walked Jackie back toward a pair of shackles that hung from the ceiling as she asked her question.

Jackie nodded. A wave of bitterness rolled off her, a scent Sarai now knew was fear. She felt guilty but didn't let up. Didn't show that she knew.

Marcelle darted forward and smoothed her cool hands down Jackie's arms from behind.

Jackie yelped a little but held still. "You don't waste any time, do you?" she whispered.

"No time at all," Marcelle purred. "And I so love watching Sarai with you. We're all very excited to get to know you like this. Be a dear and put your wrists in the cuffs for us. Then we can discuss our play session."

Sarai found it funny Marcelle worded it that way. When they'd had their first sessions and when Sarai had first slept with Marcelle and Setanta together, they'd had a thorough discussion of what would happen well before they started anything. If it was a real play session, all the talking would have happened already. But Jackie couldn't know that because Sarai hadn't told her.

Jackie did as she was told. She put her hands into the shackles, which Marcelle locked into place. Sarai tried to breathe regularly. It was working. They had her in place. She hoped Jackie didn't realize that the shackles she'd been locked into were different from most of the other restraints in the room, which included buckles and latches, or safety implements that a bottom could release on their own if they wanted to. No, Jackie didn't have those. She was chained for real.

Marcelle trailed a finger up Jackie's spine, then gripped her short hair and tugged her head back as the girl arched.

Setanta put a hand on Sarai's shoulder, and she looked up at him. For some reason, the steel in his red eyes made her want to cry. The fun was over. This was real now and time to let the vampires take over. Sarai nodded and stepped back, allowing Setanta to take her place in front of Jackie. His hand moved over Jackie's throat, up to her lips, and he pushed a finger into her mouth. It was such a sensual act, but Sarai knew better.

"You don't like men," Setanta noted. "You're a lesbian. I can read it from your body language. Or at the very least, you don't care for me or Temuulen. When I touch you, all I see is fear. Yet you give in to Marcelle and Sarai's touch. It's almost impressive how you've worked past your repulsion for us to be here. Yet despite having no attraction to myself or Temuulen, I think you hope that we'll bite you. That *I'll* bite you and drink your blood. It is sensual. Intimate. Is that what you want, to share your blood with all of us here?"

Jackie looked up at him, unable to speak with his finger in her mouth, so just nodded.

Then he gripped her mouth, forcing it open as he revealed a pair of pliers in his other hand. Jackie's eyes widened, but it was too late. With a deft move too fast to see, Setanta yanked the blackened tooth from the back of Jackie's mouth, causing her to shriek from the pain and blood to drip from her mouth. He tossed the tooth into the corner where it promptly exploded and left a hole in the wall the size of a grapefruit. Sarai breathed a sigh of relief. Jackie wouldn't die. At least, she wouldn't kill herself.

"Did you think that you could come to my palace, kill my knights, seduce my queen, and poison my sources...and I wouldn't know it was you?" Setanta hissed. "Did you think you could come to my wife's birthday celebration with poisoned blood and I wouldn't notice?"

283

That strange scent Sarai had noticed, of course. Jackie as a Vasi would use the opportunity to try and poison the king. It made her feel cold as she realized that perhaps it wasn't just the king who was the target.

"Were you trying to poison my baby?" Sarai blurted.

"I—" Jackie looked at Sarai, confusion in her eyes. "Him. I had a shot at poisoning him. The baby wasn't even on my radar. Sarai, he's a monster. Don't you understand? Help me; you know he's a monster. Remember when you came running to me because he terrified you? Because of what he's done in the past? He's a *monster*. Sarai, please…"

Sarai took a step back, shaking her head. Sure, Setanta was a monster. But he was *her* monster and Marcelle's monster, and Sarai wasn't going anywhere.

"It wouldn't have worked," Setanta informed her. "I've long taken precautions against any possible poisons that work against vampires or witches. The protections are tattooed into my flesh. You would have accomplished nothing other than harming my unborn child if Sarai had bitten you. Though I suspect you would have counted that as a success."

Jackie looked back at Setanta, at the blue ink at his barely exposed collarbone, and slumped in her chains, defeated. "Go ahead, then." She trembled as she spoke, blood and spittle dripping from her mouth. "Torture me all you want; I'm not telling you a damn thing."

Sarai was hurt to hear the girl say such a thing, despite everything. She couldn't help but think of what Jackie had said on their date. She was trapped in a bad situation. Sarai wasn't sure about her conflicted feelings wanting to rescue Jackie from herself and the Vasi, but she did know she didn't have the stomach to see her be tortured by Setanta. And she wasn't sure whether he would or wouldn't resort to such a thing. Better to talk Jackie into cooperation.

"Jackie," Sarai said softly as she took a step forward and gently touched her cheek, using her thumb to wipe away blood that dripped from her wounded mouth. "Please. It's okay. You don't need to work with the Vasi. Everything you said to me, it didn't seem like you want this."

"What I want doesn't matter," Jackie snapped in an aggressive tone Sarai hadn't expected and yanked her head away from Sarai's touch. "Fuck. I can't believe you flipped the script on me and I just went along with it. I'm a fucking idiot."

"You're not," Sarai said. "I did like you. Do like you. Maybe it was this whole weird craving thing that started it, but it got to be more than that. I didn't want this to happen. I want you to be real. I didn't want it to be you. We can help you here, Jackie. I can help you if you let me."

Jackie's expression softened. "I wasn't acting for you, Sarai. You should have run away with me." She looked back up at Setanta with a brave expression on her face despite her eyes giving away how frightened she was. "Are you going to get on with it?"

"With torture?" Setanta mused. "In my room of pleasure? I suppose that's what you're expecting. Yes, I have tortured mortals before. I've crushed limbs beneath my feet, pulled nails from their beds, branded their flesh with hot iron, and stripped humans of their skin. Then I've had them healed and started all over again."

Sarai tried very hard not to focus on the fact that his statement was entirely truthful.

"And I won't lie," he continued. "It would give me great pleasure to torture you, Jacqueline. Fortunately for you, I long ago learned torture is a tool for the incompetent and often yields poor results. You would tell me anything you think I might like to hear regardless of the truth just to make the pain stop. Or perhaps I would break your mind into useless madness before you spilled your secrets. So no, I will not torture you."

Jackie looked confused. "Then why haven't you just killed me? I'm not telling you anything."

"You will. And you will do it one of two ways. You expect to die here tonight, I assume?"

Jackie looked down at her feet, then nodded.

"That depends on you. If the crimes you committed had been done by one of my citizens, your execution would be guaranteed. But you are not a citizen. You are an enemy combatant. And I must admit a competent one to have made it this far. Few have." He leaned forward and gripped her chin to force her to look at him. "Well done. You've impressed me."

Jackie gulped, and Sarai did not envy her position. The look in Setanta's merciless eyes made it clear that impressing him was not a good thing.

"Then what happens now?" Jackie asked, her voice cracking.

"You have the opportunity to tell us the truth. Everything about the Vasi. Everything about how you managed to accomplish so much. In exchange, I will grant you your life and your freedom."

Jackie stared at him, clear confusion on her face. "And if I don't?"

"Then I will force you to drink my blood."

Terror permeated the room, and not all of it Jackie's.

286

Sarai was shocked. It had to be a bluff. She vaguely remembered a vampire law against turning the explicitly unwilling, and Setanta was nothing if not lawful. Still, perhaps he meant it. If some clause for exceptions existed in the codex of vampire law, Sarai didn't doubt he would use it.

"Your blood?" Jackie whispered.

"Yes. You will become undead under my complete control. I will order you to tell me everything, and you will obey whether you wish to or not. And only when I have every shred of truth from your lips will I grant you a proper death and turn you to dust rather than let you continue to exist. Vampires turned against their will make for poor additions to a kingdom, and I do not wish to claim you for eternity." He stepped behind her and held her head tightly with one hand while he bit into the opposite wrist and held it close to her lips as she stared in horror. "Make your choice, Jacqueline. The truth and your freedom, or the truth and your death. Either choice you make, I *will* win."

"How do you know I won't just run back to the Vasi when you let me go?"

"You can try. But you'll be branded a traitor. And I mean that literally. Your smartest move will be to start over fresh as a mere human. Not a hunter. I think that's a fair exchange. Now make your choice before I make it for you." He held the blood closer to her, so close that it touched her cheek. "Freedom or vampirism?"

"Freedom!" she blurted. "I'll tell you how I did it if you swear you'll let me go, human and alive."

"I swear." He released her to hang in her chains as his wrist healed, then he offered the wound to Marcelle, who licked the blood. "And whatever else I may be, I am a man of my word. Now. Speak."

Jackie nodded. "I'm...Artemisia's handler."

Marcelle straightened. "Handler? What do you mean?"

"She signed a contract when she was captured. She's been under orders for months, almost a year, but we only now had the opportunity to get me into the palace to give her orders."

Sarai felt cold. "Oh fuck," she whispered in horror. "She was there when you rescued me right at the beginning. She was with the Vasi."

"We've had her erasing memories of anyone who might get close to the truth. Getting information from you, Marcelle, and erasing your memory of it," Jackie explained. "We've forbidden her from talking to her brother. She got me in as a source but waited until now to not be suspicious. We knew about Sarai's blood. When we had her, the doctor who tested her managed to make some phone calls before you bastards blew the place up. When I got here...she made it so easy 'cause she liked me. I just got her to sit on a sewing needle, and I had a blood sample. Artemisia made the poison with witchcraft. It was supposed to turn them human. Just break the curse, free them from you. But..."

"Artemisia has never been good at witchcraft," Setanta murmured. He looked up at the vampires present. "I compel you all to never again be forced to obey an order from Artemisia. Any previous compulsions from her are void. You are to heed my voice first as the firstborn and elder vampire of your bloodline, and never again hers. You are free."

Marcelle stumbled and held her head. "She's been using me this whole time. I remember... She's been making me report to her. She cries about it sometimes. That poor girl. And she's not alone, is she?"

"We recruited her mother," Jackie admitted. "Without a contract, she's too sly for that I guess. She's helping plenty without one, though. She's been giving us information about the palace. Layouts, information about the protective enchantments. That kind of stuff."

"Even Giovanna would not be as daft as to work with Vasi. Her own family would execute her for it," Setanta snapped. "Why?"

"Because we promised her daughter back. She knows we own Artemisia's contract. We let Artemisia tell her just before she got banished."

"Then she knows they're unbreakable," he said.

"Almost unbreakable," Marcelle murmured. "We can kill her and resuscitate her, and it satisfies the contract, freeing her. That's how we've been freeing the witches we've found. Though I'm not sure how well that will work on a pureblood vampire."

Setanta looked relieved to hear that reminder. "Yes. We can try that." His eyes narrowed as he looked at Jackie. "Does she have a sigil in her mouth like you did?"

Jackie nodded.

"Fuck," Sarai whispered. "What the fuck, you put a suicide sigil in a child's mouth?"

"She's not a child. She's a goddamn vampire that looks like a child," Jackie snapped.

"She's a child," Setanta hissed. "Her mind matches her body. She may be thirty years old, but she *is* a child."

Jackie guiltily looked at the floor, but Setanta was having none of it. He grabbed her face again and forced her to look up at him. "She's bound to obey your orders, yes?"

Jackie nodded as much as she could with his death grip on her chin.

"Then you are going to go to her and command her not to activate the sigil. If you do not, I will kill you. Have I made myself clear?"

Jackie nodded.

Marcelle and Sarai put on robes to cover their sex dungeon attire while Temuulen unlatched Jackie's shackles so that he could fasten them behind her back. They marched her to Artemisia's room, Jackie led along as their prisoner, still bleeding from her mouth. Sarai wondered if she should have healed the wound. She could do it easily. But she didn't. Instead, she just watched Marcelle half drag, half push Jackie forward up the stairs and to the princess's room in silence.

The inside looked like a gothic dollhouse, exactly the sort of room Sarai would have expected for a spoiled princess. A whole wall of fancy porcelain dolls, comfortable pillows strewn all about, and a four-poster bed draped with dark pink and black curtains made up the most prominent décor and furniture in the room.

Artemisia stood at attention when she saw Setanta, her eyes flickering between him and Jackie.

"Artemisia," Jackie said. "Don't activate the sigil here."

Artemisia's eyes widened with an expression of hope, and she smiled. "They figured it out," she whispered.

"We're going to help you, *mo dheirfiúr*," Setanta said. "No one blames you for this."

"The half-full glass is broken," Jackie blurted out.

The hope drained from Artemisia's expression, and Sarai saw something dead in her eyes. The same lifeless, hopeless expression she'd seen before in Vasi witch slaves, in the dragon shifter. Wings burst from Artemisia's back, shredding that part of her dress so that it hung like a halter top from her body. She turned on her heel, leapt to the balcony, and flew into the night.

"Don't follow her," Jackie said as Setanta pushed her aside to do exactly that.

"Why?" he growled.

"Because it'll activate the sigil if you catch her."

"Where is she going?"

"A rendezvous."

"Where."

"I don't know. That wasn't determined by me. I have no idea where."

Setanta stood there, shaking.

"Temuulen, with me," Marcelle snapped. "We're going after her."

"You won't be able to. She's faster than you," Setanta said.

Sarai felt cold at the hatred she saw in his eyes as he looked at Jackie.

"You no longer amuse me."

In that moment, she knew he was about to kill Jackie, and she didn't know how she felt about that. Jackie had more than earned it. She'd sent off Artemisia to some other Vasi to continue as their prisoner. She'd wanted to poison them. She'd successfully poisoned most of the vampires in the palace. And yet...the irrational part of Sarai's mind knew she didn't want to watch Setanta kill Jackie even if the Vasi deserved it.

Sarai instinctively stepped between them. "We'll put her in the dungeon. She might be able to tell us more." She hoped that was enough cause to stop him from killing Jackie.

He took a step forward, looking down at her as she clenched her teeth and did her best not to be intimidated.

His red eyes narrowed.

"Why." It wasn't a question, more of a demand.

"I...don't know," she admitted. "I can't watch it."

His gaze trailed up to Jackie, and Sarai looked as well to see the girl shaking with fear in the face of imminent death.

"Please, Setanta," Sarai said. "Just put her in the dungeon until we get Artemisia back. Then we'll figure out what to do with her."

"You're too soft," he said quietly.

"You and Marcelle are too harsh. Maybe you need a little softness."

They stared at each other, and she could feel the murderous determination radiating from him. She tried to keep herself strong under his gaze. If she faltered, Jackie would be killed, and it would be bloody.

Finally, Setanta shut his eyes. "Fine. For my wife's sake. Temuulen, take Jackie to the dungeons. Marcelle, go to Lilly. We will need new plans. Sarai, please stay away from the dungeons. You can summon your friend Rosaline back from Lochlan's cabin if you wish. And I...I need to tell my father what has happened to his daughter. He should hear it from me."

Chapter Twenty-Six

The Father

Setanta felt helpless. He did not like feeling helpless. He wanted to rip Vasi bodies to shreds, tear off Giovanna's traitorous head, and save his half sister. True, he had never been close to her, but she was blood. That mattered to him. The thought that the Vasi had managed to contract her without him realizing it, to operate under his nose in his home for so long, made him hate himself. He should have realized. He should have done better. If he hadn't always been so dismissive of Artemisia due to her mother and her age, he might have noticed.

Yet in a way, he was impressed. It had been so long since anyone had gained a true upper hand over him. Even when Sarai had been taken by her family, he had easily overwhelmed and killed them all. The Vasi were different from witches. They were worse, like a thousand stinging ants. Every time he crushed a few under his foot, more swarmed to take their place.

This time, their bite stung much deeper than usual.

Setanta wasn't sure what to say to his father. He wasn't used to reporting something so personal and disappointing. Perhaps he shouldn't say a word to the old man? After all, Lugh wanted to die in peace in his sleep. Setanta wondered if he even loved Artemisia, considering he never spent time with her and started allowing himself to age before she had even been born. Yet as he went to his study, he found the man who had once been worshiped as a god waiting for him, staring at Setanta's magical spear in its case.

"*Athair*," Setanta said. *Father.*

"*Mo mhac*," Lugh replied in the same tongue. *My son.* He continued in the same dialect of ancient Irish. "I felt disturbed. It compelled me to seek you out."

"There have been many disturbing occurrences as of late. Some of which I need to speak to you on. I blame myself."

"You cannot predict everything. You should not blame yourself. Take responsibility, yes. That is your role. But holding on to the blame will destroy you over time, like it has done to me." He gave a deep sigh. "I miss your sister."

"Artemisia—"

"Aoibheann," Lugh corrected. "I know you had your differences, but she was a fine queen. Stubborn as a mule and strong as an ox. You could have been king back then instead of her, you know, as her elder. If only you weren't so resistant to the concept. I wish you hadn't waited until you were the only reasonable choice to accept the role. But she did well managing all those wars."

"Well? She had me grounded for a decade."

"As was her right as queen, and I was glad you didn't fight her on the ruling. You shouldn't have interfered in her plans for the Revolutionary War. It's your own fault you missed the whole thing." Lugh chuckled. "I'm proud of how she died, though, in World War II."

"She was impressive," Setanta admitted.

"Are you disappointed in me as your father?"

Setanta blinked. "Disappointed? Of course not, no. Where is this coming from?"

"I was never very protective of you. I let your foster father raise you when you were a child. I let you charge into situations you were unprepared for all your life. I fear I could have been better to you."

Setanta shook his head. "You gave me everything you could. I have no ill feelings toward you. I suppose I view you more as a brother than my father. We looked the same for most of our lives, did we not?"

"We did," Lugh mused. "Yet I'll always see you as my son. You know that I'm proud of you, Setanta. I'm proud of the man you are. You and I, we've seen so much, and I…"

Lugh's voice trailed off. Suddenly, his wings unfurled from his back, the blue woad tattoo design outlining a sun behind his head so that he looked like a true god for a moment. Then he threw his arms around his son and wrapped them both tightly in his wings as the world exploded.

Setanta didn't know what had happened. He could feel liquid on his body and ringing in his ears from the loud blast.

A blast…a bomb. A bomb had gone off in his office.

"*Athair*," he urged and pushed Lugh off himself, but the old man crumpled to the floor. Shrapnel stuck through the membranes of his large wings and through his torso. Blood gushed from the wounds, and for a moment, light still flickered in Lugh's eyes. Then he was gone.

Setanta couldn't move. He couldn't comprehend it.

His father, the once King Lugh, the sun god of ancient Ireland, was dead at his feet. He had been prepared for his father's passing, but not in such a violent manner. Not with a room exploding around them. Lugh had wanted a peaceful death at the end rather than a battle death. If Lugh had wanted a fight to the death, Setanta would have given it to him gladly to respect him. But it wasn't what he wanted. It was all wrong.

It had been so long since Setanta had cried that he once feared he'd forgotten how. Yet as he held his father's body close, the father who had sacrificed his body to save him, tears streamed like rain down his cheeks.

He needed to get up. He couldn't waste time crying. He needed to act. To check on the others. To find out if there were other bombs. Yet he couldn't move. He could only sit and cry as the weight of the loss of thousands of years of companionship crushed him.

Then more sounds. More bangs. Screaming from throughout the palace. Heat. They were under attack. A proper attack by the Vasi, no doubt invited into the property by Artemisia. No doubt planned by Jackie. He could not grieve, not yet. He dipped his hand into his father's blood and painted it down his face.

"To battle once more, *Athair*. Your mountaintop pyre will have to wait, but I will win this battle. I will defeat every one of our enemies, and I will build you a pyre with my own hands when I've finished."

Setanta broke the case where he kept his spear, and the bloodthirsty magic inside the weapon screamed at him the moment he touched the shaft. It had been forged with his own blood, designed for battle, and had the thirst of an untamed vampire inside. It hungered. Setanta walked to the wall that had been blown out overlooking the front of his palace and saw an army encroaching. He had defeated armies before. The weapons were new, but the concept was not.

Still, he would need help. They had obvious witches among them with unknown powers, modern firearms, bulletproof armor leagues beyond chainmail or leather armor, and the element of surprise. They were beyond prepared, he realized. They had been waiting for the bombs to go off. Jackie must have coordinated with them, anticipating that her cover would be blown or he would be poisoned. Their timing was perfect, and he had been a fool not to anticipate it.

Setanta had been too lax. Too confident in his vampires' superior prowess over humanity. This was the price. But he had one last and desperate ace up his sleeve. One that could rival even the reemergence of the dragon shifter and the threat of grenade launchers. His bloodline had a protector. Not a kind one, and there would be a cost, but she would help if he asked.

"Lady Morrigan," he murmured and felt a dark touch on his shoulders. Of course the goddess was close. She always was. He continued to speak to her in his native language, in ancient Irish. "Your line is close to extinction. If you want it to continue, this battle must be won."

She did not answer, but he could feel her still there. He knew better than to turn and look and risk insanity depending on what trifold form she might take. The floorboards creaked under her weight, and he heard something crunching, something slurping. He dared not look.

"Leave my father's body for a pyre."

The noise stopped, and the footsteps moved across the floor again until the being stood behind him. Still, he did not look.

"Protect my wives," he ordered. "Protect my unborn child. And protect me."

There will be a price for my hand, whispered the voice of a thousand women in his mind as well as from the lips near his ear.

He buckled under the pressure and fell to his knees.

There is always a price. The weak will be culled.

"If you protect my wives and my child, I'll pay your price with my own blood," he told her and forced himself to stand. "I will cull the weak for you."

You have not come to me in peacetime in many centuries, my hound. I find it displeasing. I will not abide being denied as you have denied me in the past.

"I have not yet been king for even a cycle around the sun. When I have, I will make offerings to you. You have my word. But I, my wives, and my child will need to be alive for that to come to pass."

Then beg.

Setanta ground his teeth. "Beg?" he snapped. "My Lady, it is your tether to this world that is also at stake."

Beg for my power… "Setanta…" Her voice shifted from nearly unbearable to the seductive whisper of a woman. She had lessened herself to something he could stomach to behold.

He steadied himself and looked.

She wore a red dress. Raven-black hair from which genuine ravens peeked their heads flowed in wild tresses. Her eyes glowed red with power as she looked down, towering over him. Her body was too thin, disproportioned, and long, as if something that did not quite understand the makeup of a human body had constructed one. *"On your knees,"* she told him. *"I will have what I am owed."*

He knew better than to disobey her. She wanted to be entertained, and if he had to play the jester for her, then he would. He'd learned long ago that to cross her was a fool's choice.

"My Lady," he said as he knelt. "I humbly beg your favor in battle. I need your help. I need your power. In exchange, I will pay your price in my own blood if you ask it."

She shimmered between her strange, disproportionate body and the form of a young maiden, flickering for a fraction of a second to something else his mind couldn't comprehend.

He shut his eyes. "My Lady Morrigan. Please."

He could feel her satisfied grin with too many teeth in his mind.

We have a deal.

The floorboards shifted under her weight, and a raven cried out.

Submit your body and soul to me.

Setanta took a deep breath. He knew what came next, and it terrified him. But it was necessary. "You have my body and soul, as you always have."

Pain seared through his back as a single claw scratched his skin from his skull to his tailbone. From that cut, he felt her hands peel back his flesh with the ease of peeling an orange, exposing muscle and bone. His sight was flooded by white stars, and he screamed. Some *thing* crawled along his spine, burning him.

As the Morrigan closed his skin with her delicate claws, sealing the thing inside him, something radiated through him, power like he hadn't felt in multiple millennia. It distorted inside his body, melded with the magic already at the core of his strength, and burned like the sun itself was coursing through him. The floor warped under the heat of his body as steam rose around him.

Then she flipped him on the floor as he screamed in pain and ripped out the glass eye from his socket, leaving it empty. Then she filled it with that same cruel darkness, dripping from her bleeding fingertips into his body as she used her other impossibly large hand with its impossibly long fingers to hold his head in place.

Setanta blinked with his new eye. He could feel her looking out through him and see the flow of magic in the currents of the world through her vision. He was grateful she at least hadn't taken out the good one and used the one she'd already removed centuries ago. The Morrigan had given him a boon, as tortuous as it felt twisting in his body and soul. As he pulled himself to his feet, leaning on his spear and panting, he felt something different.

Elation.

He was fearless and much stronger than before.

"Thank you." He breathed.

With that, Setanta unfurled his wings. He had more than he used to have, a second pair beneath his usual set that were covered in black feathers thrumming with power. He tested them once and leapt into the battle, screaming.

Chapter Twenty-Seven

The Water

Sarai was glad that Bear, Lochlan, and Hannah had all come back to the palace to bring Rosaline home. She invited them to her room after a quick shower and changing into casual clothes, unsure how to tell them everything that had just happened. How was she to explain that Jackie had managed to betray them yet again? That she'd stood in the way of Setanta killing her, even though she wasn't sure Jackie deserved the mercy.

She needed friends, desperately, and Marcelle was busy. Rosaline's bubbly personality was almost a relief to experience as she flounced into Sarai's bedroom for the first time.

"This is so much better than how it was before." Rosaline sighed. "I mean, the Roman stuff was fine if you're into that, but yuck on Giovanna. This looks *fresh*. It's so bright."

"It's nice." Lochlan looked around as he spoke. "Uh, I brought you a housewarming present since I've never been here. Where do you want me to put this?"

It was a potted rosemary bush with a wonderful fragrance that she was certain she'd seen at his cabin. "You didn't need to. I didn't get you anything for your place."

"Just take the dumb plant."

She smiled a little. "Thanks. I'll put it in the kitchen." She took it from him to place in the small kitchen area.

"You got a TV!" Rosaline jumped onto the couch. "That's what I'm talking about. Remember when you were in the guest room and I said that's what they need to put in these rooms? Some damn television! But they're so old-fashioned. Is this cable or satellite?"

"I have no idea," Sarai mused as she waddled over. "But that's not even the best part. Want to see something awesome?"

"Uh, duh," Rosaline said.

Sarai led them both to where Giovanna's in-floor, deep bath was located behind a folding screen.

"You kept the bath hell hole?" Rosaline exclaimed. "God, I hate this thing so much. You have no idea."

"You...hate a fancy bath?" Lochlan asked.

"Yes! It's not hooked up to plumbing! Giovanna would make us do it the old-fashioned way. We'd have to heat up big pots of water in a fireplace and bring it over to fill up that massive stupid tub. Please, you can't keep this thing."

"I improved it," Sarai said with pride and carefully knelt down to turn on the newly installed faucet.

"Sarai, I could kiss you if you weren't the queen." Rosaline clapped. "Finally, someone with common sense."

Sarai turned off the faucet and tried to stand, thinking she shouldn't have gotten so low to the ground.

"Are you okay?" Rosaline asked.

"Yeah, no worries, I'm fine." She managed to get up, and something popped. Was it possible for her pelvic bones to crack? She'd never felt that particular sensation before, and it felt a little weird, like something had moved into a new place. Perhaps it had been a kick from the baby?

"Sarai," said Bear as he stepped into the room. He looked serious by the doorway with a newly risen undead Hannah.

Sarai couldn't see if Hannah also looked serious, as she had on a mask to cover her nose and mouth, no doubt to keep from inhaling too many tempting scents.

"Something's on your mind. What happened with Jackie?"

"How's Hannah doing?" she said, ignoring his comment. "You look great, by the way, Hannah."

It wasn't a lie. Her face was more symmetrical, even if half hidden. Her gray hair looked healthier and almost voluminous. She still looked elderly and had the wrinkles of old age, but it was the old age of a movie star, the kind of strange glamour women from Hollywood who had teams to work on their appearance possessed.

"She's adjusting. We decided it's best for her not to breathe around witches, to retain control. She'll talk when she's had more time to learn self-control. Sarai, what happened with Jackie?"

Sarai's eyes swelled with tears. "I need my friends." And she spilled everything, telling them to great shock how Jackie had manipulated them all, how she had controlled Artemisia, and how Artemisia had flown off into the sky with a suicide sigil still implanted in her tooth.

"I can't help but find it funny," Bear said quietly. "Setanta checked my head for outside compulsions, but it was Marcelle. His own damn queen."

"Yeah, wild. She's working with Lilly right now, I think. They're trying to plan how to get Artemisia back." Something tightened in Sarai's abdomen, and she paused. The sensation became more uncomfortable.

"Are you okay?" Bear said with concern.

"Uh, I think so. I think it's Braxton-Hicks contractions. You know, fake contractions, not real ones. I'm only eight months along, so it can't be the real thing. I'll give my aunt a call just in case. She knows about all this pregnancy stuff so—"

"What was that?" Bear snapped, his body tensing on high alert.

"What?"

"That noise—"

The world erupted into fire around them.

Wood and stone shattered and broke. The floor was gone, and she fell away from the explosion in a whirlwind. There was screaming: her screaming, the screams of those around her, and screams from the rest of the palace, and pain as well. Sarai's head was throbbing, and something excruciating was embedded deep in her shoulder.

As dust settled, Bear's clear voice called out. "Who's not dead?"

Sarai tried to pull herself up to stand, but the pain in her shoulder and a sudden sharp contraction kept her on the floor. "I'm here!"

Bear was suddenly by her side, Hannah in one arm and Rosaline in the other, both looking as shell-shocked as Sarai felt. He put them down and knelt by Sarai.

"The baby," she whispered, her voice trembling.

"It's okay. I can still hear the heartbeat," he assured her. "There's shrapnel in your shoulder. I'm going to pull it out so you can heal."

Sarai nodded, shutting her eyes.

"On three. One." He yanked out the wood, causing her to shriek as pain splintered through her bone.

"Fucking asshole!" she shouted, gripping her shoulder as it healed.

"Two, three."

"Has anyone seen Lochlan?" Hannah said, then froze, fixated on Sarai. Specifically, on her blood. Her eyes turned bright red as fangs grew in her mouth. She lunged, and Bear just barely managed to stop her by slamming into her.

"Hey," he snapped. "Focus. Hold your breath. Remember, we talked about this. You need to stop. We don't attack the pregnant queen."

Hannah shut her eyes, gripping Bear so tightly that her nails drew blood from his arms. She was trembling, shaking as if experiencing a seizure, muttering in tones too low for Sarai to understand.

"I know she smells good, I know her heart sounds great, but you need to keep it together. We've got some big problems right now, and I don't want you to be one of them. Hold your breath," Bear instructed.

Hannah nodded, and her chest was still, her breathing stopped as she tried to maintain control.

"Are we safe with her here?" Rosaline demanded. "Can't you break her neck or something to keep her from coming after us?"

Hannah's eyes widened in an expression of fear.

"I'm not breaking her neck. Hannah, I'm not breaking your neck. You just have to keep control for me, and we'll be fine."

Sarai heard a groan from somewhere in the rubble,

and Lochlan coughed on dust. Bear took one more look at Hannah, then rushed to lift a heavy beam off Lochlan's lower half.

"Fuck, my head hurts," the fire witch said. "I can't feel my legs."

"I can fix him." Sarai stumbled forward and put a hand on Lochlan as she spoke. Her warm healing magic fixed a concussion, two broken ribs, and a broken spine.

He sighed in relief. "Thanks."

"Yeah, no problem… Oh, ow. Ow. *Ow*." Sarai bent over, gripping her abdomen as a contraction struck. It hurt. Ten times more than any period pain she'd felt in her life. More than she expected from any Braxton-Hicks contraction. She felt a trickle of liquid from her sex and looked up at everyone in fear. "I need help," she whispered. "I think maybe my water broke. But it's too soon. It's too soon for her to come."

"Oh, no, no, no," Rosaline whispered. "Okay, deep breaths. We've got you."

"We need to get you out of here." Bear went to move another beam, but the precarious ceiling of assorted pieces of floor, wall, and bedroom above them creaked dangerously. Flickers of orange light from the flames outside threatened at the cracks. He slowly put the beam down. "That won't work."

They were trapped. And the baby was coming.

****

The palace was in flames in a hellish inferno unlike anything Marcelle had seen since World War II. She could smell the explosives in the air, and her worst fears threatened to overwhelm her. Her lovers, her Setanta and her pregnant Sarai, could be dead. Explosions could kill even a pureblood. Marcelle wouldn't be able to cope with that sort of loss and guilt. Luckily, she had been with Lilly, Temuulen, and most of the knights in the palace at the time, and they darted out into the gardens to avoid the fires.

"Kill the Vasi," she said in a low voice. "Priority one is finding your king and queen. Lugh as well if you can, and rescue human sources."

A familiar war cry shook the air, and the ground trembled. Marcelle made a quick hand signal to her team to follow close, and they darted around the mansion. In the garden was their king. His spear, Gae Bulg, pulsed with red blood magic as it drank from the two bodies impaled on it. Setanta was covered in blood from head to toe, his wings stretched out wide from his back like a demon's. A black line of something that hurt to look at throbbed down his back, bubbling under his flesh, and almost seemed to be growing an extra pair of feathered wings made from what could only be described as cursed tar. Blood swirled around him as battle magic saturated the atmosphere like a cyclone.

The dead were all around, bullet casings littering the grounds. She could see beyond their corner of the gardens other Vasi engaging with vampires, some with witches flinging offensive spells. But no vampires dared to get close to whatever their king had become. Not that he needed their help. The flicking of his tar-like new wings absorbed a rain of gunfire from two Vasi he hadn't killed yet.

He turned around, unnerving joy in his eyes. One Vasi was gutted with Setanta's spear, then torn to pieces before Marcelle could blink. The other was not so lucky. Setanta thrust his hand into the Vasi man's chest and ripped out his heart before taking a rough bite, blood drenching down his front as the Vasi dropped.

"Setanta!" Marcelle shrieked. He turned to look at her, panting heavily, fangs extended, and she stumbled back in shock. The bloodlust and fury in his presence was unprecedented to her, and something was horribly wrong with his prosthetic eye. It had gone black, blacker than any known substance, with a pinpoint of glowing red light at the center staring back at her.

His expression of hatred melted away when he saw her, and he ripped his spear out of the body.

"Marcelle," he murmured. With a beat of his powerful wings, the cyclone of blood dissipated, dropping bodies to the ground, and he was suddenly before her, his arms around her. His body felt like fire, much hotter than he usually was, and Marcelle resisted the urge to pull away.

"Thank the gods you're unharmed," he said. "Have you found Sarai?"

"No. What the hell is this?"

"Jackie and Artemisia must have placed bombs in the palace. There was one in my office. My father stood between it and me when it went off."

"Your office? Then Lugh..."

"My father is dead," he said through his fangs. "And those responsible will know my wrath. With any luck, Jackie at least is buried in the dungeon."

She couldn't believe it. She'd never been close to Setanta's father but respected the man and saw him as a permanent fixture in the palace. To think that a man once worshiped as a god had been taken down by something as mundane as a bomb was almost inconceivable. "Has your sister shown? If she's forced to fight for them, we can try to take her alive."

"Still missing. I need you to find Sarai, Marcelle. They have too many witches here for me to leave the fight. I've no doubt the shapeshifter will show themselves at some point."

Shit, she hadn't thought of that. "How are we supposed to take on a dragon? We made it out by the skin of our teeth last time, and we have no portals to run through."

"I'm strong enough now." He paused. "I made a deal with the Morrigan."

Marcelle hissed. That explained the extra wings and the eye from hell. "Is that wise?"

"If it means you, Sarai, and our child survive, then I don't care. I refuse to lose any more."

She nodded. Shouting could be heard from the other side of the garden, and her fangs extended as shooting began. "We'll find them," she promised. "And we'll make the Vasi pay for this with their flesh and blood."

Setanta nodded and lifted his spear. He beat his wings and was instantly above them, hurtling toward the Vasi and their gunfire, landing like a meteor to knock them all to the ground before slaughtering everyone in his vicinity.

Marcelle looked around. "You heard him. Vasi with witches are our foes. Keep silver ready, be on the lookout for the shapeshifter. Let your king be the vanguard. Temuulen, you're with me to find Sarai. Lilly, you and your team look for human sources and work on evacuation of noncombatants. The rest of you." She grinned to display her fangs. "Kill every Vasi. Give no quarter. Take no prisoners."

Chapter Twenty-Eight

Trapped

"I wanted pain relief!" Sarai shrieked for the fiftieth time. "I was promised a magical painless childbirth, not this bullshit!"

Why had Liora left her? Her ghost mother had disappeared after killing her father, and that was so incredibly selfish. She wanted her mother there. She wanted her mother to tell her it was all going to be fine. She wanted the other mother of the child to be there. The father of the child. But she was trapped in a literal burning hell hole. When the contraction stopped, she fell backward to slump in the rubble, but Bear caught her and let her lean against his body. He was cold and the cold was soothing. Lochlan was able to keep the worst of the flames far enough from their position and mitigate the intensity of the heat to keep them safe, but Bear's coldness provided comfort on top of that safety.

Rosaline slapped Bear's shoulder. "Can't you do something?" she demanded. "Give her your blood?"

"Vampire blood doesn't take away pain. It just heals. She's not sick or wounded—"

He paused as Sarai screamed through her teeth due to another intense contraction. She wanted to do something more than fall to the floor. Could she fall through the floor? Be absorbed by the earth's molten

310

core? Anything to make the pain stop.

"It could get her a little high, right?" Rosaline insisted.

"I don't want to get high. I want the pain to fucking stop!" Sarai snapped.

"Can you do a spell?" Bear asked.

"I can't fucking focus on a spell while my uterus is trying to kill me!"

"What about you?" he asked Lochlan.

"I don't have any medical training. Fuck, I don't know fuck about this." The fire witch's eyes were wide as he spoke. "This is so far out of my comfort zone; you have no fucking idea."

"Well, one of you useless dickwads needs to do something to help her," Rosaline demanded. "Because all I'm working off are some TV shows, but you don't see me making excuses." She got down between Sarai's legs. "You're doing great, sweetie. Everything looks great."

"Fucking liar." Sarai groaned.

"No, seriously, you've got a great vagina. Marcelle's a lucky lady."

Sarai looked up to see a reassuring, joking smile on Rosaline's face, and burst into laughter that all too soon turned into sobs. "Makeitstopmakeitstop," Sarai begged as the contraction peaked. She knew they could do nothing to make it stop, but just vocalizing her need for the pain to end was cathartic.

As it finished, Rosaline squeezed Sarai's hand. "That was great, girl. You're doing great. Gotta ride them out like surf waves."

"I've never surfed."

"Neither have I."

The next round of pain and pleading came and went, and she lay back in Bear's arms. "No more, no more," she begged him. The guilt in his eyes hurt, but she just wanted someone to do something. "Can you just...just cut it out? Just get it out, make it stop. I can heal."

"I don't think an unmedicated C-section is the way to go here," Rosaline said gently. She looked up at Lochlan. "You seriously don't know any pain-relief spells?"

"Spells aren't a matter of knowing the right words," Lochlan snapped. "It's understanding how to stop pain. Understanding the nervous system and what can safely be manipulated by your power without doing damage. The words don't matter; it's the intent that matters. I could fuck her up with a bad spell."

Sarai understood his hesitation, but being on the receiving end of the worst pain of her life made her desperate. "Can you try? Someone later can fix me if you fuck up."

"What if I fuck up the kid?" Lochlan said.

He was right. Another wave of agony hit, then another a bit faster this time. She felt like she didn't have a chance to catch her breath. It was maddening. For the first time, she understood on a primal level why so many women in history had died in childbirth. The pain alone was enough to kill a person.

"Rosaline, switch with me," Bear said.

Rosaline put her hands on her hips. "Excuse me? I'm not just handing the royal cooch over for you to gawk at."

"Out of the four of us, I've actually had some experience with women in labor. I suspect I'm the only one here who has. And not just back in the day, this chick went into labor at a music festival I was at once, and I helped deliver a healthy human kid," he said. "Those last two contractions were back to back. Let me see how far along she is."

Rosaline looked at Sarai. "Is that okay with you?"

"Fine, fine," Sarai muttered. She couldn't care less who saw her naked with how much pain she was in, and she trusted Bear.

He switched so that Rosaline was holding her up, then knelt between her legs. "Do you mind if I touch you?"

"Do whatever helps, I don't care," Sarai said. Then before he could even attempt to touch her, a contraction hit. "Wait, wait, fuck, fuck, stop, please, stop, stop, stop—" The pain felt worse. When the wave stopped, she leaned back against Rosaline, tears in her eyes, but nodded at Bear. "Before another one hits."

He put his hand between her legs, his fingers inside her. She was uncomfortably reminded of when Setanta had impregnated her with the special spell they had used, pushing an enchanted pearl into her womb. She had thought at the time that if such a small pearl going past her cervix was so painful, she never wanted to push out a child while feeling the pain. She wanted anything to make it stop. Maybe they could break her spine? No, her gift would make her heal. And if she used silver to inhibit the healing, she would be putting herself at risk of complications. Perhaps even death.

Bear's face was stoic, as if he was hiding something.

"What's wrong?" Sarai demanded.

Bear sighed. "You're having very close contractions, but you aren't dilated. Maybe an inch, if that. Probably because of stress. You need to try to

313

relax."

"Relax? I bet this whole thing started because of stress, and you're telling me I won't be able to do it right because of—fuck, fuck, fuckfuckfuck!" She cried and squeezed Rosaline's hand as tightly as she could through rolling contractions. Just as they seemed to die down, they would start again, not giving her a moment to breathe. When it stopped, she glared up at them. "You know what's stressful? This goddamn pain!"

"Then we need to get rid of the pain. You said spells are about focusing intent, right?" Rosaline said to Lochlan. "Well, we need to make her not feel anything from the waist down. We need a magic epidural, okay? I've been reading up on all this pregnancy stuff since she first announced it. Epidurals stick a needle through your lower back and give some meds to block the pain. So you can't feel shit. Can you magically block off feeling?"

Lochlan shifted his weight. "I don't know."

"Come on, work with me, man," Rosaline said. "Your magic word is epidural. Say it."

"Epidural," he said, looking sick.

"Please," Sarai begged hoarsely. "Please try. Just focus on me. Keep the intent on me, and the magic won't affect the baby. I don't care if you break my spine to do it. It's fine. Just please."

"Me," whispered Hannah from her place at the side. "I know a little medical—" She held her breath again, shutting her eyes. Then she slumped over, her eyes open and glazed over. A ghostly apparition of her appeared in front of them. She had used her gift to astral project out of her body.

"Holy shit." Rosaline gasped.

"That's better. Now I can talk with you without

physical distractions. Lochlan, come, I'll instruct you on the nerves you need to numb," Hannah said.

He nodded, and they sat together. Sarai tried to listen to them but was too caught up in her own pain as another contraction caused her to sob and shout.

After a few more, Lochlan knelt down next to her. "Okay. I think I can do this. Sarai, can you sit up?"

"I don't know." Sarai groaned.

"We're gonna pretend this is a nice, normal human hospital," Rosaline said. "I'm your doctor, and Lochlan's your epidural doctor dude. I need you to lean forward so we can get this epidural in you right, just like I saw on TV. We're gonna get this right."

Sarai leaned forward, rode out another wave of begging while gripping Rosaline and Bear's hands, then nodded.

Hannah's astral form sat next to them and guided her student. "Lochlan, put your hand here. You're going to focus on just Sarai. On her spine from the waist down and on all the electric nerves that make her feel. You're going to make them stop firing, but only from here down. On three."

Lochlan's warm, almost hot hand rested against Sarai's lower back.

"One. Two. Three."

"Epidural," Lochlan said.

Sarai could feel a bit of red-hot magic tingling, but it wasn't enough. He was a powerful gift user, so his skill with magic spells was limited. But Sarai knew a trick for that. "Bear, bite me," she demanded.

He blinked in surprise. "I don't think now is the time for that."

"No, just to draw some witch blood. Setanta taught

me how to do blood magic, how to use blood to amplify spells. He used his own blood to work his spells, so we can use mine here."

"No," Lochlan interjected. "You can't waste your strength like that. I...I can do it." He lifted up his hand and offered his horrifically scarred wrist to Bear. "Bite *me.*"

It was as if time froze. Sarai knew what it meant to Lochlan to offer such a thing. He had been traumatically and violently attacked by vampires in his childhood in an assault he had barely survived. A vampire's fangs were the worst thing in the world to him.

Bear hesitated for a moment, then accepted Lochlan's hand. His eyes turned red as his fangs grew, and Lochlan tensed but held firm as the fangs sank into his flesh. The bite was quick, like a viper's strike, and Bear was done. The wound wasn't in Lochlan's veins directly, to avoid a serious puncture that would cause more problems, but it was enough. Hot blood dripped down Lochlan's hand and against Sarai's back as he touched her. Her abdomen tensed with the beginnings of another contraction about to hit.

"Epidural," Lochlan said with force.

The magic was like a cool wave of numbness from the base of Sarai's spine downward. She could feel her body tensing, but the pain was absent. She looked up at Lochlan and collapsed backward against Rosaline. "Thank you." She breathed.

"It worked?" Lochlan asked.

She nodded.

Bear put his hands against her abdomen. "You're in the middle of contractions. No pain?"

"Nope." But she was so extremely tired. "Maybe I

should take a nap?"

"I don't know, maybe that's not a good idea?" Rosaline looked up at Bear. "Is that a good idea?"

"I don't think I've ever seen a labor where the woman napped," he said. "Then again, I'm not used to having access to anything beyond willow bark around as far as pain medicine. It makes a good tea."

"Aspirin," Rosaline said. "That's early aspirin. They had that at the music festival?"

"Nah, willow bark was earlier than that. Festival was other stuff, which I would not recommend."

"I think I prefer magic epidurals." Sarai sighed. "Aspirin can fuck off. I can't feel a thing, and it's great."

Though she also couldn't move very well, almost unaware of how her toes felt. How anything felt. She could see them move a little, but it was the same sensation as her prosthetic magical hand moving. Unattached. Blissful. It gave her a moment to take in their location. The rubble around them was scorched and charred to a crisp. The creaking noise above them was more than a little concerning.

"Do we need to worry about smoke?" Sarai asked.

"I managed to get the fire back enough that I think we should be good," Lochlan said, though he did look worried.

"And with your healing, Hannah, you, and I should be fine at the very least," Bear said.

But that still left Lochlan and Rosaline to worry about. While healing powers were all well and good, Sarai could still suffocate. Or have problems imparted through her to the baby.

"Should you try to get through the rubble?" she asked the vampire.

"I would if I wasn't worried about it collapsing on us." He glanced upward as he spoke. "Also, this is probably the safest spot for you right now."

"Why do you say that?"

"Because I can hear a war going on outside." Bear tapped his ear. "The Vasi are on the grounds, and there's gunfire out there. We need to keep you hidden."

"That's a nice stress-free thought." Sarai shut her eyes. She tried to take several deep, meditative breaths. With the pain gone, she could worry more about Marcelle and Setanta. Bombs and gunfire could kill even a pureblood. She had no idea if the other parents of her child were still alive.

"I'll astral project outside and see if I can bring help," Hannah said.

Bear nodded. "Do it."

Her ghostly form disappeared through the rubble. As time passed and the fighting raged outside of their trapped sanctuary, Sarai felt increasingly tired. Bear checked on her progress periodically, and the pain relief had apparently helped enough that he wasn't worried about her not dilating. That in turn made everyone worry about having to deliver the baby.

The sounds outside got closer, scraping and shifting of stone and wood. Everyone tensed, and Bear stood protectively in front of Sarai while Lochlan raised a hand with fire growing in his palm. Sarai shut her eyes. *Anyone but the Vasi. Please, let anyone but the Vasi find us.*

Hannah's astral form reappeared, and she gave them a close-lipped smile. "It'll be all right. Help is on the way."

A wave of cool air rushed over them as rubble was

cleared and moonlight illuminated the most beautiful woman in the world. Marcelle.

Sarai released a sigh of relief and tried to sit up better but couldn't move well. "Hey." She gave her a weak smile. "Nice of you to show up."

"You have no idea how happy I am to see you." Marcelle darted forward immediately and covered Sarai's mouth with a needful kiss. "Are you hurt?"

"We need to be careful moving her," Bear warned, stooping low so as to not hit the unstable ceiling with his unusual height. "She's in labor."

"And I can't feel shit. It's great. Lochlan did a spell for me." She could have sworn that Marcelle's pallid face somehow became paler.

"But your due date isn't for weeks."

"Tell that to the kid. Is Setanta there?"

"He's alive. There's Vasi out there. It's a full-blown assault. Setanta said to look out for the shape—"

A loud roar echoed through the Appalachian Mountains, and they all looked toward the sound.

"—shifter," Marcelle finished with a tremble of fear in her voice.

"All right, you scaly bitch." Lochlan breathed. "Who's up for round two?"

Chapter Twenty-Nine

Red Like Rubies

Marcelle did not want to leave Sarai but had no choice. She couldn't sit back and watch while a literal dragon attacked what was left of her home.

"I'm going." She caressed Sarai's sweat-beaded face as she spoke. Her hands lingered. She wanted the moment to last forever so she could stay by the witch's side. Sarai looked so pitiful. She needed help. But the best help Marcelle could provide was combat. She kissed Sarai again on the lips, then the forehead. "I'll be back. You'll be all right, I promise."

She didn't know that, though, and looked up at Bear and Hannah. "I know you're still getting used to this, Hannah, but I need you two to stay with her. You'll get in the way here. Protect her, please. Get her away from here. Try Lochlan's cabin. It's warded and not someplace the Vasi should think to attack. Once you're there, I need you to astral project to the Ellis Coven and call in some backup for us. Temuulen, you go with them too. They might need an extra hand if they run into trouble."

"Sure." Bear picked up Sarai with care in both arms, who groaned from the movement. "Temuulen, can you carry Rosaline?"

"No problem," he said.

"Be safe," Marcelle whispered, seizing the moment to lovingly hold Sarai's sweat-soaked face once more.

"I'll be okay," Sarai promised. She closed her eyes and gripped Marcelle's hand, smearing dirt of some kind there. *"T'shmor la."*

"You need your own strength," she protested as she felt a surge of necromantic power.

"Shut up, I already did the spell," Sarai replied.

Something strange itched at the palm of Marcelle's hand, and she frowned. As she watched, an eye grew there, just like the one Sarai had in her palm at their wedding.

Sarai grinned and held up her own good hand where another matching eye blinked at them. "It's not henna, but it'll work. They'll keep us safe."

A roar shook the trees, and Marcelle didn't have much more time to linger or contemplate the absurdity of Sarai's ancestors gazing out of her hand. "Go," she urged, and they darted off into the forest. Marcelle stood shoulder to shoulder with Lochlan. "We need to take out the dragon. Any ideas?"

"Those scales are tougher than bullets. And that fire is hot as hell. But I can control the fire. It's a shapeshifter, not a pyromancer."

"We manipulate the fire. Do you think you can do enough damage that way to take it down?"

"Probably not," he admitted. "But fire eats oxygen. That thing needs to breathe just like us. If I can manipulate fire inside it enough, maybe I can make it pass out. Maybe even kill it."

She nodded. "Then you're our ace in the sleeve. We'll grab Setanta, and he'll be the muscle to try to crack the scales. I'll be the bait."

He squeezed her hand. "Don't die."

She smiled and squeezed back, then turned and planted a loving kiss on his lips, which he responded to by throwing his arms around her and holding her tight.

"I'm undead. Death is my bitch," she said. "Let's go kill a dragon."

They advanced together as Setanta came falling out of the sky to slam into the dragon's white, moonstone-colored neck and crash into the ground.

"Perfect timing." Marcelle breathed, and she and Lochlan split up to flank the massive beast. Guns wouldn't work against the dragon. But she had brute strength second only to Setanta himself. She would take a page out of his book and attack more viciously.

She launched herself into the air and landed on the creature's back. Its scales were hot like coals under the soles of her shoes. She didn't wait for the rubber to melt and instead jumped up and landed as hard as she could again, causing the creature to stumble. At the same time, Setanta shrieked and attacked, and Lochlan twisted the flames in the dragon's maw. Fire filled the air, swirling around the dragon's head.

"Knock the wind out of it," Marcelle shouted at Setanta. He flew up into the air and shot down like a missile, hitting it from the side so that air was forced out of its lungs in a massive fireball that Lochlan took control of.

It shook, throwing its head back as if trying to escape its own breath, then beat its wings. A wall of wind threw all three back, and Marcelle felt the stone wall of their palace crack against her body. It hurt. Ribs were most certainly broken from the way they crunched inside her. The moment they ground back together and snapped into place, she searched for the creature.

The dragon had taken flight and landed on a remaining section of roof. Immediately, the structure groaned and buckled under the massive weight before collapsing, the dragon roaring as it did. Setanta was hot on its heels, flying above and diving down into the ruins. Marcelle caught sight of Lochlan hobbling on a broken leg, face white with pain, and darted to his side.

"I'm okay," he said before she could speak. "You need my fire. Get me to that thing."

She nodded and grabbed his waist before jumping and climbing up the palace wall, digging the fingers of her free hand into the stone and launching them up over the wall and down into the hole the dragon had created. As they landed, she recognized the room. It was the throne room or what was left of it. The chandeliers were shattered and scattered, the windows blown out, the floors fractured, and the throne itself was smashed before their eyes with an errant lash of the dragon's tail.

Setanta made eye contact with Marcelle. She knew from the flicker of his gaze what to do next.

"You've got this," she told Lochlan and bit into her wrist to offer him her blood. "Take my strength, and we'll take it down."

He didn't hesitate. His mouth latched on to her wound, and he drank hard like a man possessed with thirst. She heard his leg set, and he pulled back, panting.

"Let's do this," he said.

The dragon opened its mouth once more as fire glowed brightly in the back of its throat. At that moment, Setanta unleashed the blood magic stored in his spear from killing so many and draining their lifeforce and power. Streams of violent red magic ripped through the soft flesh of the dragon's open mouth, and it screamed something ear shattering and monstrous. Marcelle lunged forward, flinging herself at full force into its belly to punch out its air, the scales cutting her skin as she did. All the while, Lochlan had control of the fire. He pulled it out as if extracting the creature's soul.

It stumbled as it gasped, unable to take a breath of air. As it struggled, Setanta ripped through the membranes of its wings so that it couldn't fly away, and Marcelle threw herself against the tail to keep it from lashing against their focusing pyromancer.

The dragon began to shrink and shrink. Marcelle and Setanta kept hitting and hitting, working in harmony to pummel the monster into submission until it collapsed, breathless and still on the scorched and shattered marble of the throne room.

"Holy shit." Lochlan gasped, breathing heavily as if he had been the one deprived of oxygen. "We just killed a dragon."

"A shame," Setanta said. "It may be the last shifter we ever see. But it should turn the tide. Keep an eye out for Artemisia and Giovanna. They may yet…"

As they watched, heat rolled in waves off the dragon corpse and it shrank until it was the size and shape of a naked, dead woman with white hair growing at a length to rival Marcelle's long locks lying over her motionless body. Her skin was not like any regular skin Marcelle had ever seen. It was red as fresh blood.

"The witch." Lochlan's eyes lit up as he spoke. "Marcelle, help me." He knelt over the woman and began chest compressions.

"What are you… Oh." *Brilliant.* She pushed him aside to take over chest compressions while he pinched the shifter's nose and blew air into her mouth. It felt like an eternity, working on a corpse, but finally the woman gasped for air, flailing her long limbs.

"Hey! Hey, hey, it's okay," Lochlan said. "It's okay. We freed you. Their contracts only last until death. You die, you come back, and you're free. It's okay now."

She blinked a few times and looked around.

"Do you feel like you still need to obey their orders?" Lochlan asked.

She shook her head.

"Great! That's great!" Lochlan sat back in relief.

The woman looked up at the tattoos on Setanta's chest, then spoke in a language Marcelle couldn't recognize, though she did catch her use of the name CuChulainn.

Setanta replied fluently in the same language, and she nodded. She turned to Lochlan and held out her hand, a large red scale forming in her palm, then detaching. She said something in her language again.

"She says it's a gift for saving her instead of letting her die," Setanta translated. "She says not to waste the transformation magic."

"Thank you." Lochlan looked at the thing in wonder as he picked it up.

The moment of stillness was broken by gunfire, and Marcelle grabbed Lochlan to push them both down against the floor, out of the stream of bullets in the air. A line of Vasi had gotten through the broken windows to take aim at them. The vampire woman's eyes darkened as she stood and faced the battle, fierce determination twisting her body as she lumbered forward. Cold snapped through the air as she shifted once more into her dragon form and launched herself at the Vasi who had just been in control of her. But this time, her scales were no longer white. Instead, they were red as if her body were covered in layers upon layers of the brightest rubies and garnets the world had ever seen, all dancing with internal fire in the light of the rising sun. She landed in front of the line of Vasi who opened fire. It did them no good, and soon they were charred into screaming oblivion. *A fitting end for witch hunters*, Marcelle thought. To be burned alive.

"Do you know her?" she asked Setanta.

"No, I don't believe we've ever met, though she knew of me. She spoke ancient Welsh and said she had decided to sleep either in a tree or as a tree a long time ago, but these modern humans found her and bound her to their will."

"Welsh, huh? I like her." Lochlan tried to get up but fell back to his knees. "I think I'm spent." He flinched at the sound of gunfire not far from their location.

"I'll get you someplace safe," Marcelle told him as she gathered him into her arms. "Setanta, I'll join you once he's clear to take out whatever Vasi are left."

"Good," Setanta agreed. "Take care, Lochlan."

****

Setanta was relieved to see Marcelle take Lochlan away to safety, but he knew he had more work to do. More Vasi to kill and a missing sister to find.

He flew up out of the ruins of his throne room, looking at the battle, listening. A familiar voice caught his ear, sobbing. It wasn't far, and he landed in a fury of tar-like feathers in a clearing. It was a fitting clearing. The one that Giovanna had once sent Sarai to via deceit so that she could be kidnapped. A very fitting clearing indeed to find Giovanna crying. But what he saw in her arms made him stop.

Artemisia's slight form lay limp in her mother's arms. The sigil in her mouth had been activated.

Setanta's heart felt numb from the sight. He had never had a bond with this newest sister, though he was grateful for her potential as part of his family. She could have been more. So much more.

Giovanna looked up at him, her cheeks stained with black mascara tears. "Help her," she whispered. "Please, Setanta. You have to help her."

Setanta shut his eyes. Artemisia had been such a small girl. Such a tragedy. With a mother like Giovanna so careless yet so permissive of a spoiled princess, Artemisia had never had a chance. He hated Giovanna but knew her pain all too well from his own experiences. He found he couldn't wish it even on her, despite his hatred of her.

"You helped the Vasi," he murmured. "You betrayed not just your family but your species. She paid the price for you."

"They said they would let me take my daughter back with me to Rome when you were dead," she whispered. "I just wanted my daughter." She hugged the corpse and caressed her face, closing her eyes.

"There's always a price." He paused. "They killed Lugh as well."

A raven landed on a branch above their heads and stared down at them. A raven...of course.

"They culled the weak," he said. Just as the Morrigan had promised would happen. The blood to be given as payment was his familial blood, but not from his veins in sacrifice. It was his sister.

"I can't live without her," Giovanna whispered.

"How could you do it? You outlived all your children. Why don't you die? I feel... Gods, my heart, I must be dying."

He didn't have an answer. He had no special trick other than a determination to live. He no longer saw that determination in Giovanna's eyes.

"Please end this," she whispered. "But let me kiss her one more time."

As she leaned over to press her lips to Artemisia's forehead, Setanta brought his spear down through her heart, then yanked it free. Giovanna slumped over, at last embracing her daughter in death. Immediately, the raven descended, and he looked away.

Setanta clenched his fists. "My Lady Morrigan, I didn't mean for you to take *her*."

The Morrigan answered in his mind. *Then you should have been more...*

"Specific."

He blinked at the unexpected familiar voice and looked back. Artemisia stood, drenched in blood, her wounds filling with black tar and healing.

"I'm going to join her," she said softly. "I think that'll be better for me."

He nodded. "I regret we were never close."

"It wasn't your fault. Mother never allowed it."

The raven landed on Artemisia's back and began to expand, the black feathers with the consistency of deep space covering the young girl.

"Thank you for fighting for me. I'll be free now. With Her." His sister's eyes went black with glowing points of red at the center, and she looked up at the sky, smiling. "I see...everything."

Then only the raven was left. Setanta unfurled his

own wings, and they took flight in separate directions.

As he looked back down at the battle to see where he was needed most, he found a large group of Vasi taking shelter in the old stables turned car garage. He landed, and a bloodlust rippled through him at the sight of their terrified faces. Bullets flew around, but he was too fast now for that to be a concern. He wanted their hearts. The desire burned inside his core like a furnace, like live wires wrapped around his spine and throat. In a daze, he ripped his way through Vasi, shrugging off their weapons, oblivious to their screams as he ate and drank his fill.

The only things to bring him out of his frenzied state were a voice calling to him once again and cold hands daring to grip his arms and try to restrain him. At first, his instinct was to attack. He pinned the person to the ground, then stopped, teeth inches from her throat. A strange sensation of a thousand hands reached out to him and held him fast to keep him from being able to complete his attack. The cold of her flesh drew him out of the haze, and he found Marcelle lying under him, looking up without a shred of fear in her eyes.

"Setanta, don't you dare." Her words were a warning as she struggled against his grip.

Breathing heavily, he nodded. "Apologies." He shut his eyes, taking deep breaths to control the thirst and bloodlust. "Did I hurt you?"

"Only my pride. Let me up."

He did, and she embraced him.

"Lochlan's safe," she told him. "And the Ellis Coven witches arrived to help through a portal a few minutes ago."

"And Sarai?"

"She's with Bear, Hannah, and Rosaline back in Lochlan's cabin. She's in labor."

He felt his eyes widen as shock rooted him to the spot. Sarai was in labor with their child. His child. His heir. He had lost his father to death and his sister to the Morrigan so fast in one night, and now his wife was laboring to save his family. Somehow, despite everything, he still had a family to save.

A roar of the dragon devouring Vasi caused him to look up. "A red dragon and the birth of a royal," he murmured. "How fortuitous."

"Does it mean something?" Marcelle asked.

"Ancient legends and coincidence, nothing important," he dismissed. "But consider it a good omen. Are there any Vasi left?"

"Stragglers. Any that aren't dead are running. Most are dead. The dragon on our side really changed the tide. We've won, my love." She raised her hand to show an eye in her palm closing and disappearing. "Sarai's protection spell is done. The battle is over."

Outside the garage, the cold ground was soaked with blood, and the dragon was once more shaped like a woman with crimson skin, whom someone lent a jacket to. Vampires worked to clear Vasi bodies from the grounds and gather them in one area. Jackie was not among them, and Setanta concluded she must have been crushed by the rubble or perhaps escaped in the chaos.

The human sources looked terrified but alive. Apparently, the human quarters had been the one corner of the palace that had not been rigged with a bomb, which spared most from even being injured. Setanta took note that there had been more than a few vampire deaths, evidenced by the smell of dust swirling in the wind, but most of them had survived, in part because Setanta and the dragon had taken on the bulk of the Vasi forces themselves.

It was a relief but short lived. Setanta could no longer control the thing inside him. His very sweat turned to steam rising off his body. With a cry, he reached up to his own face and ripped out the black eyeball the Morrigan had given him. It crumbled in his palm, and he covered the empty socket with his hand.

"Marcelle, I need your help," he whispered, leaning on her for support.

"Anything."

"Get me to the water."

She helped him to the fountain at the center of his gardens, and he climbed, trembling, into the water. More steam rose from contact with his skin.

"Please," he said, his voice tense. "I need you to take out the magic the Morrigan put in my body. Use your knife. Please, Marcelle."

She audibly gulped. He knew what she must be thinking. Just looking at the darkness he'd accepted that was burning and eating him from the inside could make a person's head hurt. But he needed her. He couldn't do it himself.

Thankfully, his love demonstrated nerves of steel and gripped one of the slippery, tar-like feathers.

As she tugged at it, he felt it pull at his mind, at his perception of reality. He could feel the way her eyes widened though he could not see them. He could feel the way she wanted to run screaming in the opposite direction. He could feel it on her skin, cold like dry ice yet hotter than the dragon's breath. He could feel the *hunger*.

Oh fuck, he could feel the hunger spearing through his mind, twisting his thoughts until he wasn't sure he could stand or even think.

She made the first cut, and black blood oozed from it, covering her hands and his back like molten, burning syrup. It almost felt as if it were trying to find a crack in their clothes and skin, to find a way back into his body or hers. That hunger… He dug his fingers into the stone foundation of the fountain. He needed to control its hunger.

With a shout, Marcelle flung a piece of the thing away into the water where it shriveled with a hiss. She cut again, and Setanta grunted. She grabbed a large fistful of the black tar and pulled. The sound of tearing flesh squelched from under his skin, and he shouted in pain, doubling over.

"Should I stop?" she asked nervously.

"No," he growled through his teeth. "All of it. I need all of it gone, or you won't like what I become." If it wasn't gone, he would lose control. He would consume everything he could. Everyone.

She pulled and cut as he screamed in the most bloodcurdling agony of his life, but she didn't stop. He felt as if all those live wires wrapped through his bones were being torn out of his soul one by one, and it was maddening. He had to think of something else, something other than the pain.

Marcelle. Sarai. And…love. He needed love. Needed them.

By the time she was done, the water had evaporated around them, and he was back to his normal temperature without anything moving under his skin. The hunger had been defeated, and he collapsed. His body lurched, and blood and flesh retched from his mouth. He'd taken too much when possessed by the thing and could no longer stomach it. He felt nothing but relief with it all out of his system and looked up to see what had become of that thing he had played host to.

It was a blackness deeper than a color now. It possessed an absence of color, like a void of everything. Yet something restless, disturbing, and beyond earthly existence stirred in that void. Something inside that wanted to consume flesh and blood and souls. As he watched, the blackness shifted into a large raven that hurt to look at for too long, and he shut his eyes as it fluttered away into the sky to perhaps join his sister in the Morrigan.

"I would like to never need to do that again." He groaned as he pulled himself to his feet, then stumbled, and Marcelle caught him, holding him close. He had never been so weak before her and found himself grateful to be held in her loving, strong arms. It was safe to be vulnerable to her. He felt safe.

"Are you going to be all right?"

"I will be now that it's gone, thank you." He took a few deep breaths, then kissed her in gratitude. He could feel such softness and love in that brief touch that despite everything being destroyed, he knew the worst was over. Everything would be all right.

"Do you need blood?" she asked.

"I've had more blood today than I need for half a lifetime. But thank you for the offer." He paused. "I think we're needed somewhere, you and I."

The battle was won, and their people were safe, and so it was time for personal matters to take precedence. It was time to be at Sarai's side.

Chapter Thirty

The Phoenix

Sarai felt like she was in a trance. She was immensely grateful to know that her spouses weren't dead when she left, but she was afraid for what the future would bring. She felt her spell end as the eye in her palm disappeared, but didn't know if it was gone because the fighting was finished or because the other half, Marcelle, was lost. She tried not to think about it, not to imagine the worst. Losing anyone was not an option.

Her relief when she saw Marcelle and Setanta both burst into Lochlan's guest bedroom where she was laboring was like she could breathe again, and she wasn't even perturbed by the amount of blood covering them or the blood-soaked strip of cloth covering one of Setanta's eyes like a makeshift eye patch. If she could have, she would have jumped up and tackled them, but all she could do in her state was smile weakly.

"Sarai," Marcelle whispered. "How are you doing?"

"I'm pushing a watermelon out of my vagina. But other than that, you know, okay. What happened?"

"We won," Setanta reassured her. "Lochlan, Lilly, they're all safe. And the Vasi have been dealt a massive blow today. They will not recover soon."

Sarai saw a flicker in his expression. "Who's dead?"

"My father. And Artemisia is...not with us

anymore, though that's complicated to explain."

Her heart sank at his words. She had never been close to Lugh, but respected the man. How odd that Setanta repressed any outward expression of grief except that one flicker.

"I killed Giovanna when she showed her face. Other than my father, we were fortunate. The palace is gone, but recovery teams are working now to salvage what they can."

"What happened to your eye?" Sarai asked.

"The prosthetic came out. Don't focus on that. You have your own work to do here." A concerned expression crossed his face. "Would you like me to leave you women for this and wait—"

"Don't you fucking dare," Sarai snapped. "You are not leaving me now that you're both here. I need you both."

He glanced at Marcelle. "I've never done this before," he murmured. "Do you need me to boil hot water?"

"You've had twelve children!" Marcelle exclaimed.

"Yes, but men weren't the ones who handled labor," he insisted. "That was handled by women, separately. They made a point of evicting us from the room."

"Well, you're staying for ours," Sarai instructed him. Not having both her lovers there now that they had made it past the fighting and to her side was unthinkable. "If you can put it in me, then you can help get it out. That's the rule."

And so he did, though after Bear pulled both him and Marcelle aside to wash the blood and viscera of combat from their bodies before he allowed them to physically assist in any way. Sarai was grateful for that and for the new ill-fitted clothes they borrowed from Lochlan's wardrobe that didn't stink of gore.

Setanta held Sarai's arm just below her prosthetic hand while Marcelle held her good hand and was subjected to having her fingers crushed with as much strength as Sarai could muster. The epidural spell worked, but the pressure was intense, and focusing on pushing while not being able to feel required everything from her. Soon, Sarai brought their screaming daughter into the world with the light of the sun illuminating them all.

She was stunning, a princess with black hair matted to her head and a high-pitched shriek that could shatter glass, trembling in the light of high noon. She was perfect but too tiny and premature. Sarai was grateful that at least the baby's lungs seemed developed as she held her in her arms. The poor creature was so small. So fragile and precious. She was everything. Sarai had never known a love so intense and instant as the moment those little red eyes squinted through the sun to try and see her parents and she screamed her confusion and discomfort.

"What a battle cry," Setanta whispered.

"Shh, it's okay," Sarai whispered and began to sing the Hebrew lullaby her mother had once sung to her. *"Numi, numi, yaldati, numi, numi nim."*

The crying quieted. The small child wiggled and looked up as if in shock. Their eyes met, and Sarai's heart melted.

"She recognizes your voice," Setanta said in awe. "Look at her. She knows you."

"Put her to your breast," Marcelle urged, guiding the infant's head.

The baby latched with a greedy need and began to

suckle. A tear dropped onto Sarai's hand, and she looked up to see Marcelle weeping with a smile on her face.

"You did wonderfully, Sarai. You made such beauty."

"We made such beauty," Sarai said. "Though I suppose I did most of the work."

Marcelle laughed and kissed Sarai's forehead.

"When should I worry about fangs?" Sarai asked.

"Not for a long while, it's safe for now," Setanta reassured.

Sarai leaned back against the pillows between her husband and wife as she felt pressure relieved in her breast. "She's perfect. I love her so much. I love...I love both of you."

Marcelle kissed Sarai on the cheek. "You have my love forever, Sarai. *Ma petite sorcière*."

"Even when you think you've seen everything...something so pure can pull you back to earth. Can remind you of what matters most. I love you, Sarai," Setanta said softly, running a finger over their daughter's brow. He looked up into Sarai's eyes, his own red irises burning with intensity. "Forever."

Sarai's eyes filled with tears. It was no longer a lovely lie but the honest truth. She was loved by Marcelle and Setanta.

"What will we call her?" Marcelle asked. "We never chose a name, did we?"

"I suppose we didn't. Is there a name you'd prefer, Sarai?" Setanta said.

"I'd like to call her Lior, after my mother, Liora. It means, 'my light,' " Sarai said.

"That sounds beautiful," Marcelle agreed as Setanta nodded.

"What's her last name? We all have different ones."

"We use something like a patronym system adapted to whoever the highest-ranking parent is rather than last names for the royal family," Setanta said. "She is Princess Lior ni Setanta."

"A princess with no palace," Marcelle mourned.

"A princess with everything to gain ahead of her," Setanta said. "We'll rebuild, better than it was. We'll be stronger than ever before. Our home is ashes now, but we will rise from them. She is our phoenix princess, born from ash to inherit the world."

Sarai smiled as she watched the phoenix princess at her breast. "Welcome to the world, my phoenix, my light," she whispered. "Our Princess Lior of New Ulster."

****

They stayed the day and a night at Lochlan's cabin. Sarai was grateful to have two lovers. One could oversee recovery of books and artifacts from the ruins of the palace and finding emergency housing for survivors of the attack. The other could stay at her side and hold baby Lior when Sarai needed to sleep. While her milk came in without complication, Sarai was unprepared for the mind-numbing exhaustion creating it came with. She needed assistance for the simplest things once the epidural wore off. Her privates felt pummeled, and only pads soaked with water and frozen or Marcelle's cold hands provided comfort. The pads were especially good since her bleeding continued for a while despite her healing powers.

They soon decided that they could not impose too long on Lochlan's cabin. Not only out of respect for the man's space, though he had no objections, but because they had no supplies. A convenience-store run got them diapers and wipes, but the three new parents possessed no crib, no baby clothes, nothing. All the preparation in Sarai's room had been blown to pieces.

Luckily, they had help. Sarai was unwilling to go on a plane with a newborn, even a private one, so Hannah procured a transportation gateway for them to walk to that led them to the Ellis Coven. Once there, they were able to take a short ferry ride, then car ride to their penthouse apartment. Sarai was grateful that, out of all the artifacts destroyed in the palace, she had kept her berberisca wedding dress there in New York.

With a baby so new, they didn't want many visitors as the family learned to adjust to Lior's needs. But they made an exception for Sarai's aunts, who hurried over with armfuls of used baby clothes they'd saved from their daughter. Somehow, hand-me-downs from her own family were so much more wonderful than any of the new items Sarai had intended to use, and she was glad to wrap Lior snuggly in secondhand, sloppily knitted blankets.

Mazal also brought a car full of ingredients and set herself to work in the kitchen, cooking up filling and healthy meals for Sarai to enjoy, which was better than anything Marcelle or Setanta were capable of cooking for her on short notice, and better than what their staff could bring her. It tasted like home and made the penthouse smell like home.

"You know you don't need to do that," Sarai would remind her.

"*Sha, sha, motek.* It's my honor," Mazal insisted. "You just focus on Lior. Do you need laundry done?"

"We have staff for that," Setanta reminded her.

Mazal huffed and shooed him away. "Go hold your baby. Sarai needs more food."

Watching Setanta coo over and cuddle the infant in his arms while Marcelle prepared turmeric tea and Mazal served Sarai heaps of lamb, roasted vegetables, and couscous was perfection. As she ate, Sarai realized something—her cravings for blood had disappeared. No matter how she tried to summon them, her fangs and other vampiric qualities were gone. She was normal again. Or at least, as normal as Sarai could ever be.

Mazal also proved herself quite useful in another regard. She helped to create a new prosthetic eye for Setanta, one that was apparently superior to his old one in that it no longer made him half blind, and he was able to leave his eye patch behind.

New York City became the temporary seat of New Ulster's government. It wasn't the same as the old palace, but it worked. Sarai focused on healing but received updates when she had the strength to. It was still her kingdom, after all. She was still a queen.

What was left of the Vasi in their territory had gone underground or fled the kingdom. The resources and members they'd lost had been a Hail Mary attempt to destroy Setanta's bloodline that failed. Despite the losses of the palace, the vampires came out on top.

Plans were drawn up to replace the palace, with an emphasis on secrecy, but that would take time. Luckily, Sarai's lovers were immortal.

They had as much time as they needed.

Epilogue

Fifteen Years Later

Sarai was proud of her daughter, Lior ni Setanta, being the first of her children to go to high school. She looked a little younger than perhaps she should in her face but had inherited her father's height and so was sometimes mistaken for a senior rather than a sophomore. She had her mother Sarai's curls with her *maman* Marcelle's black hair color. Her skin was somewhere between Sarai's and her paler parents, tan enough to indicate her ancestry wasn't strictly European, but pale enough that people called it just a tan if they didn't think about it much. She also had a light dusting of freckles across the bridge of her nose that Sarai wasn't sure which parent had given her.

And of course, Lior had inherited her father's red eyes, which she kept colored brown with a potion of eye drops so that she could blend in.

Their home had changed from the palace Sarai had been brought to so many years prior and from the penthouse in New York that their children had spent much of their childhood in. No longer was home an obvious, anachronistic building layered with old protective spells that stuck out like a sore thumb or an apartment far above a busy city. The new design of the palace placed a heavy emphasis on camouflage. It had taken a decade to construct, even for the meticulous and speedy vampire artisans who worked on the massive project in a fervor.

A mountain hidden deep in Appalachia had been chosen for the project and the inside hollowed out into a massive palace of granite. The walls were decorated with carvings painted with gold highlights.

On the outside of the mountain was a gated community. Model homes were propped up with fences around them that many vampires or guests to the palace could use should they choose to, and all were modern.

The royal family lived in a mansion at the very top. It had a view of every mountain sunset, a room for each of Sarai's children, and a uniquely designed three-sectioned bedroom for the monarchs to share together rather than continuing the usual royal tradition of each having their own suite. This was on the suggestion of Sarai, who found the whole idea of living separately from her spouses ridiculous when she wanted to spend each night curled up against them.

A boon of the mountain palace compared to the old one was secrecy. Instead of relying on magic barriers that could be shattered by superior spellcraft or bypassed with the correct witch or invitation, it physically was hidden from sight. A hunter would have to know what they were looking for to assume that the palace was anything other than a handful of vacation homes. And they could never burn down the stone.

The night of Sarai's fortieth birthday, a celebration which she shared with Lior's fifteenth birthday the next day, was a special one. They had already had a large party with their witchy family in New York, full of ridiculous amounts of delicious food and good company with all the many cousins who adored Sarai, Marcelle, and Setanta's children. On the actual date of the birthdays, Sarai wanted just her close family, their partners, and their friends.

At the round table in their dining room were Setanta, Sarai, and Marcelle, as well as all four children: Lior, the twin red-haired and brown-skinned brothers Ultan and Henry, and their little sister, the dark-haired Branna, who looked the most like Marcelle with her fair skin, though she had inherited Sarai's facial features. Temuulen was there, though he couldn't eat, and Rosaline as well. The human source had become a staple in adoring the vampire children, and was occasionally found in Temuulen's bed, though Sarai, her husband, and her wife kept their relationship with Rosaline platonic.

Bear and Hannah had been invited but were unable to make it to the occasion from their elongated second honeymoon gallivanting about Europe. They were missed, but Sarai was set on having her fortieth party on the right day, so she did not want to wait for their capricious whims to bring them home.

Lochlan, dubbed Uncle Lochlan by the children, had also been invited along with his shapeshifting partner, Emrys. He'd decided on blue hair, eyes, and nails for the evening, while Emrys appeared masculine with his usual white hair and unnatural ruby skin. Sarai had once inquired about the choice to have skin in such an unusual pigment, to which the shapeshifter replied simply that he enjoyed the color, so why shouldn't he wear it?

While Lochlan had aged well, he still had a handful of strands with gray at the roots on his head. At thirty-five years old, he looked younger than his age, no doubt in part thanks to the magical assistance of the shapeshifter helping him perfect his physical body to exactly the shape he wished to be and from Marcelle as his lover keeping him at peak health through sips of her blood.

They were all the people Sarai wanted with her on her special night. And it was a very special night not just because of the celebration, but because Sarai had made a decision.

"So tell us," Temuulen said to Sarai as he leaned against Rosaline. "Forty looks good on you. I'm not saying anything against it. But you've got us all on pins and needles."

"You mean, have I decided if I'm going to join you and Marcelle?" Sarai broke into a grin. "Well, I'm done having kids. And I am getting older. I'm tired of using a cane on bad days with my arthritis. That's never going to get better. It's getting to be time to decide, isn't it?"

"There's no rush if you're not ready," Setanta said.

"What if I want to wait as long as Hannah did?" she teased. "Would you still love me looking like a grandma?"

"Without a doubt," he reassured her. "And as Hannah's proven, you can still be a powerful vampire regardless of your physical age."

"You'll be beautiful to me no matter what," Marcelle said.

"That might be weird, though, Mom," Lior said. "No offense. You don't want to wait until you're in your eighties, do you?"

Sarai laughed. "Probably not."

"Wait, then you *have* decided?" Lochlan leaned forward as he spoke. "Are you going to do it for real?"

Sarai looked at Marcelle and Setanta. "I want to do

it. That's what I want for my birthday. I want you to turn me." She lifted her fork, laden with soft cake and frosting. "After I eat my birthday cake, though."

Marcelle clapped loudly, and soon everyone joined in, making heat flush her cheeks as Sarai felt herself blush. The cheering was interrupted by the twins Ultan and Henry flinging cake off their forks like catapults at each other, to be scolded by their *maman*.

"Your wish is my command, my love." Setanta spoke his words with a grin, apparently happy not just with his wife's choice but also amused by his boys' shenanigans.

Their youngest, Branna, rolled her eyes at the whole thing, her feet dangling from her chair, unable to reach the floor as she politely ate her cake.

"Still no chance of you accepting the offer?" Marcelle asked Lochlan as she pushed a napkin at Henry. "We could do a two-for-one special."

"Nah, I'm happy how I am." He smiled. "But I'm happy for you, Sarai."

When the dinner was done, the children had been settled into bed, and Sarai was satisfied that she had tasted everything mortal she wished to taste, Rosaline gave her a hug.

"I'm so happy for you," she said. "You be gentle when I get up there, okay? I'll wait here until they call me."

"Thank you." Sarai returned the hug as tightly as she could. "I wouldn't want anyone else."

Setanta and Marcelle led Sarai into the bedroom at the top floor of their home. Each step held a strange weight as she walked, and not just because of the usual pain in her arthritic knees. Every moment was closer to her last breath of life.

"You're certain you're ready?" Setanta asked as they sat together on the large bed. "I don't want to pressure you."

"I've had years to think about this, Setanta," she said. "I've done the blood-drinking thing when I was pregnant, so I know better than most what I'm getting into. I'm ready. I've been ready for a long time."

"We'll be careful with you," Marcelle promised. "As little pain as possible."

"I'm not afraid," Sarai lied, her heart racing.

The vampires smiled a little but didn't call out the clear fib. True, she wasn't afraid of the pain but still had some fear. Fear of change, fear that everything she knew was about to be altered forever. Fear of the concept of eternity.

When Marcelle held Sarai in her arms, that fear evaporated.

"I'd give you the usual warnings, but you know what to expect. You know how this works," Marcelle said.

"We'll do it together," Setanta said. "Are you ready?"

Sarai nodded. They held her up between them, and fangs rested at either side of her neck.

"I'm ready," she whispered.

They bit, and Sarai gasped. She was used to their bites, adored them, savored them. But they felt different. The pair usually didn't drink heavily from her but now worked together to drain her close to dry. Numbness crept into her fingers and toes and crawled up her limbs as her head spun from the blood loss. Her healing gift fought to keep up but was failing. She let her body fall limp in their arms, her heart slowing and struggling against their feeding.

Finally, her vision blurred, and they stopped.

Setanta kissed her lips.

But it was more than a kiss. He'd bitten down on his tongue, and as Sarai opened her mouth, she could taste his blood. She'd sampled it more than once when she'd been pregnant and been immune to the effects at the time. She was no longer immune.

At first, all she could notice was the sensation of need and power. It made her crave him.

Then it began to burn like lightning in her soul, and her heart began to pound faster and faster. The blood spinning through her body was on fire, and every cell of her weak mortal flesh screamed as it was forced to change.

Sarai opened her mouth to shriek in pain but heard a loud, sickening crack, and the world went dark.

When she opened her now red eyes, everything had changed. The bed was softer than it had been. She could almost feel the thread count of the pure cotton. She could see individual strands of dust in the moonlight that streamed from the wide-open windows. She could feel starlight on her skin as if it were sunlight, and everything was all so bright. She felt as if she had been blind her entire life and only now learned what colors were.

There was no instinct to breathe. No need for it in her lungs. As she sat up, even with such a simple movement, strength flowed through her muscles.

"How do you feel?" Marcelle asked.

Sarai looked at her and Setanta sitting there expectantly. Their faces, though beautiful to her before, were like works of art to her new eyes. Smooth, symmetrical, and glowing in the moonlight. They were hers. "I feel...wonderful."

And fangs grew in her mouth.

A word about the author...

Evelyn Silver is a multi-award-winning bisexual and polyamorous Jewish author who lives in South Florida with her spouse, their two children, and their two cats. She has a BFA in English and enjoys a variety of hobbies including belly dancing and singing opera. Evelyn sews her own clothes (poorly) and somehow manages to kill every plant she ever tries to take care of.

~*~

https://eternalevelyn.com/

Thank you for purchasing
this publication of The Wild Rose Press, Inc.

For questions or more information
contact us at
info@thewildrosepress.com.

The Wild Rose Press, Inc.
www.thewildrosepress.com